the shut mouth society

Also by James D. Best

The Digital Organization (John Wiley & Sons)
The Shopkeeper

the shut mouth society

James D. Best

The Shut Mouth Society

Cover photo by Mathew Brady, February 27, 1860

Published by Wheatmark®
610 East Delano Street, Suite 104
Tucson, Arizona 85705 U.S.A.
www.wheatmark.com

International Standard Book Number: 978-1-60494-012-1
Library of Congress Control Number: 2007941144

To our children:

Wayne and Erika
Joe and Jennifer

the shut mouth society

Prologue

· · ·

New York City
Monday, February 27, 1860

Amos Cummings cursed his editor.

He hated this assignment. Beyond career objections, it caused him to miss a rare opportunity to take his soon-to-be fiancée to dinner. When he had chosen journalism as a profession, he had had no idea that it would consume so many evenings.

As an abolitionist, he had wanted to influence public opinion, and he had believed that Horace Greeley's *New York Tribune* would give him an elevated platform. Instead, Greeley had assigned him to cover Thurlow Weed and his political machine. Years of gritty local politics had made Cummings a cynic. Nowadays he was more concerned with starting a family than with changing the country.

This morning, he had asked Greeley for a new assignment: anything different from his old beat. As he climbed aboard the horse-drawn streetcar that would take him up Broadway, he knew haranguing his editor had been a mistake.

Although the packed streetcar rattled and clanged, Cummings thought he overheard one of the other passengers mention Abraham Lincoln. Considering the hour, many of the people on this trolley were probably also heading to the Cooper Union. Tonight's speaker—and his assignment—was this Abraham Lincoln.

Cummings could not pick up the thread of the conversation. Just as well. He did not need to hear the banter of someone who would pay an exorbitant twenty-five cents to listen to a commonplace politician from some prairie state. Abraham Lincoln had earned a modicum of fame during his debates with Senator Stephen Douglas two years ago, but he had lost that race. Cummings could not see the fledgling Republican Party nominating a loser. How had this rough-hewn storyteller wangled an invitation to a lecture series meant to expose serious candidates to the New York political elite?

The Cooper Union was ablaze with gaslights when Cummings stepped off the trolley. Greeley had reserved him a seat in the front row, so he could hear clearly and report on Lincoln's address. Still in a foul mood, Cummings merged with the crowd and meandered down the stairs to the Great Hall in the basement. As the crowd jostled him, he noticed that tonight there seemed to be a heightened sense of energy and excitement. The audience would surely be disappointed. Homespun yarns might draw crowds in the bucolic West, but New York City demanded a more elevated style of speech making.

After some salutations with fellow journalists and friends, Cummings took his seat at the side of the auditorium. The hall buzzed with conversations and greetings, and Cummings estimated the crowd at about four hundred, leaving a quarter of the seats empty. Most of the important Republicans in this overwhelmingly Democratic city had bought tickets, but after some rough calculations, he guessed the promoters would be lucky to break even.

The windowless Great Hall felt like a church, with its sixteen massive columns and vaulted ceiling. Red leather swivel chairs rose from front to rear at a slight incline, so everyone could see over people seated in front of them. One hundred and sixty-eight gaslights in crystal chandeliers bounced light off the mirrors that lined both walls to make the room bright as day. The illumination may have been a modern miracle, but the constant hiss from burners sometimes made it difficult to hear a soft-spoken speaker.

In a few minutes, Abraham Lincoln and his hosts emerged from behind a curtain and sat on chairs lined up across the stage. Cummings heard a muted gasp as this gangly, disheveled, and ill-dressed being walked onto the stage with the strangest gait he had ever seen. Lincoln walked with a slouch and took each step with the flat of his foot instead of the heel. When he sat, he wrapped his enormously long legs around the chair and assumed a glum expression that seemed to promise a fire-and-brimstone sermon instead of one of his well-known humorous talks. Cummings looked around and saw dismay on other faces.

Lincoln had provided typeset copies of his speech to the major newspapers, but Cummings had been in a snit, so he had not bothered to read it before leaving the Tribune building. He arranged the text on his lap and made sure his four sharpened pencils were handy in his side pocket. Hopefully, he would need to make few notes and be able to submit his story to the night editor before midnight.

After the introduction, Lincoln walked to the podium with one pant leg caught about two inches above his shoe. He seemed a pathetic creature and, as he began to speak, nothing altered this first impression. He laid his foolscap notes on the gold-tasseled podium and held his hands behind his back. He spoke in a high-pitched monotone voice and made few gestures of note. As Lincoln spoke, Cummings used his finger to follow the text, but he did not bother to note the minor alterations from the typeset copy.

Senator Douglas, more than any other man, had raised the specter of slavery in the territories north of the Mason-Dixon Line, by claiming that the Founding Fathers believed the federal government held no authority to restrict slavery in the territories. Lincoln, presenting a scholarly review of the voting records of the Constitution's thirty-nine signers, showed that twenty-one of them had voted for bills restricting slavery in territories, and sixteen had left no record. Only two supported the Douglas contention.

Cummings had let the pencil slip onto his lap. He realized that he had been captured by Lincoln's words. His grammar and diction were flawless, and he artfully used repetition to drive home his points and add levity without resorting to his famed countrified stories.

About five minutes into the speech, Cummings saw a startling transformation. Lincoln made faces, threw his head, and modulated his voice to captivate the audience. When he mimicked the Douglas stentorian style, he not only succeeded in mocking the "little giant," but caused his audience to laugh uproariously and stomp their feet with abandon.

His speech had started slow, but as it picked up momentum, the energy in the hall lifted until the excited audience waited on the edge of their seats for the next opportunity to clap, yell, and bang out a rhythm with their shoes. Lincoln gave them plenty of opportunities.

Cummings watched Lincoln accentuate his great height by lifting himself on his toes and throwing his arms wide open. "Will you meet us then on the question of whether our principles wrong your region? Do you accept the challenge?" Lincoln snapped back down on his heels, and the Great Hall joined him in shouting, "No!"

"Then you must believe our principles so wrong as to demand condemnation without a moment's consideration."

Cummings looked around as Lincoln waited for the applause and cheering to subside. With wonder, he realized that these jaded New Yorkers liked the man.

Lincoln again used his voice and mannerisms to mock Senator Douglas. "Some of you are for the 'gur-reat pur-rinciple' that if one man would enslave another, no third man should object, fantastically called Popular Sovereignty by the gur-reat Senator Douglas."

Now laughter mixed with applause. Lincoln waited again. When he resumed, he directly addressed the South.

"We hear that you will not abide the election of a Republican president! In that event, you say you will destroy the Union; and then, you say, the great crime of having destroyed it will be upon us!"

Laughter.

"That is cool. A highwayman holds a pistol to my ear, and mutters through his teeth, 'Stand and deliver, or I shall kill you and then you will be a murderer!" The sudden shift of laughter to prolonged applause told Cummings that Lincoln had command of this audience.

"What the robber demands of me—my money—is my own; and I have a clear right to keep it; but my vote is also my own; and the threat of death to me to extort my money and the threat to destroy the Union to extort my vote can scarcely be distinguished."

Lincoln smoothly slid into his concluding argument. "What will convince slaveholders that we do not threaten their property? This and this only: cease to call slavery wrong and join them in calling it right. Silence alone will not be tolerated—we must place ourselves avowedly with them. We must suppress all declarations that slavery is wrong, whether made in politics, in presses, in pulpits, or in private. We must arrest and return their fugitive slaves with greedy pleasure. The whole atmosphere must be disinfected from all taint of opposition to slavery before they will cease to believe that all their troubles proceed from us.

"If slavery is right, all words, acts, laws, and constitutions against it, are wrong and should be swept away. Holding, as they do, that slavery is morally right and socially elevating, they cannot cease to demand full recognition of it as a legal right and a social blessing.

"All they ask, we can grant, if we think slavery right. All we ask, they can grant if they think it wrong." He paused dramatically. "Right and wrong is the precise fact upon which depends the whole controversy."

Lincoln held for a couple beats to punctuate his point.

"Thinking it wrong, as we do, can we yield? Can we cast our votes with their view and against our own? In view of our moral, social, and political responsibilities, can we do this?"

The hall burst with repeated shouts of "No! No!"

"Let us not grope for some middle ground between right and wrong. Let us not search in vain for a policy of 'don't care' on a question about which we 'do care.' Nor let us be frightened by threats of destruction to the government."

Prolonged applause kept Lincoln silent for several minutes. Cummings looked down at his typeset copy of the speech and saw that Lincoln had only one more sentence. With perfect timing, he delivered it with all the energy he could muster.

"Let us have faith that right makes might, and in that faith, let us, to the end, dare to do our duty as we understand it!"

When Lincoln stepped back from the podium, the Cooper Union Great Hall exploded with noise and motion. Everybody stood. The staid New York audience cheered, clapped, and stomped their feet. Many waved handkerchiefs and hats. Cummings had tried to remain professional throughout the raucous speech, but he abandoned propriety and rose to his feet to clap and cheer with everyone else. The approbation continued so long that Lincoln began to look embarrassed. The bouncing noise seemed to grow on itself, until Cummings thought it had hit a crescendo, and then it grew even louder. The audience reaction told Cummings that he was witnessing the dawning of a new political force.

Cummings grabbed his papers from the floor where they had fallen and swiveled to exit the hall. A colleague from the *Herald* grabbed his elbow. "What do you think?" he yelled above the din.

"I think no man has ever made such a good first impression on a New York audience."

"But what do *you* think?"

"I think I shall vote for him come November."

Chapter 1

· · · ·

Greg Evarts looked at the mahogany paneling and red tucked-leather booths and grew a bit anxious. The place looked more expensive than he had remembered. When the host led another couple to their table, Evarts pulled a menu from a wood rack and scanned the prices. High for a hamburger joint, but he probably could get away with two lunches on his policeman's expense account. Hopefully, the professor didn't have a taste for pricey wine with the noonday meal.

When the host returned, Evarts dropped the menu back in the rack and stepped away from his podium. The young man was so good looking, he must have been an actor slogging it out in an eatery until his big break.

The host gave him a patronizing look. "Table for one?"

"Two, but my companion hasn't arrived yet."

"Yes, I have."

Evarts turned to the voice behind him. He suddenly hoped she liked wine for lunch. "Professor Baldwin?"

"Yes." She faced the host and turned on a smile that would probably get her whatever she wanted. "I have a class in just over an hour. Can we be seated immediately?"

The host grabbed two menus. "Of course."

Of course. Evarts let her go in front and admired her athletic stride. He suddenly looked forward to lunch. As they slid into the booth, Evarts handed her his card. She looked at it and said with a touch of disdain, "*Commander* Gregory Evarts, Santa Barbara Police."

"Something amusing?"

"Do you like being called *Commander*?"

"Call me Greg."

"I shall. Commander sounds far too authoritarian for my taste." With that she lifted two fingers and flashed her smile. A waiter unceremoniously plopped two drinks at the next table and scurried over. He was equally handsome, but Evarts almost laughed at his purposely disheveled hair. Without preamble, she asked, "Is your iced tea freshly brewed?"

"Daily ... regular and mango."

"Regular and a Cobb salad." She threw Evarts an expectant look.

"Hamburger, fries, Coke." He saw disapproval on her face.

"We serve over a dozen different burgers, sir." The tone was snotty.

"Just get me a basic burger."

"Yes, sir."

Thankfully the waiter disappeared to place their order.

For some reason the professor looked amused. "First time here?"

"No. When I was a kid, my parents brought me to Westwood to see the big movies—*Star Wars, Superman, Close Encounters.* We made a day of it and we always ate here." He looked around. "But it's been over twenty years."

Westwood Village was probably as close to a village as Los Angeles could produce. A hodgepodge of exclusive stores, high-end restaurants, nightspots, old-fashioned stand-alone movie theaters, quaint shops, and 1930s Hollywood architecture made Westwood distinct from other parts of Los Angeles. The sprawling campus of the University of California protected Westwood's northern flank, and milling students mixed easily with those rich enough to afford one of the neighborhood homes. The winding streets of the business district were hidden from the major thoroughfares, so the Village seemed isolated from the hullabaloo just outside its parameter.

The rich and the students belonged. Most of the hired help, however, only dreamed of a day when they would become famous and someone in their current job would recognize them on sight and part the riffraff from their path. Hollywood, after all, was just a stone's throw down the road.

The waiter returned and carefully positioned their drinks, but he kept his eyes and his own edition of a dazzling smile on the professor. Evarts wanted to arrest him, but instead turned his attention to the task at hand. "Thank you for making the time to see me." He slid a legal-size brown envelope across the table. "This is the document I mentioned on the phone."

She made no attempt to reach for the sealed envelope. "Did you develop your taste for hamburgers on those little family outings?"

"Is that a dig?"

Instead of answering, she pulled the envelope toward her but made no attempt to open it. "This is a fraud case?"

"Preliminary investigation. A rich Santa Barbara collector thinks this may be a forgery. He said you're the best Lincoln expert west of the Mississippi."

She took a sip of the iced tea, and her expression confirmed that it had been brewed that very day. "Is the victim Abraham Douglass?"

"I'm not sure he's a victim yet, but yes, Mr. Douglass filed the complaint. Do you know him, Professor?"

"It would be odd if the number-one Lincoln expert in the nation didn't know the most prolific Lincoln collector west of the Mississippi."

Evarts smiled. "Before coming, I googled Professor Patricia Baldwin. You have very impressive credentials."

"Associate professor, but my full professorship is just a formality due to the recognition my book has brought the school."

"I've picked it up, but I haven't had time to read it yet."

"I suspect you'll find it exceedingly dull."

Evarts pulled a straw with a tiny white paper cap out of his drink and tossed it on the table. After a healthy swallow of Coke, he said, "I find arrogance dull."

She didn't flinch. Evarts decided they were both used to controlling conversations. This should be fun. "If you know Douglass, why didn't he come directly to you, Professor? Why ask for police help before he's sure it's a forgery?"

"What's a commander, by the way?"

"You didn't answer my question."

"Am I being interrogated?" Evarts remained silent until Baldwin eventually said, "That was two questions. I'll answer both, if you answer mine."

"I'm head of detectives. Commanders are right under the deputy chief."

"So why didn't you send one of your detectives? Seems like a small case—excuse me, preliminary investigation—for a *commander*." She said the last word of the sentence with distaste.

Evarts almost drummed his fingers, but he caught himself and laid his hand flat on the table. He didn't want to give her the satisfaction of knowing she had annoyed him. When he finally spoke, he kept his voice even. "When I asked you to call me Greg, I was being polite. Now I think it's a necessity to keep our conversation civil."

"You didn't answer my question."

"You owe me two answers first."

"Okay. Abraham Douglass didn't come to me directly because we dislike each other. Or at least, I dislike him … and he knows it. He sent you because he knew I wouldn't give him the time of day." She tapped the brown envelope with perfectly manicured nails. "And this is certainly a forgery."

"How do you know without looking at it?"

She started to say something but stopped. Instead, she slumped back against the booth and gave Evarts a self-satisfied smile. "Because no preinauguration address in Lincoln's handwriting has ever surfaced. On the phone you said these were handwritten notes for his Cooper Union lecture."

"Yes. February 27, 1860. Before he was nominated."

Baldwin made a little salute with her iced tea. "You did your homework."

"I'm a detective."

"Head of detectives. Now you owe me an answer."

It was Evarts's turn to feign a relaxed position against the red leather. "Mr. Douglass is an important citizen in our town. The mayor made it clear I was to handle this personally."

"The mayor?" she asked in mock surprise. "Not your deputy chief? Nor even the chief?"

"The mayor and I are pals."

"Nothing to do with our dear friend Douglass's political influence?"

Evarts shrugged. "The mayor runs for reelection soon and the police department needs him to support our budget."

The waiter arrived with their food. Evarts thought the Cobb salad looked puny for nine dollars, but the burger startled him even more. "What's this?"

"A basic burger, as you requested."

The plate held an open bun displaying a big piece of overcooked ground meat. A half-dozen huge-cut fries filled the rest of the plate. "You burnt the damn thing to a crisp."

"Unless specifically requested, we cook our beef well."

Evarts laughed and shook his head. "I suppose if I had asked for it rare, you'd have made me sign a legal release."

"I'm sorry you're not pleased, sir."

"It's okay. Just bring me some lettuce and tomatoes…and mustard."

"That would be the John Wayne Burger, and I'd have to charge you an additional dollar. Perhaps next time you should examine the menu."

Evarts wondered if a charge of police brutality outside his jurisdiction would harm his career. He settled for his hard-ass cop look. "That'll be fine. I'll deduct it from your tip."

The preening poser gave Evarts a nauseatingly sweet smile and trotted off. When Evarts returned his attention to Baldwin, she looked amused. "He's going to spit in your mustard."

"Professional hazard." To get by the embarrassing moment, he asked, "Would you please look at the document?"

"While I eat?"

"It's only a copy. Douglass retained the original."

Baldwin set her fork beside her plate with deliberate care. "That bastard," she hissed.

"Excuse me?"

"He knows I can't prove it's genuine without the original document."

"He said you'd want to review the content before any testing."

"He *wants* to lure me up to Santa Barbara."

"What's the issue between the two of you?"

Instead of answering, she practically ripped open the envelope. As she studied the nine odd-sized pages, Evarts studied her. She was pretty. Not Hollywood gorgeous but a fresh kind of pretty that promised an evergreen sort of innocence. Except for the smile. There was nothing innocent in that smile, and it surely snared any male within casting distance. This was the outside. He had learned from his Google search that she had done her undergraduate work at Berkeley and had received her doctorate from Stanford. She had written too many journal articles to count and published three books on Abraham

Lincoln: The most recent had been on the nonfiction bestseller lists for months. *Quite Contrary—Mary Lincoln Critiques Her Husband* had struck a chord with the general public and garnered elaborate praise from renowned historians and book critics. The professor was obviously smart—with a streak of arrogance that seemed to come from her intellect rather than her looks.

The one thing about her that didn't seem to fit was the glasses. Evarts supposed she thought they made her look more academic and perhaps sent a signal to her colleagues that she wasn't vain. But if that was her purpose, she should've avoided pricey designer frames and thin lenses that eliminated the glare that usually concealed the eyes. Eyes? Green? No, emerald. The eyes were what made her so striking.

Evarts had joined the Santa Barbara Police Force immediately after his military service. For years, he had dealt with the outrageously rich and merely wealthy in that exclusive enclave nestled along the California coast. He had learned to recognize two-hundred-dollar haircuts and unpretentious clothing that cost more than his weekly salary. Patricia Baldwin sported both. He guessed her cashmere sweater cost well over five hundred dollars, and her short light brown hair had the kind of blonde streaking that only exclusive salons could make look natural. She was either rich or spent an inordinate amount of money on her appearance.

Evarts knew he had no chance with her. The professor not only had an academic's prejudice against police, but she had sent none of the signals that Evarts normally got from interested women. He kept fit, and females found his California beach-boy good looks attractive, but they also said he was remote and uncompromising. As a result, the women he had known seemed to prefer prolonged trysts to serious relationships. A couple of times, just when he had thought things might progress, he had become engaged in tricky investigations, withdrawing into his own head and growing increasingly obsessive. Then he had invariably endured a string of accusations that he had found another woman or was just an inconsiderate bastard.

The professor suddenly tossed the sheaf of paper on the table.

"You look puzzled," Evarts said.

"The notes look consistent with the style of his presidential papers. Someone went to a lot of trouble to fake them."

"You're sure they're fake?"

"No, damn it." She looked away. "I need to test the originals."

"Meaning you'll have to go to Santa Barbara."

She returned her eyes to his. "Unless Douglass will release them to your care."

"He won't." Evarts finished his hamburger and wiped his mouth with the oversized white cloth napkin. "But you knew that. What's puzzling you?"

"The last page. It's just a column of numbers, and it doesn't look like Lincoln's handwriting. Why's it included with these notes?"

"I was hoping you could tell me."

"It's completely foreign to me. What did Douglass say?"

"Nothing. Never mentioned the page, but I know what it is."

"You do? What?"

"An encrypted code."

Chapter 2

· · · · ·

Evarts stood on the landing at the rear entrance to the inclined lecture hall. He guessed that the crescent-shaped rows of hardwood chairs held about two hundred students. Since the hall was almost full, Evarts surmised that Professor Baldwin must be popular or a tough grader.

With no seats available close to an aisle, Evarts walked down until he reached the middle of the small auditorium and then squeezed past the scrunched knees of several coeds. Giving a friendly nod to his neighbors, he squeezed into the narrow chair while casually adjusting the position of his gun so it wouldn't poke him in the ribs. Next, he swung up the little writing platform that swiveled from beneath the armrest. He didn't intend to take notes, but he wanted the mini-desk up so he had something to lean on.

At the end of lunch, he and the professor had made plans. Immediately after her lecture, they would travel together to Santa Barbara. Evarts would drive and bring her back the following day. He told Baldwin that he had an appointment the next afternoon at the Federal Building just outside Westwood Village on Wilshire Boulevard.

He had lied. He wanted to continue interviewing her on the two-hour drive—and he especially wanted an opportunity to ask seemingly harmless questions on the way back. He had already figured out that if Professor Baldwin suspected she was being grilled, he would be as clueless about the time of day as Abraham Douglass.

The rest of the arrangements had gone smoothly. After lunch, they had stepped outside the restaurant and both whipped out cell phones. She had arranged some preliminary tests at the University of California at Santa Barbara and secured herself a room at the university's Guest House. Evarts had called Abraham Douglass and, with no effort at all, gotten them invited to dinner at his home for that same evening. Douglass also had promised to escort the document to UCSB with Professor Baldwin in the morning. After their respective telephone calls, Baldwin had made a quick detour into a ritzy apartment building in the Village to pack a few items. She hadn't invited Evarts to come up with her, so he had stayed in the lobby, wondering if she wanted to be alone to inform a significant other of their plans.

Evarts looked around the lecture hall and felt old. At thirty-eight, he was undoubtedly the oldest person in the hall. Then Professor Baldwin stepped out of the back room. A treble tone took over the hall as the male voices hushed. As a cop, he judged ages pretty well, but she gave him a bit of trouble. In the end, Evarts guessed that he still held the unwanted honor of being the oldest, but the call was close. Whatever her age, she held the male portion of her class enthralled before she spoke a word.

She set a valise beside the podium and extracted one of those ubiquitous manila folders. Evarts knew the valise also contained the brown envelope he had given her at lunch. After fiddling with her papers, she started with, "Abraham Lincoln is the most deified president in our history. Can anyone tell me why?"

Calling on a few raised hands, she got the stock answers. Lincoln emancipated the slaves, held the Union together, won the Civil War, and suffered a tragic death at the hands of an assassin. With over a half-dozen arms still in the air, Professor Baldwin dove into her lecture.

"This is a history class, and as such, our task is to deal with the truth, not myth. So let's examine the 'Great Emancipator' issue first."

Here she stepped out from behind the podium and stood full bodied in front of her audience. "I assigned the Emancipation Proclamation as homework. My bet is that you found it dry reading, especially for a document written by Abraham Lincoln, the one who really deserved to be called the Great Communicator. Unlike his speeches, the Proclamation was a carefully crafted legal brief. It freed all the slaves in the rebellious states if those states didn't willingly rejoin the Union prior to January 1, 1863. It didn't free slaves in the loyal states, and the document carefully excluded regions in the South that the Union army had already conquered. In other words, if the Confederacy capitulated and rejoined the Union, not a single slave in the entire nation would've been freed."

She paused for effect. "President Lincoln freed slaves he had no power to free and kept in bondage those slaves he actually had the authority to set free."

Evarts shifted in his seat. He read a broad range of material, so he knew American history better than most, but this perspective was new to him. He decided he had better read Professor Baldwin's book.

"What were Lincoln's motives?" she asked.

After stepping back behind the podium, she answered her own question. "Among other things, he wanted to incite a slave rebellion in the South. In late 1862, the South was winning the war, and he needed to open another front against the Confederacy. He wanted an insurgency deep inside enemy territory. An insurrection, by the way, that would threaten the women and children left behind to tend farms and businesses. An insurrection that would siphon off Confederate troops from battlefields as they raced home to protect their loved ones."

She removed her glasses and swept her green eyes across the auditorium. "More to the point of his personal character, he reluctantly proposed this narrowly defined emancipation only after enormous pressure from his own Republican Party."

Replacing her glasses, she picked up her lecture notes. "Did Lincoln seek a legacy as the great emancipator? This need not be a point of speculation. We can ask him. Seldom have American presidents been clearer about their goals." She waved her notes as if to confirm the validity of her statement. "Lincoln believed the nation indivisible, and he fought the bloodiest war in our history for one purpose and one purpose only: to force the Confederacy back into the Union. He famously said that if it were possible, he would reunite the nation without freeing a single slave. The Emancipation Proclamation proves that he meant what he said."

She went on to support her position with an elaborate recital of Lincoln's own words and deeds. It looked like Professor Baldwin fell into that category of historians who took delight in pooh-poohing established orthodoxy. Evarts was not impressed.

Then she said something that made him pull out his Moleskine notebook. He scribbled a reminder and then snapped the attached elastic band around the outside of the little black notebook. He slid the book back into his windbreaker's inside pocket. He almost always wore the light jacket to hide the badge and gun hanging from his wide belt.

At the end of the lecture, most of the students went up the stairs and out the rear doors. When foot traffic allowed, Evarts walked down toward the speaker's platform. While a half-dozen fawning students circled Professor Baldwin, Evarts waited patiently. Maybe not so patiently. After ten minutes of her holding court, he pointedly looked at his watch. Finally, she disentangled herself from her adoring fans and made a beeline toward the speaker's door. Over her shoulder, she bid him to follow with a two-finger wave. He bet she did that a lot.

Her office on the second floor looked too neat and tidy for a professor. She had books everywhere and papers galore, but they were all stacked in apparent order. As soon as they entered, she opened a cabinet, rifled a few files, and then slipped the day's lecture into one of those muddy-green hanging folders. Evarts stood at the door. If he could hurry her, they might miss the worst of the commuter traffic. She sat down in front of her computer, and Evarts sighed audibly.

"I'll only be a moment. I need to check my memory of tomorrow's schedule and see if I have any important email notes."

"Can't you do that at the Guest House?"

She held up one finger to silence him. How grand it must be to go through life issuing commands with one or two fingers.

"My schedule is almost clear. I can take care of the few appointments with phone calls once we're on the highway."

That disappointed Evarts. He wasn't thrilled with the idea of her jabbering away on her cell phone once they got into the car. One of his pet peeves was being ignored, and it seemed to him that a cell phone shunted aside the person physically close in favor of the person who possessed the ear. Besides, he hated hearing only one side of a conversation.

"There's a note from Douglass." She clicked the mouse to open the message. "He's never sent me email before."

Now she had his attention. "What does it say?"

"Odd." Evarts watched her eyes rapidly scan the screen and then slowly go back over the text. "He asks me to leave the document copy here."

That didn't seem so odd. "He probably has more copies in Santa Barbara."

She looked up from the screen and met his eyes. "He wants me to seal the envelope and give it to a trusted colleague or friend, preferably someone not in the History Department." She grabbed the envelope he had given her at lunch and started for the door. "Wait here. I'll be back in about fifteen minutes."

"Let me make a copy for myself first."

"No."

No? What the hell did that mean? "Then I'll go with you."

She never broke her stride toward the door. "No. Douglass said my safety depended on keeping the hiding place secret."

"Not from me."

She stopped with one hand on the open door. "Yes, from you. He mentioned you by name." She disappeared into the hall and slammed the door.

Chapter 3

· · · · ·

Evarts was in a snit as they walked back through the college campus. He hadn't moved his car from the Westwood Village lot because he didn't have a UCLA parking sticker. Despite the warm July sun, he walked fast because he wanted to get back and ask Douglass what the hell was going on.

"Excuse me, *Commander*."

"I told you not to call me that." He immediately regretted the harsh tone because it broadcast his irritation.

"Well, do you mind if I shout at you?"

"What?"

"If you keep walking this fast, I'll have to yell because you'll be in the next county."

Evarts slowed down. "Sorry. My mind was somewhere else. I naturally walk fast."

"You mean sprint fast."

"Whatever." Evarts pointed. "My car's right there."

"The Odyssey?"

"Yeah."

"Is that your wife's car?"

"No, it's mine."

"You drive a soccer-mom minivan." Baldwin laughed. "What do the other cops call you?"

"They call me Mr. Tibbs."

"Huh?"

"Never mind." Evarts thumbed the unlock button, and his car made a cheerful chirp. "Just get in." He didn't bother to open the door for her.

As he started the engine, he saw her examine his van. Other than the driver and passenger seats in front, the only other seating was in the far back, with a big void in the center.

"Why don't you have a middle seat?"

"I haul stuff. Buckle up."

"Must be tough to have a conversation on a double date."

Evarts ignored her. Why had Douglass warned her to hide the document copy? His caution made no sense for a fraud case. And why keep the hiding place secret from him? He had tried to reach Douglass by phone but got his answering service. The message he left had been rude. He didn't like uncooperative victims, because they usually had something to hide.

"Why don't you wear a wedding ring?"

"What?" Evarts was trying to reach his wallet to pay the parking attendant.

"I said, why don't you wear a wedding ring?"

"Because I'm not married. Why do you wear glasses?"

"You said this wasn't your wife's van."

"No, I said it was mine." Evarts paid the attendant and screeched out of the parking lot. "Why do you always answer a question with a question?"

"What are you in such a huff about?"

Evarts sighed in exasperation. "How well do you know Douglass?"

"How—" She scooted around in the seat to face him more directly. "Douglass peer-reviewed one of my books. We've run into each other at conferences and seminars. Lincoln enthusiasts are a tight clique."

"You didn't sound like a Lincoln enthusiast in your lecture."

"Don't judge me on a single lecture. I admire the way Lincoln grew in office."

"Why would Douglass warn you about your safety? Do Lincoln enthusiasts threaten each other?"

She laughed. "Only in print." She used her thumb to pull a little slack in the seat harness. "It seemed strange to me too, but I know him well enough to give his warning some credence. How well do you know Douglass?"

"Evidently better than you."

"Really?"

He liked that she seemed surprised. "Really. We spend several evenings a week together ... at least when we're both in town."

"Douglass socializing with a cop? I find that out of character."

"We share an enthusiasm for backgammon and Macallan single malt scotch."

"Backgammon? Isn't that a gambling game?"

Evarts concentrated on merging onto the San Diego Freeway. "Yes, at least the way we play."

"Douglass is rich."

"So? We don't play for big stakes. It's the contest that counts."

"And the Macallan's?"

"Of course."

She made her calls as he drove over the Mulholland Pass and into the San Fernando Valley. After she finished, she stuffed the cell phone into her purse and said, "I don't like putting things in my eye."

"What?"

"You asked why I wore glasses."

Evarts didn't respond immediately. After a few miles, he said, "Listen, it seems like we got off to a bad start. Can we call a truce?"

"Fine by me."

"Okay, then. Do you have any idea how those papers might put you in danger?"

"If genuine, they're valuable, but the people who would want them have money." She thought a minute. "How do you know that last page is encrypted code?"

"I worked for Intelligence in the military. Trained to recognize codes."

"Did you break this one?"

"No time." Evarts honked at a car that had abruptly swerved into his lane. Traffic was starting to get bad. "But it shouldn't be too hard if it's really from Lincoln's time. We know the Civil War codes."

"Where're we going?"

Evarts had just passed the exit for the Ventura Freeway. "Highway 126. Less traffic this time of day. Have you ever encountered something like that last page before?"

"No, but Douglass didn't send that by mistake. He wanted us to have a copy."

"He wanted *you* to have a copy. And I'm the guy with code-breaking experience. Why would that be?"

For once she didn't answer with a question. In fact, she didn't answer at all for many miles of bumper-to-bumper traffic. Finally she said, "If genuine, the Cooper Union notes are invaluable, but from what I saw, not controversial. The speech was printed in countless newspapers and pamphlets, and I saw nothing in the notes that deviated from the historical text. The only thing that could pose a threat is that last page."

Evarts had already figured that out, but he would need to wait to examine the code more closely. "Tell me about this Cooper Union speech."

"That I can do. Abraham Lincoln said that the Cooper Union address made him president. That and a Mathew Brady photograph taken the same day, but we'll leave that for later. Lincoln had become somewhat of a national figure two years earlier during the Lincoln-Douglas debates. Although he lost the race for the Illinois Senate seat, the debates were published nationally. In the latter part of 1859, he received an invitation to speak at Cooper Union in Manhattan. Despite his fame from the debates, the powers that be still considered him a regional politician of mediocre note. This was his chance to make his mark among the political elite in the media capital of the country."

"Wait a minute. New York City was a media center back then?"

"Even more than today. Except for a few Boston publications, all the national magazines and important newspapers came from New York. In fact, sitting onstage with Lincoln was Horace Greeley, publisher of—"

"'Go West, young man'?" Evarts had to suddenly brake and kept his eyes on the rearview mirror to make sure he didn't get rear-ended.

Baldwin's hand leaped to the dashboard for support. When a possible fender-bender had been avoided, she continued in an even voice. "In his time, Greeley was famous for more than a single quip. He published and edited the *New York Tribune*, the most influential newspaper in the nation." The traffic opened up a bit and she shifted in her seat to face him more directly. "Back to the speech. Lincoln was only one in a series of politicians invited to speak in the run-up to the Republican convention. No one expected anything eloquent from a man renowned for his homespun yarns and humorous stories, but Lincoln gave what today we would call a presidential address. It was masterful. The speech not only impressed the sophisticated New York audience, but it also read well in newspapers. You have to know Lincoln to understand what a feat that was."

"Explain."

"Well, Lincoln was a highly animated speaker. He looked like a rube, but once he got going, he mesmerized an audience. They interrupted his speech numerous times with cheers or laughter, but Lincoln told no jokes, no stories. That night, he captured his audience with repetition, tone of voice, and facial expressions. He knew every laugh line and played them with the timing of a modern-day stand-up comic. Those types of speeches normally don't read well in print, but he had carefully crafted it for both audiences."

Evarts had to brake again. Not hard this time, but firm enough to irritate him. He hated the fitful nature of California freeway traffic. Why couldn't drivers pay enough attention to drive smoothly? Too many cell phones, radio station changes, and other activities he didn't even want to contemplate.

When once more in the clear, he said, "That doesn't sound like the morose man that's been eulogized in marble. Wasn't he an accidental president?"

"Hardly. Lincoln was undoubtedly one of the greatest speakers in history, but he was also a wily politician. There was nothing accidental about his presidency ... or his reelection in 1864."

"You sound like you admire him."

"I do."

"It didn't sound like it during your lecture."

"A man must be judged in his times. Lincoln held the Union together and despite his instincts, eliminated slavery. The man was human, not a saint. Lincoln by any measure was a racist. He also violated the Constitution to such an extent that he should've been impeached."

Evarts felt himself get irritated, not at the traffic this time, but at the professor's comments. "How so?" he asked.

"He suspended habeas corpus, arrested newspaper editors, jailed Northerners without hearings or trials, bypassed Congress, ignored the Supreme Court, and even arrested a member of Congress. He justified these violations as part of the Executive's War Powers and claimed that he violated the Constitution for the sole purpose of protecting it."

"If he had lost the war, there'd be no Constitution."

"That's debatable. The Constitution of the Confederate States of America wasn't that different from the Constitution drafted in 1787."

Evarts felt Lincoln still had a sworn duty to win the war, but he didn't want to start another argument, so he let the subject drop.

He took Highway 126 toward Santa Paula. Evarts liked this drive. As soon as they exited the busy freeway, orange trees lined both sides of the highway that ran up a picturesque narrow valley. Every couple of miles, brightly tented stands sold produce from local farms at prices that must have embarrassed supermarkets. This stretch of two-lane road preserved the last remnant of a rural Southern California—the Southern California that his father and grandfather knew. He feared the day he would make this turn to find the orange trees bulldozed so developers could build even more scrunched-together, humdrum houses.

He had been fuming ever since Baldwin quit talking. He had enjoyed the last half hour of civility and hated to ruin it. Making a decision, he said, "Professor, I should tell you that I get angry when someone throws the racist accusation around."

"Oh." She hesitated. "There's a dictionary definition of racist, and Lincoln fits within that strict definition. His own words indict him, but I didn't mean it to be as derogatory as you might think. Remember, I said a man must be judged in his time, and nearly everyone was racist back then." When Evarts didn't comment she asked, "You have some scar tissue?"

"As any cop, especially one that grew up and works in a rich white enclave."

"Doesn't your friendship with Abraham Douglass grant you absolution?"

"It means nothing to those who use the epithet politically, and it means everything to real racists."

After a moment she asked, "How is Douglass received in Santa Barbara?"

Evarts laughed. "Just fine. In the insular Santa Barbara social circles, his enormous wealth counts for more than his black skin."

Chapter 4

· · · · ·

Most tourists can't find the Southern California the movies promise. Luckily, they don't venture as far north as Santa Barbara, or Evarts's favorite coastal town would be polluted with checkered shorts and black socks. Sandwiched between the Pacific Ocean and the Santa Ynez Mountains, a twenty-five-mile stretch of relatively unspoiled California coastline separated Santa Barbara from Ventura, the largest town to the south, and no big city loomed from the north for nearly a hundred miles. Less than a two-hour drive from Los Angeles, Santa Barbara's geography and no-growth temperament protected it from the kind of sprawl that cluttered the coastline between San Diego and Los Angeles.

Evarts had grown up in Santa Barbara, but he didn't live there now. The city had become too expensive. Real estate in the city that old-timers called the American Riviera had always been outrageous, but recently prices had gone beyond absurd. The median home price had escalated to over a million dollars, with even small California bungalows a mile from the ocean going for seven figures.

He had dropped Baldwin off at the UCSB Guest House to get situated. Douglass had promised to send his driver to pick her up for dinner at his home later that evening. Evarts decided to drive directly there so he could talk to Douglass before her arrival.

He knew he ought to stop at the police station, but he picked up his cell phone instead. His department consisted of eighteen detectives under the direction of himself and a lieutenant. In short order, Evarts found out that nothing significant had happened that day.

Property crimes demanded most of his resources, and catching the Rock Burglar presented his biggest challenge. The nickname was a misnomer because his department felt confident that a gang committed these crimes, not an individual. The criminals carefully cased a neighborhood, learned the routine of the residents, and then threw a rock through a window when the owners were away. In less than five minutes, the gang swooped up everything of value and disappeared before the police responded to the alarm. Worse, they would commit a couple of burglaries and then move to another prosperous city, only to return to Santa Barbara after the residents had again become complacent. This had been going on for nearly eight years, and despite cooperative investigations between various police forces, the gang had not only eluded capture, but had left no forensic evidence that pointed in a consistent direction.

By the time Evarts got off the phone, he had approached the busy commercial district. Santa Barbara advertised Old Town as the most beautiful downtown in America, but Evarts thought Carmel and a few other cities might challenge that claim. Despite the exaggeration, Old Town, with its Spanish architecture, abundant sidewalk cafés, curio shops, fine restaurants, and countless coffeehouses, exuded the charm and relaxed atmosphere of a Mediterranean coastal village.

Like all the truly wealthy in town, Douglass lived high up a secluded canyon in the foothills of the Santa Ynez Mountains. Evarts drove the serpentine road carefully and then pulled onto a gravel path facing a wrought-iron gate. He pushed the call button on the security box, and the gate opened without an inquiring voice over the squawk box. Evarts had examined the Douglass security system and knew that a camera showed his face on a monitor inside the house. After passing through the gate, he drove along a private road that followed a ridgeline until he reached the house that had been built on the apex of an outcropping.

Although the white stucco house had a red tile roof, it veered from the contemporary architecture that realtors called the Santa Barbara style. The flat facade, crushed rock driveway, and minimalist landscaping gave the impression of an ordinary house, but this unpretentious entrance disguised an exquisitely decorated, rambling single-story home of over eight thousand square feet. From the driveway, the house also blocked the panoramic view of the California coastline that could be seen from the patio on the far side of the traditional Spanish hacienda.

Douglass's manservant opened the door before Evarts rang the chimes. Evarts nodded to the familiar face. "Hi, Pete."

Without preamble, Peter said, "Mr. Douglass is on the back patio."

"Thank you." Evarts walked about twenty feet through the

antique furnished foyer and out a set of double doors. The hacienda was built in a square around a huge tiled courtyard. Mexican-style furniture had been arranged into four sitting areas that surrounded a bubbling fountain in the center. He had attended charity functions where over a hundred people had comfortably sipped cocktails in this central square, but it wasn't his destination today. He traversed the length of the courtyard and entered the house again through an identical set of double doors. They led to an enormous common room that could hold another hundred people for Douglass charity events. As he walked through the great hall, Evarts saw that all of the atrium doors lining the back of the house stood open, making the room feel more like an extension of the rear patio than part of the house.

Evarts picked one of the twelve doors and stepped out onto the patio. For first-time visitors, the grandeur of the view came as a surprise and a treat. Douglass had had the patio designed so that the ground seemed to disappear at the edge of the tiled surface. A person walking through one of these doors had the impression of being cantilevered over some of the most beautiful coastline in California. This was Abraham Douglass's favorite spot in the world, and the two of them often spent the evening sipping scotch whiskey and watching the sun slowly sink into the Pacific Ocean.

"Good evening, Mr. Douglass," Evarts said to the man's back.

Douglass turned with his evening scotch already in hand. "Mr. Douglass? What's got your dander up?"

"I think you know." Evarts took his usual seat in the chair on the opposite side of a glass-top table. He noticed the backgammon game was nowhere in sight.

"Peter, can you get *Mr.* Evarts the usual?"

Douglass, of course, meant a glass of Macallan's, neat. "No thank you, Pete. Not just yet. I have official business first."

Douglass turned toward the sunset and took a shallow sip of his scotch. Abraham Douglass kept his craggy face clean-shaven and his gray hair cropped so close that his black skull showed through. Evarts knew Douglass was seventy-three, because he attended his gala birthday parties each year. An exceptionally handsome man, Douglass wore Hollywood-style attire from the forties, which made him look like a gracefully aging movie star.

In truth, he had made his fortune in Southern California's other great industry. When John F. Kennedy set the country's sights on the moon, the Los Angeles area had already become the aerospace center of the country. Northrop, North American, Douglas Aircraft, Lockheed, TRW, Hughes, and others had bustling factories that contributed far more to the local economy than the entertainment industry. Douglass had had the foresight to understand that these factories would need millions upon millions of fasteners certified to stringent government specifications. His Aerospace Supply Company provided all these companies with explosive bolts, rivets, screws, and esoteric single-use fasteners that cost more than the outrageously priced hammer of Apollo fame. Douglass built a highly profitable business, but his huge wealth came from selling his company at the height of the eighties acquisition and merger craze.

"I presume you have questions," Douglass said.

"A few. Where did you get the Lincoln document? Who'd you buy it from, and how did they make contact with you? Why did you have Baldwin hide the copy from me? How can this document endanger her? Why did you include that page of code? And finally, has there actually been a crime committed, or are you using me to run errands?" Evarts paused. "You may answer in any sequence you choose." He said this last with a bit of an edge.

Douglass seemed amused. "Is this the way you normally grill suspects?"

"Damn it. Is everyone going to answer my questions with questions today?" Evarts turned toward the rear door. "Pete, on second thought, I'll take that scotch now." Evarts's irritation grew because Douglass wore an enigmatic smile that said he found his friend's annoyance amusing.

Douglass waited until Evarts had been served. "You called it the Lincoln document. I take it you believe it genuine."

"Abe, you're too damn smart to get scammed, and fake documents don't raise a warning to third parties. My bet is that Baldwin will prove this document real."

"Probably not, but she won't prove it fake. Harder to prove the positive."

"Did you use me just to get her up here?"

Douglass took a deep breath. "Yes. But it's bigger than that. Much bigger. I'll explain everything when she gets here."

"I can wait a few minutes, but tell me now why you had her hide the document from me."

"Greg, I couldn't trust your chivalrous nature. If someone threatened Professor Baldwin in your presence, you would disclose the location of the document in a heartbeat. Now the decision will be hers alone."

"What about the encrypted page? I'd like to take a crack at that code."

"Use your own copy."

Evarts stopped. "How do you know I have one?"

"You might not care about the Cooper Union notes, but you could never resist that encryption." Douglass chuckled. "I knew you'd make a copy for yourself before you drove down to UCLA."

"You used a priceless Lincoln document as bait? For what?" Evarts took a sip of his drink and set the heavy crystal glass down hard enough that the glass tabletop rattled. "Abe, why? You've never been devious with me before."

"Ah, but I wish that were true." Douglass held up the flat of his hand to signal that he wouldn't explain. "Please be kind enough to wait until Professor Baldwin arrives."

Evarts took a deep breath and picked up his drink. "Are you getting me involved in something illegal?"

"An outrage, yes, but illegal … no, I don't think so."

"That doesn't sound reassuring." Evarts thought about leaving but decided against it. He knew and trusted Douglass, so he would wait to hear the explanation. "No backgammon this evening?"

"I thought you'd be more interested in spending the evening with an attractive woman."

"Professor Baldwin doesn't like me, and I think she hates you."

Douglass laughed. "That ought to make for an interesting evening."

Evarts remembered the notation he made during Baldwin's lecture. "Abe, are you a descendant of Frederick Douglass?"

"Yes, I'm a direct descendant. That's why I donated some of his papers to UCSB." Douglass took on that enigmatic smile again. "I'm surprised you haven't asked that question before now."

"Never occurred to me. I don't care about people's ancestry."

"Ah, but you should. Family's important. You ought to look into your own genealogy."

Evarts finished his drink. "What the hell for? I know my parents. They're good people. Anything beyond that is useless trivia."

Chapter 5

·····

Professor Baldwin arrived in less than an hour. She had on the same casual slacks, but now she wore a green raw-silk blouse that accented her eyes. She also wore a frosty demeanor that made their little social gathering a bit scratchy.

The first words out of her mouth set the tone. "Good evening, Abe. Can I look at the originals of that document?"

"Patricia, my dear, relax a moment first. I've taken the liberty of ordering you a nice port."

"I didn't come here to socialize." She didn't take a seat or acknowledge Evarts's presence.

"But it would be polite. Please, humor an old man. After all, you're about to examine a singular piece of antebellum history. One worthy of a learned dissertation by a preeminent Lincoln scholar."

"Flattery? I thought that beneath you."

Douglass chortled, as if privy to an inside joke. "In truth, very little is beneath me."

"If you think I'm a preeminent Lincoln scholar, why did you ravage my last book?"

"Because your premise was wrong, my dear," Douglass said with a cheery lilt.

Exasperated, Baldwin slipped into the open chair. She picked up the glass of port and sniffed without tasting. "My, you pulled out one of your best bottles."

"A celebration. It's not every day that a new Lincoln document surfaces."

She turned to Evarts for the first time. "You told me Abe thought the document was a forgery."

"Evidently, our host is playing games. I suspect the document's real and that Douglass knew it all along."

"Impossible." She shifted her gaze to Douglass. "Where would you get a preinauguration address in Lincoln's own hand?"

"From the descendants of people entrusted with Lincoln's early papers."

"What? Who?" Baldwin sat bolt upright, looking flabbergasted. "You mean to say there's more? Do you have them?"

"I'm only in possession of the Cooper Union manuscript. You may examine it momentarily, but first, enjoy your port and the sunset. They're both spectacular."

"Spectacular, hell. The sun sets every night. A previously undiscovered Lincoln document comes along once in a lifetime. Abe, you're enjoying this far too much." She looked peeved but tasted the port and made an appreciative nod. After another sip, she asked, "Why me?"

"Why us?" Evarts interjected.

Douglass appeared to choose his words carefully. "Patricia, you're one of the foremost Lincoln experts in the country, and our friend Evarts here has the right background for his piece of our little enterprise."

"You mean my intelligence experience, don't you?" Evarts said. "You used the Cooper Union manuscript to get me intrigued about the encrypted code."

"You're a fine detective, which you just demonstrated." Douglass raised his glass in a salute. "Your deduction is correct."

"Who wrote it? The code doesn't appear to be in Lincoln's hand." Baldwin went right to practical matters.

"I don't know. That message was sent to Lincoln prior to his departure for New York to deliver that address. The code has never been broken."

"I find that hard to believe." Evarts felt growing annoyance at being used for nonpolice business.

"But true, nonetheless. People have tried, but no one has found the key to unlocking the encryption. All we know is that Lincoln was in secret communication with someone, and that someone probably lived in New York."

"Because the two documents were kept together?" Evarts asked.

"Another astute deduction." Douglass smiled at Baldwin. "See, I've paired you up with someone useful to your research."

"Paired? What are you talking about? I thought you just used Detective Evarts to get me up here."

"The task ahead requires both of you."

Douglass spoke with such solemnity that Evarts began to question his competence. He leaned forward. "Abe, perhaps you should explain this mystery ... from the beginning."

"An excellent suggestion." Douglass sipped his scotch and gazed at the horizon a moment. "This mystery, if you will, goes back to the Civil War. Beyond, actually. It involves one of the most powerful political families in our nation's history. A family that was instrumental in securing our independence, engineering our republican government, and moving us ever forward toward the vision espoused in our founding documents. A family that not only had a hand in fomenting the Civil War, but to a large extent prosecuted that conflict."

Douglass took another moment to enjoy the view. Evarts might have been concerned, but he had seen this behavior on numerous occasions. Right in the middle of a roll of the dice, Douglass would almost go into a trance. It had never bothered him before, but now he wondered if these periodic distractions were an indication of an unraveling mind.

When Douglass spoke again, it was as if there had been no interruption. "I believe the encrypted page will unveil a good piece of the mystery. And I can't think of two better minds to put on it. It's why I brought the two of you together."

"Which family?" Evarts asked.

"Later. You need to understand more first. But I can assure you this family makes the Adams, Kennedy, and Bush families look like featherweights."

Evarts watched Baldwin scoot her cushioned chair around so she had a better view of the coastline. The way she sipped from her glass and sighed contentedly said volumes. She had dismissed Douglass's recital as the ranting of an old man who was starting to lose it. Her posture and lack of further questions indicated that she had decided to take her host's initial advice and enjoy the glow of an ending day, savoring the outrageously expensive port.

Evarts, however, hoped this cagey old man might still be in possession of his faculties. He tapped the glass tabletop and used his hard cop voice to get Douglass's full attention. "Where did you get the Cooper Union manuscript?"

"From the Shut Mouth Society," Douglass said. "An organization founded by members of the family I told you about."

"And the encrypted document?"

"Same source." Douglass actually seemed pleased with the questions.

Suddenly, Baldwin whirled around, now interested in the discussion. "The Shut Mouth Society? That's how Lincoln's law partner described him. He said he was the most shut mouth man he had ever encountered."

"Correct, my dear. The Society took its name from that description."

"That's ridiculous. Lincoln's family wasn't powerful... politically or otherwise. His ancestors were dirt poor. His son Robert was secretary of war, minister to Great Britain, and president of the Pullman Corporation, but there were no other prominent members of the Lincoln family."

"You misunderstood. The Shut Mouth Society idolized Lincoln, but neither he nor his family members belonged to it. A loose family cabal existed before Lincoln, but they became a secret society only after his death."

"A secret society? That sounds like the kind of hokum I'd expect to hear on a radio talk show in the wee hours of the morning," Evarts said.

"Have you ever heard of the Shut Mouth Society?" Douglass asked with a sly smile.

"No," they both said in unison.

"That proves they're a secret society, because I can assure you, it's been in existence for nearly a hundred and fifty years."

"Doing what?" Baldwin asked.

"Oh, you know secret societies. Much ado about nothing. The appeal is the secret association and some arcane little rituals. Once you get inside the Masons, Skull and Bones, or the Illuminati, the supposed secrets always disappoint."

"Are you a member of the Shut Mouth Society?" Evarts asked.

"Me? A black man? Heavens, no. I told you the Society is comprised of descendants of a powerful political family that goes back to our founding. You'd be hard-pressed to find a Negro family that fits that description."

"Then how do you know it really exits?" Evarts asked.

"Because my family has had dealings with the Society over the years. I knew about them from my father … and they provided the Cooper Union manuscript as their bona fides. A sample of their treasure trove, so to speak."

"Treasure trove?" Baldwin said incredulously. "Just before the Lincolns left for Washington, Mary burned stacks and stacks of papers in the alley behind their house. Historians always assumed that these weren't just personal letters but all her husband's political papers."

"Historians assumed wrong." Douglass appeared to enjoy this exchange way too much.

Baldwin's voice showed impatience. "Abe, if they have Lincoln preinaugural papers, they have real secrets, not just arcane little rituals."

"Perhaps, but I don't believe the Shut Mouth Society has a malicious purpose."

"Listen," Evarts said. "I'm not a historian, so I need some help here. Professor Baldwin said the Cooper Union manuscript doesn't conflict with recorded history, so why withhold this so-called treasure trove from the public?"

"Exactly," Baldwin added.

For some reason, Evarts enjoyed the comradely glance Baldwin threw him as she said this. Douglass chuckled in a way that told him that he had noticed as well.

"What secrets are they hiding?" Evarts demanded.

"That I can't answer. I only know that they approached me to ask a favor. They wanted the papers out, but without fanfare. I was asked to keep the circle of people small and professional."

"Why? And why now? What's their purpose?" Baldwin demanded.

"That should seem obvious. They want the code broken. Why now, I don't know."

"You know more," Evarts said in an accusatory tone.

"But I won't tell more."

Evarts noticed he didn't deny the charge. "Why not?" he asked.

"Because you're both skeptics. Further information will only convince you that I've succumbed to senility. You each must investigate the information I have already provided using your respective skills."

Night had fallen, and Douglass stood to indicate they should move indoors. "We'll meet one week from today, and I'll tell you everything...after you've learned enough on your own to give credence to what I have to say."

"This is ridiculous," Baldwin said. "We have nothing to investigate."

"On the contrary. You have the Cooper Union manuscript, an unbroken code, and a family to identify."

"And the Shut Mouth Society," Evarts said.

"And the Shut Mouth Society."

Chapter 6

· · · · ·

When they stepped indoors, Douglass led them into his library. Interior decorators often assembled ersatz libraries for rich clients with intellectual pretensions. The library in Abraham Douglass's home had none of the telltale signs of a decorator's touch. The dark wood shelves extended to the ceiling and were stuffed with hardcover books, but the books had the jumbled appearance of actually having been pulled out to be read and then replaced without forethought. Some had dust covers, other did not. Some books lay in horizontal piles, while gaps existed on other shelves. The room was furnished with great easy chairs and ottomans instead of a *Town & Country* desk. Lighting was indirect, but each chair had its own floor lamp positioned just over the reader's head. Evarts had perused the shelves enough to know that the books ranged from esoteric history tomes to popular novels.

Evarts thought he knew the room, but Douglass went to a column of shelves that looked indistinguishable from the others and pressed a button on a remote he had taken from his pocket. A soft motor whirred, and the column moved out toward the room and pivoted to the side to reveal a massive walk-in safe.

"My god, Abe," Evarts said. "The Rock Burglar would never get through that before a police response."

Douglass spun the huge tumbler, shielding the combination with his body. "That's why they make safes. More people should use them." After he snapped the stainless steel handle down, Douglass effortlessly swung the precision-balanced door open. Evarts expected the inside to display modernistic stainless steel, but instead the interior looked like an extension of the library, with the same dark wood shelves and jumbled up stacks of books and portfolios.

"I expected gold, currency, or jewelry. What's this?" Evarts asked.

"His priceless Lincoln collection," Professor Baldwin answered.

"Not priceless, my dear. Just pricey."

"Abe, I've seen exhibits of your collection, but nothing you've made public compares with this."

"And you may peruse it all at your leisure after next week, Patricia."

"A bribe?"

"Of course. It's about time you got a proper handle on your specialty."

"You do know how to ruin a moment."

Douglass chuckled as he reached for a folio and handed it to Baldwin. "Let's step back into the library so you can examine this properly."

"Can you have Peter bring my laptop? He took it away when I came in."

"Of course." Douglass made a shooing motion with his hands so he could exit the narrow vault. When they had reentered the library, Douglass locked the safe and closed the hiding partition before summoning his servant, using the same remote control unit. He pointed to a small writing table in the corner. "Why don't you set up over there?" When Peter arrived, he asked for Baldwin's case and new drinks.

Baldwin walked over to the table and lay the portfolio on the surface with a delicacy that reminded Evarts of his father when he worked with his stamp collection. She carefully lifted the cover of the folio. Evarts was surprised to see odd-sized blue paper.

"Foolscap," Douglass explained. "Thirteen by sixteen inches. Not used today."

"But the copies were standard legal paper?" Evarts said.

"I digitally photographed them and printed reduced-sized pages. Easier for us to handle nowadays."

Peter came into the library with a black Tumi case slung over his shoulder and a tray that carried two scotches and another glass of port. After distributing the drinks and the case, he retreated without a word.

Baldwin immediately pulled out her laptop and set it beside the manuscript. She ignored the port until the machine was booting up. "I'm going to compare the text to the *Tribune*."

"Of course. We'll leave you to it. Dinner will be served in an hour." With that, Douglass motioned Evarts over to two of the easy chairs on the other side of the room. They settled in with their scotch, and Douglass explained, "After Lincoln gave his address, he went to dinner with the sponsors of the event. They dropped him off at the Astor House to get a good night's sleep, but Lincoln left his hotel and walked across the street to the *Tribune* office. He stayed until the wee hours, editing the text of his speech for the morning edition. Witnesses say he compared the typeset speech against a handwritten foolscap copy. Many newspapers printed the speech, but only Greeley's *Tribune* had the privilege of being edited by the author. Many variations appeared in broadsides and books during the campaign, and they all had slight variations. Patricia wants to compare my manuscript with the most authoritative source, which she undoubtedly has preloaded onto her laptop."

"Greeley? Professor Baldwin mentioned him."

"Professor Baldwin? I would've thought you two would be on a first-name basis by now."

"I'm trying to get her to use my first name but only because I don't like the way she says 'Commander.' The professor thinks I work for the Gestapo."

"She was raised by a couple of heavy establishment types, rich but progressive nonetheless. Something rubbed off, I suppose."

"That explains her dress."

"Her dress? She couldn't dress more conservatively."

"I didn't mean the progressive part—I meant the rich part. Her clothing and accessories would make your female neighbors envious."

Douglass laughed. "Yes, indeed. Patricia is a good person, but she has her frailties. Vanity among them. Unfortunately, it affects her research. Too damn smart for her own good, but she's right that Greeley was a player in this drama. He helped found the Republican Party. By all opinions, William Henry Seward should have grabbed the Republican nomination for president in 1860. Greeley hated him for past transgressions and believed an ardent abolitionist could never win, so he supported a series of New York speeches by other Republicans, Lincoln included."

"Were Greeley and Lincoln allies?"

"Depended on the month and the year ... and possibly the phase of the moon with Greeley. The man rode political issues like a teeter-totter. Lincoln and Greeley were probably too similar to get along for an extended period. Both had desperately poor upbringings with little formal education, each passionately approached politics with unbridled ambition and a craftiness that would make Machiavelli proud, and they both used the English language with the finesse of a master. Greeley helped set up and publicize the series of lectures, but he thought Lincoln was a lightweight, and Lincoln held a grudge against Greeley for supporting Douglas for the Illinois Senate seat."

"Douglas? I thought he was a Democrat."

"Right you are, Greg." Douglass chuckled. "Greeley had this grand idea that Stephen Douglas had so pissed off Southern Democrats that the party would split into warring factions if Douglas won the nomination for president. To secure the 1860 Democratic presidential nomination, Douglas had to win the 1858 Senate race, so Greeley went against his party and supported Douglas against Lincoln."

Douglass chuckled again. "Greeley's strategy worked. The collapse of the Democratic Party made Lincoln president, but Lincoln kept a wary eye on Greeley for the rest of his life, despite Greeley's ardent support for him after the Cooper Union address."

"Baldwin said the Cooper Union speech made Lincoln president."

"Well, it gave him the chance to become president. Prior to that, he was just another interesting regional politician. He developed a national reputation in the race against Senator Douglas, but during the debates he became renowned as a rube that entertained ignorant farmers with humorous stories. He also didn't appeal to the radical abolitionist wing of the party, because he repeatedly promised not to interfere with slavery where it already existed."

"The professor says he was a racist."

"A seismic fault in her reasoning." Douglass went into one of his brief reveries before continuing. "She's a captive to her discipline. Historians are all about sources. When they find a new or rarely used source, they treat it like scripture." Douglass laughed. "They don't believe half the things a sitting president says, but they ascribe truth to any contemporaneous quote from a historical figure."

"Meaning what?"

"Meaning politicians lie, or at least mislead. It's their nature. Today, yesterday, and in the future."

"You're saying Lincoln lied?"

"Of course. Everything the man said or did prior to 1858 opposed slavery. But in an overtly racist time, equating a black man to whites would not only doom a political career—it would also get a man ostracized from the community. Steven Douglas understood Lincoln's predilections and the temperament of Illinois voters, so he kept goading Lincoln to say that he supported voting rights for blacks or that they were equal to whites. The two great bugaboos of the age were that the black man would take the workingman's job and seduce white women. The opponents of emancipation artfully propagated the notion that if slaves were freed in the South, they would stream north to grab the poor man's money and his wife. Even the radical abolitionists approached the issue somewhat like today's animal rights activist. They wanted only to stop the cruelty, not to elevate blacks to an equal plane."

After another one of his long pauses, Douglass added, "Lincoln just said the things necessary to avoid being painted as an extremist."

"Is that the problem you had with her book?"

"Yes... but she's the one in the mainstream. My ideas are ridiculed."

"Does Lincoln's election have anything to do with this mystery?"

"I don't know... perhaps. Once you break that code, we may get a peek behind the curtain."

Evarts withdrew a trifolded piece of paper from his windbreaker. He looked at the sheet for a long moment before speaking. "A simple code that's hard to break uses a book known only to the sender and receiver. Numbers relate to pages, paragraphs, and words. These numbers almost fit that pattern."

"Others have come to that conclusion, but no book has been found that works."

Evarts studied Douglass. "How much more do you know?"

"Next week, my friend, next week. Let's see how our researcher is doing. Dinner must be ready."

Before Evarts could ask another question, Douglass had bounded out of his chair and briskly walked across the room. He had no alternative but to follow.

Baldwin immediately looked up. "Almost perfect match."

"What does that mean?" Evarts asked.

"Only that I can't dismiss it. If it's a forgery, the artists were clever enough to use the right source."

"What next?"

"Tomorrow morning, Abe and I take the document to UCSB. I have a friend in the Special Collections Department. He'll do some rudimentary tests."

"How long for conclusive tests?"

"Never, here. It's beyond the University's capabilities. Tomorrow, we can only prove the negative. If the tests prove positive, it'll have to go to a specialized lab. Probably the National Archives."

"Tomorrow you may test only one page of the speech," Douglass said.

"No. All the pages should be tested," Baldwin countered.

"I promised to keep the circle small. A single page won't disclose the significance of the document, but it's enough to test the ink and paper. When we go to a lab, we'll discuss it again, but tomorrow we take only one page." Douglass used a tone that brooked no further argument.

Baldwin turned to Evarts. "Are you going with us?"

"I have a job that demands my attention. Call me when you're through, and I'll drive you back to L.A. You can fill me in on the ride."

"You're still reluctant to get involved," Douglass said.

"I have responsibilities, Abe. And very little time to devote to an intellectual exercise."

"But we can skip our backgammon evenings next week. Think of this as another game between us."

"It *is* a game, and I don't like your rules. I solve mysteries at work. I prefer games of chance for recreation."

"Greg, this is *more* than a game. I know you disapprove of my way of handling it, but I'm asking you to trust me."

"Secret societies, newly discovered historical documents, encryptions, and we need to keep our investigation quiet." Evarts shook his head. When he said it out loud, it sounded ridiculous. "Abe, what's going on?"

"I need your trust. Just for a week."

"You want more than that. You want me to get enthralled with the chase. You're seducing us. I'm not going to take the next step until I know that this has a serious purpose."

Douglass drifted off for a few moments. When he came back, he put his hands on Evarts's and Baldwin's shoulders. "I know you'll find this hard to believe, and I can't say anymore right now, but there's a calamitous conspiracy about to overtake our nation, and you two represent our best line of defense."

Chapter 7

· · · · ·

Evarts got the call at two thirty. Professor Baldwin wanted her ride back to Los Angeles. The prior evening's dinner had been subdued. The food, as usual, was excellent, and the wine the best California had to offer, but no matter from which direction Evarts and Baldwin had approached the subject, Douglass had refused to offer any additional information on the Shut Mouth Society or the supposed conspiracy.

Evarts found his department workload light and made time to do a few web searches. No hits on the Shut Mouth Society, and the search on secret societies produced a host of disturbing paranoiac sites. He had scratched out some notes on the possible key to the code. He was certain the numerical code was based on a book. Before computers, amateurs often used this elementary technique. Breaking the code simply required finding the right book, then matching up the numbers with page numbers, paragraphs, and word count. This code had too many numbers on each line to correspond to page, paragraph, and word count, but the extra numbers were probably meant to confuse and were meaningless.

He dismissed the Bible, the most common choice of neophytes. Douglass said others had tried, and they certainly would have examined Bible alternatives thoroughly. One of his detectives had been an English major, and he asked him about nineteenth-century American writers. Off the top of his head, he listed Nathanial Hawthorne, James Fenimore Cooper, Ralph Waldo Emerson, Herman Melville, Harriet Beecher Stowe, Henry David Thoreau, and Henry Wadsworth Longfellow. The detective promised to make a comprehensive list and include English authors popular in America.

As Evarts drove to UCSB, he had an idea. Lincoln was a lawyer, and a law book might be the key. He always told his detectives not to run with hunches, but this one seemed tantalizing. The more he thought about it, the more it made sense. He bet law books were expensive in that age and had limited editions. Someone in New York might not know Lincoln's reading habits but could guess which law books he owned or that he could access easily. Evarts knew little of law beyond the criminal code, but he wondered if the extra column of figures could relate to statute numbers. Hunch or not, he decided to pursue this line of investigation first.

He parked in a loading zone in front of the Guest House, but before he opened his door, Baldwin marched out from the lobby of the temporary residence hall. She carried only her overnight bag and her computer satchel slung over her shoulder, so Evarts didn't rush to help her but went around the van to slide open the side door.

"Good afternoon, *Commander*."

"Oh, back to that, are we? What have I done to piss you off?"

"Well, for starters, you left me sitting in that lobby for nearly an hour. I thought you had a four o'clock appointment at the Federal Building? I expected you to be waiting. Nervous about my tardiness."

Evarts had forgotten that fib. "Sorry, rescheduled for another day. I should've called you in case you needed more time." He threw her bag and case in back.

"Hey! Be careful. My computer's in there."

"Sorry." It would be a long drive.

After they had taken their seats and buckled up, Evarts asked, "Any conclusions?"

"Only that we can't prove they're fake." She seemed to pout for a moment. "Abe wouldn't even leave me the single page. Just took off with it as soon as we finished the tests." She knocked her knuckles against the side window and then suddenly turned toward Evarts. "What's that bastard got us into?"

"Abe is a friend and of sterling parentage. Please just call him an asshole."

No laugh. After a moment, she said, "I suspect the manuscript is genuine. If it is, then how much else is true? A conspiracy that threatens the nation? How bizarre…and paranoid. I have my own research. I don't have time to oblige an old man's fantasies."

"Scared?"

"You betcha. The best-case scenario is that I get enmeshed in an elongated wild goose chase. The worst case could be dangerous."

"I doubt there's a physical threat." He smiled and made his tone light. "Besides, I carry a gun."

Still no laugh. "I was talking about my career."

"Sorry." Three "sorries" in less than five minutes. It definitely was going to be a long ride. He decided to mollify her with agreement. "Listen, I'm not happy about this either. I have a demanding job, a class I need to prepare for, and I like to spend my free time at the beach. I don't—"

"What class are you taking?"

"I'm a college instructor, not a student. Night school at California State University at Channel Islands." Evarts tried a light tone again. "You can quit calling me Commander. I'm a colleague, of sorts."

"Police science?"

"Yes."

"A part-time lecturer in a nonacademic subject at a third-rate college." She folded her arms across her chest. "My colleagues come with better credentials."

"That was nasty."

She unfolded her arms. "I'm sorry." She sounded genuinely contrite.

Three to one on the "sorries." At least he wasn't losing ground. "I just meant I have a full life, and I don't need this any more than you." He paused. "Listen, I keep my private life compartmentalized from work. I do what I want, when I want. Maybe I'm selfish, but I feel like this is an invasion of my privacy...and I don't like being manipulated."

"Me either. So what are we going to do about it?"

Evarts thought about her question. Douglass was his only real friend, so the situation presented a problem. He kept a professional distance at work and didn't socialize with the other cops on the force. He had many acquaintances in his private life, but none he would classify as a friend. People called him a loner—at least those who liked him. Others called him worse. He knew people thought it odd that his only friend was double his age, but Douglass never bored him. He liked his life just the way it was, and he felt content. He needed to set his own agenda, but he didn't want to lose his sole friend.

"I guess we run this out," he said. "At least for the week."

She didn't answer at first but then said, "Yeah. I'm willing to invest a week. Especially if I can get close to more Lincoln papers. That bastard sure knows how to seduce me."

"I have an idea. Can I bounce it off you?"

"Go ahead."

"I told you the code key was probably a book. An elementary encryption but hard to break. I looked into nineteenth-century publications, but I think it might be a law book."

"Makes sense. But it would need to be a federal law book. Probably one on Supreme Court rulings. Someone in New York would have limited access to an Illinois law book."

Evarts hadn't thought of that. Perhaps Douglass was right, and they would make a good team. "How many of those would there be?"

"Not too many, but the trick would be to get the right year. They published updated editions annually."

"That sounds promising. By the way, you're right about the paranoia. I googled secret societies, and every loony on the planet has a posting."

"And I'll wager that none of the societies were benign."

"No, they all want to rule the world . . . or already secretly do rule the world."

"You're a trained investigator. What do you make of Douglass's charges?"

"I'd dismiss them, if I didn't know him. And then we have the manuscript." He thought a minute. "I think there might be something there but probably not ominous. Maybe someone is using Douglass to ramp up the value of the remaining papers."

"Exactly. That's what I think. Someone happened upon some Lincoln documents, and how better to increase their value than to shroud them in mystery? Sucker an old man who has a reputation of paying dearly for Lincoln memorabilia."

"Except Douglass is no fool."

"You know only one side of him. He's fanatical when it comes to Lincoln."

"You're right, I don't know that side. Why the Lincoln fixation?"

"Douglass's great grandfather admired the man, and Douglass believes Lincoln freed the slaves. Not of small import to a black man."

"You disagree?"

"It's a matter of opinion. Lincoln proposed the Thirteenth Amendment that outlawed slavery at the end of the Civil War. But he was a reluctant convert to the abolitionist cause. I mean, hell, he won the nomination because of his moderate position on slavery. He fought to preserve the Union, not to free slaves. Emancipation just came later."

"So the Civil War wasn't about slavery?"

"Of course it was—nothing else, despite what some historians say. The Republican Party was formed for the sole purpose of stopping slavery in the territories, and the South seceded because a Republican won the presidency. They didn't care if he was a moderate. He was a Republican, and they knew that if slavery was stopped in the territories, eventually the delicate balance in the Senate would tip away from slaveholders."

"Why do so many say the war was about something else?"

"Because everybody, North and South, pretended to fight about something else. To this day, many Southerners continue to pretend it was about States' Rights, except only one state right was threatened— the right to own other human beings."

"Okay, I understand avoidance in the South, but why in the North?"

"I bet you don't totally understand why the South confused the issue. At the time of the war, only one in five men of fighting age owned slaves in the Confederate States. If the CSA ever admitted they were fighting over slavery, eighty percent of their army might question dying to protect the property of rich men. All contemporaneous Southern writing and speeches put the war on an elevated rights basis, and some historians have carried the pretext all the way to the present."

"But the North had moral right on their side. Why would they pretend?"

"Because they were racists. Not a sprinkling of racism, but a consensus that the Negro was a lesser being. The Union couldn't field an army if the working class suspected they were fighting to free slaves, because only slavery kept the black man shackled to the South. Free blacks would stream north and steal their livelihood. Only after the North won and got to rewrite history did the war take on moral righteousness."

Evarts waited for her to catch her breath before asking, "Does Douglass believe Lincoln consciously went to war for the purpose of destroying slavery?"

"Yes. And he doesn't have an iota of proof."

"You mean he doesn't have any contemporaneous documentation?"

"Exactly. Historians can't make stuff up out of whole cloth."

"Especially when all the contemporaneous political figures are lying."

She turned in his direction. "What are you implying?"

"Only that Abraham Douglass would say you just made his case. Lincoln pretended to have a moderate position on slavery to win the election. He'd probably add that Lincoln didn't fool the South, who saw him for what he was—a closet abolitionist."

"That's—"

Evarts's cell phone rang. He dug it out of his pocket and flipped it open. "Evarts."

"You need to return to Santa Barbara immediately." He recognized the deputy chief's voice. He had worked for Chuck Damon for two years, and he liked him as a boss and as a police officer.

"I can't right now. I'm transporting a witness back to Los Angeles."

"Now. This is an emergency that demands your immediate attention."

"Can't Lieutenant Clark handle it?"

"Greg, were you at the Douglass home last night?"

"Yes."

"Did you see him today?"

"No. What's this about?"

"Did your passenger see him today?"

"Yes."

"Then we need you both back here immediately. Turn around and come directly to the Douglass estate."

Evarts wondered what kind of mischief had gotten his friend involved with the police. "Has there been a crime?"

"Yes."

"Well, damn it, tell me."

"Abraham Douglass has been murdered."

Chapter 8

. . . . .

As soon as Evarts snapped his cell phone shut, he cut over three freeway lanes in a manner sure to infuriate other drivers. Instead of slowing for the next exit, he gunned down the off-ramp and braked hard at the bottom. Without making a complete stop, he screeched through the surface street and barreled up the on-ramp in the opposite direction.

"What are you doing?" Baldwin screamed halfway through the change in direction.

"Gotta get back."

"I have classes tomorrow." She grabbed the handle above the door for support. "Let me out. I'll call a taxi."

"You have to return too." He took a deep breath. "Someone murdered Abe."

"No! I just saw him this morning."

Evarts drove well above the speed limit with an eye in the rearview mirror. He had no fear of a ticket, but he didn't want to be delayed by the Highway Patrol. Despite his concentration on driving, he stole a glance at Baldwin. She was ashen. He guessed violence didn't often intrude into her sheltered life. As a matter of fact, violence of a personal nature had never intruded into *his* life. He realized the news had shaken him and slowed down to only ten miles an hour over the speed limit.

"What does this mean?" she asked.

"I don't know. They gave me no specifics. Could be related, possibly not."

"Come on, Greg. Do you believe in coincidence?"

"No." Despite the tense moment, he noticed that she had finally used his first name. "It means we have to take his warnings seriously." He stole another glance to see how she took the news. What he saw made him wish he had kept his mouth shut.

"What's he gotten us into?" She sounded frightened.

"How secure is the Guest House?"

"A hell of a lot less secure than the Douglass house, for god's sake. Besides, they're full." After a moment, "I won't get home tonight, will I?"

"Probably not…and depending on the circumstances, it might not be a good idea anyway."

"You're scaring me."

"I can sugarcoat it, but you're too smart. Listen, we'll find you a safe place. Police protection, if necessary. I suggest you make a call and get a substitute for your classes. Don't mention Douglass. We can't let the evening news get hold of this yet."

As she made the call, Evarts thought. After she got off the phone, he slowed down even more. "Have you had a relationship with any professors at UCLA?"

"That's none of your business."

"I'm afraid it is. If this is associated with last night, then there might be only two copies of the encryption left. One's in my pocket. The other you hid on campus. After your office, lovers are the first place someone will look."

"My god." She looked down at the folded hands in her lap.

"Am I right?"

"Yes."

"Current or former?"

"A little of both."

"Damn," Evarts thought. "Okay, I think it's better to be safe than sorry. Call him. Tell him to take the document and go to…no, ask him to come up to Santa Barbara. I can protect him here. Tell him you'll meet him at the Santa Ynez Inn. I'll have a couple of cops pick him up and bring him to us."

"What reason should I give?"

"Use the 'current' part."

"It would be embarrassing for you to listen in."

"This is too important for a bout of modesty."

She dug out her cell phone and speed dialed. "Hello, Greg. Trish."

No wonder she showed reluctance to use his first name.

"I got stuck in Santa Barbara this evening. I was wondering if you could join me." She listened for a bit. "Play hooky. I did. Someone can cover for you." Her voice turned sensual. "I'll make it worth your while, and in the morning, we can walk on the beach. You love Santa Barbara." Another pause and then she laughed seductively. "Yes, that too. Room service and the whole nine yards." Another laugh. "Okay, maybe less than nine yards. Will you come? Great. Meet me at the Santa Ynez Inn. Ask for me at the desk...yeah, me too."

Evarts quickly pulled out his copy of the encryption and snapped it in her face.

"Oh yes, by the way, will you bring that envelope I left with you?" She paused. "No, I won't be working. I just want to give it to a colleague at UCSB." After listening a long moment, she said, "No, Greg, this isn't an errand. Not unless you think what we'll be doing is only a favor to me. If you do, don't come." Another agonizing pause. "Good. I'll see you in about three hours." She hung up.

"You worried me with that 'don't come' line."

"I had him."

"What's his last name and department?"

"Why?"

"Because we'll probably be tied up, and I need to give his name to the patrol officers. Also, I want to monitor campus police for office break-ins."

"Marston, Art Department."

Evarts threw her a glance and thought she looked better than when he had first told her about Douglass. "You did well. I'm probably being overly cautious, but it can't hurt. Now listen, I need to tell you what's going to happen. Other than the killer, you're the last person to see Douglass alive. When we arrive, a detective will take you someplace private for questioning. I won't be with you. Can you lie convincingly?"

"I think you just saw a demonstration."

"Good. I don't think you should bring up the Douglass conspiracy stuff. If the murder has nothing to do with it, then it won't harm the investigation. If it does, I'll explain the whole thing to the chief later."

Evarts stole another quick look at her face to make sure she understood. After she responded with a nod, he continued, "Douglass was an important person, and we have to control the news. Cops talk, and I don't want him tagged as a crazy. Also, if this *is* connected to some grand conspiracy, I don't want the perpetrators to learn how much we know. Are you okay with this?"

"Yeah. What do I tell your detective?"

"Everything except the conspiracy allegation. No Shut Mouth Society or encrypted codes. Just that I brought you up as a favor to look over a new Lincoln acquisition. Dinner was a social occasion. My attendance is ordinary. Tell her that you went with him to UCSB this morning to do some testing. Give her your credentials and don't be modest."

"Her?"

"Departmental practice. We question female witnesses with a female detective. Makes the witness more forthcoming."

"No good cop-bad cop routine?"

"That comes later. And only for uncooperative witnesses, and you're going to be the epitome of cooperation." Evarts gave her a reassuring smile. "Now our immediate problem is where to stash you and Marston for the night."

"What will you tell the patrol officers?"

"That you decided to stay in Santa Barbara for the night. You had set up a date, but you can't meet him because you're being interviewed. He'll be treated respectfully."

"Seems like you have everything figured out."

"Except where you'll stay. There's a plate collectors convention in town."

"A what?"

"Some people collect Lincoln memorabilia, other people collect plates. This convention fills every room. Dealers come from Europe and Asia. We like them. They're a well-behaved bunch." He pulled out his phone. "I'll get my assistant working on it."

"Separate rooms," she said suddenly.

"Excuse me?"

"You may have never heard this, but I'm not in the mood."

"Great, you just doubled the problem. I hope you like Ventura." He made the call and got more whining than he expected. His assistant reminded him it was high season and late in the day. He sympathized but told her that he didn't want to hear from her again until she had secured two rooms.

After he hung up, he thought things through again. If this looked connected to the Douglass conspiracy tale, he would ask the chief to bring in the Feds. The chief would resist, but Evarts would remind him that the murder of a well-known black man in his predominately white city would be a national scandal. His mind had been racing since the news, and its impact suddenly hit him. He wasn't driving to just another crime scene. He had been so focused on how to handle the situation that he hadn't realized his own loss. He felt relief when Baldwin interrupted his thoughts.

"Do you want to know about my relationship with Marston?"

"*That* would be none of my business."

"Just the same, I want to tell you. We had a serious relationship for about three years. Everyone assumed we'd get married, but it didn't work out. We parted friends. More than friends, really. We get together occasionally, but now it's not serious and we keep it quiet."

"Why are you telling me this?"

"I don't want you to think I'm attached to someone."

Evarts threw her a glance. "Why's that important?"

She looked out the side window. "Because I've been attracted to you since yesterday."

"You have an odd way of showing it."

"Self-defense. Men hit on me, so I've built a shield to keep them at arm's length." She returned her gaze to him. "When I was young, I went for the macho type. More to piss off my parents than anything else, I guess. But they always disappointed, so I switched to academics. No luck there either."

Evarts cursed to himself. If only this conversation had occurred under normal circumstances. He knew that emotionally distraught victims often turned toward someone in authority for protection. He sighed. "This is not a good idea. You've been shocked and you're scared. Suddenly you find a guy with a gun attractive. It doesn't take someone from your psychology department to figure this one out."

"That wasn't an invitation to a relationship." Her voice had regained a testy note. "I just didn't want you to have the wrong impression about me and Marston." She leaned her head against the heel of her hand and looked out the side window again. After a long moment she added, "Besides, I'm not good at relationships."

"Work comes first?"

"First or instead. I haven't worked that out yet."

Evarts needed to halt the direction of this conversation, but he didn't want to preclude future possibilities. He was similarly unconnected, and Baldwin so far appeared to be someone he would like to get to know; at least when she wasn't biting his head off.

"Listen, we've both been emotionally rocked. After things calm down, I'd love to take you to dinner, but I should tell you I have my own warning label. It also says 'Caution, Bad at Relationships.' Only I've worked it out. I get absorbed in my cases. It's not a professional hazard—it's my personality. My partners say I withdraw emotionally, but to be honest, that's not exactly true. I seldom get emotionally engaged in the first place." He glanced at her, but couldn't read her face. "If you want, we can talk about this later, but right now I have a job to do."

Her silence extended for several miles. Just before he pulled off at the Santa Barbara exit, she said, "If that was an invitation to a date after this is over, I accept."

Chapter 9

· · · · ·

When Evarts pulled up to the Douglass estate, the gate was open but blocked by an unmarked police car. He ran the window down to stick his head out, but the duty officer recognized him through the windshield and backed up to give him entry. He navigated the narrow access road but couldn't pull up to the front of the house because police vehicles of every sort blocked the path.

He turned to Baldwin. "Ready?"

"Yes."

"Okay. Deep breaths if you get nervous, but it's all right if you're shaken. Abe was a colleague and friend. Don't make up anything. Just stick with the facts."

"But not all the facts."

"Stick with the facts, not the insinuations or gossip. Let's go."

Evarts opened his door and came around to the front of the car to wait for Baldwin. He took her by the elbow and led her up the drive to the front door. A patrolman stationed at the door said in a cheery voice, "Commander, the chief will sure be glad to see you ... oh, damn; I forgot ... you and Mr. Douglass were friends." He looked embarrassed. "My condolences."

"Thanks." Evarts reminded himself to stay professional. If he allowed his emotions to surface, the case would be taken out of his hands. Keeping his tone businesslike, he asked, "Is Detective Standish on the scene?"

"Yeah." He spoke into his shoulder mike and got a response in his ear. "She'll be right out."

"We'll wait."

In less than twenty seconds, a woman appeared at the door, wearing a dark skirt and matching jacket over a white blouse. Evarts gave her a welcoming nod. "Detective Standish, I'd like you to meet Professor Patricia Baldwin. She and Abraham Douglass went over to UCSB together this morning. Could you take her someplace private and get her statement?"

"Of course. I'm sorry. Were you and Mr. Douglass friends?"

"Close acquaintances. Colleagues, actually."

"Well, you have my condolences. Could you step this way? I'll make this as easy as I can."

After the two of them went into a sitting room off the entry, Evarts turned to the patrolman. "Where's the body?"

"Bodies. This was a double homicide. Mr. Douglass is on the back patio. They strangled his servant in the pantry." The patrolman looked puzzled. "You don't know?"

"No, but I'll find out soon." Evarts retraced his steps from the previous evening. Before he stepped out onto the patio through one of the atrium doors, he saw the scene through the glass and stopped in shock. He was still standing there when his chief and Deputy Chief Damon approached him.

The chief said, "Are you okay?"

"No. That was my friend."

"Damn it, Greg, I need you," Damon said. "The shit's gonna hit the fan on this one."

Evarts gave his boss a hard look and let irritation creep into his voice. "Just give me a sec, will ya?"

"Yeah, sorry." Damon didn't look sorry.

Evarts tried to get his emotions under control. Abraham Douglass hung naked from a cross that faced his prized view of the Pacific. Several forensic specialists worked on the remains, but Evarts could see around them enough to know that he had been set on fire. He winced as his nostrils pick up the stench of charred skin.

He took a deep breath and faced his boss. "Has a time been determined?"

"Early this afternoon. Probably close to 2:00 PM. A neighbor called the fire department at 2:27 because she saw smoke on this ridge. We'll get a better fix after the autopsy." Damon suddenly looked embarrassed. "Sorry you had to see this, but the chief thought you better see the scene as we found it."

Evarts turned to the other man. "Right call, Chief." He took another look at the scene and then turned back to the chief. "Anything I should know before I talk to my men?"

"There's something I need to know. Can you handle this?"

"Yeah. The scene just startled me for a minute. I want the bastards who did this, and I'm the best you got, so let's get on with it." He held the chief's eyes until he saw him nod. "Now what do I need to know?"

"Okay. We can't find any evidence of robbery, except for a small amount of cash missing. Lots of valuables in the house left untouched. Looks amateurish. There's some vandalism. Tore up some stuff, but it appears haphazard. Right now, it looks like a hate crime. Probably youths." The chief stole a glance at the corpse and then returned his eyes to Evarts. "Were you here last night?"

"Yeah. With Professor Baldwin, the woman I picked up at UCLA yesterday. The two of them went to UCSB this morning, so she may have been the last person to see him alive. I have Detective Standish taking her statement."

"Good. I want to see the report. Tonight."

"You will. Anything else?"

"Yeah, the FBI will arrive in a little over an hour. Get as much of a head start as you possibly can, but don't fuck up. Also, don't move either body until they give the okay. It's going to be their show."

"Civil rights?" Evarts asked.

"Yeah. I hate to bring them in, but I had no choice."

Evarts bet the chief and city officials welcomed the opportunity to dump some of this political mess onto a federal agency.

"I better get to work" Evarts said. He turned away from his two bosses and stepped out onto the patio. In the open air, the awful smell grew stronger. Before going to the body, he walked the perimeter of the patio. He knew it had already been examined, but he wanted to look for himself. He found nothing and realized he had been stalling.

As he approached the corpse, the stench made him wince. The forensic team had positioned a six-foot ladder in front of the body so they could examine the remains without disrupting the crime scene. Evarts leaned around the ladder and peered up at the corpse. It hung limp from a cross that had been screwed together from galvanized pipe. Fire had charred nearly all of the flesh, and the loss of body fluid had shrunk the skin to reveal the skeletal form. Despite a monotone coal black hue, Evarts could still recognize the face of his friend, Abraham Douglass.

Evarts turned and walked to the edge of the patio, looking out to sea. Countless evenings he had sat here with Douglass and a glass of scotch to watch the sun set. Never again. He took one deep breath and then another. At first he felt an overwhelming loss, but he was able to get his emotions under control by reminding himself that he had a job to do and that job made him the one responsible for catching his friend's killers. He told himself to mourn after arrests had been made.

He returned to the makeshift cross and motioned the lead forensic specialist over. "What have we got?"

"Dead before the burning, but it looks like he was tortured. We found lacerations around the scrotum and face. Appears to be death by strangulation, but I can't be sure yet."

"Any physical evidence?"

"None out here. Still dusting inside."

"Who's chasing down the galvanized pipe?"

"Matthew's working on that, but so far it looks like generic pipe available at a half dozen plumbing supply houses."

"It won't be local. Tell him to make inquiries throughout the L.A. basin."

"Greg, that'll take—"

"Damn it, I don't give a shit! Just tell him to do it."

"Yeah. Sure."

The man appeared to be shaken at his outburst, so Evarts patted him on the shoulder and said, "Okay, thanks. You can get back to work." The specialist started to turn, when Evarts asked, "The lacerations?"

"Razor sharp. Probably was a razor … or an exceptionally sharp knife."

"Find out." A razor might mean kids, but a honed knife could hold other implications.

When he turned toward the house, Evarts saw Damon alone at one of the atrium doors. He started with a routine question. "Who's doing the house to house?"

"Four patrol officers. No one's radioed in yet. The property's pretty isolated."

"Yeah. What bothers me is that kids don't leave a clean scene, and that pipe looks premeditated."

Damon looked over his shoulder to see who was behind him. "The chief hopes it's kids. I don't think so."

"Professional or cult?"

The deputy chief shrugged. "All the visuals point toward amateurs or a cult, but the lack of evidence looks professional."

Evarts waved at the scene behind him. "The torture may have been to gain information, not just for cruelty. Douglass was rich. We'd better get someone looking into his financial holdings in case this is a diversion for an identity theft."

"Shit. I should've thought of that. You check the teams in the house, and I'll get Haden on it."

Evarts first headed to the other murder scene. Peter had been strangled in the pantry, obviously caught unawares. The second forensic team had no enlightening information, so Evarts left to check the rest of his teams' work. He found everyone carefully going by the book. No one wanted criticism from the FBI.

If the perpetrators tortured Douglass for financial access information, they had already cleaned out his accounts. Identity thieves were increasingly controlled by organized crime, and they moved fast. Evarts wanted to eliminate the possibility of either youths or organized crime. If neither could be implicated, it lent credibility to Douglass's shadowy allusions of the prior night.

He found his key subordinate, Lieutenant Clark, blocking the door to the master bathroom. Evarts nodded toward the room. "Torture site?"

"Yeah. Only a cursory examination so far. Not enough technicians. I'm keeping anyone from disturbing the scene."

"Anything obviously unusual?"

"No." Clark looked back into the room. He evidently decided to share his concerns. "Except this is the innermost room in the house, and the scene looks clinical. I, uh, closed the door and yelled. Standish said she could only hear my screams from inside the bedroom." He looked over Evarts's shoulder to make sure no one had entered the bedroom. "I know the chief thinks kids did this, but if so, they were better prepared and smarter than the average punk sickos."

"I want that in your report. Don't worry about the chief. He doesn't want us to look like a bunch of rookies to the FBI." When Clark nodded, Evarts made a sideways motion with his head. "I want to get a sense of the scene."

When Clark moved aside, Evarts stepped across the threshold. A straight-back chair sat in the middle of the blood-splattered bathroom. Nothing else looked out of order, except for some apparently crazed destruction. Mirrors had been broken and some toiletries swept onto the floor, but cabinets remained closed, and the walk-in closet beyond didn't look rummaged.

He saw an open wallet next to the washbasin and a pile of clothes in the corner. He used his pen tip to lift the edge of the wallet. No cash, but credit cards remained in place. He then used his pen to lift the slacks by the belt loop so he could check the pocket. No remote control.

"Rope?" Evarts asked.

"Assume they used the same rope to tie him up outside."

"Doesn't look like the closet's been disturbed."

"I walked in there and saw no evidence of a search. Professionals know people keep valuables in the closet, but a youth hate crime still doesn't feel right to me."

"Could've been after assets Douglass didn't keep in the house. Haden's checking out an electronic theft motive." Evarts had already started to move toward the bedroom door before adding, "I'll send a patrolman to guard this door. I want you to rotate between the teams and be ready to help me brief the FBI when they arrive."

Evarts next went to the library. He had glanced into the room as he made his rounds and saw a few books strewn around, but nothing else to indicate that the library should be a priority. He stood in front of the movable partition and bet the remote unit that had been in Douglass's pocket now sat inside the safe. Then Evarts remembered that Douglass had used the same remote to summon his servant. He returned to the master bedroom and used his pen to slide open the bedside table drawer. Just as he hoped, another remote sat cradled in a wood trough meant to hold change. He picked it up with his handkerchief and returned to the library.

Although he had pressed all three buttons in sequence, the partition refused to move. He examined the edge but didn't see any wedge or other obstruction. Standing back, he thought a moment and then tried two-button combinations. The third try worked. That was the easy part. He stared at the stainless steel vault door for several minutes and then walked briskly to the front of the house.

Evarts found Baldwin and Standish still in the small sitting room off the entrance. He said, "This seems to be taking a long time. Any problems?"

Evarts was relieved to hear Standish say, "No problems, but we need a few more minutes." If she had said 'We're about to take a break,' it would've been a preestablished code that meant Standish needed to talk to Evarts out of earshot of the witness.

"Professor Baldwin, when was Lincoln born? The date."

"February 12, 1809. Why?"

"I want to open Douglass's safe. I thought he might use it as the combination."

"Nice try, but wrong. If he used a Lincoln date, it would be March 4, 1861."

"What happened on that date?"

"His inauguration. Douglass believed that date changed the destiny of this country."

"Thank you." He started to leave.

"Excuse me, Commander." Standish stopped his progress. "Miss Baldwin had a date this evening. She said you promised to send someone to meet him."

"I forgot. Can you take care of it?"

"Of course."

Evarts left, relieved that the question didn't have more serious implications. He hurried his pace, because he knew the chief would want an update prior to the FBI arriving. When he got to the library, he stared at the large dial that ranged from zero to sixty. He decided to try a four number combination: three, four, six, one. With the last number, he heard a satisfying click, and the handle slid down with almost no effort. Opening the door, he was disappointed to find what he had expected. On the shelf that last night had held the Cooper Union manuscript now sat a remote control. Nothing else looked disturbed.

As he thought through the implications, he heard his boss's voice behind him.

"You knew about this?"

"Yes, Abe showed it to me last night. This is his Lincoln collection."

"Valuable?" Damon asked.

"Exceptionally."

"Kind of fits with the teen gang scenario. Professional would've gotten the combination out of him."

"If they knew he kept his collection in the house. I'd like Professor Baldwin to assist in taking inventory."

"Why?"

"She's a Lincoln expert. That's why she was here last night. To look at his latest acquisition."

"How long will you need her?"

"Couple of days I suspect, but I'd like her to take a quick perusal tonight. She's familiar with his collection."

Damon thought a moment. "When Standish is done with her. Good excuse to keep her around for the FBI." He looked at the empty library but still appeared nervous. "Greg, we need to talk in private. Get someone to watch this and meet me in front of the house."

Evarts put an idle-looking patrolman to the task and walked outside. This rendezvous made him nervous. Had Damon found out about the supposed conspiracy? At first he didn't see his boss but then spotted him down the lane about fifty feet.

"What's this about, sir?"

"The mayor and the county supervisor are on their way. This is gonna get dicey. Douglass was a substantial figure in the black community."

"Abe was a substantial figure in the community, period."

"No disrespect meant. He was a substantial figure in our community, but he was a national figure in the black community."

"Meaning?"

"The politicians are worried about the city's reputation."

"And the chief?"

"I said the politicians, didn't I?" Damon's voice had an edge. "Listen, Greg, they want to control communication with the media. This is national news. The chief is the only police official to talk to the press—the *only* one. You need to make this clear to your people. Anyone quoted directly or indirectly will be fired, with a 'conduct unbecoming' recommendation to other departments. Got it?"

Evarts sighed with relief but hoped it sounded like frustration. "I'll make the message clear, sir."

"Good. That includes you and me."

Evarts smiled. "I got that. Don't worry, I hate the press."

"Not as much as you will in a week or two. But there's more."

"Give it to me."

"You're off the case in the morning. Clark will handle it. When the press learns about your relationship with Douglass, they'll hound you relentlessly. Lead your teams this evening but see the chief first thing in the morning. He's gonna find you a seminar far away. Even if it doesn't start until Monday, he wants you ready to leave from the office."

"That's ridiculous. You need me on this case…and I'm a witness."

"If the FBI wants your statement, they can have a local office take it, but you're outta here. Away from the press. Got it?"

"Yes, sir." Evarts thought this development provided both opportunities and problems. He decided to think about it before arguing.

For the next three hours, Evarts watched his men scour the house. Nothing. The FBI showed up and were immediately scurried away for a meeting with the political types. They agreed to joint jurisdiction but then went ballistic when they actually saw the crime scene. Evarts heard lots of angry shouting. The FBI called in another investigation team and their own forensic people. Evarts later learned that they acquiesced to continuing joint jurisdiction but insisted that the autopsy would be done in Los Angeles.

Baldwin spent the time doing a survey of the Lincoln collection. When Evarts had a chance to pull her aside, she said she noticed nothing glaringly missing besides the Cooper Union manuscript. His assistant called to say she had reserved two rooms at a Days Inn thirty miles away in Oxnard. Things weren't going well, and then the officer dispatched to pick up Greg Marston told him that Baldwin's boyfriend had returned to Los Angeles. Now he would need to convince the Los Angeles Police to provide Marston protection. Luckily, Marston had left the envelope for Baldwin with the patrolman. Evarts had to assume that Marston wasn't interested in hanging around overnight merely to hold Baldwin's hand.

He stepped outside onto the freshly cleaned patio for some quiet time. He had to make a decision. Being relieved of responsibility for the investigation would give him time to break the code, but he would lose control of the investigation. He decided in favor of taking the seminar route because the FBI looked to be in control anyway. If he went off on a junket, he couldn't order police protection for Baldwin, but he could be her personal bodyguard. Separate rooms were already reserved. He was a gumshoe, not a street-smart cop, but how much danger was she in? Or Marston? Marston no longer had a copy of the document, but the perpetrators wouldn't know that he had returned it to Baldwin.

Everything depended on how much Abe had revealed under torture. It all came down to one point. If he told the whole fantastic story to his chief, would the chief believe him? If the chief did believe him, would he consent to expensive protection for nonresidents? Evarts decided he would not, or at least not for more than a day or two. Finally, the FBI was salivating over a high-profile civil rights crime and wouldn't be receptive to an alternate motivation based on shadowy secret societies.

He had no evidence except an indecipherable page of numbers. This case revolved around the code, and he had to break it before anyone would believe the Douglass allegations.

He looked at his watch. It was late, after ten. He decided to gather up Baldwin, take her to the motel, and stay in the other room. Besides, he couldn't get the chief's attention right now, and he had a private appointment with him in the morning. Before leaving the patio, he stared at where Douglass had been hung in mock crucifixion. He felt sorrow for the first time since he had left the army. Douglass had been his only truly adult friend. He purposely kept a respectable distance from his subordinates, and he had never been close to his bosses. His weekend buddies were mere playmates. Damn. He would miss Abe.

After he and Baldwin got into the car, Evarts sat staring through the windshield.

"Did you tell the FBI?" Baldwin asked.

"No."

"Is that a mistake?"

He started the motor. "That's what I was trying to figure out."

Chapter 10

• • • • • •

"**T**his is real, isn't it?" Her voice cracked.

Evarts steered his Odyssey onto the freeway. "Yes." He wondered how much he should tell her and decided she deserved to know. "I reviewed Douglass's security system. Only professionals could get around it to surprise Peter. This wasn't some kids or some white supremacy cult. They went after the documents, so we have to assume this secret society exists and has some ugly ambitions."

"How much do you think Douglass told them?"

Evarts gave her a smile. "Good question. You should be a detective." He waited until he had transitioned to the fast lane. "Douglass was old but tough, competitive, and not easily beaten. He had five levels of information valuable to his tormentors, and he would stall as long as he could stand the pain before revealing each level. The first was the safe combination, and we know he gave that up. Next would be my involvement. The third would be that he had delivered to me a hard copy of the document and the encryption. Your involvement would be the fourth level. The fifth level is that you have hidden a copy with someone at the university."

"You're forgetting a level," she said. "The source of the documents."

"Damn it, you're right. I was too focused on us." Evarts thought that through and came back to a question he had been mulling earlier: How did the perpetrators discover that Douglass had the document? That information could only come from the source itself—the Shut Mouth Society. But why would the Society give Douglass the material and then kill him to get it back? The only answer that made sense was a rebellious faction inside the Society. Evarts guessed that either one faction wanted to expose the Society's secrets, or a radical arm disagreed with an inner council decision to reveal the Society's existence to Douglass.

Baldwin interrupted his thoughts. "Do you think he told them about us?"

"I doubt it. They were probably waiting for him when he returned home from UCSB. He had only one innocuous page on his person, so nothing should've raised an alarm with them. Especially after they found the manuscript intact in the vault."

"Where are we going?"

"Oxnard. We could only get two rooms at a Days Inn." He gave her an appraising look. "Since Marston left, I thought I should stay in the other room. Just in case ... I don't expect any trouble."

Baldwin didn't respond at first. When she did speak, she sounded worried. "If your place isn't safe, then neither is mine."

"What? No. I assume my place is safe. I just thought you'd feel better with someone within shouting distance."

"If you really believe your place is safe, then let's go there."

Was this a test or an offer? He decided it was most likely a test of his truthfulness. He had equipped his house with a better security system than the one installed in the Douglass home, and because of the forewarning, he could take precautions that wouldn't have occurred to an unworried Abe. Besides, these people worked hard to make the Douglass murder look like a juvenile hate crime. They obviously didn't want the police excited about a mysterious murder of a prominent figure, probably wouldn't attack a police officer in his home, and likely wouldn't bring attention to themselves by going after Marston.

She broke his reverie. "Aren't we going back?"

"No, I live ahead." He checked her reaction, but she just continued to stare through the windshield.

He lived about forty minutes south of Santa Barbara at Hollywood Beach, in Oxnard. The community had taken Hollywood as its name because, in the Clark Gable era, movie luminaries had come to the local marshes to duck hunt. Oxnard had to be the most uninspired city in Southern California. Farms and strip malls surrounded the Point Mugu Naval Air Station and Port Hueneme, home of the Navy Seabees. But Oxnard owned a hidden gem. Hollywood Beach preserved the nineteen-fifties Southern California beach culture for posterity.

He had bought his house twelve years ago, before the intrusion of recreational marinas and condo complexes in the surrounding area. Despite an influx of weekend sailors and their yuppie accoutrements, Hollywood Beach remained hard to find. The small community was tucked away from the main thoroughfares, and it had successfully restrained the growth that had ruined the rest of the coastline.

He drove through a labyrinth of surface streets, expecting Baldwin to ask where the hell he lived, but she seemed in a reverie of her own. When he reached the small beach community, he turned down a narrow, unkempt street with sand piles built up against every fence and wind-exposed wall.

"You live here?"

"Yeah, don't you like the beach?"

"I love the beach. Just not what I expected."

He pulled a remote unit out of his center console and opened a garage door in the middle of the block.

She laughed. "See those buttons above your rearview mirror? You can train them to open the door."

Evarts pulled into the immaculate garage. "Not this door." He held up the industrial-looking remote. "Secure automatic opener." He pressed the button again and put a hand on her arm to keep her in the car until after the door closed. He smiled. "Just being cautious."

When she stepped out of the van, she said, "What have you got hanging from the ceiling?"

"My quiver."

"Your what?"

"Surfer slang. Those are my boards. A different one for each type of surf condition."

She looked back inside the van at the missing middle seat. "You said you hauled stuff." She pointed up. "You meant these?"

"Yeah."

"Aren't you a little old to be a surfer?"

"Thanks."

"No, I just I thought surfers were lazy dropouts. Beach bums."

"Most are, not all. Thieves too."

At the door leading into the house, he put his thumb on a scanner, and after it beeped, keyed in a combination. When a whirring noise quit, he knew the deadbolt had receded into the doorjamb.

He turned to Baldwin. "That's why all the security. I can assure you that if you leave a coffee mug on the front stoop overnight, it'll be gone in the morning. Luckily, in my town, the police advise residents on their security systems, so I can deduct from my taxes what the department doesn't foot."

They stepped into a room furnished entirely with gray metal cabinets, gray metal shelves, and gray metal closets. "Nice house," she said. "Who's your interior decorator?"

He laughed. "Storage room. Living's upstairs."

She pointed at what looked like metal wardrobe closets. "You must have a lot of off-season clothes."

"Wet suits. Beach gear. Gun safe."

He led her up a staircase. "The beach has narrow lots, so they build up, like city townhouses. This house has three stories, each with a high ceiling so you can get an ocean view from the rooftop patio." He continued to lead her up another set of stairs. "Living's on the top floor."

"How far are you from the beach?"

"Half a block. Normally two rows of houses, but I'm lucky. The lot behind me is vacant, so only one house stands between me and the ocean."

"I've made enough money on my books that I've begun to think about buying a house where I can step out right onto the sand."

"Yeah, that's my dream too, but here oceanfront houses cost four times as much as this one, and it's only spitting distance from the beach. Did you see that schoolyard across the street?"

"Yeah. You like kids?"

"These kids are okay. Elementary school. They made this house affordable for me because it faces the parking lot."

They entered the living level, and she said, "Nice house... and I mean it this time."

"Thank you."

He had decorated the house with comfortable contemporary furniture and accented it with glossy white custom cabinets to hold his entertainment center. The kitchen had natural maple cabinets and shiny white tile with light brown grouting. Bright blue pillows and glass art added splashes of color. He always enjoyed people's first reaction.

Baldwin walked over to a white-framed painting on the wall. "This is original artwork."

"Local artist. Lots of them around, and they get hungry occasionally."

She turned to face him. "In the movies, cop houses are always a disheveled mess. Beer cans strewn around, dishes in the sink, nothing eatable in the refrigerator."

"Street cops, maybe. Not detectives. Good detectives are meticulous."

"Then you must be very good."

Another laugh. "Let's hope so. Drink?"

"You got anything other than scotch?"

"No port, I'm afraid, but—" He went to a cabinet in the dining room and handed her a bottle. "I don't know much about wine, but my brother gave me this for Christmas."

She handed it back. "Yes, please. And your brother does know wine."

"He lives in Napa. If you don't mind, I'll revert to type and have a beer."

Now she laughed. "Not at all."

Evarts handed her a glass of wine and then led her to a front living room that he had converted into a library with facing love seats. Upon entering the room, she made a quick scan of his books but made no comment. After her inspection, she sat down on the love seat across from him.

Evarts wondered why she had wanted to come to his place instead of the motel. Normally, he would welcome a pretty woman into his house, but today wasn't a normal day. She didn't appear insensitive, so she must have motives unrelated to her comments about being attracted to him.

"I think we dismissed the Cooper Union address too quickly," she said, without preamble.

"What do you mean?"

"Douglass said the Shut Mouth Society members came from a powerful political family that went all the way back to the founding. Before Lincoln's address, Stephen Douglas had been saying that the framers of the Constitution firmly believed that the federal government had no power to regulate slavery outside the states.

The Dred Scott decision and the Kansas-Nebraska Act destroyed the Missouri Compromise, and the expansion of slavery into the territories would be the overriding issue of the next election. At Cooper Union, Lincoln took his audience through the fifty-five delegates to the Constitutional Convention to show how their votes and actions after the Convention demonstrated that they *did* believe the federal government had the power to regulate slavery in the territories. He decimated Stephen Douglas, the likely Democratic candidate, with logic, facts, and ridicule."

"How does this fit?"

"In the speech, Lincoln reviewed the political histories of all of the delegates to the Constitutional Convention. The text may provide a clue to the Shut Mouth family."

"Something no one has picked up?"

"Something no one would notice if they didn't know about the Society."

Evarts finished his beer and motioned to Baldwin to ask if she wanted her drink refreshed. Getting a positive nod, he picked up their glasses and went into the kitchen. From the kitchen, he yelled, "What do you propose?"

"Do you have broadband?"

He returned to the library. "Of course."

"Then if you think the house is safe, I'd like to stay here tomorrow and do some research."

"No problem. Tomorrow will be a short day for me. I won't be gone long."

"What do you mean? Won't you have a lot to do on the Douglass case?"

"I'm being sent to a seminar, one far away. Because of my personal relationship with Douglass, they want me out of the way so the press can't grill me."

She sipped her wine and then asked, "The Shut Mouth Society?"

"No. It smells too strong of city politics. Besides, their tentacles can't reach everywhere."

"What about me?"

"I'm going to pretend to go to the seminar, but I'll stay with you until we get to the bottom of this. I need time, and probably your help, to break that code. Until I break it, nobody will believe that far-fetched story."

"Speaking of that, I have some additional thoughts."

"Let's hear them."

"The law book idea is good, but there are more possibilities than I originally led you to believe."

"How many?"

"Possibly a hundred, maybe more. We need to include books any lawyer might reference, like John Marshall rulings and dissertations on Constitutional law."

Evarts smiled. "In the code-breaking business, a hundred or so possible keys isn't overwhelming." He finished his second beer and said, "Hungry?"

"No. I had some of that pizza your cops brought in."

"Tired?"

"Yes." She took the last half swallow of her wine and rose from the loveseat with the empty glass. "I'm eager to go to bed."

Evarts was tired as well, but he suddenly felt a need to be close to someone. "I have two guest rooms. Unless..."

"No unless. I'm sure either of your guest rooms will do just fine."

She walked to the orderly kitchen, rinsed the wine glass in the sink, and then held it aloft in an unspoken question. Evarts opened the dishwasher, and they both added their glasses to the neatly stacked top rack. Before showing her to her room, Evarts showed Baldwin the security features of the house.

After he led her downstairs to the bedroom level, he pointed to the first door in the hall. "This room has its own bathroom. You'll find disposable toiletries in a basket by the sink."

She gave Evarts an encouraging smile, but in a tone filled with finality, she said, "Thank you. Good night," and closed the door.

Chapter 11

· · · · · ·

After he showered the next morning, Evarts became annoyed when he found neither of his newspapers on the front stoop. Living at the beach had disadvantages, and petty thievery ranked at the top of his list. He bounded up the stairs to the kitchen to find Baldwin at his breakfast table, sipping coffee and reading the *Los Angeles Times*. He had caught his thief.

"Good morning. I see you found the coffee."

She pointed over her shoulder with a single finger. "Right next to the coffeepot. Papers on the stoop. Simple deductive logic." She looked up from the paper and smiled. "Would you hire me as a detective?"

"Depends on how neat you left my guest room."

She made a point of surveying his spotless kitchen. "Perhaps I'll withdraw my application. I can never be this tidy."

Evarts poured himself a cup of coffee. "I get that a lot." He returned to the kitchen table. "Anything in the papers?"

"Nothing in the *Times*. I guess the story broke too late."

"I'll check the local paper."

They read their respective papers and sipped coffee like this was something they did every morning. In less than ten minutes, Evarts said, "The story's here, front page, but no details and no mention of a hate crime."

She folded up her paper and said, "I'll bet your police didn't let any reporters onto the property."

"You got that right. The city leaders are nervous as hell." He folded up the local paper and stood to carry them over to the trash compactor, when the phone rang. The ringing continued incessantly until he reached the library to take the call out of earshot.

When he returned, he said, "Chief's tied up. They told me not to come in until afternoon."

"What'll we do?" she asked.

"Breakfast. We need nourishment for our research."

Evarts checked outside from the vantage of his rooftop patio and kept Baldwin inside until he had reviewed the situation again from street level. With no visible threat, they walked the couple of blocks to a beach shanty that called itself Mrs. Olson's Coffee Hut.

When they entered, the waitress—probably once a hot item, but now paunchy and time beaten—looked over Baldwin's expensive attire and said, "Slumming, are we?"

"Greta, be kind or I'll tell her you molest children."

"Matt just needs a place to stay. Besides, he's twenty-seven years old."

"A child, nonetheless."

Greta laughed. "Wouldn't have it any other way. Seat yourself."

The Hut had been cheaply furnished with Formica-top tables covered with strawberry-patterned oilcloth. Evarts picked a small table for two in the rear. Greta followed them over. "What ya have, hon?" she asked Baldwin.

"Oatmeal. Do you have any fresh fruit?"

"Of course, we opened the can just an hour ago."

"Then just oatmeal with raisins, walnuts, and maple syrup. Whole wheat toast."

"Got the oatmeal, got the raisins, got the whole wheat bread, but I'm betting you won't like our imitation maple syrup, and I sold all the walnuts to that gent over there." She hooked a thumb behind her at an empty table.

"Then just bring brown sugar on the side."

"Of course." Greta turned to Evarts with a look that said, "Where did you pick this one up?"

Evarts said, "Bacon and eggs, over easy, hash browns, and rye toast. Coffees."

"Like I couldn't have guessed that," Greta muttered, as she walked away to place their order.

Baldwin looked around, concerned. "Are we safe here?"

"I think so. Locals only. Inlanders stand out like a sore thumb."

"Like I did?"

"Yup."

Greta brought their coffee. After a sip, Baldwin looked down and said, "Greg, I'm scared." When she lifted her head, her designer glasses failed to hide eyes that looked ready to tear.

"Me too."

"Really? I'm not sure that's reassuring. You're supposed to be the tough-guy cop. Have you ever been scared in the line of duty?"

Evarts thought about it. "No."

"Not even in the military?"

"I was in Intelligence. A desk job. No spy stuff. We're both actually just a couple of researchers."

Baldwin smiled. "Colleagues, in a matter of speaking."

"Yeah." Evarts liked the familiar way she said that. "Can I ask you a question? About Marston?"

"Sure."

"What time are his classes?"

"You expect me to know his availability? What do you think we did? Schedule trysts between classes?"

"Just the facts, ma'am, just the facts."

"Jack Webb, *Dragnet*. Pretty old allusion."

"Sorry, bad habit." Evarts thought she looked relieved that he had sloughed off her defensiveness.

"I figured out the Mr. Tibbs reference too. *In the Heat of the Night*, Sidney Poitier."

"Correct."

"Do you just like detective movies or all types of movies?"

"All movies." This was good. She wanted to know about him. "I own over two hundred DVDs, and I go to the movies once or twice a week. By the way, Professor or Doctor seems a bit formal. May I call you Patricia?"

"Of course." She smiled, but she didn't look happy. After looking around warily, she said, "Greg, we can't fight a secret society alone."

"My department will back us soon ... and with luck the FBI. I see my chief this afternoon."

"Are you going to tell him about the Douglass conspiracy?"

"First, I'm going to find out where the investigation has led. Then I'll platform off that and give him the reasons that we shouldn't rule out a professional hit. If he's still listening, I'll explain the Douglass conspiracy allegation." Evarts reached across and took her hand. "He's a smart man, and I have standing in the department. Don't worry."

She smiled, but this smile looked rueful. "I wasn't worried until we left the house." She looked around again. "Do you always carry a gun?"

"Always."

"Even when surfing?"

"I won't surf until this is over."

"I want a gun."

Evarts was surprised. "Do you know how to use one?"

"Unless you can forget. An early boyfriend taught me. I liked the thrill at the time."

"Automatic or revolver?"

"Both. And rifles and shotguns. We blew up half the Mojave Desert." She suddenly looked embarrassed, and Evarts guessed they did more than shoot in the desert.

"I still want Marston's schedule."

"Why?"

"We involved him, and now he's dangling out in the cold. I want to call him, but I don't want to pull him out of a class and unduly alarm him."

"I really don't know, but I'll log on to the UCLA website when we get back to your place."

Before Greta returned, Evarts reached under the table and taped an envelope to the bottom, near the center post. Since Marston had returned Baldwin's copy of the encryption, they now had two, and Evarts wanted to keep them separate. This would work as a hiding place for a few days.

After Greta distributed their breakfasts, Evarts asked, "Any strangers about?"

"You're pretty strange."

"I mean people that don't belong here."

"Nope. Could use a few more customers, though."

"Let me know if you see anyone suspicious."

"Police business?"

"No." He nodded at Baldwin. "Irate boyfriend. Guy's got some tough friends."

Greta turned to Baldwin. "Honey, you forget my kiddin' around. Hold tight to this one. Given a chance, Greg could make a woman happy."

Baldwin gave him a wink. "I suspected as much."

After breakfast, Evarts took Baldwin back to the house. He took a Glock 9mm out of his gun safe in the storage room and made her show him how it functioned. She knew. Next, they went to the computer. Within minutes, Baldwin determined that Marston had classes all morning. Evarts made a mental note to call him as soon as he left the chief. He then asked her to start the list of law books prominent in the middle of the nineteenth century. Once she became engrossed in the task, he told her he had an errand and would return in a half hour. She gave him an absentminded nod and said, "Lock the door on your way out."

Evarts walked a couple blocks to a surf shop. Nowadays, no store could survive selling only boards. In fact, you had to navigate past untold racks of clothing, cold-water gear, magazines, books, DVDs, and thirty varieties of sunblock before you even saw a surfboard leaning against a back wall like an afterthought. Women increasingly took up the sport, but the numbers still weighed heavily in favor of the male side of the population. Despite the arithmetic, women's clothes dominated the racks. Surf shops had discovered that girls liked to shop in places where the cute boys hung out.

After fifteen minutes, Evarts stood at the counter with two bright polo style shirts, a pair of beige shorts, two different styles of sandals, and a pair of full-length drawstring pants. When the store clerk grabbed the clothing to scan it, Evarts said, "Pete, do you have any women's underthings?"

"Nope, but those bikinis are on sale." Pete gave Evarts a wicked grin. "Do in a pinch."

Evarts looked at Pete anew. He guessed the girls considered him a hunk. "Help girls pick out suits much?"

"You think I'm here for the minimum wage?"

"Okay, I need your help. I'd guess she's about a size 4. Something stretchy and thin and in a neutral color."

"The first two are easy." He raised an eyebrow. "Black's not neutral but sexy as hell."

"That'll do. Two."

"Two? Dude? Cops aren't supposed to shelter runaways. Don't trust 'em if they say they're eighteen."

"Relax, Pete. The airline lost her bag. She's almost old enough to be your mom."

In less than a half hour Evarts returned to the house and found Baldwin buried in his computer. "Any progress?"

"What's in the bags?"

"Clothes … for you. But we don't have designer shops hereabouts, so this is casual beachwear."

She rummaged through the sacks and then kissed him on the cheek. "You're a dear." She held one of the sacks up. "Thanks for not getting me the top with the psychedelic mermaid."

Evarts feigned surprise. "You've shopped at Scotty's before!"

"Indeed, I have. I think it's a chain." She bounded off for the bathroom.

Evarts noticed the Glock beside the keyboard. In the future, he decided to announce his entry into any room she occupied. He examined the automatic and saw that she had racked a round into the chamber.

He heard a noise behind and turned to a delight. Baldwin wore a yellow polo shirt, shorts, and sandals. She fit the house, and he realized that he was beginning to hope they could get to know each other better. "You make even cheap clothes look expensive."

"Thanks, but I wear this kind of stuff all the time." She smiled. "Bikinis? Aren't you the innovative detective?"

"Let's hope so. The laundry room's on the first level."

"Already found it." She held up a pair of panties and bra. "I'm going to add this to the load."

After she left, he looked at the computer screen. Something caught his eye. She had pulled up the genealogy of the Evarts family.

Chapter 12

· · · · · ·

Evarts pulled the Odyssey into his reserved parking spot alongside the Spanish-style police building. Just before turning off the ignition, he glanced at the console clock. Not quite one o'clock. A bit early, but he hoped the chief could see him. He wanted to hurry back to Oxnard.

As soon as he appeared in the upstairs office bay, Chuck Damon came bounding out of his glass-front office. "Greg, sit in my office a sec and I'll see if the chief's free." Before Evarts could comment on his nervous behavior, he had disappeared into the chief's solid-wall office.

In a moment, Damon returned and gave him a "follow me" wave through the glass. When Evarts took a seat in front of the chief's desk, the palpable tension put him on edge.

"Has there been news?" he asked.

"Were you in Westwood the day before yesterday?" the chief asked without preamble.

"You know I was," Evarts said.

"What took so long?"

"Excuse me?"

"You went to interview Professor Baldwin. Why'd that take all day?"

They must have found out she had stayed overnight in his house. She was a witness, but not a material witness, so it probably didn't violate departmental guidelines. Although nothing had happened between them, he felt defensive for her and didn't want them to think she had sex with him after only one lunch meeting. "She had a class after our appointment. She also had to handle her email and complete a few chores before she could leave."

"What did you do during this time?"

"I attended her lecture."

"Can anyone verify that?"

"Dozens of people. What the hell for?"

Damon cleared his throat and said almost sheepishly, "You're a person of interest to the Los Angeles Police for a crime."

"What crime?" He directed his question at Damon.

"The Rock Burglaries," the chief answered.

Evarts got angry. "Douglass was my friend, goddamn it. I'm not in the mood for roughhouse cop humor."

"This is no joke," his boss said. "They've found physical evidence for the first time."

"What?"

"A parking receipt from a Westwood lot. It was on the burgled property and ... well, the LAPD says it has your fingerprints."

Evarts thought quickly and didn't like the implications of what they had just told him. "Where's the property and when was it hit?"

"Last night in Westwood. Technically, this morning, about 3:00 AM."

"I was with someone," Evarts said.

The chief looked down at his desk. When he looked up, he wore a sympathetic expression. "Greg, LAPD always believed the Rock Burglar was a cop who cased the jobs but sent a different crew to do the deed. An alibi for last night will not remove you from suspicion." As if to emphasize his point, he tapped his pen on the lone document that sat on his desk. "You fit their profile."

"Where'd they find this ticket?"

"In the alley, one door away."

"That's not on the property."

"That sounds lame," Damon said.

It sure did, Evarts thought. He took a deep breath and got hold of himself. "I'm not the Rock Burglar, nor am I in any way affiliated with this crime or any other."

The chief looked relieved. "Thanks." He called for coffee and then said, "Do you have any explanation for that parking ticket?"

"Yeah, but you won't like it."

"Try me."

"I put that ticket in my center console where I keep all my receipts for my weekly expense report. The only time I left my van unlocked was at the Douglass estate ... when it was surrounded by cops."

"Meaning?"

"Meaning someone at the crime scene lifted it from my van."

"What? You don't expect me to believe that?"

"Well, I sure as hell didn't lose it, and I wasn't in any damned alley in Westwood." The chief and Damon just stared at him, so he added lamely, "Damn it, that parking receipt was for twenty-four dollars."

"Greg, you can't just blame another cop."

"I paid for parking as I left. How could I lose it casing a neighborhood that afternoon?"

"LAPD thinks you went back after dark. We know the Rock Burglar does a careful canvas at different times of day."

Evarts turned. "Chuck?"

"Greg, I want to support you, but you gotta give me something more than that one of my officers stole the receipt out of your van."

Evarts couldn't believe how easily they abandoned him. "Am I under arrest?"

"No. You're not officially a suspect, yet. But this is a shitty time for the city. We're going to be splashed all over CNN, FOX, and MSNBC tonight. They all went out and scheduled every black loudmouth in the country. The mayor doesn't need any more bad publicity plastered all over the news channels." He pulled a sympathetic expression again. "I'm sorry, Greg, but I have to put you on suspension."

Evarts debated using Baldwin as an alibi, but then he remembered that after dinner with Douglass, he had dropped her off at the UCSB Guest House and gone home alone. With a night unaccounted for, he simply asked, "How long?"

"Until this is resolved." The chief held out his hand. "I need your badge and gun."

Chapter 13

. . . . . .

Evarts left the police station and got into his van. His parallel parking spot was alongside the building in an alleyway that led to the main parking lot at the rear of the station. Few people walked the alleyway, and he saw no one paying attention to him. He reached under the driver's seat, and after fumbling with a touch keypad, extracted a SIG-Sauer P229 .40 caliber automatic from a lockbox he had installed there. Taking a suspended officer's gun away made little sense, because everyone on the force owned several guns. The city just wanted their property back.

Technically, he no longer had a carry permit, but since he hadn't been suspended for a violent crime, his fellow officers would probably turn a blind eye. At least to a handgun. They probably wouldn't tolerate the Vang Comp modified Mossberg short-barreled shotgun he had hidden under the rear floor panel of his van. Before leaving for the station that afternoon, he had gone to the lower level of his house and packed his van with some essentials in case of an emergency. He had stored the shotgun, ammunition, camping gear, and clothes in the back and stuffed whatever extra cash he had in the glove box.

He had to get back to Oxnard as quickly as possible. If they framed him as the Rock Burglar, then that meant Douglass had given up his name under torture. He knew Douglass and believed him a true friend. If he couldn't withhold *his* name, then he probably gave up everything he knew. Patricia was in danger.

How powerful were these people? They had gained entry into a secured estate, penetrated his own police force, knew his movements, understood how law enforcement people think, and tortured and killed in a way that showed neither remorse nor scruples. Whoever these people were, he needed help, and help depended on breaking that damned code.

Evarts's heart jumped when he turned onto his street. Two strangers, dressed in what could only be described as "business casual," stood sentry across the street from his house. They didn't stand together; instead they spaced themselves at the opposite edges of the school parking lot. If it hadn't been summer vacation, he would have called the Oxnard police and filed a complaint about strange men suspiciously hanging around a schoolyard.

He stopped the van in the middle of the street and used his cell phone to call Baldwin. As the phone rang, the sentries watched him with curiosity, not menace. She answered, crying. "Patricia, almost home. What's wrong?"

"Marston's dead."

Evarts pulled the SIG from his holster and stuck it barrel first between the seat and the center console. "How?"

"Out his office building window. They said it looked like suicide."

"I'm almost there. Any problems in the house?"

"No, not here, but somebody ransacked my office. Greg, what's happening?"

Evarts kept checking the rearview mirrors. Nothing. Nor did these two guards make any threatening gestures… but they probably guessed he had called Baldwin, and they must know she was in his house. Damn. They wouldn't interfere with him going home. They wanted him inside the house. They would just not let him leave. Could they breach his security? Evarts decided that if they could get around the Douglass system, then his would present few additional problems.

"Greg?" Her voice sounded near panic.

"Patricia, I'll be there in less than two minutes."

He snapped his cell phone shut and punched his remote garage door opener. He waited until the door completely opened before he touched the throttle. He thought about revving the motor to warn the two watchdogs that he would ram them if they moved, but they stayed put as if they didn't have a care in the world. As he screeched toward the garage, he punched the remote again and flew under the door before it closed. Leaping out of the car in a crouch, he went down on one knee and swung the SIG back and forth across the closing space beneath the door. No threat. He could see no legs running toward the house. As soon as the door closed, he slammed the steel deadbolt closed with a report loud enough for them to hear outside.

Evarts found himself breathing hard by the time he ran up two flights of stairs. Baldwin must have heard him, because she came crashing into his arms as soon as he crossed the threshold. "They killed Marston!"

Evarts pushed her to arm's length. "Yes. Now I need your attention. We're in trouble. Pack everything you've got. Hurry. Stay away from the windows. I'll be right back."

"They're outside? Now?"

"Yes. Do you trust me?"

She didn't hesitate. "Yes."

"Then you need to do what I say. Okay?"

She took a step away from him, squared her shoulders, and took a deep breath. Then she returned to the computer desk and picked up the Glock. "Okay."

"Pack. I'm going up to the roof to check things out."

"You have a plan?"

"I have a plan."

"Do you want me to pack some stuff for you?"

Evarts ran out of the room and shouted over his shoulder, "I put some things in the van this morning! Hurry!"

He ran up another flight to the rooftop patio. A three-foot wall surrounded the perimeter, but he stood erect and walked the circumference. The two men across the street hadn't moved, and he found two more watchers at the back of the house, leaning against cars parked along the oceanfront street. He stared at one of the men on the other side of the empty lot, who casually stared back. Evarts raised his empty fist and made a make-believe gun with his hand. Sighting down his finger, he moved his thumb up and down like he was firing a pistol. The watcher just stared blankly back at him. Then he slowly raised his hand and gave Evarts the finger. Shit. Professionals.

He found Baldwin in the hall outside the bedroom carrying her overnight bag and computer case. "Let's go," he said and led her downstairs. He hoped that if they moved fast, they could catch them by surprise.

When they reached the garage, he put his index finger against his mouth to signal quiet. Then he carefully unlatched the van side door and slowly slid it open. When he had it fully open, he grabbed her bag and computer and shoved them toward the back of the van, under the rear seat. Then he signaled for her to follow him to the garage door and whispered for her to gently step on the handle to seat the door against the floor. When she had done this, he very slowly slid the deadbolt open. So far, so good. He then stood on the running board and reached up to release the automatic door opener mechanism because it was too slow for what he planned to do.

Now he put his hands on her shoulder and whispered, "Are you okay to drive?"

She looked nervous but simply said, "Yes."

"Okay, I'm going to fling the garage door open and when I do, you start the car and barrel out of here. Don't worry about me. I'm going to jump in the open side door." He pointed north. "Drive that way; turn right at the corner and then right again at the signal." He continued to hold her shoulders, with his mouth close to her ear. "Can you do it?"

"Yes."

"Get in the driver's seat as quietly as you can. Put on your harness and have your hand on the key in the ignition, ready to start the car when you hear the door open." He gave her a reassuring squeeze on the shoulders.

Without further discussion, she got into the car with only a slight click as she pulled the door shut. Evarts went to the garage door and reached down for the handle. Taking a deep breath, he slung the door open. The car started immediately, and she squealed out of the garage with the front wheels smoking. Evarts barely leaped into the van as it accelerated out of the garage, and he rolled out of control against the opposite door as she careened into the street. Before he got his balance, she accelerated and made a wild turn at the corner. He never saw the men's reaction, because he was rolling around the back of the van. It took all his concentration to slam the side door closed and clamber into the passenger seat.

He feared she would forget to turn at the signal, but she got it right, and they were heading south. "Did you see the men?"

"One."

"Did he look surprised?"

"No. He smiled at me."

"Damn it."

"What does that mean?"

"It means they wanted us to run. It makes me look guilty, and they can deal with us away from my house." He turned in his seat and looked behind him. Soon a full-size sedan careened out of the Hollywood Beach enclave. Damn, these guys were quick.

She saw them through the rearview mirror. "Greg! They're chasing us."

"I expected that," he lied. "Don't worry. I have a plan." He did have a plan, but he worried about whether it would work. These men were professionals. He hoped he had at least lost the second team behind the house, but in a few seconds he saw another rental car about a half mile back barrel out onto the major surface street.

"What now?" She sounded close to panic.

"Keep driving. We're going into the Point Mugu Navel Air Station."

She looked visibly relieved. "How far?"

"A few miles. Don't worry, for right now, they just want to follow."

They surprised Evarts by coming right up on the Odyssey's rear bumper. He crawled into the back and reached under the rear seat to extract his shotgun from the back storage compartment. When he made himself visible above the back seat, showing the shotgun, the car receded, but the driver smiled at him. For now, they only wanted to make him nervous. They had succeeded.

They still followed close enough that when they pulled up to the guarded military gate, he could see the worried look on the driver's face. He scurried back in the passenger seat and showed the guard his retired army identification. Another guard lifted the gate and waved them through: a husband and wife going shopping. As soon as Baldwin saw the gate lowered behind them, she exhaled a great sigh of relief.

"Turn left up here," he said.

"Where are we going?"

"Out the back entrance."

"Can't we stay inside?"

"No. Retired officers only have PX privileges."

"They have two cars. One of them might cover the back entrance." She sounded near panic again.

"They probably don't know about it, and if they do, it's a long way around on the outside surface streets. We'll be long gone before they can get over to it."

"Then what?"

"San Diego."

"Greg? I'm scared. Why can't we go back to your police head-quarters?"

He told her.

"Oh, shit. I can't believe this."

"Left here and out that gate." After they passed through the checkpoint, he directed her down Highway 1 along the ocean toward Malibu. When they reached a secluded area along the coast, he had her pull over to switch drivers. Then he told her the rest of his plan, at least his plan for a diversion. He hadn't thought beyond how to throw them off their trail.

After a long silence, she said, "I know one place where we can go."

"Where?" He didn't believe she knew how easy it was to track someone through financial records.

"My family has a walk-up apartment that's owned by my family trust."

"They can probably penetrate a trust."

"Not this one, and if they did, the place isn't on the books as an apartment. It's carried with a nonsignificant number instead of an address."

"Why?"

"Taxes. Or I should say tax avoidance." She smiled weakly. "The rich hide things from the IRS."

"Have you ever used it?"

"No. When I guest-lectured at Harvard or BU, I stayed at a hotel. No one knows about it, except my parents."

"It's in Boston?"

"Yeah."

Evarts thought a minute. "Okay. We drive to Boston as soon as we finish our business in San Diego."

Chapter 14

······

Evarts didn't breathe easy until they headed east on Interstate 8 out of San Diego. On the trip down, he had explained that the government watched foreign currency transactions over two thousand dollars. When they reached San Diego, they made maximum withdrawals at ATMs using all their credit cards and then went into a bank and charged twenty-five-hundred dollars' worth of Mexican pesos against the same cards. If asked, Evarts had told her to say she was going camping in Baja and wanted enough pesos to buy her way out of trouble if necessary.

With a trail clearly leading to Mexico, they started their long drive to Boston. On the way down, Evarts had described how he had been implicated in the Rock Burglaries, what it meant about the reach of this secret society, and how strongly they wanted to collect all copies of the manuscript. She wanted to know why they didn't actually cross the border into Mexico, and he explained that it would take too long and there would be a record of them going and returning. Better that they just dropped off the map with wallets bursting with Mexican pesos. He explained that they would convert the pesos back to dollars at one of those currency kiosks at the Denver airport.

On the way out of San Diego, he occasionally changed lanes as if he was about to make a quick exit from the freeway, but the maneuver never exposed anyone following them. Baldwin had remained unusually quiet. They had decided to wait until nighttime to call her dean, when Baldwin was sure to get her answering machine. She would explain that she had a family emergency and needed to start her sabbatical a month early.

"You're awfully quiet," Evarts said, as he checked his speedometer to make sure he wouldn't attract the attention of the Highway Patrol.

"Thinking."

"What about?"

"How safe is it to drive this van?"

"Safer than other options," he said. "Hopefully, they'll think we found a way across the border, so once we leave California, we should be fine. The LAPD probably won't put out an interstate bulletin for a property crime, and the Shut Mouth Society can't cover every highway."

"Don't we need to change license plates or something?"

"Later. Right now, we need to get far away fast. Speed is the enemy of detection." He considered what she had said. "We'll switch plates in Phoenix at the airport long-term parking. Cops reflexively check the state first, so I'd rather not have California plates on the car. Besides, Arizona is better than California because they only require a back plate." He hesitated again as he thought it through. "That'll only last a couple days, so I need to figure out a way for us to get a different car."

"If we switch plates, why only a couple days?"

"Because switching plates only works in the movies. As soon as the plates are reported stolen, the numbers are entered into police computer systems and alerts go out to law enforcement."

"Maybe the driver won't notice they're gone."

"Maybe not, but the parking attendant will when his camera shows no plate to verify against the parking stub."

She sat quiet a minute and then asked, "If we switch cars, how will you haul your *stuff*?"

Evarts felt encouraged that she had made a weak attempt at humor. "Got no stuff to haul anymore." He threw her a smile to disguise how disappointed he really felt. "Remember, we left the garage door wide open."

"You lost a friend, your career, and your surfboards. I'm sorry. I was thinking only about myself."

"Not your fault. I can handle most of it, but it bothers me that my friends and family will think I'm guilty because I ran. Just what those bastards wanted." Evarts thought some more and then muttered, "I need to break that code."

"I found the family."

"What family?"

"The powerful political family Douglass told us started the Shut Mouth Society."

"Really! Who?"

"Us."

"What?"

"You and me. We're part of it."

"That's not funny."

"I'm not being funny. I found the family on the Internet. It wasn't even hard. It's all I've been thinking about since we left Oxnard. I'm confused and scared."

"Explain."

"It's called the Baldwin, Hoar, and Sherman family. Descendants of Roger Sherman, one of the Founding Fathers."

"Never heard of him."

"Most haven't. Not today, but he was a major player in his day. Only founder to sign all of our historical documents: the early resolves, the Declaration, Articles of Confederation, Peace Treaty, Constitution, and many others. He was on the committees that wrote many of these documents."

She reached into the back and pulled out her laptop case to extract a spiral notebook emblazoned with the UCLA logo. She flipped through the pages before continuing. "As best I can gather from a quick perusal, his progeny included twenty-three members of the Senate or House, eight cabinet officers, five governors, a Supreme Court justice, another nominated for the Supreme Court but not confirmed, five career diplomats, and a presidential chief of staff. And the names read like a Who's Who of our political history."

"Wow. I've never heard of him or his family." Evarts stole a look at her, but she was buried in her notes. "Are you saying you're one of the Baldwins?"

"Yes. I just didn't know the extent of the family." She looked up from her notes. "How did you meet Douglass?"

"At a police benefit. He came over and introduced himself. We had a good conversation and discovered that we shared a passion for backgammon and Macallan's."

"He probably hated both," she said.

"What?"

"Had he lived in Santa Barbara long?"

"No. Just moved there. What are you getting at?"

"I think he moved there to get close to you. Just like he seemed to hover over my career."

"Douglass and I were friends."

"I'm sure, but I suspect he engineered the friendship." She turned in her seat to face him. "The Evarts are one wing of this family."

"Bullshit."

"You were given this manuscript and then sent to me. That seems far too unlikely for a coincidence."

Now Evarts felt confused and a bit scared. "We're related?"

His face must have betrayed his feelings, because she laughed with joy for the first time since he had returned to the house. "Don't worry. As best I can figure we're cousins, six or seven times removed."

"Thank god." Now he felt embarrassed. She had given him no reason to be concerned about being related to her. "I, uh—"

"Yeah, me too."

Now he laughed in relief. After they traded smiles, she said, "Want to hear more?"

He gave her a fresh look. "Just a sec: Are you a member of the Shut Mouth Society?"

"No. Never heard of it before this. Are you?"

"No." Evarts shook his head to emphasize his denial. "Nor do I believe my parents are. They're so nonpolitical I have to harangue them to vote."

"No one in my family has mentioned it either, but I'm not sure they don't know about it. I always sensed there was something overly secretive about the way we handled our affairs."

"Can you talk to them?"

"You're kidding? I can't wait to talk to them. I may even ask you to apply your police interrogation skills." She laughed. "Nonviolent, of course."

"Where do they live?"

"New York. Upper West Side."

"Can't call them." Evarts thought. "We'll stop on the way to Boston. See them in person. By the way, did you have a chance to make a list of nineteenth-century law books?

"Yes. I narrowed the list to about twenty prime candidates."

"Great. Now all we need is a library that has old law books. Maybe in New York."

"That's not a problem. I'm a member of the Boston Athenaeum, the oldest private library in the country."

"Maybe that's not a good idea. If you're a member, they might watch it."

"The Athenaeum is private and elitist. They don't give information to nonmembers. My father bought me a lifetime associate card in prep school, so I pay no dues." She hesitated. "I bet it's safe. I haven't been back in nearly ten years."

"I'll think about it. What else did you learn about this family?"

"Lots. Listen to these names: Susan B. Anthony, William Jennings Bryan, Henry Stimson, Archibald Cox, and Sherman Adams."

"I've heard of them."

"The family helped found the American Bar Association, the ACLU, the Counsel of Foreign Relations, the Smithsonian, the Rockefeller Foundation, and the Brookings Institute. Members were heavily involved in the Warren Commission, the Manhattan Project, and both Yale and Harvard. Do you remember Douglass said the family was instrumental in the Civil War?"

"He actually said they had a hand in fomenting the Civil War and to a large extent prosecuted that conflict."

"You've got a good memory."

"Detectives are trained to listen."

"A man who listens. That may be unique."

Evarts smiled. "Perhaps, but remember, we're always trying to trip people up, so be careful."

"I will. Anyway, you've probably already guessed General William Tecumseh Sherman, but did you know his brother held the Senate seat from Ohio and wrote the Sherman Antitrust Act?"

"I hadn't even thought as far as General Sherman."

She flipped back to her notebook. "General Thomas Ewing and General Charles Ewing both married into the family. Major Hoyt Sherman served as paymaster for the Union army. General Nelson Appleton Miles won the Congressional Medal of Honor. Roger Sherman Greene commanded the 'colored regiment' and Dorothea Lynde Dix served as superintendent of nurses for the Union army. She later became a social activist for women's issues. Key generals, highly regarded politicians, head of nurses, control of the army payroll—this family covered all the bases."

"You're saying all those people were related?"

"Either a direct line from Roger Sherman, or they married one of the women. But there's more. Simon Cameron, Lincoln's first secretary of war, was also a family member, as well as William Maxwell Evarts."

"That's the first Evarts." He took his eyes off the road a second to look at her. "Who was he?"

"Lincoln's envoy to Great Britain during the war. A critical post because Lincoln's top foreign policy imperative was to deny recognition of the South by world powers and to withhold European aid from the Confederate States. Actually, there were Evarts all over; William was just the most prominent. He even defended President Johnson during his impeachment hearings."

"Johnson? He wasn't impeached."

"Wrong century. Andrew Johnson, Lincoln's successor. In fact, this family was involved in the most dramatic trials in our history. William Jennings Bryan prosecuted the Scopes Monkey Trial. Archibald Cox, the Nixon impeachment. Roger Sherman Baldwin defended the Amistad captives."

"I thought that was John Adams."

"Movies. Adams didn't get involved until the case reached the Supreme Court. Actually, Matthew McConaughey played Roger Baldwin."

"Did you know he was a relative?"

"Yeah, I knew that. Part of my family lore."

"We just left California," Evarts said.

She looked up from her notebook and said, "Are we safe then?"

"I'll feel better when we reach New Mexico. California and Arizona police cooperate a lot."

"How long?"

"Five or six hours. I know a back way that avoids Interstate 10, so we should be okay."

"You want me to drive?"

"You done with your notes?"

"With the facts, yes, but not with my conjectures."

Evarts pulled into a rest stop. After they had relieved themselves and switched drivers, Evarts said, "Tell me your conjectures."

"Roger Sherman had fifteen children. It seems all the prominent family members came from the daughters, not the sons."

"What do you make of that?"

"You said you never heard of Roger Sherman, but have you heard of the Great Compromise? Sometimes called the Connecticut Compromise."

"If I remember my high school civics, that was the compromise at the Constitutional Convention that gave equal representation to the states in the Senate."

"Correct, but it was actually far more complicated. The end result enshrined slavery in the Constitution and gave the South the mechanism to protect their peculiar institution. That compromise led directly to the Civil War. The biggest prewar political battle involved the extension of slavery into the territories. During the eighteen-fifties, the slaveholding states had overturned the delicate compromises of the last seventy-some years and would at some point control the Senate if slavery were legal in states admitted in the future."

She gave him a look to see if she still held his interest. Evarts gave her a nod to go on. "Roger Sherman engineered that compromise. It violated his morals and ethics, but he knew that without accommodating slavery, a single nation wouldn't emerge from that convention. It was a compromise he was forced to make. I think it bothered him, and he conveyed his misgivings to his daughters. Whether with him or without him, the women probably made a pact to erase this stain on the family. When you look at the abolitionist movement, the daughters', their spouses', and their children's fingerprints are all over the place. I think the key to the Shut Mouth Society is through the women."

"Except … something doesn't make sense. The Shut Mouth Society murdered my friend and probably your former fiancé. Everything you've relayed shows idealistic motivations. How do you account for that?"

"I don't. I told you I was confused and scared. But do you still think Douglass threw us together by accident?"

"No way. Nor was it an accident that he sidled up to me at that benefit. He even gave me a clue the other night. He told me to investigate my family genealogy. Obviously we have been watched and recruited. But for what? And why now?"

"What do you mean?"

"The Shut Mouth Society kept their secrets for a hundred and fifty years. Possibly longer. Something has changed the landscape and pulled us into a maelstrom."

"But what? There's nothing on the news."

"That's what we've got to figure out. That's the key to this mystery."

Chapter 15

· · · · · ·

When they reached the outskirts of Denver, Evarts took the west exit onto Interstate 70.

"Where are we going?" Baldwin asked.

"To get a car."

"In the mountains?"

"Copper Mountain to be exact."

"The ski resort? Why there?"

"Out-of-state skiers store SUVs in the subterranean parking under their condos. A stolen car won't be missed until next ski season."

"You're going to steal a car? A cop?"

"Borrow. I'll return it when we finish this business...which better be before snow falls in the Rockies." He turned from the road and smiled. "I'll leave an envelope in the glove box with cash for the miles."

"How much?"

"I think the IRS allows forty-eight-and-a-half cents a mile."

"Four thousand miles will cost you nearly two thousand dollars." She smiled and her voice was teasing. "Pretty expensive for a civil servant."

He duplicated her tone. "I was hoping you'd pick up half."

"Deal. Let's go a few more miles up the road to Vail and steal something fun to drive. Same rate."

Evarts laughed. "Do you ski?"

"I go to Vail twice a season. Yourself?"

"I'd rather ski than do anything except surf. I own a threadbare condo at Copper Mountain with three other cops in the department. I usually get up there three times a season. Sometimes more."

"Then we should make a ski date. I'll race you down the hill."

"I'll win, but not on style. Never had a lesson."

"When I was a child, my parents took me to Vail several times a year, but they always left me with an instructor." She laughed. "I've probably had a year's worth of lessons."

"Expensive at Vail. Copper Mountain's down the hill and down the food chain. We'll get our car there, and it will be a three- or four-year-old Ford or Chevy. Something common and nondescript."

"What other sports do you like?"

"Tennis."

"Singles or doubles?"

"Singles."

"So... surfing, skiing, and singles tennis. Not much into team sports, are you?"

"I never thought of it that way, but I guess you're right. I didn't play sports in high school because they would've kept me away from the beach." He considered what she had said. "As I think about it, I guess I do prefer individual sports." Evarts threw her a smile to show he was kidding. "I go to the gym regularly. Does that count as a team sport? Lots of people."

"Hardly. What's regularly?"

"Two, three times a week."

"I go most every day. Even on days when I play tennis."

"Singles or doubles?"

"Doubles. Faculty league. I like the social aspects."

Evarts drove a few minutes before asking, "Are we getting to know each other or just making idle conversation?"

"Good question. I've been stuck in this car with you for two days. That's more time than I've spent talking to a man in... well, maybe in my entire life."

"Not even with Greg Marston?"

Evarts regretted the question as soon as it left his mouth. He glanced over and saw that she seemed disturbed by the reminder of her ex-boyfriend's demise. But when she spoke, her voice sounded even. "We never talked. Probably the reason we broke up. After the first few dates, he even brought a book to restaurants."

"You didn't complain?"

"I needed to research my own book, so I fell into the habit with him, but after a while I realized I needed a companion, not a reading mate."

Evarts frequently took a newspaper to breakfast. He vowed to squelch that habit if this turned into anything serious. He liked women and seldom had trouble making conversation, but just as seldom enjoyed the dialogue. Probably why he seemed to end things after a couple months. But he had been cooped up in a rolling box with Baldwin for two days and enjoyed every waking moment. When they weren't speculating about the Society and their predicament, she captivated him with her explanations of history. He loved her enthusiasm and the way she tied events together to expand their meaning and consequence. She also enlivened her little talks by revealing the odd or nasty peccadilloes of historic figures. She knew all the dirt about the forefathers and used it to turn history into stories about real people. She had begun to charm him, and he seldom let anyone tug on him emotionally.

During the long hours of driving, they also shared their personal histories. She had evidently been a handful as a teenager and an outright rebel at Berkeley. She grew up in New York City, but insisted on going to college on the West Coast. This devastated her parents, who believed that all schools west of Trenton, New Jersey, were minor tributaries of mainstream education. Which, of course, was why she chose the school with the most radical image in the nation. Despite banging around the radical fringes her first two years, she grew up in her junior year and outgrew Berkeley by her senior year. In graduate school, she fell in love with Stanford, history, and her first academic. She laughed and said she would need to be careful because Evarts was a throwback to her wild days. When she said this, she made it sound as if they already had something more than a flirtation.

He told her he had graduated from California State University at Northridge with a degree in economics. Thankfully, she didn't ask why he didn't attend UCSB. High school had too many distractions for him to earn grades good enough for the UC system. He explained that he attended under the ROTC program and joined the army after graduation to fulfill his financial obligation. Economics somehow led the army to believe he had the proper credentials for an intelligence career, and he served most of his four years attached to the Pentagon. When she asked about his East Coast experience, he said that he knew only Washington and the surf beaches along the eastern seaboard.

They had dissimilar upbringings. He grew up middle-class in a rich community; she grew up wealthy and played with poor kids. She rebelled, while he embraced his parents' values. The irony was that he still clung to a surfing culture that irritated his parents, while she had become a card-carrying member of the establishment. Both sets of parents seemed intent on indoctrinating them with opposing philosophies of life. Baldwin's parents wanted her to take responsibility for the broader world, and Evarts's parents constantly warned him against being sucked up into other people's passions and agendas.

Despite the differences, or perhaps because of them, they enjoyed being together and had grown comfortable with each other. A question had been nagging Evarts, so he decided to ask it. "Why did you want to stay at my house the night of the Douglass murder?"

"I wanted to see how you lived. Why?"

"That's my question."

"It's how I size up someone."

Evarts wanted to ask how he fared, but she started rummaging in her purse for lipstick, which Evarts had learned was a woman's way of stifling a conversation. She had said she was attracted to him and wanted to check out how he lived, but other than friendly conversation, she had intimated nothing that went beyond their bond as two unwilling participants in this drama. What was she thinking and why did she not give him a clue?

Baldwin broke his reverie by asking, "How do you propose to gain entry to one of these subterranean garages?"

"Easy. I consult on building security. Touchpads at these large complexes always have a backdoor code for the hired help and maintenance. I'll look for a manufacturer I'm familiar with and try the service codes until we get lucky."

"What about your own building?"

"That's where we'll stash my car. No one will pay it any notice in our condo's assigned parking slot."

In about forty minutes, they pulled into Copper Mountain. Evarts had seen it only in winter with snow, cars, and people scattered everywhere, and for a few minutes he felt disoriented. The parking lots and roads appeared expansive without snow mounded on the periphery. He couldn't believe how much a change in the dominant color from white to green altered the appearance. The ski runs looked like vertical meadows, and Evarts was surprised to see how many boulders and stumps sat implanted in runs he had skied hundreds of times. Copper Mountain also looked like a scene from one of those disaster movies where only the main characters remained among the living. He soon picked out a condominium complex and pulled down a driveway that descended beneath the huge building.

He tried a code and the gate slowly swung inward. "See. Piece of cake."

"Is hot-wiring a car standard police training?" she asked.

"No need. When I pull up to a car, you slide over to the driver's seat."

The garage held more cars than Evarts had expected. A lot of people must fly into the Denver airport and take public transportation up to the resort. He parked directly behind two Ford Explorers sitting side by side. After he leaped out of his Odyssey, he reached under the back bumper of the one on the right and ran his hand along the entire length. Finding nothing, he repeated the procedure with the next Explorer. Eureka. He held up a little magnetic box for Baldwin to see.

"Hideakey," he said with a grin. "Pull forward so I can get out and then follow me."

It took less than fifteen minutes to deposit his Odyssey in his own parking space, transfer their belongings, and get on the interstate leading back toward Denver. The white Explorer seemed in good working order and had less than forty thousand miles registered on the gauge.

They had pulled into Copper Mountain at twilight and had been on the road since six that morning. The night before, they had slept in sleeping bags on the floor of the van at an independent campground. Evarts said, "How about a motel tonight?"

"Sure. I'm ready to call it a day."

"As soon as we get to the Denver suburbs." He gave her a glance. "We'll need to stay at a low-end place so they won't think it odd to pay in cash."

"Anything, as long as it has a private bath."

Evarts had hoped to share a bath, but he kept this to himself. In another half hour, they saw the Denver skyline, and he pulled off at a sign for a Motel 6. As he threw the Explorer in park, he asked, "One room or two?"

"One," she said flatly. "We need to conserve our cash, don't we?" He fumbled his next question, and she laughed. "A single king bed will do just fine, Mr. Evarts."

After he checked in, Evarts reminded himself not to run to the car. He wanted to be cool, but his heart and other organs wouldn't cooperate. When he restarted the car and gave her a glance, she gave him the fetching smile he had first seen in the Westwood restaurant.

When he dropped the room key and then mishandled the lock, she waited patiently but looked amused. After they entered the room and dropped their bags, Evarts said, "I don't know how to—"

Patricia Baldwin interrupted him by throwing her arms around his neck and kissing him with a passionate urgency he never expected. The rest came naturally.

Chapter 16

· · · · · ·

The next morning, Evarts bounced out of bed. Last night hadn't been an unusual experience for him, but it sure beat all his previous first encounters. Nothing was more exciting than an excited woman. A professor? With a doctorate, yet. As a lifelong surfer, he knew adrenaline as an addictive drug. The danger of their situation probably had something to do with it, but Evarts thought he might like this to last beyond their current predicament. Surprisingly, he really enjoyed being in the company of this woman when they weren't in bed.

He used the bathroom and then admired the form of her back as he pulled on a pair of shorts. He stumbled getting one leg in and woke her.

"Where are you going?" she asked.

"To the front office to get a newspaper. Back in a jiff." He waved at the bathroom door. "I've used the bathroom, so it's all yours."

She laughed. "Okay, I get the hint. Brush my teeth."

Yes, he enjoyed being around this woman.

When he returned with two black coffees and several newspapers, he found her sitting up in bed with her hair arranged, a smile, and the blanket tucked below her bare breasts.

"Adequate?" she asked.

"Patricia, that's not only a great understatement but too self-effacing. You look delicious."

She gave him a wicked smile. "Thank you … and call me Trish."

"I will." He jumped into bed beside her and laid one of the newspapers in her lap. "Scan for articles on Douglass." Evarts stopped, embarrassed. "I'm sorry. I warned you I get obsessed about a case. Do you want to talk?"

"No. I want to see if we made the newspapers."

Evarts looked to see if she was serious. She smiled again, but this time it was friendly and, in a much different way, more intimate.

As she pulled the sheet up, she said, "So there's no distractions."

The news stories played up the race issue and portrayed the killing as a hate crime. He could guess from the disparaging remarks about Santa Barbara that the city fathers had their hands full. Also, because no one in his department would slant the story to make the town look like a hotbed of bigotry, he assumed that the FBI had fed the story line to the press. He found no reference to himself, Baldwin, or the Rock Burglaries.

Evarts threw his newspaper on the floor. "Anything about us in your paper?"

"Nothing." She shook her head. "Whoever did this sure knew how to divert attention away from the real motive."

"Yeah, we're dealing with smart people."

She looked worried. "How powerful do you think they are?"

Evarts decided not to equivocate. "Their intelligence is first-rate. They discovered what Douglass was doing before he got very far, they found us, and they even connected Marston to you. They've got some heavyweight professionals doing their dirty work, and those kinds of people are expensive, so we have to assume they have strong financial backing. My bet is that they also have substantial political clout. Hell, they even got someone in my own department to help frame me." He watched her face to see how she took this news, but he could see she had already figured out most of this for herself. "Trish, I'd say we're up against a pretty tough bunch. Our biggest problem is that they know who we are, but we don't know who they are. That makes breaking the encrypted code imperative. We need to discover who we're fighting."

"Maybe my parents can help."

"I hope so, but we're still a hard three-day drive away from New York."

She threw her paper on the floor as well. "Then I guess we better get at it."

"Agreed." Evarts threw back the blanket and then paused. "Were you referring to a shower, sex, or breakfast?"

"All the above, in that order, if you please."

Chapter 17

· · · · · ·

Evarts reached into his pocket to pay the toll at the George Washington Bridge. They had made it from Denver to New York City in three days by driving fourteen to sixteen hours a day. When they stopped, Evarts had insisted that they stay at independently owned campgrounds. They used the showers, sat outside and talked while Evarts cooked on a hibachi, and slept together in the back of the SUV.

They had discussed the danger of meeting her parents. Evarts assumed their New York apartment would be watched, especially if they had some knowledge of the Shut Mouth Society. The Mexico gambit might have worked, but they couldn't count on it. The people chasing them would assume that contacting her parents might be the first thing she would do.

As they turned onto the Hudson Parkway, Evarts said, "Remember everything?"

"Yes, but I'm nervous again."

"It'll be okay if we follow our plan."

They had tried to think of a place they could meet undetected away from her parents' apartment, but decided that if someone followed her parents, the two of them could be spotted leaving the rendezvous. Baldwin said her parents' apartment had excellent security, but it was a large building, and hundreds of people wandered in and out all day long. All they had to do was figure out a way to enter the building without being recognized. He suggested some disguises, but she came up with a better idea. They stopped in a mall in New Jersey and went into a maternity shop. Just as she predicted, each dressing room had a pregnancy apparatus that fit around a woman's middle so shoppers could see how things would fit after they became larger. Baldwin wore one out of the store under her clothes, but it wasn't for her. He tried it on and discovered how a beer belly altered his appearance and even the way he walked. His disguise included calf-length shorts and an NYU tee shirt, finished with a bright red baseball cap. When he tried on the whole outfit, he laughed at his appearance. No one trying to remain incognito would dress in that garb.

He had suggested that she pull her hair straight back and wear no makeup, but her idea was to wear an exorbitant amount of makeup and bright red lipstick. At Target, they found a tawdry outfit and accented her new clothes with a pair of dark framed glasses from one of those one-hour optical shops. She also accepted his suggestion to buy a cheap purse to replace her Prada bag. Her only condition was that the new purse should be big and sturdy enough to carry the Glock. She had become attached to her security blanket.

They exited the Hudson Parkway at Seventy-ninth Street and meandered along the streets until they found a legal parking place. No small feat, even in the middle of the day. Baldwin had explained that her parents habitually went out to breakfast to leisurely read three newspapers. After breakfast, her father returned to the apartment and religiously wrote on his blog until midafternoon. Believing the entire world awaited his daily musings, he never changed his routine or skipped a day. Her mother often left him to his toils, but they decided to chance catching her at home.

They walked six blocks to Central Park and then waited on a bench along the perimeter of the Circle Walk. In a few minutes, a young man and a girl approached leading six dogs.

"Hi, Sandy," Baldwin said.

"This is strange as hell," she responded.

"I know, but you owe me a favor."

Baldwin had explained to Evarts that she had written Sandy a letter of recommendation to Columbia. She and her boyfriend made ends meet as dog-walkers, the most ubiquitous nonresidents on the West Side.

"You look terrible," Sandy said. "Why the masquerade?"

"Too complicated to explain. I got into some trouble."

Sandy and her boyfriend gave Evarts a nasty look. They obviously thought him a scoundrel who had taken a fine lady and turned her into a painted hussy and gotten her into some predicament. He merely reached out his arm, and they handed over the leashes.

"Where do they go?"

"Number 11, next door to your parents. We do their building next." She handed Baldwin a three-by-five card. "Those are the apartment numbers by breed. On the back are the dogs we pick up in your building. If anyone asks, tell them I have finals."

"Okay, we'll meet you back here in one hour."

"We'll be here. Don't screw up. This is our livelihood."

Evarts and Baldwin each took three dogs and walked to West Eighty-first Street. He pointed at an incongruous building across the street. "What's that?"

"Natural History Museum. I grew up in there, but now I'm more likely to visit the New York Historical Society on the other side."

"I meant that glass monstrosity," he said. A huge white globe enclosed in glass had been grafted to the side of the nineteenth-century Natural History Museum building.

"That's the planetarium. Built in 2000. I think it's kind of ugly, except at night."

"Ross Geller worked at that museum."

"Ross Geller is fictional. Are you trying to distract me?"

"I'm trying to look like we're talking and having a grand old time with these pups. Are you sure *Friends* wasn't a documentary?"

"Pretty sure, but I've had students who thought it was a reality show. They kept waiting for one of the six to get voted off Manhattan Island."

Evarts spotted a limo double-parked where the driver had a clear view of the entrance to number 15. "What are kids coming to nowadays? We were raised on a program where real friends stick together, while they prefer reality shows where everyone backstabs their fake friends."

She gave him a tolerant smile and directed him into number 11.

In the elevator, Evarts said, "That limo driver was a lookout."

"How could you tell?"

"The eyes. He wasn't waiting for a passenger; he was watching the entrance to your building."

"Did he see us?"

"Yeah ... but that's good. Now he has us catalogued as part of the terrain."

After they dropped off the dogs, they walked out of the building laughing. As they passed in front of the limo driver, Evarts patted Baldwin on the butt, and she slapped his shoulder. When they entered the outer lobby of her building and out of sight from the street, she reassumed her identity as Patricia Baldwin. They found the doorman stooped over to give a doggie biscuit to a resident's wheaten terrier.

Evarts examined the massive lobby and almost whistled. The public area appeared to encompass the entire first floor, but it was the décor that grabbed his attention. The lobby had been decorated in an odd mixture of art deco and medieval. The lighting fixtures, floor, and doors all had classic art deco flourishes, but the walls had been hung with Old World tapestries, the furniture looked like it came from a Spanish castle, and light streamed through stained-glass windows that illuminated knights in shining armor. Somehow it all worked together to give an impression of wealth and permanence.

When the doorman stood up, Baldwin said, "Hi Frank. Still giving treats to the dogs."

He looked surprised at her appearance but didn't mention it. "Yeah. And the toddlers, when the parents allow." He looked embarrassed and then added, "I'm terribly sorry about your parents."

"Sorry? About what?"

He looked nonplussed. "Aren't you here for the funeral?"

"What funeral?"

"My god, you don't know?" He glanced around as if looking for someone else to tell her. "Where have you been?"

"Traveling. What's going on, Frank?"

"Your parents were both killed in a car accident in Connecticut. I'm sorry. I shouldn't have to be the one to tell you."

Chapter 18

· · · · · ·

Evarts had a hard time calming her down enough to collect the building's dogs, but her parents' death made it even more imperative that they leave the building undetected. She had wanted to stop to calm herself in their apartment, but Evarts's instincts told him to get out.

He stared at Baldwin's mascara-smeared face. "If that limo guy sees you, it'll call attention to us. As we leave the lobby, stay on the far side of me and turn right."

She took off her glasses and wiped her cheeks with the back of her fingers. It smeared the mascara worse. "Dog walkers go to Central Park."

"Not these and not today. Trish, we've got to get out of this building without being noticed."

"Then let's go out the back onto Eighty-second Street. It's an exit only."

"No. I know the position of the guy in front. We didn't case the back. You have to pull yourself together." He tried to make his voice sympathetic. "Trish, I'm sorry. Just until we get out of here."

She nodded. Just as they were about to leave the building, Baldwin told Evarts to stop, and she fumbled around in her purse and finally extracted two twenty-dollar bills.

"Frank?"

He had been pretending to be busy at his little stand-up desk, but Evarts saw him peek at the dogs. "Yes, Ms. Baldwin?"

"How long have you worked here?"

"Over thirty years. I gave you treats when you were a toddler."

"Thank you, if I forgot to say it then."

"Your parents always made you say thank you."

"The apartment is mine now, and I've noticed how you protect the privacy of the residents." She reached over and pressed the twenties into his fingers. "You never saw me. I wasn't here." She paused as she held his eyes. "Do you understand?"

He seemed confused by the dogs but just said. "Yes, Ms. Baldwin."

"I'm sure the co-op board appreciates your discretion."

He looked taken aback but added only, "I'm sorry for your loss."

"Thank you." Baldwin squeezed his arm to reassure him, and without waiting for a response, she and Evarts left the building and turned right toward Columbus Avenue, in the opposite direction of Central Park and the phony limo driver.

Evarts admired the deft way she had handled Frank. Her tone of voice would scare the creased pants off any doorman at a ritzy co-op building. Out of uniform, bereaved, and mascara smeared, she kept her head and covered their tracks.

As they walked the half block to Columbus, Evarts resisted a temptation to glance back at the limo driver. Instead, he focused ahead, sweeping his eyes over both sides of the street to make sure they hadn't stationed a second watcher. At the corner, he got himself purposely tangled up in the dog leashes so he could get a good look behind them. The limo and its driver hadn't moved. Good. With any luck, the Shut Mouth Society wouldn't discover they had made it to the East Coast.

It took about fifteen minutes to make the circuitous route back to the real dog walkers. Evarts got some more nasty stares from Sandy and her boyfriend due to Baldwin's obviously distressed state, but they completed the transfer of the dogs with a minimum of conversation and made their way back to where they had parked the car.

When they had both slammed their respective car doors, Evarts said, "Trish, I'm sorry." He checked the street one more time. No visible threat. "We're safe. Would you like a few moments before we get under way?"

She pulled the Glock from her purse. "What I'd like to do is to go back and kill that son of a bitch limo driver."

Evarts put his hand on her shoulder. "That wouldn't accomplish anything but let them know we're here. He wasn't the one that killed your parents."

She looked so sad that Evarts felt her anguish. What if it had been his parents? Oh my god. "I've got to call my parents." Evarts threw himself out of the truck and ran to the Barnes and Noble on Broadway. Running up the escalator, he found a pay phone next to the restrooms. Damn. He needed a calling card. After he bought one at the register back downstairs, he returned to the phone and punched the numbers as fast as his fingers could move. After one ring, he heard his mother's voice say hello. He hung up immediately.

What did this mean? Her parents were involved but not his? Did they want him to call so they could pick up his location? Did they have the same murderous intent for his parents but hadn't carried it out yet? Think. As soon as he remembered that the calling card disguised his area code, he dialed again.

"Lieutenant Clark," said the voice on the other end of the line.

"Bob, this is Greg."

"Where the hell are you? Everybody's looking for you. The goddamn FBI, the LAPD, the chief. What the hell's going on?"

"Bad stuff but not by me. Do you believe that?"

"Of course." Evarts felt relieved not to hear any hesitation before Clark answered.

"Listen, I can't explain now, but my parents might be in danger. Could you keep them under surveillance? For a cover, convince Damon that it's the surest way to find me."

"They're already under surveillance. Did you call a minute ago?"

"Yes. Thank god. Bob, please, keep an eye on them."

"Greg, we have them under surveillance to get a handle on your whereabouts."

"I don't give a shit why, just do it." Evarts hung up.

When he jumped back in the Explorer, Baldwin looked impassive. "Were they all right?"

"Yes, they're under police surveillance in case I tried to contact them."

They sat there for several minutes. Not sure what to do, Evarts touched her forearm and then gently tugged her toward him. She startled him by leaning across the center console and throwing her arms around his neck. The sobbing quickly escalated into a crying fit that shook her so hard, Evarts found it difficult to hold her. He had no idea how long they stayed in that position, but when she finished, she went so limp and quiet against his wet shoulder that he thought she had gone to sleep.

In a few moments, she said, "We better get out of here."

"Yeah." He stroked her hair. "Boston?"

"New Canaan...Connecticut." She sat upright and wiped her eyes. "Thanks for giving me a few minutes. I just—" She started to sob again but got herself under control. "I went out of my way to hurt them, but I never lifted a handset to tell them I loved them." She pulled a fresh tissue from a box under the dashboard. "I quit being angry years ago, but I never told them."

"They knew."

"How?"

"The hurting stopped."

She sat still a long moment and then said, "Thank you." Her smile hadn't disappeared as deep as Evarts had feared. "I never told them in words, but you're right, I told them in actions." She lifted her chin. "Did you know that they stage the balloons for Macy's Thanksgiving Day Parade on their street?"

"Did you come every year?"

"Every year, since graduate school." She straightened up in her own seat. "I'm ready. Let's go."

"What's in New Canaan?"

"My grandmother's house."

"I don't think that's wise."

"Don't worry, I haven't been there in fifteen years, and I don't want to go to the house anyway. She died many years ago. My parents used it as a weekend retreat away from the city. I want to go to the public library. My parents were considered locals, so the town newspaper will have articles about the accident."

Evarts started the car. "Good idea. Sure no one will recognize you?"

"My parents' friends don't patronize public libraries."

"Okay, tell me how to get the hell out of this city."

Baldwin directed him back the way they had come to the Hudson Parkway and then through the transitions to the Merritt Parkway. Thick trees shielded both sides of the divided roadway, and stone overpasses gave the parkway a genteel, picturesque appearance.

"No wonder they call this a parkway," Evarts said. "Nothing like this in L.A."

She seemed distracted but said, "We have an ugly Los Angeles-style freeway just a few miles east of us. Anyone with sixteen wheels or in a sixteen percent tax bracket has to stay on I95."

"You kidding?"

"Not about the sixteen wheels. The poor can sneak onto the Merritt, but we gouge them at the gas pump."

They passed a scenic gas station nestled among thick trees in a wide grass median. The posted price was twenty cents higher than they had last paid in New Jersey. "Now, you're serious."

"Now, I'm serious."

They exited at the New Canaan off-ramp. After a few miles of country road, a quaint town came into view, looking exactly the way Evarts imagined a New England village should look.

After they pulled into the library parking lot, Baldwin grabbed her overnight bag, which contained her regular clothes, and asked Evarts to start scanning local papers for articles about her parents' accident while she cleaned up in the ladies room. He found six articles spread over three days.

When Baldwin returned, she had changed into her own clothes, but her freshly scrubbed face still showed raw eyes behind her regular glasses. "What did you find?"

"They died two days ago, here in New Canaan. Hit a tree at forty-five miles an hour in a vintage 1956 Porsche Roadster. No bumper, no airbags."

"That car was my father's pride and joy. He kept it in pristine condition and paid more to park it in the city than the payments would've been on a new luxury car." She sat down. "He had the bumpers replaced with these little chrome bars."

"The New Canaan police found no indications of foul play, but they haven't closed the investigation."

"Why not?"

"Doesn't say, but I'll get Lieutenant Clark to give them a call." She grabbed one of the newspapers and started to read the article. Evarts interrupted her. "They were returning from a lunch engagement at the Roger Sherman Inn."

"So it was probably midafternoon."

"I meant, does the Roger Sherman Inn have any significance?"

Baldwin looked up as if a new thought had struck her. "That inn has always been part of the landscape in New Canaan. It never occurred to me that it might have implications for this."

"Could it?"

"I don't know. After we're done here, let's go see. I want to know how much they had to drink at lunch anyway."

"Okay, you read the articles, and I'll get out of these silly clothes and call Clark."

Clark sounded unhappy to hear from Evarts again, but he agreed to call the New Canaan police. When he returned from the pay phone, Baldwin stood ready to go. "Anything more?" he asked.

She shook her head. "Let's go."

The Roger Sherman Inn sat back from the road, as picturesque as the town. The grounds had been groomed perfectly, and the white clapboard converted home looked like the kind of intimate inn where, in better days, he would've liked to bring Patricia Baldwin for a long weekend. A portrait of a stern-looking man with a big square face hung in the lobby. Evarts checked the plaque and saw that it read "Roger Sherman."

"How many children did you say?"

"Fifteen, two different wives," she answered.

"He looks passionless."

She studied the portrait a moment. "John Adams said he was the opposite of grace...and Adams was a friend. Contemporaries universally described him as awkward and clumsy, but they also said he was brilliant and a savvy politician. Thomas Jefferson said Sherman never spoke a foolish sentence in his life. An odd man to propagate a family that has exerted such a strong influence on our nation and our lives."

"Yeah." Evarts glanced toward the dining area. "Are you hungry?"

"Starved."

"Let's eat. By the way, we're journalists following up on the death of a prominent New York couple."

"Sounds good. Let's say we're from the *New York Daily News*. A tabloid would do a follow-up on this type of story."

The host sat them on a cozy patio with trees overhead, shrubs along every sight line, and brightly colored flowers at their feet. The fine china and three glasses per place setting made the small, cloth-covered tables look crowded. While Evarts studied the menu, it occurred to him that the hamburgers in Westwood Village now appeared reasonably priced.

After they had ordered, Evarts asked to see the host. The young man who approached their table possessed the élan of the well-to-do and asked how he could help.

"We're reporters doing a follow-up story on the tragic Baldwin accident. We understand they ate lunch here just before the incident."

"Yes, they did."

"Did they drink alcoholic beverages with lunch," Baldwin asked.

"I'm sorry ma'am; we try to protect the privacy of our guests."

Baldwin waved her arm around the half-empty patio. "A mention of your fine restaurant in our paper could fill these tables."

"Perhaps you should talk to Mrs. Greene."

"Mrs. Greene?"

"She and her husband had lunch with the Baldwins that day. They're the inn managers."

"Could you get her for us?"

"And Mr. Greene, if he's available," Evarts added.

"I'm afraid Mr. Greene took a business trip to Omaha, but I'll see if Mrs. Greene is available."

A few minutes later, a sophisticated older woman started toward their table but made an abrupt stop when she spotted them. She immediately retraced her steps.

"Did she recognize you?" Evarts asked.

"I can't imagine how. It's been fifteen years since I've eaten here."

The woman didn't reappear before their food arrived. Evarts was famished, so he took three quick bites and then said, "I'm going to go find out what's keeping her."

Just as he entered the inn, the host came up to him. "I'm sorry, sir, but Mrs. Greene had to leave suddenly."

"I insist on seeing her."

"That would be impossible. She left five minutes ago. She did leave this for your companion." He handed Evarts a sealed envelope. In exquisite penmanship, the envelope had three words written on it that stunned Evarts: *Miss Patricia Baldwin.*

Evarts walked back to the table and handed the envelope to Baldwin. "We're blown."

"Good god," she said as she ripped open the envelope. She read it at least three times before she handed it over to Evarts.

Dear Patricia,

You have my sincerest condolences for your parents. They were good friends. I assume that is Greg Evarts with you. I don't know what you are doing here, but they told us you would fight the union.

Please forgive me, but I must leave. Don't try to contact me. I'm far gone.

Nancy Greene

"Fight the union," Evarts said. "That's odd wording."

Baldwin looked around nervously. "I think we should get out of here ourselves."

Evarts got up and threw two twenties on the table. "Right now."

Chapter 19

· · · · · ·

"Pull over and let me drive," Baldwin said.

Evarts had just pulled off the Massachusetts Turnpike onto Boston surface streets. Baldwin had been unusually quiet on the four-hour drive, but that seemed normal considering the circumstances.

"Why? We're almost there."

"This is the worst driving city in America. All one-ways with tiny street signs you can't read until you've committed yourself to go straight. Bostonians don't believe you should be driving here unless you're a local."

Evarts didn't argue. He hated being lost. After they switched seats, he was glad that she had gotten behind the wheel. Even with her knowing the city, it seemed like they drove in circles. Eventually, they reached a road that passed through a park, and she explained that the Boston Commons were to the right and the Public Gardens were to the left.

When they stopped at a red light, she pointed ahead. "The apartment's just off Charles Street up ahead."

"The street with all the oncoming traffic?"

"Yes. It's one-way on the other side of this signal. We need to go around Beacon Hill and approach it from the other side."

Evarts thought it odd to have a two-way road suddenly turn one-way, but they had already encountered three of these marvels of civic engineering. After they turned right, four- and five-story brick townhouses faced the Commons in tight formation. Baldwin explained that early settlers had established the Commons in 1634, and that public hangings had occurred in the park until 1817. In the early days, women convicted of witchcraft had their death sentences carried out in the Commons so everyone could witness the penalty for consorting with the devil.

When they reached a gold-domed edifice on the left, Baldwin said, "That's the new statehouse ... built in 1798."

"New?"

"We'll see the old one later. They built it in 1713."

"In Los Angeles, we tear down anything over fifty years old."

"Try that in Boston, and they'll probably reinstate hangings in the Commons."

They drove around the periphery of Beacon Hill and entered Charles Street from the north side. Evarts couldn't believe the audacity of the pedestrians. In California, cops ticketed jaywalkers, but in Boston anyone waiting for a green walk sign would feel foolish as people brushed past them into the street against the red light. To successfully navigate the slalom course between the dashing pedestrians required a driver's full attention.

"How many pedestrians do Bostonians kill each year?"

"No one knows. They just brush them aside so the street cleaners can pick them up in the wee hours."

When they reached mid-block, Baldwin stopped and put on the flashers. As she opened the Explorer door, she said, "I'll run in and get the key."

"Wait. Do you have to show ID?"

"No, just whisper the secret password."

"What secret password? What are you talking about?"

She nodded toward a real estate office. "My dad set up a system with these people. They give the keys to anyone that asks for them and says they're with the S&M League. I thought it sounded kind of kinky at the time."

"Trish?"

"What?"

"League is a synonym for society."

She looked irritated for a brief moment until she made the connection. "Damn, the thought never occurred to me. My brain must be addled. I keep worrying instead of thinking."

"Run in and get the key before a cop tickets us for double parking."

"Don't worry about that. I put the flashers on."

"That makes it legal?"

"In Boston, custom overrules law." She bounded out of the car and disappeared into the real estate office.

Evarts kept an eye on the street. The heavy foot traffic and the approaching dusk made it difficult to isolate individuals, but he spotted no one watching the real estate office. Charles Street looked like an incongruous mishmash. The quaint red brick storefronts, narrow gas-lit street, and undulating brick sidewalks made Charles Street look like a tourist destination; except nestled between the antique stores, art galleries, and fine restaurants were coin Laundromats, video rental stores, pizza joints, and a grocery store so cramped that it probably also had one-way aisles. Most pedestrians looked like tourists browsing one of the oldest mercantile districts in America, but a few appeared to be harried residents running into a neighborhood establishment to complete some errand before heading home for the evening.

Baldwin returned in less than five minutes dangling a set of keys in an outstretched hand. After she slammed the door, she said, "Now for one more tour around Beacon Hill."

"Excuse me?"

"The apartment's on Pinckney Street, behind us. One-ways, remember."

"This is so convoluted; no one'll ever find us."

"That's the idea. It's on the west side of Charles, which, metaphorically speaking, is on the wrong side of the tracks." She pointed to the left. "The rich live east of Charles on Beacon Hill."

"Parking?"

"You've got to be kidding. After we unload we need to find a garage."

Evarts thought about his shotgun and other specialized gear he had thrown in his van before they left his house. "Quiet neighborhood?"

"Extremely. The street dead-ends at the Charles River just a half block away, and it's off the tourist footpaths. The street's central but, at the same time, almost completely isolated."

"Let's get unloaded quick, and I'll run the car over to long-term parking at the airport. Is it far?"

"No, but I better take it. The route's tricky."

"Why doesn't that surprise me?" Evarts turned around to check the traffic behind them, but saw no one suspicious. "We either go together or I take it."

"I can handle it."

"I'm not letting you wander this city alone."

She gave him a nasty look. "Then together." She double-parked, threw the car in park, and flipped off the ignition with a sharp movement.

Before she opened the car door, Evarts said, "Hold a sec." After he inspected the street and the windows, he asked, "Which one?"

"That door over there. It gives access to a second-floor apartment."

Evarts saw a plain door at the extreme edge of a two-story brick house. The building had been a single residence at one time, and sometime in the past, an enclosed staircase had been built on the side of the building to provide a private entrance to the second floor.

"Okay, let's check it out."

They both got out of the car. Baldwin had her hand in her purse, and Evarts guessed her fingers didn't clutch the keys. The commercial-grade lock turned easily when she inserted the key. As she opened the door, Evarts nudged her aside and had his hand on his own gun. The open door revealed only blackness. She reached around him and fumbled against the wall with her hand until she found a light switch. Three bright bare bulbs came on to illuminate a narrow staircase painted a dull brown. Evarts checked the street and buildings one more time and then started up the stairs.

"Wait," she said. "The door at the top is locked as well." She handed him the keys, and when he had moved up a few steps, she closed the street door behind them and twisted the lock closed.

Evarts felt trapped in the staircase, so he hurdled up the steps two at a time. At the top, it took him awhile to find the right key on the ring, but when he did, he felt the heavy-duty deadbolt slide free. He opened the door a crack and reached his left hand inside until he found a light switch. After pulling out the SIG, he motioned for Baldwin to stay down a few steps. He noticed she had her Glock out, and more important, she had it pointed straight up with her trigger finger extended along the barrel. Evidently, her ex-boyfriend had taught her good gun safety.

Evarts bent into a crouch, flung the door open, and swung the automatic from side to side. Nothing but draped furniture. He entered the room and wished he had backup that understood the proper procedure to clear a series of rooms. He glanced back and saw that Baldwin had stayed about two steps down the staircase and had assumed a shooting posture, but with her gun still in the air. He was going to have to ask her about her ex-boyfriend.

In less than a minute, Evarts had cleared the one-bedroom apartment and signaled Baldwin to come in.

"That was scary," she said.

"Cops hate clearing rooms." Evarts smiled, partly from relief. "You did good. Was your old boyfriend a cop?"

"Drug enforcement. How'd you guess?"

"Because he taught you more than how to shoot." He moved toward the door. "Let's get our stuff up here."

In a little over an hour, they had hauled their few belongings up the stairs, stashed the car at an airport off-site lot, and taken a taxi back into the city. Inside again, Evarts checked out the place more carefully. He found it odd that the hardwood door at the top of the stairs would give a police ram trouble and that the windows had blackout curtains. Checking the windows, he discovered a fire escape that provided a quick exit to a rear alley. He opened the window and checked out the drop ladder on the fire escape. Someone had used a spring-loaded C-clamp to lock it in the up position so someone from below couldn't pull it down.

When Baldwin returned from the single bedroom, she held aloft a brick-size stack of currency. "Money's not a problem."

"Trish, what did your father tell you about this place?"

"He brought me here when I was seventeen and said I should use it only in an emergency. That I should think of it as my safe haven in case of trouble."

"That's it?"

"Yeah." She looked embarrassed. "I didn't ask questions. I assumed he used it to cheat on my mother. I thought it weird that he took his teenage daughter to see his lair."

"Did he show you where he hid that money?"

"He showed me the floor safe and said one of the keys would open it. He didn't show or tell me about the contents."

"What else did you find in the safe?"

"Foreign currency, unsigned traveler checks, and this." She pulled out a .45 automatic she had tucked behind her in the waistband of her shorts.

Evarts ran his fingers through his hair. "Trish, he didn't use this apartment for illicit rendezvous. In the intelligence business, we call this a safe house: secure, off the beaten track, hidden ownership, and provisioned for emergencies."

Baldwin looked miserable. "My parents belonged to the Shut Mouth Society, didn't they?"

"I'm afraid everything points in that direction. S&M League is a bit too much of a coincidence."

"A lot of my rebellion had to do with things like this. Hidden apartments, trusts inside trusts, secretive absences, special phones, and an elitist attitude that our family had a responsibility to take care of the people too ignorant to understand the real world. I didn't understand it, but as I grew older, I eventually came to believe that my parents were basically good people." She held up the money in one hand and the .45 in the other. "Despite this, they couldn't have been members of a secret society that kills people."

"All secret societies have layers, and each layer keeps secrets from those outside the inner echelons. It's possible that the Shut Mouth Society is relatively benign, but that a rogue clique wants to take over or possibly stop it from going public."

"Are you trying to make me feel better about my parents' involvement in this?"

"I'm just saying we know too little to jump to conclusions. The good news is that your father prepared a safe place for us, so we can relax for the first time since this started. Right now, I'm hungry, tired, and filthy. Let's start our research in the morning."

She looked around, and her voice sounded weary when she spoke. "First things first. Let's get these covers off the furniture, make the bed, and buy a few staples at the grocery store."

Evarts thought she looked forlorn. "Yeah, it's been a tough day. I'm sorry."

She walked over to a couch and flung the cover off. "It's been a series of tough days." She suddenly began to cry and used the cover to hide her face. As she collapsed onto the couch with her head in her lap, Evarts heard her muffled plaint. "When will this end?"

His sympathies went out to her, but he had a different question on his mind: How would this end?

Chapter 20

. . . . . .

The next morning, they got up late and had cereal and bananas for breakfast. Baldwin suggested that they dress more formally so they wouldn't look out of place at the Athenaeum. Evarts put on the khaki pants and black polo shirt that he had worn into the office to see the chief, and Baldwin dressed in the same outfit she had worn to dinner at the Douglass home.

The regular bed and the sudden feeling of safety allowed them a sound night of sleep. They had finished their chores the previous evening and then devoured a takeaway pizza in less than ten minutes. When they hit the bed, both instantly fell asleep.

Baldwin placed her bowl in the sink and looked at her watch. "Let's walk to the Athenaeum. I'm anxious to get started."

Evarts thought she sounded distracted. He wanted to get started but worried about her frame of mind. "We can wait a day, if you want."

"No, I need to keep my mind busy."

They walked up Pinckney Street into the Beacon Hill neighborhood and then headed right on Joy Street until they got to Beacon Street. She pointed left. "It's only a couple blocks this way."

The ten-minute walk fascinated Evarts. Beacon Hill looked like something Disney would build to give the illusion of a quaint district in a distant part of the world, except here the brick sidewalks and gas lanterns were real and older than almost anything in Southern California. Of course, Disney's sidewalks would be laid with precision so visitors wouldn't stumble. These brick paths undulated and required a bit of attention to keep your footing. Evarts could tell nothing from the face of the townhouses that rose anonymously right next to the narrow sidewalk, but Baldwin explained that they were all expensively furnished with antiques and artworks normally associated with museums. When she mentioned that an intact townhouse in this neighborhood could command fifteen million dollars, he thought about the Douglass estate that cost half as much and offered a panoramic view of the California coastline. Evarts couldn't understand rich city dwellers who chose to cramp themselves into outrageously priced tight quarters with only a view of their neighbor's window.

"Do you have the list of law books?" Evarts asked.

"In my briefcase," she answered matter-of-factly.

Evarts thought her tone distant, but he dismissed it as a product of her grief. Maybe she was right about getting her mind busy on something else. "While I work on the code, I thought you might start with William Maxwell Evarts," he said.

"Why him?"

"Douglass said the family didn't form a secret society until after the Civil War. Evarts lived in that period."

"So did others." Her tone had gone from matter-of-fact to testy.

"You said he defended President Johnson during the impeachment hearings. The three seminal events around that time were the Civil War, Lincoln's assassination, and the Johnson impeachment. One of those events probably drove the family underground as the Shut Mouth Society. I think the impeachment might hold the key." Evarts walked a few more steps before adding, "On the other hand, perhaps the impeachment interests me because I know the least about it."

"I've got to start somewhere, so William Evarts is as good a place as any." Baldwin had returned to her matter-of-fact tone. "The impeachment was a political power play, and this whole affair seems connected with politics."

When Evarts got sight of the Athenaeum, he thought it looked more like a sturdy old bank than a library. The gray stone building, adorned with faux Federalist columns and arches, gave the impression of a structure designed to protect something of enormous value. Even in its day, it must have been exceptionally expensive to construct. Evarts appreciated the value of knowledge, but in the age of the Internet, it seemed like an antiquarian idea to elaborately house paper-based books in such an edifice. On second thought, maybe in the not too distant future, books would find a secure home only in a museum.

Baldwin stopped Evarts on the steps of the Athenaeum. "Let me explain the access procedure. I'll have to give the guard my real name and show ID, but I don't have to sign in. Don't worry. These guards are only interested in getting back to the baseball game or whatever else they're listening to in their earpiece. Visitors do sign in, but they don't show ID, so use whatever name you like."

"Why haven't you told me this until now?"

"Because you wouldn't have come here." She pointed toward the Athenaeum. "The answers to our questions lie inside that building. No one knows we're in Boston, and no one knows I'm a member."

Evarts took a deep breath. "Okay, on one condition. If I signal to leave, you don't hesitate a second."

"Agreed, *Commander*." She used the same disdainful inflection as she had on the first day he met her.

Evarts wanted to ask her if she had a problem with him, but she marched up the steps and into the building. He had no choice but to scurry after her.

The interior of the building didn't disappoint. A chest-high dark wood counter curved around from the entrance to a reception counter. An oriental rug muffled footsteps, and huge original oil paintings adorned the walls. Glass doors separated a beautifully decorated reading room to the left, and Evarts could see an elegant room ahead with rows of bookshelves. He felt relief when he saw the man behind the counter. He looked like an indifferent rent-a-cop.

"Patricia Baldwin, life member."

He barely gave her a glance before checking his computer screen. "ID."

She showed him her driver's license, and he waved them in without asking about Evarts. Definitely a rent-a-cop.

As soon as they entered the library, Baldwin turned and walked through a narrow hall until she reached a tiny elevator door. She pushed the call button.

"Where are we going?" Evarts asked.

"Upstairs to the law stacks. We'll get a private research room so we can talk."

On the third floor, Baldwin went directly to a small room furnished in Federalist antiques or excellent reproductions. As she entered, she flipped a plaque mounted next to the door so it read "occupied." She immediately opened her briefcase and spread out her papers and laptop on a small table. "Welcome to the Athenaeum."

"You seem pretty familiar with a place you said you hadn't used."

"I said I hadn't used it in years. I did some of my doctoral research in this very room."

The small room had two easy chairs along with a worktable and original oil paintings. The atmosphere had been carefully crafted to look refined and soothing.

Without preamble, she handed him the list of law books. "I think you should get to work."

Over the next three hours, Evarts tried seven law books without success. After finishing with one, he would leave the room to replace the book in the stacks and get the next book on her list. Baldwin, on the other hand, pulled several dozen books into the reading room and stacked them on the floor until it was hard to move around.

Evarts needed a break, so he flopped into one of the easy chairs. "When I visited your office, you kept everything neat."

She didn't look up from the book she was reading. "I am neat. I know what's in every stack."

"Find anything?"

She gave him an exasperated look. "Have you finished the list?"

"No. I need to rest my eyes ... and I'm hungry."

"Later. I want to finish this."

Evarts looked at her stacks of books. "That could take days."

She reached down to one of her stacks and threw him a book. "Look up William Evarts in the index."

He did. What he found made his hunch seem plausible. William Evarts was Roger Sherman's grandson. He graduated from Yale, where he joined Skull and Bones. He got his law degree from Harvard. He was U.S. District Attorney in New York and led the New York delegation to the 1860 Republican National Convention. President Lincoln sent him on two secret diplomatic missions to Great Britain in 1863 and 1864. He served as attorney general under President Johnson and acted as chief council in the Johnson impeachment hearings. President Hayes appointed him secretary of state, and he later served in the U.S. Senate.

Evarts looked up to find Baldwin buried in two books. "What do you make of this? It looks like he had the trust of at least three presidents."

She took off her glasses and rubbed her eyes. "That's encyclopedia stuff, surface history. We've got to get deeper. Did he influence

Lincoln's nomination at the convention? What instructions did Lincoln give him for the Great Britain missions? What cases did he pursue as attorney general? Right now I'm checking the Skull and Bones connection, and it looks promising. So far, I've identified eight Sherman family members that belonged to the Order of Skull and Bones at Yale." She looked up and caught Evarts's eye. "You were in army intelligence. What do you know about the connections between Skull and Bones and the CIA?"

"Nothing. What do you mean?"

"There's been a supposed connection between Yale and intelligence ever since Nathan Hale spied for George Washington. Hale and three other Yale graduates made up the Culper Ring, America's first intelligence operation. Since then, Yale and spying have gone hand in hand. William H. Russell founded Skull and Bones at Yale in 1832, and ever since then, the secret society has been intertwined with our country's intelligence operations."

"Why do you say a supposed connection?"

"Because secret societies and intelligence organizations don't publish minutes of their meetings. It's all speculation."

"Well, it may surprise you to hear this, but army intelligence and the CIA don't get along."

"You must have heard scuttlebutt," Baldwin insisted.

"It's common knowledge that the CIA recruits at Yale, and it makes sense that they would prefer people who have already shown an affinity for secret societies. Where do you think this leads us?"

"The Shut Mouth Society might be connected to either the CIA or Skull and Bones or both."

"Too Hollywood. I think Skull and Bones is a clique of sophomoric snobs who get a kick out of playing stupid games. They like to pretend they're going to rule the world."

"Many of them do rule the world. They're notorious for helping each other out in their careers."

"As do all fraternity brothers. I don't think we ought to jump to conclusions. Let's follow the facts we know."

"Which are?"

"The Shut Mouth Society was a loose family alliance until Booth assassinated Lincoln; then they turned into a clandestine society. The Society's founding family has wielded enormous political power, and we think we've identified that family as the Sherman progeny. They have Lincoln documents in their possession, including some encrypted messages. And most important, somebody is killing people to keep something secret."

"What about the eight Sherman family members who joined Skull and Bones?" Baldwin countered.

"If you go to Yale and you're from a prominent family and you're not a total loser, then you'll likely get invited to join the most exclusive fraternity on campus."

"Is that an army intelligence officer talking or a descendant of William Evarts?"

Evarts felt annoyed. "I'm not interested in my ancestors. I just don't want to waste time following false leads. An inner CIA conspiracy sounds like a bad movie script. I ran into a bunch of those people, and most of them can't find their way to the toilet without written directions."

"Now you *are* talking like an army intelligence officer."

"Touché." Evarts thought a minute. "Listen, let's get something to eat. I can't concentrate with only a bowl of cereal. Afterwards you can pursue the Skull and Bones connection, and I'll get cracking on the code again. It wouldn't have been given to us unless it held the key to unraveling this mystery." Evarts stopped. After a moment he said, "Damn it, I'm getting slow. Somebody gave us those documents, which means that someone is trying to help us. They may have drawn us into a dangerous game, but they gave us clues."

"So?"

"That means good people are out there somewhere. I've been focused on identifying the bad guys, but we should also be looking for our allies. We're going to need all the help we can get, especially if your theory about Skull and Bones proves correct."

"How do you propose we find these so-called good guys?"

Evarts smiled. "That's easy. Follow your parents."

Chapter 21

. . . . . .

Since they had plenty of money, Baldwin suggested the Federalist Restaurant almost directly across the street from the Athenaeum. The high-end establishment catered to lobbyists trying to schmooze state legislators, so the establishment arranged the tables far apart and used partitions between some for additional privacy. The décor surprised Evarts. The restaurant name and the Athenaeum led him to expect an Early American interior, not a contemporary style using a gray and brown muted color scheme.

Once they had a table, Evarts excused himself and found a pay phone to call Lieutenant Clark. One o'clock in Boston would be ten o'clock in California. Evarts didn't like making these calls, so he hoped Clark had an answer by now.

He returned from the phone and slid into his chair. "The New Canaan police haven't closed your parents' case because her purse contained no wallet or keys. For the time being, they assume someone came along afterwards and stole them from the wreckage."

"But we know different, don't we?" She looked ready to cry again, but she squared her shoulders and lifted her chin. "Sorry. Part of the reason I didn't want to leave the library was because the research distracted me."

"I know, but you have to eat ... and you're right. They took her keys and ID so they could search the apartment."

"They won't get past the doorman. That's a tough building. Even if you arrive in a ConEd truck wearing all the appropriate gear, they won't let you upstairs unless you're on the day-list, keys or no keys. Firemen might gain access ... but there better be smoke." Then Baldwin's voice suddenly faltered. "Oh shit, cops. They could get in, huh?"

"Yes."

"How will they do it?" she asked.

"Pretend to be New Canaan police and tell the doorman they're investigating the death of a couple from the building. Probably show a forged search warrant. Search warrants aren't hard to pull off, because most people have never seen one." He started to reach for her hand but held back. "Trish, they've probably already gained access and searched the apartment. Nothing to be done now." This time, Evarts did reach over and cover her hand with his. "I'm sorry."

She slipped her hand out from under his. "They didn't find what they're looking for."

"How do you know?"

"My dad kept secrets … and he was very good at it." She picked up the menu. "Let's eat."

"First, tell me what's wrong. Why are you angry with me?"

"Nothing's wrong. Don't you think I deserve a day or two in a foul mood?"

"Of course, but I want to help and you seem to be pushing me away."

"There's nothing wrong. At least nothing I want to discuss."

That told Evarts that she did have an issue with him. Did she blame him for getting her involved in this series of tragedies? For her parents' death? He didn't know, but he decided to give her her day or two before broaching the subject again.

The Federalist menu made Evarts cringe, but he ignored price and ordered a steak sandwich. Baldwin chose a Caesar salad with chicken.

"Why did you say we should follow my parents to find the good guys?"

"Because you said your parents were basically good people, and I don't believe Douglass had a mean bone in his body. Something about this whole thing doesn't make sense. Throughout history, the extended Sherman family has shown an idealist and progressive bent. None of these people have ever demonstrated a penchant for the kind of violence we've witnessed. I think we should proceed on an assumption of warring factions within the Society."

"You think Douglass and my parents were on the good side?"

"I do. Douglass said he didn't belong to the Shut Mouth Society, but it looks like your parents may have belonged, so we follow their trail."

"How?"

"First, tell me everything you know about your parents. Everything, no matter how trivial or how much it hurts. Start at the beginning, when you first noticed something askew."

The food arrived before she got very far in her story. She looked at Evarts's steak sandwich with fries and said, "I need a gym. I haven't worked out in six days, and I feel paralysis creeping up on me. Besides, I need to release some tension."

"I saw one above the Starbucks on the corner. We can go after we finish for the day."

"I prefer morning workouts."

"I prefer surfing in the mornings. Evening workouts hype the appetite for dinner."

"There's no surf here, so we'll work out in the mornings. Speaking of the beach, I need to go to Macy's. Other than that beach attire you bought me, I have one and a half outfits."

Evarts decided not to argue about the gym. "I need a computer store too. Can you check books out of this library?"

"Yes, but I hate to limit myself to just a few books. Why do you need a computer store?"

"I want to mount a camera in that staircase and tie it into your laptop. One in the alley would be a good idea too."

"We better eat quick."

As Evarts devoured the small steak, all the fries, and even the grease-soaked bread, Baldwin explained that ever since she could remember, her parents had tried to instill in her a deep sense of obligation for less fortunate people or people ignorant of the constant threat of oppression. At about fifteen, she accused her father of patronizing the "little people" and pointed out that noblesse oblige reeked of elitism. Her subsequent rebellion took the form of adopting everything common, including boyfriends.

She began to seriously wonder about her parents during her first menstrual cycle. Her mother had supposedly taken a trip to visit her sister, but when Baldwin tried to reach her mother by phone to ask her what to do, her aunt said she had neither seen nor heard from her. On her return, her mother had mumbled something about a change in plans, but Baldwin remembered only that her mother had abandoned her in an hour of need.

This incident represented a pattern. Her parents would individually take off for days and then give the vaguest excuses for their absences. Baldwin grew increasingly suspicious after her father showed her the Boston hideaway. As a senior in a "sophisticated" prep school, she decided her parents had what some people called an "open" marriage.

Her father always seemed consumed with some complex dealings, but he belonged to the idle-rich class. When he did make time for her, he spent it explaining the intricacies of their nested trusts and elaborate banking arrangements. She interpreted his preoccupation as distance. She never knew their intimate friends, whom they kept separated from their casual social gatherings. Although she could never put her finger on what bothered her, she knew they wanted to mold her into something she didn't understand. Her independent streak pushed them away for many years.

"That doesn't give us much to go on," Evarts said. "We can try to trace the Greenes from the Roger Sherman Inn, but if they're in a safe house like ours, it'll be difficult."

"Last Thanksgiving my parents asked me to come back in the summer for an extended stay. My father told me he wanted to explain about our family. I put the trip off because I feared that what he'd tell me would destroy our reconciliation."

"What do you think now?"

"That extramarital affairs weren't the reason for their unusual behavior." She absentmindedly picked at her salad and then met Evarts's eyes. "The Shut Mouth Society could account for all that secrecy."

Evarts swallowed the last of his Coke. "My parents never showed any secretive behaviors. Just the opposite: They made an obsessive point about none of us ever having any secrets from the rest of the family. But I did feel they were trying to mold me as well. They're pretty controlling. I always sensed something was amiss, and I guess my obstinacy about being controlled is my way of rebelling against them."

"But you don't think they were part of a secret society?"

"I'm certain they weren't. They wouldn't even join AARP. They hated organized religion, governments, homeowner associations, even the PTA. They weren't even pleased that I joined the ROTC in college."

"Well, it sure looks like my parents joined the Shut Mouth

Society." She shoved her salad away. "There's another thing that points in that direction: My parents loved that I became a Lincoln scholar."

Evarts drummed his fingers on the table. "We've focused on the Sherman family and the Shut Mouth Society, but the encryption came attached to Lincoln papers. There's a reason those papers have been withheld from the public." He thumped the table. "Let's pay the tab and get back to the library."

As they walked back, Evarts asked, "If Lincoln had a big secret, what do you guess it would be?"

She didn't answer immediately. "Let's walk around the block." After a few more moments, she said, "Fort Sumter."

"Where the Civil War started?"

"That's where the shooting part of the war started. After Lincoln's election, but before his inauguration, seven states seceded from the Union and formed the Confederate States of America. The CSA seized eleven U.S. forts inside its territory on the premise that a sovereign nation had the right to expel a foreign power from inside its borders."

When they got to the corner, Baldwin signaled that they should walk straight ahead. "Some historians believe that Lincoln instructed the Republicans in Congress to do nothing to mollify the rebellious states. After his inauguration, Lincoln agonized for weeks over what to do about Fort Sumter, one of the two remaining U.S. military installations in the South. The commander of the fort refused to surrender, and a standoff ensued. The Confederates harassed the fort but didn't attack. They issued warnings that any attempt to reinforce or reprovision the fort would be viewed as a hostile act of war.

"Starvation threatened the garrison, so Lincoln told the Confederacy he had dispatched a ship with food and medical supplies only. On April 12, 1861, the day before the ship arrived, the South Carolina militia open fired on Fort Sumter. The following day Congress declared war on the rebellious states. Immediately, four more states seceded and joined the Confederacy." She nodded that they should cross the street. "There's an ironic twist to the story. The South heavily bombarded the fort for thirty-four hours before the garrison surrendered, but there were no casualties on either side in the battle that started the bloodiest war in our history."

"Fascinating, but what could be the big, dark secret?" Evarts asked.

"A few historians have accused Lincoln of purposely manipulating the Fort Sumter crisis to start the war and paint the South as the aggressor. Abe Douglass subscribed to this theory. A few even suggest he designed his inaugural address to position any forthcoming crisis to the Union's benefit. They see some of his words as evidence of premeditation."

"Any proof?"

"Circumstantial only." She pointed. "That's the old statehouse."

Evarts had never seen a more incongruous building. The three-story, red brick building had cream-colored trim and a cream steeple positioned in the center of the roof instead of at one end, like a church. The statehouse looked like a miniature model crowded in on all sides by giant glass and steel giants. A preservation group must have saved the building, but bustling Boston just built right up to its edges and ignored the landmark.

Evarts's gaze shifted between the skyscrapers and the little brick building. "It looks like the building's about to suffocate." All of a sudden, the old statehouse disgorged an unending stream of rushing people. "Where the hell did all those people come from? It looks like a panicked mob scene from one of those B horror flicks."

"Subway stop. The street exit comes right up through the old statehouse."

Evarts laughed. "A three-hundred-year-old building converted to accommodate a modern conveyance. I might learn to like Boston."

"Not such a modern conveyance. They built the Boston T over a hundred years ago. It's the oldest subway system in the United States. Come here. I want to show you something." She walked to the front of the building and pointed to the congested street. "See that rock circle in the middle of the road?"

"Yes."

"Five men died on that spot in 1770. The radicals who wanted war with Great Britain called it the Boston Massacre. In truth, a large mob of drunken thugs started throwing stones at eight Red Coats, who fired either in self-defense or by accident. John Adams acted as defense counsel for the British troops and got them acquitted, but that didn't stop the rabble-rousers from using the incident to enflame hatred for the British and push the populace closer to war." She turned toward him. "You're standing on the very spot where those frightened young soldiers faced an angry mob just fifteen feet away."

"Hard to imagine, with all these honking cars and scampering pedestrians."

"Some historians believe the radicals purposely incited the riot for political gain."

Evarts nodded. "An engineered provocation like the battleship Maine anchored in Havana harbor, the Gulf of Tonkin incident, or cutting off Japanese oil supplies." Evarts turned to face her. "And possibly Fort Sumter."

"If you were one of my students, you'd earn a good grade by submitting that as a thesis. Now let's go back. You need to crack that code."

Chapter 22

· · · · · ·

When they returned to the reading room, they found everything as they had left it. Baldwin explained that as long as the room displayed an occupied sign, the librarians would treat it as sacrosanct.

Over the next four hours, Evarts exhausted Baldwin's list with no success. He felt frustrated. True, he had dedicated only one full day to the code, but he had started the day convinced that his law book idea would blow this whole case wide open. After some contemplation, he realized he had grown anxious to test the theory on the drive across the country, and that the five days between the formation of the idea and being able to test its validity had built overblown expectations. He had become overconfident because he assumed a hundred-and-fifty-year-old code would appear primitive to a modern cryptologist.

Baldwin had chased her Skull and Bones lead to more success. One or more Bonesmen always seemed to hover around key turning points in American history. Baldwin saw this as ominous; Evarts thought it common sense that the elite of an elite institution would end up in positions of power. She confirmed that a close connection existed between Yale and the Sherman family, all the way back to Roger Sherman, who served for many years as the college treasurer. She even thought Lincoln's signing the Land-Grant College Act, which his predecessor had vetoed, might have been a political payoff to Yale or possibly even to Skull and Bones. The act provided each state with thirty thousand acres of federal land for each Senator and House member representing the state. Yale received its federal land scrip before any other college in the nation and grabbed all of Connecticut's allocation so fast that no other Connecticut college had a chance.

After returning from the book stacks, Evarts said, "No luck and that was the last book on your list."

"You didn't expect to break it in one day, did you?"

"As a matter of fact, I did."

"That was foolish...and unprofessional." Her voice had an edge.

Evarts choked down a retort. He was getting tired of her snippiness, but then he remembered that he had decided to give her a few days before bringing it up again. He looked at his watch. "If we're going to hit Macy's and a computer store, we need to get going."

Baldwin glanced at her own watch. "You're right, it's nearly six thirty." She worked the touchpad on her laptop a moment and then turned it around for him to see. "Copy this list down."

He looked at the screen. "Are these law books you rejected from your first list?"

"Greg, these aren't rejects. Don't you think it more likely that the key would be an obscure book?"

He shrugged. "Probably."

"Make the list and then grab two or three of them to check out overnight. We can work at home after dinner."

"Home?"

She looked up, startled. "Did I say home?"

"You did."

"Well, I guess it's all we've got now."

"Silver linings."

"Excuse me?"

"I like the idea of living together."

"I like the idea of living." She bent back over her work. "Make your list."

After checking out their books, they walked a few blocks to Downtown Crossing. The shopping area looked too downscale for Baldwin. Downtown Crossing forbade cars, so foot traffic clogged the streets. The city probably wanted to create a personal, neighborly feel, but a kind of rowdy disorder permeated the district. Scantily dressed teenagers meandered everywhere, the homeless and pretend homeless worked the crowd, and vendors hawked street food at the top of their lungs. Evarts knew the heavy police presence indicated that the retailers had a concern about crime. Downtown Crossing certainly couldn't challenge Santa Barbara's claim to the most beautiful downtown in America.

"Not the caliber of shopping I expected you to suggest," Evarts said.

"It'll do. The upscale shops are on Newberry Street. Too far to walk at this hour. I can find adequate outfits here."

Baldwin's tone was curt, so Evarts headed toward a computer store, telling her that he would meet her later, inside Macy's. He needed a little time to himself anyway. He had started to chafe under her irritable and dominating behavior. She was getting far too controlling for his taste. If her parents hadn't just died, he knew he would have reacted in a way that would have ruined any chance of their relationship developing further.

Evarts thought they had taken some promising steps toward something more than a chance sexual encounter, but Baldwin had been dismissive of any comment or action he took that reminded her of their intimacy. Her behavior might have resulted from the sudden death of her parents, but in his experience, tragedy drove people together, even if only for temporary solace. True, her initial frosty demeanor hadn't totally returned, but he definitely felt that she held him at arm's length and kept their conversation on the business at hand.

He didn't expect her to show off her sexual prowess or give him a light kiss when he didn't expect it, but he found disheartening the erosion of the camaraderie they had shared crossing the country. He thought it odd that he feared losing their intimate conversations more than losing their intimate physical moments. This was a new one for him, but he would think about it later. For now he decided to leave it alone. Then a thought occurred to him. Perhaps he was seeing Professor Baldwin for the first time. Not Professor Baldwin in front of a class, but the scholar immersed in research and distracted. He could understand that behavior, because when he became engaged in an investigation, he was often accused of becoming distant. The thought gave him hope.

Evarts bought his supplies at the computer store and went to the men's department in Macy's. In twenty minutes he had everything he needed and wandered around the women's departments looking for Baldwin. He finally found her when she emerged from a dressing room.

"All set?" he asked.

"No." She discarded an armload of clothing onto a bench. "I need to try on a few more things. I'll let you know when I'm done."

Evarts hated waiting in women's wear, but he sat down in what he hoped was a patient pose and started reading the instructions on the cameras and the baby monitor he had bought. The simple instructions held no surprises, but he wondered about the technical configuration of her laptop. She had put her case beside him to watch, so he took out the laptop and opened the lid. The computer snapped out of its slumber, and the cursor started blinking. He was about to check the memory and system capabilities when he noticed a file on the desktop titled "notes." He assumed these were the notes from her research at the Athenaeum.

He opened the file, thinking it might be more interesting than reading computer instructions he already knew. She had formatted the Microsoft Word file in the Outline view. As he reviewed the contents under the various headings, he found nothing she hadn't already conveyed to him. He moved the cursor to close the file when he noticed a heading he had missed: GE, his initials. He opened it.

Can I trust him?
    Scared Mrs. Greene!
        "We were told you would fight the union"
        Ran away from him
    Running from police—guilty?
Parents unharmed
Conspired with Douglass?
    Parents' apartment
        Would not let me visit
        Hurried me away
        Apartment now probably searched
Won't let me out of his sight
Discouraged research on Skull & Bones
Lied about appointment in Westwood
Escape from Oxnard too easy

Evarts stared transfixed at the screen. When he looked up, Baldwin stood arms akimbo outside the dressing room, looking white-hot with fury.

"What the hell are you doing in my computer?"

Chapter 23

. . . . . .

"I was just—" Embarrassed, Evarts snapped shut the lid of the laptop. "You don't trust me?"

"Damn you, Greg. Do you think rummaging around in my personal property makes you trustworthy? How dare you?"

"I ... I thought the file contained your research notes from today. Aren't we working together?"

She stepped over and jerked the laptop out of Evarts's hands. "Are we?"

"If you're this upset about me seeing your notes, perhaps not. Especially if you think I'm part of the opposition."

"Are you?"

"No! Damn it, come on, Trish. You know me."

"I thought I knew my DEA guy too, until they arrested him for scamming drug dealers."

"I'm not accountable for your past boyfriend's sins."

"Oh, yes you are." This came from a man who sat about six feet away. "Believe me buddy, you are." He made a gesture toward the dressing rooms. "Charlotte's prior boyfriend boffed her best girlfriend. For some reason, she kept the girlfriend but makes every man pay for that dumb-shit's transgression."

Baldwin gave Evarts a look that said that she didn't want to discuss this in public. "I'll check out." She turned her back on him and said over her shoulder, "Meet me at Au Bon Pain across the way."

Evarts left Macy's and walked across the pedestrian way to the small café. He ordered a coffee for himself and one for Baldwin. As he stepped out, heading for the outdoor seating, Baldwin intercepted him, charging like an enraged lioness. "How do you expect me to carry coffee with all these bags?"

"I thought we should sit down and discuss this."

"In public? After that? Are you crazy?"

"Let me take the books and a couple of your bags."

"Fine." She dropped several of the bags on the sidewalk, grabbed the coffee, and started toward the apartment. Before Evarts could sling all the bag handles over his arms and juggle his own coffee, she was gone.

By the time he caught up with her, she had already entered the Commons. "Trish—"

"Wait until we get to the apartment."

They marched across the Commons and up Charles Street in silence. The arm Evarts used to carry the books began to ache, but Baldwin wouldn't slow her pace enough for him to shift loads. He tried to keep up and ignored the pain. By the time they had unlocked the door, climbed the stairs, and unlocked the second door, Evarts's initial embarrassment had transformed into anger.

He dropped the book bag onto the hardwood floor. "Goddamn it, Trish, I've done nothing wrong." He threw the second armload across the room onto the divan. "Your attitude stinks."

"My attitude?" She plopped her load onto the floor. "Damn it, why were you spying on me?"

"Spying on you? What the hell are you talking about? I got bored waiting for you to try on all those damn outfits and decided to check your computer specs for the cameras. I saw the file on your desktop and thought I'd read your notes from today's research. I thought we were—" Evarts ripped off his windbreaker and threw it. "Then I found out what you really think of me."

Baldwin let her computer case slip off her shoulder and held it out in front of her by the strap. "This is mine."

"I'm afraid not. It's the only computer we have, and while we're in the apartment I need it to hook up the cameras."

"I have personal stuff on here, and you have no right to ransack through it."

"I won't look at your damn files, but I have to use the machine. You can watch me if you want."

"I want."

"Fine, but we still need to work together, so how do we get beyond this?"

Suddenly she looked spent and exhausted. Collapsing onto one of the dinette chairs, she said, "I'm not sure. I didn't mean for you to see that. It's not what I believe; it's what I fear. Those questions just keep bothering me."

"How long have they been bothering you?"

"Since New Canaan."

"How about we get a glass of wine and talk through your points?"

She looked ready to cry. "Greg, I don't—" She did start to tear. "I want to believe in you, it's just—"

"I know. Your parents, all this trouble. At least let me explain."

"Can you?"

"Some. I did lie about the appointment in Westwood, but it wasn't to keep you under my control. I... I thought you were pretty, and I wanted to be alone with you for the two-hour ride."

She made a dismissive wave with the back of her hand. "That's minor. What about Mrs. Greene?"

"Is that what started you on this train of thought?"

"Can you blame me? She wrote a note warning me about you."

"Is that the way you read it? I didn't know what to make of it."

"It seemed obvious to me. You frightened her. She didn't expect to see us together because she thought I would fight our union."

Evarts went to the tiny kitchen, poured one glass of wine, and pulled a beer from the refrigerator for himself. After he had handed her the wine, he sat in the opposite chair. "I can't explain that note, but it never occurred to me that she meant us. At least, not until you brought it up."

"What else could she have meant?"

"I don't know, but at that point I believed our relationship had grown into something meaningful, so perhaps I was blind to how you might read it." He sat silent awhile and when she didn't speak, he added, "Perhaps she meant the Shut Mouth Society when she said union."

"That's a stretch and you know it."

"You're right."

They sat silent for a long while, just looking at each other. Finally, Evarts said, "I never lied about anything else on your list. In each instance, I did what I thought was right in the moment." When she still didn't react, Evarts grabbed at the only thing he could think of that might persuade her. "I gave you a gun when you asked for one." No reaction. "And I never tried to separate you from it."

"Did you know I've been carrying the .45?"

"Yeah, but I just thought you preferred the heavier caliber."

She looked embarrassed. "I was afraid you might have tampered with the Glock."

"Then keep the .45."

"I will."

"Trish, this is a dangerous situation and we only have each other. How can we work together if you feel this way?"

"Carefully. And from this point forward, we need complete honesty."

"I have been honest. What about you?"

"What do you mean?"

"What's on that computer?"

She failed the flinch test. "None of your business."

"Excuse me. I thought you said we needed complete honesty."

"Some things are personal. I'm not ready to share them yet."

"When?"

"When I know I can completely trust you. When I know I can let you back into my personal life."

"I'm out?" Evarts felt an unusual emotion. It went beyond disappointment, and he realized it was fear. He feared losing her. He took a sip of his beer. "What about our relationship?"

"That can only be healed with time and events."

Chapter 24

. . . . . .

Evarts finished his beer and worked on installing the cameras. He started with the entrance and pointed the camera down the enclosed staircase toward the door that led to the street. He put the camera high above the upper-landing door and ran an extended USB cable down the doorframe and under the door. After he installed the software drivers on Baldwin's computer, he got a clear picture of the staircase on the laptop. Baldwin sat in a chair with one of her books, but Evarts noticed she kept an eye on him while he worked on her computer. He made sure it always faced her and sat to the side so she could see the screen.

After the camera, he installed a baby monitor at the bottom of the staircase so any intrusion could be heard from inside the apartment. Next, he worked on the staircase lights so they would always stay on to provide enough illumination for the camera. He rewired the fixtures so the switches no longer controlled the lights and then rewired the switch at the bottom door so that, if someone threw it in an attempt to turn off the lights, a buzzer would sound inside the apartment.

Entering the apartment again, Evarts reexamined the back alley and the fire escape. He had two more cameras, but he had a problem. No matter how he positioned them, there would still be blind spots. He decided to point them in either direction down the alley and hoped they would catch movement before someone got directly beneath the apartment window. When he finished, he called Baldwin over and showed her how everything worked.

"How much did all this cost?" she asked.

"Less than three hundred dollars."

"I'm impressed. I feel safer already."

"Even with the enemy inside the apartment?"

"Greg, I'm sorry. I—"

"Forget it. We have other business." He didn't want to reopen the subject. "I had a chance to think while I worked. I no longer believe the law book idea will pan out. I want you to tell me about

Lincoln: his personality, his interests, everything ... especially prior to his inauguration."

"This time I'm hungry."

"Okay, let's find a quiet restaurant."

They left the apartment and walked the half block to Charles Street. Baldwin picked a high-end Italian place named Ristorante Toscano. When Evarts saw the white tablecloths and upscale place settings, he wondered how much money the safe had contained. Most of the time, Evarts viewed food as fuel. He would have preferred to conserve their assets, but he didn't want to start another argument.

After they ordered and their drinks arrived, Baldwin said, "Lincoln is the most studied president in history, but he remains an enigma. Since 1968, over sixteen hundred books have been published on Lincoln. Every author looks for new ground and almost all of them find it ... or make it up. The Library of Congress has digitized over two hundred thousand Lincoln documents, more than any one researcher could peruse in a lifetime, and yet nobody has successfully revealed the flesh and blood man."

"Not even you? Your last book stayed on the bestseller lists for months." Evarts had a copy of *Quite Contrary*, but with the driving schedule and other activities, he had read only a small portion of it.

"I told Abraham Lincoln's story from Mary Lincoln's perspective. In the beginning, I thought I could flush out the man by looking at him through the eyes of his wife, but she destroyed most of their personal letters, so I had very little new material. It only appeared fresh because of the point of view ... and the book sold well because it appealed to women, who buy most of the books nowadays."

"Why can't anyone get a handle on the man?"

"Despite all that documentation, almost nothing of a personal nature survived ... if it ever existed. Lincoln didn't keep a journal like others in his cabinet, and his letters seldom revealed his feelings. Since Lincoln rarely made a record of his meetings, the notes we have about his private conversations come from the other participants." Baldwin sipped her wine before adding, "He had to balance every power base in the country, so he might lead one party to believe he supported them and then appear to take a different slant with the next visitors."

"Douglass said you didn't appreciate that politicians lie."

"It's not whether historical figures lied or not, it's whether a responsible historian can tag a specific utterance a lie without a sound basis for the assertion. If historians can dismiss any part of the record that conflicts with their point of view, then you lose all restraint on the discipline."

The waiter brought them each a bowl of lobster bisque. One spoonful and Evarts knew food could go well beyond mere fuel. After another sip, Evarts asked, "How did Lincoln make different parties believe he agreed with them?"

"People left meetings believing that he would seriously consider their positions, rather than that he agreed with them. If Lincoln encountered a particularly strident petitioner, he frequently told entertaining stories until the meeting time ran out. Sometimes the stories could be interpreted to support or oppose a position, but in either case, the petitioners took away no presidential declarations they could use. The man mastered several techniques to deflect people and issues when he didn't want to get involved or thought the timing inopportune."

"And these deflections make it hard to get to the man beneath the myth?" Evarts asked.

"Yes. He kept his own counsel." She took a sip of her wine. "Due to the scanty or conflicting record, authors portray the man as evil or great, straight or gay, clinically depressed or a paragon of mental stability, decisive or vacillating, a racist or the Great Emancipator, a stalwart protector of the Constitution or someone who desecrated the Constitution and refused to accept any limitations on his powers."

"What do we know... for sure?"

"We know that despite less than a year of formal education, he held his own with a cabinet impeccably educated in the best institutions in America. We know that despite his rail-splitter image, he actually ran a prominent and lucrative law practice. We know that despite his caricature as an inexperienced buffoon who accidentally won the presidency, he seemed to always get his way when confronted by powerful and experienced politicians. We know that despite his aw-shucks country-lawyer image, the man was driven by an implacable ambition that made him lament that he could never accomplish anything as great as George Washington. We know that despite his reputation as honest, Horace Greeley once famously said, 'I can't trust your Honest Old Abe. He's too smart for me.'"

Evarts had a thought. "Do you think Greeley could've been the one in secret communication with Lincoln?"

"Doubtful. By that time, Lincoln distrusted Greeley's mercurial disposition."

"Who then? It had to be someone in New York."

"William Cullen Bryant, maybe." She didn't look certain.

"I've heard the name, but I don't know where."

"A distinguished poet who helped found the Republican Party. He presided over Young Men's Central Republican Union, which sponsored the Cooper Union lectures. For his day job, he served as the editor of the *New York Evening Post*. He actually met Lincoln for the first time during the Black Hawk War, when Lincoln was a militia captain."

"Lincoln was in the military? I didn't know that. When?"

"1832. The Black Hawk War wasn't much of a war, and the Illinois militia wasn't much of an army. The Indians east of the Mississippi were being pushed west, and Sauk Chief Black Hawk repudiated a treaty he said was coerced under the influence of alcohol. At that time, militias elected their own leaders, and the men chose Lincoln to be captain. He never saw action and loved to claim the only blood he shed came from mosquito bites." Baldwin sipped her wine. "Lincoln always said that being picked by his neighbors as their captain was his proudest election victory."

"I never heard that... or forgot if I did. What else?"

She hesitated. "He was one of the greatest public speakers in history."

"You said that before. Why? Because of the Gettysburg Address?"

"That would be like saying Shakespeare should be considered a great playwright because of *Hamlet*. The Gettysburg Address represented but one speech in a long line of persuasive speeches."

"Persuasive? I thought that speech eulogized the dead and wounded."

"Read it again. He used the occasion to push emancipation further along in the public mind. He crafted all of his speeches to persuade, sometimes subtly, sometimes directly. He made his points with words, but he used emotions to make them forceful—gaiety, sorrow, hope—or perhaps he appealed to—"

"Wait a minute. Something you just said has been nagging me. Did Lincoln read Shakespeare?"

"All the time. Lincoln loved Shakespeare. Frequently read his plays aloud, which drove his law partner crazy. He wrote poetry as well, albeit rather mediocre poetry."

Baldwin had lost him when she said Lincoln loved Shakespeare. She continued describing Lincoln's literary interest and talents, but his attention had focused on the Shakespeare angle. Excitedly, he interrupted her midstream. "How many plays did Shakespeare write?"

"What? About forty, I think. Were you listening to me?"

"Sorry, but I think Shakespeare might be the key. I thought about fiction but considered only contemporaneous publications. I have a former English major in my department, and when this whole thing started, I asked him to make a list of popular nineteenth-century fiction, but then I got sidetracked with law books. Fiction over four hundred years old never occurred to me."

"Greg, don't throw away the law book idea too soon. At least check out the new list I gave you."

"I'll test the books I've already checked out, but tomorrow I want to try a few plays. It makes sense, especially if William Cullen Bryant sat at the other end of these encrypted messages."

"William Cullen Bryant was a radical abolitionist."

"So?"

"Lincoln never endorsed abolition."

"You just said the Gettysburg Address pushed the idea of emancipation forward?"

"That was later, after he had been convinced that the Civil War had to have a grander purpose than just preserving the Union."

"Perhaps he never had to be convinced. You said we don't know what he really thought."

"We have his words," Baldwin said.

"Yes, we do. We have the words of a politician. Remember the old joke: How can you tell when a politician is lying? When his lips move."

Chapter 25

· · · · · ·

Evarts woke up stiff. Without discussion, he had bedded down on the couch in the front room. He tried to stretch out the kinks after rolling off the too-short divan. He saw Baldwin making coffee in the kitchen and realized that the sound of running water had awakened him. As he raced to the bathroom to relieve himself, he noticed that she had already dressed in a loose-fitting gym suit.

"I don't know if I can work out this early," he said as he came out of the bathroom.

"Then don't."

"You're not going to the gym without breakfast?"

"Banana and orange juice."

"That's not food," he said as he reached for a coffee mug.

"I'll eat a bowl of bran with yogurt after I get back."

Evarts gratefully sipped the coffee. "If I insist on going with you, are you going to get all paranoid?"

"No." She peeled a banana and broke off a small piece to put in her mouth. "I may have overreacted." She tried a smile, but it looked weak. "I guess if you wanted to kill me, you'd have done it already."

"So ... everything back to normal?"

"Nothing's been normal since I met you." She broke off another piece of banana. "Greg, when I said I needed time, I had something more than twelve hours in mind."

He took a step back, and in an exaggerated gesture, threw his hands up, palms out. "Okay. I'm not pushing."

Evarts wolfed down some cereal and another cup of coffee before they left for the gym. After they paid twenty dollars each for a one-day pass, Evarts went to the free weights, where he was able to watch Baldwin go through her routine on the abs lounger. No wonder she had an athletic body. She knew how to breathe and she pushed herself hard. Very hard. Evarts followed suit, and by the time he moved to the elliptical machines with her, he knew he would be sore the following day.

"Did you enjoy that?" she asked, when he climbed on the elliptical next to her.

"Yeah. It's been over a week since I had a chance to work out."

"I meant watching me."

"I didn't realize I was staring."

"That's why I wear loose clothing when I go to a coed gym. I can do without the leering men."

Evarts matched her rhythm at about seventy strides a minute. "Do you belong to a women-only gym in Westwood?"

"Yes."

"And there you wear tights?"

She smiled for the first time in days. "I may not like men gawking at me like I'm some kind of pole dancer, but I do enjoy the envious looks of other women."

"Do any of them ever hit on you?"

She threw him a puzzled glance and said, "Occasionally."

"Then I don't see the difference."

"Women make a direct bid and then leave you alone. Men keep pestering, if not with their stupid lines, then with their eyes."

Evarts increased his pace to about eighty strides a minute. "Men don't care as much about impressing their own sex."

She matched his rhythm. "Bullshit."

"Yup. Bullshit."

She actually laughed at his admission, and Evarts hoped it signaled that they were making progress. After a half hour on the elliptical, he thought they were done with the workout, but she moved over to a stair-stepper. Evarts hated the stair-stepper, so he stayed on the elliptical. After another fifteen minutes, they both moved over to the treadmill and cooled down for a mile.

As they walked back to the apartment, Evarts said, "I need protein."

"Fry up some eggs when we get back."

"Let's go out for breakfast."

"Not all sweaty. Besides, look around. Do you see any coffee shops? Rent's too high, and Bostonians like to pretend they're European anyway. Croissant and coffee. If you want an American breakfast, you'll have to go to a hotel."

"A hotel? You gotta be kidding. At fifteen bucks a head?"

"Closer to twenty."

"I'll fry up some eggs."

"Good idea."

In just over an hour, Evarts and Baldwin found themselves back at the Athenaeum buried in books. Evarts tried several Shakespeare plays but had no more luck than with the law books.

After he failed with *Macbeth*, Evarts said, "I can probably get through all the plays in a few more days, but can you suggest a shortcut?"

"What do you mean?"

"A play that would appeal to Bryant and Lincoln."

"It's a big leap to assume Bryant wrote that code."

"Humor me."

She set her own book down. Evarts could almost see her think through the long list of Shakespearian plays. "I don't know about Lincoln, but Bryant would choose *The Tempest*."

"Why?"

"*The Tempest* was Shakespeare's final play and the only one to take place in North America. More important to Bryant, it carried an antislavery theme."

Evarts said thanks and reopened a thick book containing Shakespeare's complete works. In less than twenty minutes, he yelled, "Eureka!"

"You're kidding."

"I don't think so."

Baldwin didn't go back to her book. Instead she watched Evarts with such intensity that he grew nervous. In about twenty more minutes, he looked up and said, "This might be the key, but it will take me about an hour to translate enough of the message to be sure."

In just under an hour, he handed her a slip of paper. "See these numbers?"

The paper listed the following numbers: 413825, 129062, 217434, 41194, 4120108, 221117, 129197, 111024, 517242, 2113537, 5127116, 126127.

"If you use these numbers for act, scene, speaker, line, and word, then they translate into this sentence."

He handed her another slip of paper. It read, "meet bees her at play mouth place of worship sun day service."

"Mean anything to you?" he asked.

Baldwin studied it a minute and then exclaimed, "You did it! You broke the code!"

"What does it mean?"

She ran her fingers through her hair. "Nothing historians don't already know. On the Sunday before his Cooper Union address, Lincoln went to services at Plymouth Church in Brooklyn Heights. The minister at this famous church was Henry Ward Beecher, an antislavery crusader and renowned speaker."

"Meet Beecher at Plymouth Church, Sunday service." Evarts smiled. "Makes sense."

"No, it doesn't. We know Lincoln went to Plymouth Church that Sunday. There were hundreds of witnesses."

"But did you know he arranged a secret rendezvous?"

"No, but why set up such a meeting? Henry Ward Beecher was a celebrity in his day, and his church was a pilgrimage for aspiring politicians. Everyone would've expected Lincoln to attend Sunday services."

"Was he religious?"

"No, probably a deist, but like everything else personal, he left few telltale signs."

"Would it have been appropriate for Lincoln to have a private conversation with Beecher?" Evarts asked.

That stopped Baldwin for a moment. "If he wanted to maintain his reputation as a moderate on slavery, it probably wouldn't have been a good idea. Beecher and his sister were radical abolitionists."

"His sister?"

"Harriet Beecher Stowe. She wrote *Uncle Tom's Cabin* in 1852, and it fomented the radical abolitionist movement." She gave Evarts a long look. "Are you suggesting that Lincoln was in cahoots with the radicals prior to his nomination?"

"I'm not suggesting anything... yet. But the more public you can make a clandestine meeting, the better. It reduces suspicion."

"What could they possibly talk about?" she asked.

"I'm not the historian, but it would seem like they had only one thing to discuss: Lincoln's run at the White House."

Baldwin became thoughtful. When she finally spoke, her voice sounded as if she were talking to herself. "If that were the case, then Lincoln would be the supplicant."

Baldwin stood and paced the tiny room. "Back then, just like today, the radical elements of a party provided the energy and ardent campaign workers. Candidates had to appeal to these elements or at least to appease them."

"If Lincoln wanted to contact Beecher, would he use William Cullen Bryant?"

"Possibly. Bryant was one of the radicals accepted by the moderate wings of the party. He even introduced Lincoln the next evening at Cooper Union." She quit her pacing and stood over Evarts. "Lincoln might have used Bryant as a conduit to the radical Republicans, but Greg, there's something I don't get. At the most, this is an interesting factoid. It doesn't enlighten the historical record that much. Why were we given this code, and why have people been murdered because of it?"

"Three reasons. First, someone gave us those documents as bait. Remember, the Cooper Union document held nothing new either. They gave us two innocuous documents to suck us into their labyrinth. Douglass said more papers were stashed away. Whoever pulled these two particular documents out of their treasure trove wanted to entice us to take the next step, but didn't want to expose anything really vital in case we didn't bite. The second reason is to give us a sample so we can break the code. After we found the key, we'd be able to read other encrypted messages."

"What's the third reason?"

"The second sentence of this message." He handed her another piece of paper. It listed only three numbers: 122681, 121016, 5150117. The three corresponding words read, "subject house divided."

"Do you know what this means?" she asked in a tone that said she knew.

"Yes. You told me all about Lincoln's House Divided speech on the drive from the West Coast. Remember?"

"He delivered that speech when he accepted the nomination to run against Steven Douglas for the Senate. That was 1858, two years before his run at the presidency. It was the last time he sounded alarmist about slavery." She looked up from the decoded message and met Evarts's eyes. "He said the nation couldn't survive half slave and half free."

Evarts nodded. "I've read it."

"When?"

"Just a few minutes ago. I translated those last three words first. I find code breaking easier back to front." He lifted a book of Lincoln speeches. "I read the House Divided speech to make sure I hadn't just randomly found three words that didn't sound like gibberish."

Evarts opened the book and read, "A house divided against itself cannot stand. I believe this government cannot endure permanently half slave and half free. I do not expect the Union to be dissolved. I do not expect the house to fall but I do expect it will cease to be divided. It will become all one thing or all the other. Either the opponents of slavery will arrest the further spread of it, and place it where the public mind shall rest in the belief that it is in the course of ultimate extinction; or its advocates will push it forward till it shall become alike lawful in all the states, old as well as new—North as well as South."

Evarts plopped the book back onto the table. "This man believed a pivotal moral issue gripped the nation, and he publicly announced on which side he stood." Evarts pushed the book a few inches toward Baldwin. "I think he might have gone after the presidency to facilitate the 'ultimate extinction' of slavery."

"That's too simple. You need to study the entire man. He said nothing during the Lincoln-Douglas debates that condemned slavery. Quite the opposite, in fact. At Cooper Union, he reassured the South that Republicans wouldn't threaten slavery where it already existed. His platform as a presidential candidate again reassured the South and attacked only the extension of slavery into the territories. You can't take this one speech and say this is the one true reflection of the man's inner feelings and that all the rest of his utterances were just bunk he said to get a job he wanted."

"Listen, I'm not a historian and I sure as hell haven't examined all the evidence, but as a detective I'm trained to uncover the real motives for why people take a particular action. I'm not suggesting that everything Lincoln did after the House Divided speech was bullshit. I'm just saying that maybe he had a higher purpose than just getting a job. Maybe he wanted enough power to destroy slavery in America."

"You're not proposing that he purposely started the Civil War?"

Evarts hesitated. Then he started to speak but closed his mouth. Finally, he looked Baldwin in the eye and said, "I don't know."

Chapter 26

. . . . . .

"**W**hat now?" she asked.

"I'm not sure. We broke the code, but this encrypted communication didn't tell us much. I presume that after we had broken the code, Douglass or one of his accomplices would've slipped us additional documents. With Douglass dead and us in hiding, I don't see how we can get our hands on the secret cache." Evarts leaned forward across the small table that separated them. "The Greenes remain our sole lead, and she skedaddled when she spotted us at the Roger Sherman Inn."

"Omaha?"

"Possibly … but they might have mentioned Omaha to the staff to build a false trail … like our feint toward Mexico." Evarts stood and paced the small room. He finally sat back down. "I keep coming back to the document cache. It must contain revelations that will shake the foundations of some power base." He picked up the decoded message and read it again. "Someone used this encrypted message to rouse our curiosity so that we'd be drawn into their little intrigue." Evarts covered Baldwin's hand with his own. "Trish, it could've been your parents that engineered our coming together."

"I know." A tear emerged from the corner of her eye.

Evarts squeezed her hand. "I'm sorry."

Baldwin lifted her chin and made a defiant toss of her hair. "We need to think about ourselves now. How do we get our life back?"

Evarts let go of her hand and leaned back in his chair. He loved her use of the plural pronoun, but pursuing that issue could wait. "We can't waste time. Unless we missed something, I don't think the documents that Douglass already gave us will provide much more help. Our focus should shift to finding the storehouse of documents."

"How? They've been successfully hidden for a hundred and fifty years."

"Few even knew they existed, so probably nobody has looked for them. Besides, I can't think of an alternative."

"Neither can I." She sat a moment. "How do we proceed?"

"Someone killed Douglass and your parents to protect a really big secret. I still think it must involve the end of the Civil War, Lincoln's assassination, or the Johnson impeachment."

"Which?"

Evarts laughed. "Hell if I know. What's your guess?"

Baldwin drummed her fingers. "There's so much nonsense about Lincoln's assassination … almost as much as Kennedy's, except with Lincoln, we know a conspiracy actually existed."

"A CSA conspiracy?"

"Confederate loyalists for sure, but it probably wasn't sanctioned by the government. The picture's confusing because there was so much spying going on, especially by the South."

"I studied Civil War intelligence in the army, but I want the historian's perspective. Start with why you said there was more spying by the South."

"Opportunity, I guess. Washington was a Southern city surrounded by slaveholding states. In fact, at the beginning of the war, slavery was even legal in D.C. Lincoln's biggest political accomplishment might have been keeping Maryland in the Union, but he still fought a war from a city filled with enemy sympathizers, hemmed in by Virginia to the south and Maryland to the north. The Confederates had no trouble finding people willing to pass them information or sabotage things like telegraph lines."

"Didn't Jefferson Davis authorize kidnapping Lincoln?"

"Probably, but whether he later authorized the assassination remains an unresolved question. Most historians don't believe he did."

"Why not?"

"Several times, nefarious characters approached Davis with plans to assassinate Lincoln. It would've been easy, because he traveled with only a light guard. Davis turned them all down, until he learned that Lincoln had approved a clandestine operation to kidnap him. Circumstantial evidence indicates that, after he gained this knowledge, Davis authorized a small group of Southern partisans to kidnap Lincoln. Davis wanted to hold him hostage in exchange for the release of Confederate prisoners. He needed them to replenish his army. The plan—"

"That group included John Wilkes Booth, didn't it?"

"So?" Her voice sounded irritated. "At the time, he was just another rebel sympathizer. What's your point?"

"It's a direct link from Davis to Booth."

"Not direct. Davis only knew the ringleaders. Besides, few historians believe Davis would've endorsed fruitless revenge. His early reluctance to attack Lincoln substantiates this view." Baldwin used her fingers to tap a closed book in front of her as if to indicate that the contents shored up her argument. "Davis envisioned himself as a Southern gentleman, and he practiced personal honor like a religious creed." She shook her head. "No, I don't believe he would back a band of murderers."

"If I remember correctly, the assassination of Lincoln included a simultaneous attempt against the secretary of state and the vice president. And after the authorities finally cornered Booth in a barn, he ended up dead."

"What're you driving at?"

"That Lincoln's assassination was a big conspiracy, big, with roots that went back to the Confederate States of America and Jefferson Davis. Booth may have been killed to keep the organizers' identities secret. Perhaps these Lincoln papers expose other villains. If Johnson knew something, they might have impeached him to shut him up. Whatever happened back then, someone may have squirreled away a bunch of documents so posterity could eventually learn the truth."

Baldwin took off her glasses and rubbed her eyes. "Where did you get this stuff?"

"From the web, back in Santa Barbara when I did some research on secret societies." Evarts felt embarrassed. "I'm not saying I know, I'm just saying maybe."

"One question." When she lowered her hand to give Evarts a direct look, he again noticed her striking emerald eyes. "Why would anyone care so much about the exposure of people long dead that they would traipse around the country killing people today?"

Evarts collapsed against the back of his chair. "Shit."

"Shit?"

"I mean, you're right. Why would anyone go to such extreme measures to protect an ancestor's reputation? Something more has got to be at stake."

"Agreed." She slid her glasses back onto her face, using two fingers to hold the bridge.

"Money or power," Evarts mumbled.

"What?"

"Sorry. I said, money or power. We don't prosecute descendants for the crimes of a forebear. My bet is that these documents threaten some currently active organization's power base or financial resources."

"The Republican Party? They controlled the government at the time."

"Democrats were around as well, but the problem is that neither qualifies as a secret society."

"Perhaps the Shut Mouth Society provides hidden funding."

"Not likely, with modern campaign finance laws. No ... I think they hide their power as well as their identity. It won't be anything so obvious as a political party."

"Then I'm at a loss."

"Who, what, when, where, and why." Evarts got up and paced again. "We know when: right after the Civil War; and we think we have a handle on who: the Sherman bunch. I think we should concentrate on where. Where did they hide the documents?"

"Washington or Springfield seem obvious choices." She gave Evarts an irritated look and waved her two fingers to indicate he should sit. "You're making me nervous."

"Let's walk outside. I can't stay in this tiny room any longer."

"All right, I want to show you something anyway."

With that they gathered up their possessions and each picked a couple books to check out overnight. After leaving the library, Evarts followed Baldwin's lead, and they walked the long way around Beacon Hill. In a few minutes she stopped and said, "That's the Lewis and Harriet Hayden house."

Evarts saw a four-story brick townhouse that looked no different from the rest of the houses on the block. "The name doesn't mean anything to me. What's the significance of that house?"

"Lewis Hayden was an escaped slave, and he and his wife harbored runaways on their way to Canada. That house is a famous Underground Railroad station. Come on. I'll show you where Abe Douglass's ancestor preached."

After a few minutes she stopped in front of another large brick structure. "This is the African Meeting House, the oldest black church in America. Frederick Douglass spoke here many times."

Evarts stared at the building. "Why did you bring me here?"

"I'm not sure, but Abe Douglass visited here many times and helped finance the restoration." Baldwin turned and looked at Evarts. "You keep saying that the three big events at the time of the formation of the Shut Mouth Society were the end of the war, the assassination, and the impeachment. You forgot the Thirteenth Amendment."

"The amendment that abolished slavery?"

"Yes. In 1865 … after Lincoln's assassination."

"Damn, you're right. Abe Douglass may have misled us. The Shut Mouth Society might be black."

"Or a secret society that works against blacks. Like the Ku Klux Klan."

"My mind's reeling. Let's drop these books off at the apartment and get some dinner."

They brought in pizza again and continued their research. They worked until they both felt exhausted. Evarts went over to the couch and fell fast asleep before eleven o'clock.

Buzz!

At first Evarts felt disoriented, but in a flash he realized that someone had breached the outer door and had tried to turn off the staircase lights. He threw off the blanket and scrambled to the laptop on the small table near the entry. What he saw on the camera display made him gasp. Two men stood at the bottom of the stairs. Each held a gun.

Chapter 27

· · · · · ·

Baldwin rushed into the front room. "What was that god-awful noise?"

Evarts put his finger over his lips to signal Baldwin to hush. Damn. He should've spent more money on the damn buzzer. It was so shrill and loud, they must have heard it. He glanced back at the screen, and what he saw indicated they had. The men single-filed carefully up the stairs, staying to the side with guns aimed at the door at the top of the narrow confine. How secure was the top door? How much time did he have to prepare for their entry? From the cameras, he could see no threat out the back in the alley, but he couldn't believe they would leave it unguarded.

Looking over his shoulder, Baldwin saw the screen and struggled for breath. Evarts turned and grabbed her by the shoulders. "Go throw some things in a bag. Hurry," he whispered.

She bolted for the bedroom and Evarts went to the rear window. When he threw it open, he felt a sharp pain above his left eye. Jerking his head back, he swiped his face and saw blood on his fingers. Silencer. He had heard nothing. He made another quick inspection of his face and decided that only a wood splinter had nicked him. Damn. How had they found them?

By the time he had gotten back to the computer screen, the first man had reached the upper door. When they had moved their stuff into the loft, he had staged his shotgun against the front doorframe. Now he reached for it while keeping an eye on the computer screen. By the time he swung the shotgun into his arms, the first man had reached up and used the barrel of his automatic pistol to break the camera. They had lost their view of the outside world. Damn. Damn. Damn.

Evarts snapped the lid of the computer shut and jerked out the USB cables that connected the cameras. He took a quick look at the door handle and made a decision. He raced to the bedroom doorway and stage-whispered, "Dress. Fast." When he saw acknowledgment of what he had said in her eyes, he whipped around and threw on his own clothes, all the while keeping an eye on the doorknob for any movement that would indicate they had succeeded in picking the lock. After he pulled up his pants and buckled his belt, he tucked his SIG in his back waistband and dropped some extra shotgun shells into his pocket.

Evarts had just switched from tying his left shoe to his right, when Baldwin came bounding out from the bedroom fully dressed, carrying her purse and the same Tumi overnight bag she had brought with her from Westwood. He started to ask if she had any of his things but decided that was ridiculously inconsequential.

This time he laid a gentle hand on her shoulder and leaned into her ear. "Trish, I'm sorry, but we're going to have to shoot our way out."

She gave him a worried look. "Greg, you're bleeding."

"Just a nick. It's how I found out they're covering the fire escape."

She wiped the blood away from his eye and seemed satisfied that the wound wouldn't kill him. "I want my computer," she whispered. Without waiting for his reply, she grabbed the laptop and power cord and jammed it into her matching Tumi computer case. With bag straps slung over both shoulders, she reached into her purse and pulled out the .45. She pointed the automatic straight up and extended her finger along the barrel. With more composure than he felt, he heard her ask, "How do we do it?"

"Put the gun away a sec. I need you to help me push this chest against the door." He pointed at a low chest that sat against the opposite wall.

She gave him a brief questioning look, but she put the .45 back in her purse. They raced over to the chest and carried it over to the entrance. Evarts was surprised how heavy it was, but then he remembered that he had inspected it on arrival and found it full of books.

Whoever picked this apartment knew the closed-in staircase provided a good defensive obstacle. It was so narrow, assailants would need to climb single file, and the tiny landing in front of the door had enough space for only one person.

Evarts explained in a low voice, "They'll have the door lock picked soon, and they know we're ready. If they're as professional as I think, they'll snap the door open and throw in a percussion grenade."

"Shit."

"Exactly. We want the door to open, but only an inch or two. Enough for this." Evarts held up the shotgun by the barrel. After Baldwin nodded, she helped him position the chest close, but not tight, against the door.

"What do I do?" Her voice broke a little, and Evarts actually felt relieved to see her show a little anxiety.

Evarts whispered even lower. "Sit with your back against the chest. That will add additional resistance."

She took out her gun and pointed it straight up in both hands.

"And don't shoot me," he added.

"Where will you be?"

"Right here." He lay on his back along the baseboard and pointed the shotgun over his shoulder so it was positioned to shove through the crack in the door when it opened. He wanted to be low and out of the first line of sight.

She sat behind the chest and looked around its edge to catch his eye. "This'll never hold the door."

He whispered, "I don't want the door jammed tight. I want it to give an inch or so, with just enough resistance that the bastard's instinct will be to throw his shoulder against it. I need that split second before he tosses in a flash grenade or starts shooting."

She suddenly looked scared. "This might not work."

Evarts put his finger in front of his mouth to signal quiet.

"Greg, I'm scared."

"Me too. Just don't panic." He made another quiet gesture with his finger and then whispered low, "We'll get through this."

In another thirty seconds, Evarts saw the doorknob move ever so slightly. He pointed the shotgun almost straight up over his right shoulder. The door banged open against the chest, and Evarts instantly shoved the shotgun through the crack pointed at about where the assailant's chest ought to be if he threw his shoulder against the door.

He pulled the trigger. Bang!

He cycled the pump action, adjusted the aim, and fired again. Bang!

He rolled over onto his knees against the wall and blindly pointed the shotgun around the now open door and pulled the trigger again. Bang!

After he cycled the gun, he peered around the corner and saw both men tumbling down the stairs. He jumped up and ran after them. When the one toward the bottom bounced clear of his partner, Evarts pulled the trigger with the barrel aimed at the middle of his chest.

Bang! That one was no longer a concern.

Evarts raised the shotgun to his shoulder and aimed at the second tumbling body. He almost shot again, but in the last instant he saw that the man's face had been blasted into a bloody mash. He continued down the stairs, making high steps like a football player running through tires until he got past the bodies. When he got to the lower door, he dropped to one knee and threw it open, swinging the shotgun left to right.

He heard a shot slam into something close by, but he couldn't see where it came from. Reflexively, he snapped back into the stairwell with his back against the wall. Reaching into his pocket, he pulled out two 00 buckshot shells and rammed them into the gun. Suddenly he became aware of Baldwin beside him. No time to waste. The stairwell was a trap. It had been a trap for the two men he shot and now it trapped them. He had to get out, and the only chance for escape depended on a startling and savage attack. He leaped out the door.

Evarts bounced his shoulder against a parked car and whipped his head left and right. Where were they? Then he heard someone on the other side of the very car he had taken shelter behind. He stepped back, keeping low, and holding the shotgun at his waist. He pulled the trigger, shooting through the front side windows, spraying glass everywhere. Someone yelled and he dropped to a knee just in time to see a head appear briefly above the doorframe on the other side of the car. Bang! The way the head recoiled told Evarts that he no longer had to worry about that particular threat.

He cycled the shotgun and stood up hoping the assassination team had only four members. Evarts figured the guy in the alley probably had orders to stay put.

Just as he started to swivel around, Evarts felt a gun barrel punched into the back of his neck. "Drop the fucking gun, asshole. Now!"

Chapter 28

· · · · · ·

"**D**on't shoot! He knows the combination."

"What? What combination?" The man holding the gun to his neck seemed startled to hear a voice behind him. Evarts felt the greatest fear of his life when he realized the voice belonged to Baldwin.

"Why the hell do you think you were sent here?" she screamed.

Evarts felt the slightest release of pressure from the pistol barrel, and then he heard an unbelievably loud roar as a gun went off near his ear. It seemed like an eternity before he realized his skull hadn't been blown apart, but probably no more than one or two seconds had really gone by before he reached for the SIG in his back waistband. When he turned around, he felt the greatest joy of his life: Patricia Baldwin stood behind him, seemingly in one piece. Despite being unharmed, her appearance startled him. She wore a fierce expression and she held her .45 aimed at about head height. Evarts felt more than saw a body sliding down against the car beside him. She had shot the guy in the head while he held a gun on him. Shit.

Evarts looked around but saw no one, not even an innocent neighbor. Good. He took Baldwin by the elbow and urged her to run. "Come on. Let's get out of here."

She pulled her arm free. "What about your prints on the shotgun?"

He regrabbed her elbow. "We gotta get outta here. Now!" When she started moving he added, "Besides, we left our prints all over the place."

"But that's the murder weapon."

She trotted beside him now. "My prints are on those shell casings anyway." They had reached the corner of Charles Street, and he automatically turned them away from the alley behind the apartment. At this hour, nobody clogged the usually busy sidewalk, and he could spot no one awakened by the gunfire. Then he heard what sounded like a woman's scream about a block behind them. They didn't have much more time to make a getaway.

"Where are we going?" Baldwin asked.

"Away from here."

"Is the car safe?"

Evarts thought a moment. He felt sure that they hadn't found them by tracing the car, because they had separated themselves from it so early. He also doubted that it had been reported stolen already. He had driven well out of the normal route to steal the SUV, and he had parked his own van in a different condominium complex. Even if the Explorer had been reported stolen, it seemed a stretch that the theft would already be connected to him. He kept up their rapid walking pace and said, "The car should still be safe, but we need a taxi to get to it."

They had reached Beacon Street and she pointed to the park across the street. "That way," she said.

Once they had entered the quiet park, Evarts asked, "Where are you leading us?"

"To the Ritz Carlton." She pointed. "Just on the other side of the Public Gardens. It's the closest cab stand."

Evarts gasped for air, while she panted only slightly. He needed to do more aerobics or get back to his jogging routine. He checked his watch. Eleven thirty. Evidently few people wandered the Gardens at this hour, and they found themselves alone as they hustled along on a diagonal path through the park.

"Thanks," he said.

"I almost got you killed," she said with a quivering voice.

"No, you saved my life."

"I didn't think... I couldn't think."

"Thinking gets you killed in a situation like that. You did great."

When they reached the Ritz Carlton, Evarts saw a lone cab at the stand. They jumped in, but before he could say anything, Baldwin leaned toward the opening in the Plexiglas divider and said, "South Station, please."

Evarts started to ask a question, but she pinched his thigh in a way that told him to keep his mouth shut. After they paid for the short ride, she led him down some stairs to the subway. When they stood on the nearly empty platform waiting for the next car, she said,

"This may not have been such a bright idea. We have to take the Red Line two stops, switch to the Green Line, and then switch again at Government Center to the Blue Line."

"The Blue Line takes us to the airport?"

"Yeah. Sorry." She stood staring straight ahead with an exhausted expression. "Then we'll need to catch the shuttle to off-site parking."

"Perfect." He gave her a kiss on the cheek and felt pleased she didn't recoil.

"I... I thought cops could trace a taxi." She continued to look straight ahead.

"They can... and at this hour, they'd probably get a tag on it before we even made it to that long-term parking lot. Smart girl. Smart and brave."

"Right now, I just want to get to the car so I can have a nervous breakdown."

Just as she spoke, a subway car rattled into the station. A transit cop emerged from an office at the end of the platform, but he didn't look alert. They stepped into the car, and Evarts directed them to a seat on the opposite side so he could keep an eye on the cop. Evarts looked at his watch, startled that only ten minutes had passed since they had sprinted across the Public Gardens.

When the car doors closed with no sign of interest from the cop, Evarts felt himself exhale deeply. In less than three minutes, they were at the second stop. Baldwin grabbed his arm and said, "Hurry. That's the car we want and they're few and far between at this hour."

They raced across platforms and jumped on the Green Line just before a monotone voice announced that the doors were about to close. After they had taken seats, a rough-looking vagrant walked over and grabbed the pole above their heads to steady himself. With a shit-eating grin aimed at Baldwin, he said, "Hey buddy, can you spare ten dollars?"

Evarts immediately went on high alert. A bum asks for a dollar. Only a petty criminal who thought they looked vulnerable would ask for ten dollars. He wanted to hurt the guy. In fact, he badly wanted to hurt the guy badly. Despite his need to release some tension, Evarts didn't want to draw attention. "We're cops, asshole, and you're going to blow our cover. Go find someone else."

He looked dubious. "You ain't cops."

"Karen, darling, shoot this son of a bitch, please."

Without missing a beat, Baldwin opened her purse and half extracted her .45. "With pleasure."

The perpetrator jumped back and went to the furthest seat away from them. In a few minutes they were at Government Station. This time their luck wasn't as good. They had to wait on the platform for nearly ten minutes for a Blue Line car. The ride to the airport seemed to take forever, but his watch said it took only a little over eight minutes. When they found the shuttle area outside the terminal, Evarts smiled as he saw a minibus painted with the long-term parking logo. His relief evaporated, however, after they boarded the van, and the driver showed no inclination to leave the terminal.

"When do we leave?" Evarts asked.

"Few minutes. You're the first to arrive."

"First? What are you talking about?"

He caught Evarts's eye in the rearview mirror. "Didn't you just arrive on flight 617?"

Evarts first impulse was to offer him twenty dollars to go now, but he realized that would make him memorable. "Yeah. First class, no luggage, so we made it out quick. I guess you need to wait for the rest."

"Yup. Only bus at this hour." He turned and gave them a questioning look. "Why no luggage?"

Evidently flight 617 didn't just fly in from New York or some other short commuter route. "Lost at an international connection. Pissed me off, but what can you do?" Evarts put on a tired face. It wasn't hard. "This was our last leg. We had three connections, and we've been traveling for almost twenty-four hours. Now we just want to get home."

The driver's eyes in the rearview mirror showed that he had absolutely no interest in listening to another traveler's tale of woe. Evarts felt relief when he saw people exit the terminal. "Here they come." He closed his eyes. "Wake us at the lot."

"Sure thing, bud." Evarts heard him leap out of the bus to help people with their baggage. Good. That conversation had gone deeper than he wanted.

It took almost a half hour to load people, drive over to the lot, start the Explorer, and pay the parking fee.

As they pulled out of the lot, Baldwin asked, "Where are we going?"

"I'm still on the 'away from here' agenda."

"Then follow the signs to the Ted Williams Tunnel, and we'll get on the Mass Pike."

"Is there any other way out of town? It's been over an hour since the shooting, and the cops should be on full alert."

"Let me think. Yeah. When we get through the tunnel, I'll tell you how to get to old Route 9."

"Surface street?"

"Yes, but it should be pretty quick at this hour."

"Sounds perfect. Your feint to South Station will put a lot of attention on the trains. Next priority will be the airport and turnpikes. If we can get outside Boston city limits in the next thirty minutes, we should be clear. I can't think of a reason for state troopers to pull over a generic Explorer with Colorado plates."

"Because it contains a couple killers on the lam." Her voice didn't sound as light as her words.

Evarts threw her a look. She had been exceptionally capable in as tough a situation as he could imagine. Perhaps he should make up a list of questions about her. After a few moments of silence, he tried to mimic an airline attendant's announcement voice. "You're now free to mope about the cabin."

"What?"

"Bad joke. Sorry. You said you couldn't wait to get to the car so you could have a nervous breakdown."

"I'm thinking," she said distractedly. Evarts decided to leave her to her thoughts. After a few moments, she said, "Greg, I owe you an enormous apology. I never should've doubted you. Can you forgive me?"

"Of course."

"I ah—" She started crying. "You can't know how scared and miserable I've been since my parents were killed."

""It's alright. I can imagine how I'd feel if it had been my parents."

She started crying harder, and it took a few minutes for her to get enough control to continue. "I've been miserable thinking bad thoughts about you." She pulled a tissue and dried her leaking eyes.

"I fell for you and it hurt because I was afraid I had made another huge mistake. Men have had a way of disappointing me."

"I may disappoint you, but I promise, not in the way you suspected."

After he had driven several miles, she asked quietly, "Greg, is it possible for our relationship to go back to the way it was?"

Evarts grinned to show that he was kidding. "That can only be healed with time and events."

"Hell." She smiled weakly. "I sure don't want to repeat an event like that."

"Me either, so we'll have to rely on time." He looked at his watch for a few beats. "Wow, they're right. Time does heal all." He gave her a tug on the shoulder, and she leaned over the console and hugged his arm.

They stayed in that position for several hours. With the break of dawn and more traffic on the road, Evarts began to feel comfortable that that they had escaped. After he had driven away from Boston on the surface street, they had caught the Massachusetts Turnpike heading west. When Baldwin moved in a way that told Evarts she wasn't asleep, he said, "We need to figure out where we're going."

"Omaha," she said.

"Trish, we don't know for sure that the Greenes actually went to Omaha."

"Maybe we do." She sat up straight in her own seat. "Last Thanksgiving, my father downloaded onto my laptop all the trusts and financial records for the family. That's what I didn't want you to see when I was being an idiot."

"Are you telling me there's a safe house in Omaha?"

"I think so. At least there's an asset entry that looks suspiciously similar to the Boston apartment."

"Meaning no address?"

"I'm afraid so. Only an asset number." She gave him a genuine smile. "But, Commander, I'm sure you can find it."

This time Evarts liked the way she said "commander."

"Thanks for the vote of confidence, but Omaha might be a blind alley, and it'll take two days of hard driving just to get there."

"Yes, but we can stop at Hoyt Sherman Place on the way."

Evarts looked at her. "What's Hoyt Sherman Place?"

"Lincoln appointed Major Hoyt Sherman paymaster for the Union army. After the war, he left Washington and moved to Des Moines, where he founded Equitable of Iowa, among other businesses. Hoyt Sherman Place, his former home, now serves as a cultural center for Des Moines."

"And why do you think we should stop there?"

"I did some web research at the Athenaeum. If the Strategic Air Command hid their headquarters outside Omaha, maybe the Shut Mouth Society thought the heartland would be a safe place to hide Lincoln's papers."

Chapter 29

· · · · · ·

"You think Hoyt Sherman took the documents to Des Moines?" he asked.

"Someone took them somewhere. It looks like there's a safe house in Omaha, which would be a convenient base for accessing the records. We said a secret society probably wouldn't kill merely to protect an ancestor's reputation, but what if the Sherman family formed this society to protect a huge illicit fortune?" Her voice started to rise. "Hoyt could've embezzled large sums of money while serving as paymaster for the Union army, and he may have had help from all those other Sherman descendants in Washington during the war."

"How closely was Hoyt related to the rest of the family?"

She smiled. "Close. He had two older brothers you've probably heard about: General William T. Sherman of Georgia fame and Senator John Sherman, the same senator who later wrote the Sherman Anti-Trust Act. I'm not sure about his relationship with Simon Cameron. As Lincoln's first secretary of war, Cameron adopted corruption as a way of life. We know Hoyt had money when he left the capital. After he retreated to Des Moines, he built a mansion that cost nearly one hundred thousand dollars—a huge sum in those days."

"So why do you think he had control of the documents?"

"I'm not sure he did, but maybe he took the Lincoln papers for protection. He could've threatened to disclose some dark, ugly secret if they came after him for embezzlement."

"That's it? That's your whole theory?"

"You have anything better?"

Evarts thought. "No ... I guess we've got to go somewhere."

"Seems like an unlikely place for them to look for us."

"Unless they discovered that the Greenes went to Omaha."

"I'm open to other suggestions."

"Well, I don't have any, so Omaha it is."

"Good." Baldwin folded her arms across her chest in a way that conveyed a sense of purpose. "The further we get away from Boston, the better I'll feel."

"No remorse?"

"About what?"

"You seem pretty blasé about killing a man."

"If you're waiting for me to break down, you'll have a long wait. Those men killed my parents, or were associated with the men that did. Fuck 'em. It was self-defense. They meant to kill us and I'm happy we killed them first."

"Trish, I don't want you to feel bad. I agree. I just wanted to give you a chance to vent if you needed to get anything off your chest. You acted like a professional and it just surprised me."

"I guess my pent-up anger helped me do what needed to be done. I have no regrets." She grew sullen and leaned against the passenger door. Finally she asked, "What about you? Have you ever killed someone before?"

"I can't answer that."

She straightened up in her seat. "Why not?"

"Because I signed a secrecy oath in the army."

"That means you have."

"That means I can't talk about it."

"Then let's talk about something else."

"Sure." But instead they rode silent for many miles. Eventually Evarts said, "If you don't mind, I would like to look at the files your father downloaded."

"Of course. I ... I just felt confused for awhile."

Evarts continued to watch the road ahead, but he felt relief. Perhaps their relationship could get back to the way it was before the cryptic note from Mrs. Greene. He doubted that he loved Patricia Baldwin, but he certainly knew he wanted to find out how far this relationship could go.

After a moment she said, "I have a question about what just happened."

"Shoot."

"Are you trying to be funny?" Her voice sounded irritated.

"No. Poor choice of words. Sorry."

Evarts felt her move in the passenger seat. "This is uncomfortable for me, and I'm not harboring new doubts, but back there in the apartment you acted like you knew what you were doing."

"Training."

"SWAT?"

"Some of that ... and other."

"You weren't always behind a desk in the army, were you?"

"No, but I told you I can't talk about it."

Baldwin took her glasses off and cleaned them with a lens cloth from her purse. After fidgeting a moment more, she said, "I went on a drug bust once."

"What?"

"My DEA boyfriend talked me into it. He needed a decoy."

"Was he crazy? No professional would drag a civilian into an operation." Evarts hesitated. "Were you on drugs?"

"I told you, I had a few rebellious years in college." She spent more time than necessary to finish cleaning her glasses. She put them back on before adding, "He said all I had to do was walk by in a bikini. I thought it would be exciting."

"Where was this?"

"Under the Santa Cruz pier."

"He was running his own operation, wasn't he?"

"Yes and things went wrong in a big way. Two people were killed, and my boyfriend got shot in the leg and arrested. It was gruesome. Seems that he and a few of his buddies intended to rip off the dealers for their own gain."

"He didn't need your help. He was recruiting you."

"For what?" She hesitated. "No, you're wrong. He—"

"I'm right, Trish. He supplied you with drugs, taught you how to use firearms, and then asked you to do something that looked simple on the surface. He intended to drag you in one baby step at a time." He stole a glance at her. "Listen, the Tijuana drug cartel recruits young people by the dozens to do high-risk work. They all have the same profile: upper-middle-class or rich families, recreational drug users, club groupies desperate to be cool, and eager for excitement. They're called "juniors" and they generally end up dead or in jail. You're lucky that meet went sour."

"Are you suggesting he was part of a drug cartel? He was ripping them off, for god's sake."

"Trish, your boyfriend was taking payoffs. That means a cartel had him in their pocket. He was probably stealing from a different organization, a competing gang or start-up. His own cartel probably encouraged him. Happens all the time."

"Maybe you're right. I don't know and I don't care anymore. I'm only happy I escaped indictment. That's when I started pulling myself together."

"Why did you tell me all of this?"

"I'm not sure. I just wanted you to know I had been around shooting before, and maybe I'm trying to figure something out about myself."

"Like what?"

"I used to crave adventure, the riskier the better. In high school, riding fast on the back of a boyfriend's motorcycle was enough, but I kept pushing further out on the edge. I've skydived, bungee jumped, bodysurfed the Wedge, and—"

"You bodysurfed the Wedge?"

"Several times."

"How big?"

"Six, eight feet."

"Good god, that's the most dangerous surf on the California coast ... maybe on any coast. You are a druggie."

"No, I'm not." She seemed indignant. "I haven't taken drugs in over ten years."

"Adrenaline, girl. You're addicted to adrenaline."

She sat silent a long time. "Maybe that's it. I do feel like I'm still on a high." Now she looked embarrassed. "Greg, I hope this doesn't sound awful, but I'm horny as hell. Can we find a place to stop?"

Evarts accelerated to the next off-ramp.

Chapter 30

· · · · · ·

Evarts found a cheap motel where, at seven in the morning, the innkeeper obviously thought they had stopped at his tawdry roadside establishment for a prework quickie. The stop hadn't been quick. In fact, Evarts had a hard time convincing her around noon that they needed to get back on the road. They drove late into the night, got a few hours' rest at another motel, and then drove all the next day, arriving in Des Moines after the Hoyt Sherman Place tours had closed for the day. Evarts found another cheap motel within a few miles and they got a solid night's sleep.

In the morning, Evarts rolled out of bed spent and famished.

"Let's eat."

Baldwin put on her glasses and looked him over appreciatively. "Shower together first?"

Evarts didn't hesitate. "Eat first, shower after. I need fuel."

Baldwin bounded out of bed nude and gave him a passionate kiss. Her body pressed close to his bare chest almost changed his mind, but he said, "I'll be better after I eat."

"Better's better." She squeezed past him and charged into the bathroom first.

To Evarts, this was starting to become more than sex, but he wondered if it meant anything more for her. He had never enjoyed being around a woman so much. He liked to listen to her talk, and he certainly enjoyed looking at her. In truth, he had been attracted first by her cute face and athletic body, but now he knew that underneath that apparently naïve facade ran a ruttish streak that belied her innocent features.

She never ceased to surprise. Smart and driven to compete in her profession, she also had interests far afield from history. She could be tart-tongued at times and playful at others, but whatever her mood, she always kept him interested. Interested? That was the difference. He needed to have a serious talk with her before things went any further, but not today. He didn't want to scare her away. She was too good to look at, too fun to talk to, and too exciting to make love to. Besides, she was pretty good in a fight.

Suddenly, he had a revelation. Abe Douglass had been the only other person he enjoyed talking to for extended periods. His conversations with Baldwin had a similar flavor. They ranged all over the place, and he constantly felt like he learned something new. What was it about the two of them? Then he realized that they both listened and sought out his opinions about a variety of subjects, even subjects he knew little about.

Before he could think it through, she stepped out of the bathroom wearing nothing but a smile. "Last chance."

"For real?"

"Well, for the moment."

"You're going to wear this poor boy out."

"I'm trying to make up for a year of near celibacy."

"Glad to be of service."

Baldwin looked uncomfortable. "Greg, you're more than—" She looked down at herself. "Listen, this is embarrassing to talk about undressed, but I—" She walked over and gave him a gentle kiss. "Let's eat and then talk."

"Are we getting serious?" he asked.

"I think so. Now, let's get dressed and find you some fuel."

That was all Evarts needed to hear. Time and events would tell. They had a mystery to unravel and they needed to get cracking on it.

One of the things they required was wireless Internet access. Their cheap motel had no amenities other than anonymity. He wanted to check the Omaha papers and online crime reports to see if he could pick up any clues on the Greenes' whereabouts. They probably went underground, but if others had already found them, foul play might have generated some public record. He also wanted to pull up the *Boston Globe* to read the news story about the shooting near Beacon Hill.

They found an upscale inn with wireless access down the road and ate in their restaurant. Evarts wolfed down mountains of food while Baldwin had a bowl of oatmeal. As they ate, Evarts made a number of searches on the laptop for Omaha but found nothing interesting. He considered that good news. The *Globe* put the story about their escapade on the front page, but the facts were scanty. The paper reported that, although the police had no suspects, the scene looked like a gangland hit that had gone awry. Evarts knew the police would selectively release what information they had, so he felt no relief at not being named.

After he told Baldwin that there was no crime news in Omaha that could be related to the Greenes, she asked, "How will we find them?"

"I'm going to look where I would put a safe house. Downtown. Good safe houses don't require maintenance, so that rules out a suburban home with gardening needs. I'll know better when I get a look at the landscape."

"We can't just hang around to see if we spot her."

"If they feel safe, they'll do the same kind of things we did in Boston. Shop for food, eat in restaurants, buy newspapers...maybe go to a gym."

"Well, at least we can get some exercise."

"You're not getting enough?"

She smiled and ignored his quip. "The files you want to look at are in a folder called BT for Baldwin Trusts."

He opened the folder and immediately felt lost. The volume of data itself was daunting, and the information looked like arcane financial records. When Baldwin saw the puzzled look on his face, she switched to his side of the table and escorted him through the records. As he expected, he could glean nothing from the Omaha asset except that it stood alone, which was unusual because most of the other assets were clustered in major cities. He also saw that the trusts held an enormous amount of assets that had to equate to tens of millions, possibly more. Patricia Baldwin was very rich.

After breakfast, they returned to the motel, and their lovemaking caused them to miss the ten o'clock tour. When Evarts finally pulled into the Hoyt Sherman Place parking lot he had a shock. The lot could accommodate nearly a hundred cars, and a large addition had been appended to the impressive red brick house.

"What the hell is that?"

"I told you the Des Moines Women's Club converted the house into a cultural center. That's the auditorium. Most of the touring entertainers perform there."

Evarts put the gearshift in park and opened the door. When

Baldwin came around the car to meet him, he said, "Trish, the size of that project involved architects that would've made an extensive study of the house's infrastructure. If anything had been hidden inside, it would've been discovered long ago."

"Maybe Hoyt hid the documents behind a loose brick in the fireplace."

"Too Hollywood. Since they were able to give us the Cooper Union papers, the documents must be accessible." He walked out onto the lawn to get a better view of the entire complex. "This looks like a large commercial enterprise. I doubt the Society can just waltz in and check out documents."

"Why not? Maybe there's a library associated with the center."

"The Society would never give up physical control of the documents."

"We're here now. Let's at least take the tour. I want to learn more about Hoyt Sherman anyway."

They entered through the front door of the mansion and found themselves in a tastefully decorated vestibule that offered a view of the rooms to either side. The downstairs had been immaculately restored with period furniture and wall decorations. On the opposite side of the mansion from the auditorium, the Women's Club had appended two large rooms that served as an art gallery. A sweet old docent toured them through the house and the art collection but didn't tell them much they didn't already know. Although she could describe and answer questions about the building and the regional art collection, she knew little about Hoyt Sherman that went beyond what had been posted on their website. The only thing Evarts took away from the tour was that Hoyt Sherman had built and furnished a magnificent home that today would cost seven figures. It looked like it might have been a mistake to drive halfway across the country.

The tour ended on the upstairs landing, the docent asking if they had any final questions. Evarts asked if she knew anything about Roger Sherman. "Of course," she said and swung a door away from the wall to reveal a framed document that probably measured three feet square. At first glance, the white etchings against a black background looked like someone had made a chalk line drawing of an autumn tree without leaves.

"This is the Sherman family tree," she said. On closer inspection, Evarts could see that a calligrapher had penned the family tree so carefully that each name looked like a straight line until examined up close. There were hundreds and hundreds of names going back to before Columbus discovered the Americas.

"This tree was made over a hundred years ago," the docent said. "We'd really like to see it brought up to date, but so far we haven't had any volunteers."

Evarts's first thought was that any family that would meticulously pen a family tree took ancestry very seriously. He used his finger to trace the lineage between Roger Sherman and both the William Evarts line and the Hoyt Sherman line. Then he traced another branch until he felt comfortable that he wasn't closely related to Patricia Baldwin.

As they started down the stairs, Baldwin asked, "Is the director of fundraising available? I'd like to make a sizable contribution."

The docent looked like a fisherman who had just snagged a big bass. "Of course." She reversed course and led them back up to the landing. "If you'll just wait here a moment, I'll get her for you."

Evarts wondered what Baldwin was up to, but the quarters were too close to ask. When he glanced at her face, she just gave him a sweet smile.

In a few minutes a woman in her late seventies approached with an extended hand and a smile. "I'm Mrs. Leah. How can I help?"

Baldwin extended her own hand. "Sheila Prentice. I manage a charitable foundation based in Lincoln, and we're looking for worthy endowment candidates." She introduced Evarts as her husband. "We're actually here on a day trip, but it occurred to me that Hoyt Sherman Place might fit our requirements. Do you have some background literature I can take back to my board?"

"Of course. Please follow me to my office."

As they followed the woman's halting pace, Evarts became even more puzzled. She took them to a large room with desks pushed up against alternate walls. As the old woman took a seat, she pointed to two office chairs at one of the other desks. They each grabbed one and sat facing her old swivel chair. Evarts guessed that Hoyt Sherman Place had less money than the Athenaeum in Boston.

"Which foundation are you associated with?" Mrs. Leah asked.

"If you'll excuse me, I'd rather not say at the moment. My board has a strong bias toward Nebraska endowments. I'll do my best, but in the meantime, I don't want to get your hopes up."

She smiled. "Nor do you want to be pestered."

"I assure you, I'll get back to you whatever the decision. But I'm hopeful I can arrange something."

Mrs. Leah spent about fifteen minutes putting together a thick folio of promotional material and talked nonstop about the worthiness of the cultural center. Baldwin's upbringing taught her all the right things to say and how to say them to build credibility.

As they got up to leave, Baldwin asked, as if it were an afterthought, "By the way, I heard an old friend from New Canaan is visiting Omaha. I get no answer at her Connecticut number. Do you happen to know Mrs. Nancy Greene?"

"Of course. This is a small world, isn't it? She's one of our benefactors, and she visited us just last week."

"Excellent. I'll ask her for a letter of reference to support the submission to my board. Do you know how to reach her in Omaha?"

"As a matter of fact, I do. She left a number for me to call when our curator finished restoring a Velasquez painting. She wants to examine it before it goes on public display."

"That's wonderful. Could you give me the number? I'll see if we can meet. If she's already a benefactor, her recommendation would add weight to my proposal."

Without another word, Mrs. Leah twirled her Rolodex and pulled out a three by five card. After writing the number down on the card, she proffered it and said, "Please do all you can with your board. We have numerous plans on hold due to a lack of funds."

"I'm sure we can do something; it's just a matter of how much." Baldwin accepted the card. "Thank you for this. Mrs. Greene is a dear friend of my parents, and I'm in your debt."

As they left Mrs. Leah's office, Baldwin waved the index card in Evarts's face hard enough so it snapped in the air. "And you thought I was only good for sex."

"Actually, I keep you around because of your firearm skills."

Chapter 31

. . . . . .

As they walked down the stairs, Evarts asked, "How did you know she would come here?"

"I hate to give you some of the credit, but while we were touring, I remembered you said at breakfast that they would do certain activities if they felt safe. I figured that after awhile, she would need a culture fix." She made a sweeping motion with her arm. "This may not be the Metropolitan Museum of Art, but it has a nice, if small, collection." She smiled. "Zebras don't change their stripes."

Evarts put a hand on Baldwin's arm to stop her progress. "You need to go back and convince Mrs. Leah to use her phone."

"Why?"

"Caller ID. Mrs. Greene may feel safe enough to take a day trip over here, but I doubt she'd pick up for an unknown caller."

"You're right. Let me think a sec." In a moment, she reversed direction and marched back up to the office they had just left. "Mrs. Leah, could I possibly impose on you for one more favor?"

"Of course, dear. What do you need?"

"A phone. My husband and I decided to call Mrs. Greene to invite her and her husband to dinner." She gave Evarts an irritated look. "I ran my cell dry on the drive here, and my wonderfully inept husband forgot his."

She pointed at her desk. "You can use mine."

"Do you have a phone somewhere more private? I know she's going to ask about my father's operation, and I'd just as soon not discuss it in front of people." She looked genuinely embarrassed. "It's pretty serious and I might break down."

"Oh, I'm sorry to hear that." She pointed across the empty room. "Will that do? I need to go downstairs to check our inventory for a fundraising affair this evening. I'll be gone for at least a half hour, so take your time."

"Thank you." She gave one of her radiant smiles. "Now I really promise to twist the arms of my board."

As soon as she heard Mrs. Leah's footfall on the stairs, Baldwin started punching numbers into the desk phone on the far side of the room. Evarts watched her raise fingers to indicate the number of rings. Her hand gesture turned to an okay sign after the fourth ring.

She spoke quickly. "Hello. This is Patricia. You saw me in New Canaan. Please don't hang up, I must talk to you.... Can we meet? The telephone isn't a good idea. ... No, you're safe. I'll explain later.... Des Moines. I can be in Omaha in two hours. Where?... I have Greg Evarts with me. Is that a problem?" Long pause.

"Good-bye." She hung up.

"Five o'clock. A restaurant called Trini's in downtown Omaha."

Evarts looked at his watch. "Plenty of time, but it's always a good idea to arrive early at a rendezvous. What did she say about me?"

"No problem. I, uh, must have misinterpreted her note. Sorry."

"Easy to do. Forget it." Evarts walked around the desk and kissed her lightly on her forehead. "I'm impressed. You've handled this brilliantly." Her face turned pink like a schoolgirl, so Evarts gave her another light kiss. "Now I know how to make you blush."

"That's fair." She gave him a coy smile. "Because I know how to get you to preen like a proud little boy."

"How?"

"Later," she said. "Time to go." She walked around the desk and hooked her left arm through his, and as they walked away she rubbed his bicep with her right hand.

Evarts straightened slightly, proud to have such a pretty and smart woman on his arm.

"Just like that," she laughed.

"What?" Then Evarts realized he had just been played. "You're a very wicked girl."

"Indeed."

Chapter 32

· · · · · ·

They arrived in Omaha a little after three o'clock in the afternoon. Evarts had expected a flat landscape, but the Great Plains started a few miles further west. The hills of eastern Nebraska rolled with a pleasing rhythm. He exited Interstate 80 and stopped to buy gasoline and pick up a city map. Mrs. Greene had told Baldwin that Trini's lay hidden in a narrow alley called the Passageway. Evarts had no trouble finding it on the map, so he pulled out of the gas station intent on cruising the area to gain a general grasp of the surrounding cityscape.

Omaha didn't surprise him. Although it looked more cosmopolitan and wealthy than he had expected, the city matched his vision of the Midwest. Wide streets, well-behaved traffic, nicely dressed pedestrians, and a general tidiness combined to give the city a wholesome, middle-America feel. In his high school surfing days, Evarts had owned a tee shirt that said, "There's no life east of Pacific Coast Highway." Now, over a thousand miles east of his home in Hollywood Beach, Evarts saw a lifestyle that apparently pleased the citizenry. Polite, friendly people walked the streets and many stopped on the sidewalk to chat instead of huddling inside a Starbucks. In most cities, glass and steel boxes hung over narrow sidewalks, but the architects in Omaha had set their buildings back from the street and used brick or stone to give the downtown district a warm character that reminded him of an earlier era. It appeared that life had actually seeped from the coastal areas all the way to the heartland, but he still couldn't imagine living this far away from an ocean.

"Handsome town," he said.

"That's an odd but fitting description," she responded as she looked out the window. "Are you driving in circles for a reason?"

"Yeah. I'm looking for anything suspicious."

"See anything?"

"Nope. Everything looks normal and ordinary. I haven't even seen anything that would raise the curiosity of a patrolling cop."

"You sound surprised."

"I am. Not many American cities can make that boast." Evarts steered around a corner. "Where did all this money come from?" he asked.

"Breakfast."

"What?"

"Food. Omaha serves as a commercial center for the Midwest agricultural belt. Almost anything a farmer needs can be supplied from here: equipment, banking, insurance, Internet commodity quotes, food processing, even entertainment. When Americans eat, part of the cost of the meal flows through this town and some of it sticks."

"How do you know so much about Omaha?"

"Internet. Did you know the only person in the Forbes 500 who made his fortune from the stock market lives here? Warren Buffett believes that living this far away from Wall Street makes the difference. He said it gives him a clearer perspective, so he can spot opportunities that New Yorkers miss due to their myopic view of the country."

"Just fly-over country to a New Yorker."

"Exactly."

Evarts pulled into a civic parking garage about two blocks away from the restaurant. "Let's walk the neighborhood," he said.

"Nervous?"

"Careful."

Evarts led Baldwin around a four-block circuit twice. The Old Market district had been restored to the Victorian period. Brick paved streets, low-rise brick buildings, horse-drawn carriages, old-fashioned tin overhangs, and sidewalk cafés created a relaxed and appealing atmosphere. The city had even painted the sides of the red brick buildings with white lettered signage and advertisements from the Victorian era.

He saw nothing threatening on the street, so on the next circuit, he approached the glass doors that led to the Passageway. When he opened the door and stepped inside, he cursed.

"What?"

"Amateurs like secluded rendezvous. I'd prefer a place with multiple exits."

The alley had been converted into a closed menagerie of novelty shops and restaurants. The Passageway was so narrow that if two couples approached each other, one set would need to step aside to let the other pass. Again, red bricks dominated two dimensions, and a glass roof had been added to retain the feel of being outdoors. Two three-story buildings framed the slender footpath, and plants hung from every window and outcropping. The otherwise pleasing ambiance made Evarts feel claustrophobic.

They entered Trini's, which happened to be a Mexican restaurant. At four thirty, it was almost empty. Evarts asked for a back table facing the door. After ordering drinks, he excused himself. When he returned, he said, "At the end of the alley, there's a back exit that goes up to the next street. If anything happens, run out and to the right, away from the door we entered. I'll meet you inside the courthouse across from the car."

"Are you expecting trouble?"

"If they found them, they may follow in the hopes of catching us all together. I just want to be careful."

The Greenes showed up about ten minutes early, looking nervous. She had found a nondescript dress that still managed to look sophisticated. He wore an academic-style suit with an expensive tie. On closer inspection, Evarts decided the apparently casual suit had been custom tailored to perfectly fit his lean body. He also sported one of those super-thin prissy mustaches. Evarts had never liked anyone who wore facial hair that required meticulous grooming. He bet Mr. Greene knew the thread count of every piece of clothing on his body.

After taking seats opposite, they asked, "Did anyone follow you?"

"No. Did anyone follow you?" Evarts asked.

"No. We've been walking around for an hour. We ducked into a store when we saw you on the street."

"I wish you had signaled us. I don't like this place."

"In a few minutes this place will fill with people dropping in for an after-work drink. We thought we'd be inconspicuous in a crowd."

Evarts looked around and saw people already filing in to grab empty tables. It would have to do, but he vowed to make the meeting short.

After they ordered a round of drinks, Mrs. Greene leaned across the table and whispered, "Do you have a lead on the union?"

"The what?" Baldwin asked.

"The union. The people after the documents."

Evarts and Baldwin traded glances. "What about the Shut Mouth Society?" Baldwin asked.

"The Shut Mouth Society? We're the ones committed to keeping the documents away from them. Don't you know?"

"We know very little," Evarts said. "That's why we're here. To find out what's going on."

Both the Greenes looked incredulously at each other. "Didn't Douglass tell you?"

"Someone murdered him before he told us anything. He just gave us the Cooper Union documents and said they came from something called the Shut Mouth Society. We assumed the Society were the ones chasing us and killing people."

"Oh my god," Mrs. Greene said.

Baldwin leaned forward. "Tell us."

They both looked around and grew very apprehensive. "Not here, it'll take too long," Mr. Greene said. He started to get up but stopped. "You do have the document archive don't you?"

"No. We hoped you knew where they were hidden," Baldwin said.

"Oh my god," Nancy Greene repeated. "We haven't the slightest idea where your father stashed them."

Evarts threw thirty dollars on the table, and the four of them scrambled out of the restaurant before the drinks arrived.

Chapter 33

· · · · · ·

Evarts didn't breathe easy until they emerged from the Passageway onto the open street. He touched Mr. Greene's shoulder to stop his progress and asked, "Are you staying in a Society safe house?"

"I guess you could call it that. Do you think we should go there?"

"I'm not sure," Evarts said. "People at the Roger Sherman Inn know you went to Omaha. The bad guys can find you as easily as we did."

"They're not looking for us. If they come here, it's because they followed you."

"No one followed us … why wouldn't they be looking for you?" Evarts asked.

"I'll explain after we get off the street." He pointed to a factory building about three blocks away. "We're in that building. Loft 21. Second floor, corner unit."

"That's an apartment building?" Baldwin asked.

"An old slaughterhouse converted into lofts for New York wannabes."

"Thoroughly hosed, I should hope." Evarts looked over the street scene. "We walk separately. I go with Mr. Greene, and Trish and Nancy go together."

"Why?" Mrs. Greene looked puzzled.

"The bad guys are looking for couples. Two men and two women walking together won't register."

"They're called the union, but I agree they're bad people. And, please, call me Benjamin." Mr. Greene said magnanimously.

Evarts nodded and crossed the street. Benjamin Greene followed. They walked a block before Greene asked, "Do you know your part in this affair?"

Evarts felt irritated thinking that someone had defined a part for him in what Greene referred to as an affair, but he simply said, "No."

"You're a direct descendant of William Evarts. Do you recognize the name?"

"Yes. We've researched some things and deduced others."

"Did your parents tell you about our little society?"

"No."

"That's because they wanted nothing to do with the Shut Mouth Society. Most of the members live along the eastern seaboard. Your parents moved to an isolated town as far away as they could get from us."

"Why did they reject the Society?"

"They wanted a normal life."

"So do I."

"It's far too late for that. Besides, you can't say you've enjoyed a completely normal life."

"What do you know about me?"

"I know everything about you," he said with a self-satisfied grin. "The Society may not have the strength of the union, but we have our resources. Enough to get a freshly commissioned second lieutenant assigned to Intelligence."

Evarts's irritation suddenly turned to anger. These people had been manipulating him for years. He wanted to punch Benjamin Greene, but when he looked at the wizened face of the patrician gentleman, he restrained himself to merely say, "You sons of bitches. How dare you interfere with my life?"

Instead of taking offense, the old man smiled. "We really aren't to blame, you know. You were recruited by your great great grandfather."

"I presume you mean William Evarts?"

"Surely, your parents told you about him, at least."

"My parents never talked about our ancestors."

"Didn't you think that odd?"

"No. I think it's odd to be obsessed about people long dead."

This actually got a chuckle out of the old man. "I presume Miss Baldwin would disagree with that opinion."

"That's different. She studies the great and treacherous men that molded history."

"Then she should investigate both of your families." He pointed with an uplifted hand. "This is where we live now. Despite its appearance, our loft is quite comfortable."

The building's exterior looked like a factory, but the lobby started the transformation of the slaughterhouse into a trendy condominium. The décor had that minimalist modern style popular with trendy hotels. Evarts thought the style more befitting ascetic monks than avaricious young professionals. The architects kept up the pretense by retaining the old freight elevator, but they had stripped and refinished the wooden doors and flooring to a high sheen.

The second-floor loft had easy access to a stairwell, and Evarts saw an industrial steel door securing the living space from the hall. At first he saw no cameras, but then he noticed the kind of fiber-optic device provisioned to the Santa Barbara SWAT team. When Greene turned the key in the lock, Evarts heard the satisfying slide of a deadbolt. "Do you know the people on this floor?" he asked.

"This floor is very quiet. Agricultural companies own most of the units and loan them to visiting lobbyists, government officials, and customers. The permanent residents bought on the upper floors to get views."

"That means a stranger wouldn't look out of place."

"Nobody pays any attention to us."

"I meant the union or whatever you call them. A stranger wouldn't raise an alarm for you."

"The union is what they call themselves: spelled with a lowercase *u* to help hide their identity. They're probably the most powerful nongovernmental organization in the world."

After they stepped into the loft, Greene closed the door and pointed to a monitor. It displayed the hall, the stairwell, and a fire escape. Evarts assumed that the fire escape could be accessed through one of the large wood-cased windows that lined two walls of the loft. "We never leave without checking."

On the monitor, Evarts watched Baldwin and Mrs. Greene step off the elevator and approach the loft door. Mr. Greene saw the women as well and quickly opened the door for them.

"See anything suspicious?" Evarts asked as they entered the loft.

In answer, Mrs. Greene gave Baldwin a peck on the cheek. Then with a smile that said she enjoyed the masquerade, she said, "No one in this town bothers a mother and her daughter taking a walk together."

Evarts could see from the distaste on Baldwin's face that she didn't appreciate the quip, with her real mother so recently dead. Partly to slide by the moment, Evarts asked, "Can we sit so you can tell us what's going on?"

"May I offer you something to drink first?" Mr. Greene said.

Before Evarts could object, Mrs. Greene said, "A glass of chardonnay, please." She gave Baldwin one of her innkeeper smiles. "Patricia?"

"The same, thank you."

"Coffee black." Evarts still felt angry and wanted his wits about him. This wasn't a social occasion.

They made small talk as the Greenes prepared the drinks. Then they sat in four opposing easy chairs in a sitting area that had been arranged beside one of the oversized windows. The loft appeared to have one bedroom, one bath, and a great room that served as the kitchen, dining room, living room, and everything else. The furnishings looked new but inexpensive, with more thought to functionality than consistent design. Evarts saw the telltale signs of a safe house rather than a home. He guessed the aristocratic Greenes would prefer a high-end hotel.

Evarts got right to business. "Why did you say the union isn't looking for you?"

Mr. Greene replied, "Because we aren't part of the Mute Circle within the Shut Mouth Society."

"Please explain," Evarts said impatiently. Benjamin Greene took far too much pleasure in doling out information.

"The Shut Mouth Society is composed of three degrees. The highest and innermost degree is the Mute Circle, which keeps the Society secrets and makes most of the decisions. There are three voting members in the Mute Circle. The next degree is the Mute Council, which advises the circle and communicates to the rest of the Society. That's how we keep general members from discovering the identity of circle members." He looked at his wife. "We're members of the council."

"And the general members?"

"Their job is to secure positions in government, business, or foundations so they can promote our agenda and advance themselves up to council membership."

"How many people are in the Society?"

"Now…only about forty. At the turn of the last century, there were as many as two hundred, but the children lost interest and fell away."

"Who are the members of the Mute Circle?" Evarts asked.

Mrs. Greene answered. "Patricia's parents, Abraham Douglass, and a fourth person we presume dead."

"Why?"

"Because the union killed the other three."

Baldwin interrupted. "Douglass told us he didn't belong to the Shut Mouth Society."

"Members are disciplined to never admit membership."

"How did the union discover the identities of the Mute Circle?" Evarts asked.

"We don't know," Mrs. Greene said.

Evarts knew. The Society had been infiltrated. Which led him to his next question. "How do you know the members of the Mute Circle?"

"We know only the Baldwins for sure, because they sponsored us into the council and they were our contact with the Mute Circle. Council members never discussed their sponsors, so we don't know for sure, but…well, Douglass's death confirmed his standing." Mr. Greene looked at his wife. "I guess we're the Mute Circle now, but we never went through the ceremony, so we don't know the location of the documents. That's why we're not hunted."

Evarts thought there might be another reason. "Earlier, you said there were three voting members of the Mute Circle, but you listed four people."

"Married couples only have one vote between them." He patted his wife's knee. "As would we, if we had been elevated as a couple." The prissy man tried to smile, but it looked more like a smirk to Evarts. "That is, if we're both alive at the time of our elevation." He shifted his attention to Baldwin. "Your parents also held the additional honor of being the Keepers."

"Meaning the Keepers of the documents?" Evarts asked.

"Yes."

"Did the other two members know the hiding place?"

"No. We were told during our indoctrination that only the Keepers knew."

"Sounds risky," Evarts said.

"That why the Keeper designation always went to a married couple. It's worked for a hundred and fifty years."

Evarts thought a minute. "Did the Mute Circle recruit new members?"

"Of course. We all did. Douglass meant to recruit you as his disciple."

Evarts had guessed that would be his answer. He contemplated his next move and came to a decision. He leaned forward in the love seat and reached behind him. In a flash, he had his SIG pointed at the Greenes. "Who was the fourth member of the Mute Circle?"

"What are you doing?" Mr. Greene asked, but his voice remained unconcerned.

"Please, answer my question. Who was the fourth member of the Mute Circle?"

"Or what?" Mr. Greene seemed amused.

Evarts suddenly felt woozy. He glanced at Baldwin and saw her eyes roll up. Damn. They had been drugged.

He had only seconds. As he leaped from the love seat, Evarts flipped his SIG to hold it by the barrel like a club. With all the strength he could muster, he pistol-whipped Benjamin Greene on the side of the head. Without hesitation, he swung the pistol at Nancy Greene, aiming for her nose. With his last moment of consciousness, he glanced back at Baldwin and saw her head lolling against the back of the easy chair. He meant to go to her but instead collapsed onto the floor.

Chapter 34

· · · · · ·

Evarts felt an awful throbbing in the back of his head. He rolled over onto his back, confused and bewildered. Who hit him? Then he became conscious enough to remember he had been drugged. The Greenes! He bounded up into a sitting position and fell back immediately. He tried again, slower this time. Damn, his head hurt. He suddenly realized he hadn't yet opened his eyes. Forcing them open, he saw that the Greenes and Baldwin were still unconscious.

With a determined effort, he picked up his gun and tucked it inside his waistband as he rose up onto wobbly legs. He willed enough concentration to walk to the kitchen to look for something to bind the Greenes. Leaning heavily against the counter, he rummaged through drawer after drawer until he found a roll of duct tape. He returned to the sitting area and gently pushed Benjamin Greene forward, so he could tape his hands together behind his back. When he tried the same thing with Nancy Greene, she slumped forward like a tipped bag of potatoes. Moving around to examine her from the front, he saw that she was dead. He had aimed for her nose, but his disequilibrium caused him to smash her throat and crush her windpipe.

Before checking on Baldwin, he went into the bathroom and searched the medicine cabinet until he found aspirin. He popped four into his mouth and used cupped hands under the faucet to capture some water to wash them down. After he swallowed, he splashed handfuls of water onto his face. He felt only marginally better as he carried the aspirin bottle and a wet washcloth back into the great room.

Baldwin hadn't moved. He checked her pulse and sighed in relief when it throbbed with regularity. He laid the cold washcloth across her forehead but did nothing more to revive her. Time would bring her around, and he had things to do that she probably shouldn't witness.

He threw the remains of his almost-full cup of coffee and Baldwin's near-empty wine glass down the kitchen sink, thoroughly washing cup and glass. He searched the inert body of Benjamin Greene and then his dead wife. Other than keys and wallets, he found nothing of interest, not even a cell phone.

After an unproductive search of the kitchen, he moved to the single bedroom. He discovered a floor safe in the closet, and despite his headache, fumbled around until he found the right key. The safe contained more money and another .45, something the Greenes evidently didn't feel obliged to carry. He took all the money out to see if it covered any papers but discovered nothing more. Next he searched the pockets of all the suits, pants, and dresses hanging in the closet. Nothing. After a further search of the single bathroom, he decided that anything of interest to their predicament must be hidden in the great room.

When he returned to the living quarters, he stuffed the brick of currency he'd found into Baldwin's purse. Then he leaned over to check her breathing and listened for moans or other signs of her coming out of her stupor. She was still out cold.

Benjamin Greene, on the other hand, had started to revive, but his eyes said he wasn't quite aware of his surroundings. Evarts pulled over an ottoman and sat directly in front of Greene so that their knees touched. Then he slapped him. Hard. When he saw his eyes show some recognition, he said in a gentle voice, "Tell me about the union."

"I know little." He struggled only momentarily against his bounds.

"Tell me what you do know."

Greene still looked disoriented and didn't even throw his wife a glance. "They were formed during the Grant administration. At least, that was when they were formally organized along lines similar to today. They actually extend back to before the Civil War, but prior to Grant, they were just people connected because of money interests in the antebellum South: for the most part, New York financiers and big plantation owners."

He finally looked over at his spouse. "What's wrong with my wife?" he asked in a most matter-of-fact tone.

"She's dead. How long have you worked for the union?"

"Pity. She ran the inn fairly well." His eyes grew steadier. "Why should I tell you anything?"

"Because you'd just as soon avoid pain. You're narcissistic, are you not?"

"Unrepentantly so, but I don't believe you'll harm me."

Without preamble, Evarts threw a cushion onto Greene's lap, pulled out his gun, and using the cushion as a muffle, shot the old man in the fleshy part of the thigh. Before his scream left his throat, Evarts used his hand to cover his mouth and force his head back uncomfortably. "I thought you said you knew all about me."

After the old man appeared to regain some control, Evarts grabbed the duct tape and made a crude tourniquet. He sat back on the ottoman and stared at Benjamin Greene.

Breathing hard, Greene wheezed, "Perhaps I underestimated some of your more brutal traits."

"That was warm-up. If you're not going to use that mouth to tell me what I want to know, then I'll duct tape it and introduce you to serious pain." When he didn't respond, Evarts added, "Do you believe me?"

Greene actually seemed to contemplate the question. Wilting under Evarts's silence, he said, "I've been feeding information to the union for over two years."

"How?"

"Email. I've never met anyone in person."

"Why?"

He winced. "In the beginning, because they promised to make room for us in the Mute Circle."

"Meaning they would murder the Baldwins?"

"I prefer to think of it as just arranging their death a bit prematurely. We'd not only be elevated to the Mute Circle but also become the Keepers."

Evarts had interrogated dozens of men and women in both the army and the police force. Greene had broken faster than most, but Evarts had only used such drastic tactics once before. That time, the lives of his infiltration team depended on immediate answers. This time, his own life and that of Patricia Baldwin depended on truthful answers, and again he didn't have time to waste. The preliminary questions confirmed that Greene had broken, so he proceeded to his most urgent question. "How long before the union arrives?"

Greene looked at a clock on the opposite wall, which partly answered Evarts's question. "They land in forty-seven minutes."

"How long from the airport?"

"Fifteen minutes. Maybe another fifteen to deplane and exit the airport."

Evarts looked at Baldwin. When he turned back, he caught Greene wiping a smirk off his face. "How long will she be out?"

"Hours. She drank most of her wine."

Evarts knew how to accelerate her recovery from the drug, but if he turned his attention to her, he wouldn't get all the answers he wanted from Greene. He decided to spend fifteen minutes with the old man and then try to revive Baldwin. He calculated that it would be close, but the union men would either be unarmed or delayed because they stopped to pick up weapons en route ... unless someone met them at the airport terminal with weapons at the ready. Damn. He had to hurry.

Evarts decided that Greene needed a reminder, so he smacked his wound with the butt of his gun. He made no attempt to stifle Greene's scream. Evarts relied on their description of the floor as nearly empty and on the industrial sounding between the lofts. Mostly, he wanted Greene to see him as desperate and crazed.

When Greene recovered some composure, Evarts asked again, "Who was the fourth member of the Mute Circle?"

"Jennifer Hathaway."

"Dead?"

"Yes. Virginia."

"How did the union expect to find the documents if they killed everybody?"

"The Baldwins were the only ones that knew the hiding place. The union didn't kill them. It was a real accident."

He remembered that Baldwin said her parents always traveled separately but evidently not by car. That had proved to be a mistake. Evarts put his hand lightly on the wounded leg. He saw the fear in Greene's eyes. "Tell me what the union is after."

"Your great grandfather's documents. The ones the Keeper protects."

"Where are they?"

The old man shook his head back and forth, and his fear became terror, confirming for Evarts that he didn't know. He squeezed the leg ever so slightly. "*What* are they?"

Relief suffused Greene's face and the words tumbled out. "Evidence. Proof that the union plundered the South after the Civil War. They stole millions, tens of millions. Shut Mouth estimated it could have been as much as sixty to a hundred million. Now, nearly a hundred and fifty years later, we estimate their assets at over two hundred billion dollars. Your great grandfather put some of the evidence together during the Johnson impeachment. He wanted to use it against the Radical Republicans. He collected more when Johnson made him attorney general. The Keepers have it all: criminal investigations, affidavits, and confessions from bribed officials."

"Who comprised the union?"

"Prior to the Civil War, New York City business interests had loaned over two hundred million dollars to the South, a good part of it collateralized with slaves. Lincoln never won an election in New York, and moneyed interests in the city never supported the war because of their investments in the South. After the war, a few New York titans teamed up with some members of the Southern plantation class to recover their money. They took everything not nailed down." The old man actually chuckled. "At the time, one of the robber barons actually said that whatever is not nailed down is mine, and whatever I can pry loose is not nailed down."

Shock seemed to have alleviated Greene's pain, but Evarts got him a glass of water and four aspirin. When he sat back down, he said, "And they continue to exist to this day?"

"In an altered state. At first, it was only about money, but somehow the Southerners grabbed control. Since then it's been about empire."

"Why didn't Evarts stop them with his documentation?"

"Remember—they were all Republicans, but the Radical Republicans controlled Congress and much of the media. The Radical Republicans, as they were called in their day, wanted the South treated as conquered territory, and they wanted enfranchisement of the freed slaves. Several influential Radicals conspired with the men who eventually became the union. Exposure of the scandal would've ruined not just the Radical Republicans, but all Republicans, so Evarts cut a deal with them during the Johnson administration: The plunderers would cease and desist, and he would destroy the evidence. They reneged, of course, and went underground."

"Evarts evidently reneged as well."

"The man was no fool."

"When he saw they continued to plunder, why didn't he bring forward his evidence?"

"At about that time, Hoyt Sherman left the capital for Des Moines, and Evarts gave the documents to him for safekeeping. When the looting accelerated under Grant, Hoyt refused to return the evidence. His older brothers, especially General Sherman, remained unquestionably loyal to Grant and didn't want to embarrass him. When Grant left office, Hoyt returned the documents, and after a family reconciliation of sorts, the key principals recommitted themselves to opposing the union. It was during that period that the Shut Mouth Society was formed to use and protect the documents. They managed to get Reconstruction under control, and the Sherman Anti-Trust Act put manacles on the New York robber barons."

"Is that when the leadership transitioned to Southerners?"

"That would be my guess."

"Why the assault on the Shut Mouth Society now? What's changed?"

"The union is about to gain control of the government of Mexico."

Chapter 35

· · · · · ·

Evarts glanced at his watch as he undressed Baldwin. He only had about a half hour to revive her, maybe a little more if he abandoned a safety margin. Earlier, he had thoroughly washed the coffee pot and brewed an extra-strong new batch. Once he had her undressed, he stripped himself, and then carried her to the bathroom.

Consistent with the rest of the trendy condominium, the shower had five showerheads pointing in every direction. He turned on the cold water, lifted her under both arms, and walked her into the freezing maelstrom of sprays. He recoiled when the water hit him, but she initially remained lifeless. Finally, she made a soft yelp and wrapped her own arms around her body. Evarts gently took her head and leaned it forward until the main spray hit her full force in the back of the neck. He turned her to face him, but when her eyes opened he saw little recognition.

After about three minutes, he turned on the hot-water tap and leaned her against the shower stall wall. Reaching out, he grabbed a biscuit he had found in the kitchen and forced her to eat. After two more soggy biscuits, he turned the water on full cold again. She started to revive but remained groggy.

When he helped her out of the shower, her entire body shivered spasmodically. Good. He needed her body's survival instincts to kick in. Soaking wet, he walked her back and forth in the small bathroom for about five minutes and then led her back into the cold shower, which he had not turned off. Gratefully, he heard her curse in anger this time. When he took her out to walk again, she needed him only to guide her, not support her. After he determined that she had enough control, he held the coffee in front of her mouth. At first, she sipped gingerly and then greedily drank the hot liquid. He looked at his watch. Less than ten minutes. Damn.

Just as he considered leaving her alone, so he could set some kind of trap for the union men, she spoke her first words. "Can I have a towel?"

He handed her a towel and helped her dry off. Then he sat her on the edge of the tub with more coffee and raced into the living area. In a moment, he returned with her clothing. "Can you dress?"

"I think so. What's happened?"

"Not now. We're in danger. Try to dress."

Instead of helping, Evarts watched to see how much control she had of her body. She staggered when she first stood but managed to stay on her feet and step into her panties.

"How's your head?" he asked.

"Pounding. They drugged us, didn't they?"

Evarts took it as a very good sign that she had started to regain cognitive capabilities. "Yes and people are on their way to kill us." He handed her aspirin and a glass of water. "I'm sorry, but we need to move."

"You're naked."

Shit. He ran into the great room and threw on his clothes. After a quick check of the monitor, he raced back into the bathroom to find Baldwin dressed but slumped against the tub holding the coffee cup with both palms. "Gotta go. Can you make it?"

"Have to." She stood, a bit less wobbly, and walked toward Evarts. He helped her out of the bathroom and toward the front door. She saw the Greenes. "What did you do?"

"What was necessary."

He checked the monitor and his watch. He didn't feel confident she could handle the stairs, so he decided to chance the elevator. If they showed up in the next few minutes, they would be unarmed, unless someone had met them at the airport. The lift ride seemed to take forever, but he used the time to walk Baldwin back and forth across the oversized freight elevator.

When they reached the ground floor, Evarts leaned Baldwin in the corner and kept a hand on his gun as he pulled the strap to open the horizontal wood doors. The lobby looked clear.

He raced her out of the building and across the street. Now what? He had parked the car four blocks away, and Baldwin's breath already came in sharp bursts. He didn't want to be caught on the street and had no idea from which direction someone would come from the airport. He spotted a deli with high chairs facing a counter that ran along the front window. He glanced at the sky. Another hour until dark. He decided.

He helped her onto a tall chair in the corner of the deli facing the window and then went to the counter to get food. Evarts realized he felt much better. The cold shower had helped him as well. He returned with turkey club sandwiches, chips, and steaming coffee. Baldwin immediately opened the sandwich and started eating the turkey and cheese with gusto. Evarts took a bite and peered out the window. "Did you happen to see anyone enter the building?"

"No . . . and I watched. What are we doing here?"

"We'll wait until they enter the building and then make our break. Feeling better?"

"A little. I can make it to the car."

"Good." He took another bite and washed it down with coffee. "You know, this is the third time we've had to run."

"One time we might not make our escape."

"Exactly."

She looked at him. "Meaning?"

"We need to go on the offensive."

Her expression changed from confused to anxious. "What are you thinking?"

"Taking these guys."

"Greg!"

"I'll only do it if it looks like I have an advantage."

"What did you do to the Greenes?"

"Later. After we're out of here."

"How did you know about them?"

"No one else knew we were on the East Coast. They knew about the Omaha safe house, and I guessed they knew about the one in Boston. Besides, her running away when she saw us at the Roger Sherman Inn made no sense."

"They were my parents' friends."

"No they weren't."

He saw two cars pull up in front of the building and discharge four men before the drivers pulled away. Evarts sensed they were armed. He realized the drug had addled his brain. After Boston, they wouldn't waltz in unprepared despite any assurances from Benjamin Greene. Time to go.

Evarts took Baldwin by the elbow and led her to the back of the deli. Earlier he had spotted a back door that probably led to an alley. He found it unlocked, and they ran stiffly through the alley to the street and then walked as fast as possible without drawing attention. The extra time and food helped, and they reached the car without incident. After paying the parking fee, he drove in the opposite direction from the condominium. He had no idea where he was heading.

He found Interstate 80 but drove under it to remain on surface streets and continued to head north.

"Where are you going?"

"I'm on the 'away from here' agenda again."

She sat quiet and rubbed her forehead for a while. "The cops are looking for us in California and Massachusetts. When they find the Greenes, they'll be after us in Nebraska. I'm beginning to feel like Bonnie and Clyde."

"They won't find the Greenes. Those men will remove the bodies."

"Bodies? You mean you killed them? Why?"

"I killed her by accident. I left him alive, but he won't be for long."

"Why do you say that?"

"Because I left a note on the kitchen counter. It read, 'He told us everything.'"

Chapter 36

· · · · · ·

As they drove north into South Dakota, Evarts told Baldwin everything that had happened with the Greenes and everything he had learned.

After he relayed all the new information, she seemed to puzzle over it awhile and then said, "It makes sense. The real conflict after the Civil War revolved around whether to treat the South as conquered territory, with all the spoils that entailed, or as recalcitrant states that should be blended back into the Union with restrained retribution."

"Lincoln favored the second approach, right?"

"Yes. After they conquered some of the western states, he implemented a policy of allowing them back into the Union after only ten percent of the voters signed a loyalty pledge—with full representation in the House and Senate. Congress balked, but while the war raged, they couldn't override him. He wanted the same policy after the war for the Deep South."

"Johnson?"

"At first, he appeared to endorse Lincoln's leniency, but the Radical Republicans soon saw that he actually leaned heavily toward the South." She rubbed her forehead again.

"Still hurts?"

"Not as much as the Greenes' disloyalty. Do you believe my parents' death was an accident?"

"Yes, but I suspect they were being chased. The union needed information from them."

"Damn the Greenes. How could my parents have been so wrong?"

When he told her he had accidentally killed Nancy Greene, she had shown no emotion. Perhaps death had become commonplace for her. Evarts hated that prissy bastard with the smug expression, but he felt bad about the woman. The union had forced him to do things that his parents had tried to protect him against, and the sudden deaths, relentless running, and unanswered questions made him feel sick at heart and fatigued beyond endurance. He was ready to stop for the night and began to look for a motel.

Baldwin turned from the side window that had seemingly held her attention for miles. "I'm beginning to think that the Lincoln assassination, Johnson's impeachment, and the Grant election are all related. In each case, the Radicals benefited."

Evarts sighed. He could see nothing but empty road in front of him. Partly to pass the time he asked, "What were the grounds for Johnson's impeachment?"

"The grounds are easy to explain, the cause more difficult. All Republicans, Radicals and mainstream, feared the Southern states rejoining the Union. They were heavily Democratic, and the Republicans might have lost control of Congress and the executive branch. The Thirteenth Amendment abolished slavery, but the Republicans wanted to go further; they wanted to enfranchise blacks and disenfranchise CSA white leaders in order to weaken the Democrats. Johnson vetoed their bills."

Baldwin turned in her seat and faced more toward Evarts. "I got ahead of myself. When Lincoln ran for reelection in 1864, the war was going bad for the North, so he jettisoned his vice president and ran on a ticket with Johnson. Johnson was a Southern Democrat, but he was an antislavery Democrat. After Lincoln's assassination, the Republicans never trusted Johnson and feared that he would try to restore the Democratic Party to prominence. The Radicals passed a law that said the president couldn't fire a cabinet member without the advice and consent of the Senate. They meant it as a trap, and Johnson leaped into it. He fired Edwin Stanton, the secretary of war and the last remaining Radical Republican in the cabinet. Technically, they impeached him for violating this law, but they really impeached him to maintain Republican dominance of Congress." She paused and as an afterthought added, "Much later the law was deemed unconstitutional."

"And my great great grandfather defended him."

"Very ably."

"So he might have assembled a dossier on the misdoings of the Radicals?"

"Very likely. Today we call it opponent research, but digging up dirt on an opponent has a long and ugly history in this country."

"We have to get on the offensive."

"What?"

"Sorry, my mind's somewhere else." He drove for a while. "I'm tired, Trish. I'm tired of all these narrow escapes, I'm tired of being on the defensive, and I'm tired of someone else setting the agenda. We need to take the battle to them—to the head of the union."

"How?"

"With the only weapon they fear—the William Evarts documents."

"But we don't know where they are."

"Your parents would've given you a clue. I don't believe they ever gave up on you joining their cause. I'm not asking you to think about it now. We need sleep and fresh minds." He slapped the steering wheel with his palm. "Damn it, are there no motels on this godforsaken road?"

"In South Dakota? We're off the beaten track. We need to head toward the next town."

Almost as she said it, a signpost indicated a town eight miles to the right. Evarts took the turn. In about ten minutes, they came to a small farming community, and Evarts gratefully saw a seedy motel. They rented a room from an equally seedy desk clerk, and after dropping their sole bag on the floor; Evarts collapsed on the bed and fell asleep.

Chapter 37

· · · · · ·

Evarts woke disoriented. The drug and stress had sapped all his energy. When he rolled over, he found Baldwin fully dressed and sound asleep. He stayed still as long as possible, because he feared any movement would wake her. Finally, he had to relieve himself too badly to wait any longer. He tried to keep his movements even, but she rolled over and looked at him with wide-awake eyes. She had been playing possum so he could sleep.

"Good morning. How long have you been awake?" he asked.

"I don't know. I've been fading in and out for awhile."

He heard the last as he closed the bathroom door. He couldn't let her sneak in first this time.

When he came out, she sat on the edge of the bed looking disheveled. "Do you feel better?" she asked him.

"Yeah. Bit of a headache but better. Yourself?"

"Something beyond a bit of a headache." She rubbed the back of her neck. "Any of those aspirin left?"

He held the bottle in his hand and threw it to her. She immediately went into the bathroom, and in a few minutes he heard the shower going.

When they had both showered and redressed in their dirty clothes, they grabbed their overnight bag, threw it in the backseat, and went in search of a coffee shop. They found the only one in town that served breakfast.

They went over what Greene had disclosed one more time. After a pause in the conversation, Evarts said, "I figure we're less than a hundred miles from Omaha."

"How many miles are enough?"

"Who knows? They seem to keep finding us."

He motioned to the waitress for more coffee. After she refilled their cups, he said, "Our last remaining clue is the computer files your father downloaded. We've developed an MO of always running far away. Maybe this time we should stick close. If we settled in one spot, we could use the time to carefully examine those files."

"We've looked through those files already."

"Now we're motivated. We have nothing else to do and nowhere else to go."

"How about Canada? Straight up north. You're a cop—don't you know how to get us new identities?"

"I thought you wanted your old life back."

"The price scares me."

"Well, I want my old life back. I liked it and I'm beginning to believe I would like it even better with you in it." He watched her face carefully. He wanted confirmation that she felt the same way. He got an encouraging smile but no words. He plunged ahead anyway. "Trish, the life I want with you doesn't include running from place to place hiding from bogeymen. We must win this fight."

"Alone? You said we could find help by following the trail of my parents. Look where that led."

"We discovered some new information, at least."

Evarts thought about what Greene had told him. Sketchy, due to lack of time, but it gave him something to think about. According to Greene, in the latter part of the nineteenth century, the union partners from the South took control of the secret organization and directed their investments toward Mexico. By the nineteen-seventies, they had built strong financial positions in Mexican businesses, especially in banking and defense-oriented enterprises that dealt with the government on a national level. The union kept in the background and put Mexican nationals in apparent charge of the supposedly independent companies.

Somehow the union had recently gained control of the newly popular Mexican Panther Party and José Garcia—the standard-bearer for the populist movement and very possibly the next president. According to Greene, the Shut Mouth Society had missed the move south and merely watched the union's United States investments, which were relatively benign. The Society had recently learned about the union's ambitions in Mexico because they had finally infiltrated someone into the union's inner sanctum.

Last spring the Shut Mouth Society had made three decisions, and the Mute Council approved these directives. The council comprised eleven voting members, and the Greenes held a single-vote membership together.

The first decision was to finally make public the William Evarts Reconstruction files and to distribute them to the American and Mexican governments after sending copies to the press in both countries.

To forestall wholesale renunciation, the second decision was to secure a noted historian verification of the documents' authenticity.

The union ruthlessly used violence and bribery to make difficulties go away, so the council's third decision was to authorize a small security force.

Abraham Douglass had been assigned to recruit Patricia Baldwin and Gregory Evarts to carry out the actions related to the last two decisions prior to international disclosure of the files. Unfortunately, the Shut Mouth Society never learned that their informer had been discovered, and one of their own trusted members had been turned against them.

Before time had run out with Greene, Evarts had learned one more piece of troubling news: The union had become a silent partner with the Mexican drug cartels. The cartel connection made the violence Evarts and Baldwin had witnessed more understandable.

Yesterday, when he had explained all this to Baldwin in the car, she had wrapped her arms around the purse that held her .45.

She set her cup down in a way that rattled her saucer. When she spoke, it seemed that she had been reading his mind. "These drug cartels are bad people, aren't they?"

"The worst."

As a Southern California policeman, Evarts knew enough about the Mexican cartels to be scared, but he debated how much to tell Baldwin. He hadn't held anything back so far, so he decided to tell her.

"The Mexicans started out as small-time smugglers for the Columbians, initially not much more than loose gangs willing to risk border crossings. But the Columbians made a strategic error: They paid the Mexicans in cocaine. The Mexican drug traffickers were already distributing their own marijuana, heroin, and methamphetamine, but after they acquired an inventory of cocaine, they grew to dominance over their partners from the south."

"I thought the Columbians were the major drug threat to this country," she said.

"Not for years. In the eighties and early nineties, the American War on Drugs diminished the Columbian cartels and made smuggling into Florida difficult. The Mexicans benefited. In short order, drug wars broke out and a few gangs emerged as preeminent: The Mexican cartels were born. They're a nasty bunch. Much more dangerous than the Columbians. They bribe the corrupt and kill the honest ... without a moment's hesitation. Police, politicians, opponents, informants— doesn't matter."

Baldwin sat silent for a minute. "Who're we fighting: the union or drug cartels?"

"I don't know. Possibly both. That's what's bothering me. I wish I knew how tight the union is tied to the cartels ... and which one."

Baldwin shoved her plate away to signal she was through eating breakfast. "If the union is more concerned with Mexican politics than drug trafficking, does that make it easier?"

Evarts swiveled his neck, first in one direction and then the other, in a futile attempt to expel the remnants of his headache. "Politics and drugs are intertwined in Mexico—at least at the local level. The Fox and Calderón administrations made some headway against drugs, but if the union can get their man in the presidency, they'll create a risk-free zone for the drug trade." Evarts gave her a glance. "Remember when I said something must have changed to bring all this to a head after all these years? This has got to be it. I'm guessing the union and one of the cartels are about to make a grab for control of the $142 billion U.S. drug business."

"How many cartels are there?"

"Three big ones—the Gulf, Juarez, and Tijuana cartels—lots of small contenders. Hopefully, the union isn't tied into one of the big three."

Evarts also wanted to know how the union had weaseled their way into such a lucrative enterprise. Suddenly, he knew the answer. Banking and defense contracting. Money and weapons. With the way the cartels corrupted or intimidated almost every aspect of Mexican society, it would actually be surprising if the union had been able to keep their operations clean. What he didn't know was whether they had been coerced or joined up willingly with some of the worst criminals on the planet.

Evarts wished he had had more time to interrogate Greene, but the quick arrival of the union henchmen proved that he had been right to get out of the loft.

"What do you know about Mexican politics?" Evarts asked Baldwin.

"Not much, but I've been thinking about the Greene allegations." She wiped her mouth with a napkin. "In Lincoln's day, the Mexican War and the admittance of Texas as a slave state emboldened some leaders in the Deep South to envision a slaveholding empire that would eventually annex Mexico and Cuba. If these sentiments got passed down generation to generation, then I can believe they aimed their investments south of the border." She shrugged. "Buy what they couldn't conquer." She paused. "Plus, the violence we've witnessed reminds me of my days hanging around the DEA."

"Then you believe him?"

"Don't you?"

"I believe what he said. I'm scared about what he didn't say. What I didn't ask."

"At least we know the names of the eleven members of the Mute Council."

"Greene told the union as well. Douglass, your parents, and the third member of the Mute Circle are dead. I bet both Greenes are dead now. If any of the others are still alive, they can't help us find the documents."

"What didn't he say? Do you suppose he actually knew the identities of people in the union?"

"No, they're too good for that, but I can't get rid of a nagging fear that the union has an ace in the hole."

Chapter 38

· · · · · ·

After breakfast, they returned to the motel to examine the laptop files once again. A little after three o'clock, Baldwin said, "There's a small workout room. Let's exercise and come back with clear heads."

Evarts snapped the computer lid shut. "Let's go."

They had the tiny exercise room to themselves, but Evarts pointed out a security camera in the corner, so they didn't discuss the day's work. After they returned to the room and showered, Evarts plopped down in the sole side chair and Baldwin reclined on the bed.

"If we ever get out of this mess, you're going to be a wealthy woman."

"I'm already wealthy."

"Your books can't have earned that much money."

"When I turned eighteen, my father funded a trust for me with three million dollars. When I graduated from Stanford, he added two million. They annually distribute to me all but two percent of the earnings."

Evarts made a quick mental calculation. "In Santa Barbara, they'd say you were comfortable, but when you get those proceeds from probate, you'll be rich by any standard."

"Then I guess you'll have to sign a prenuptial agreement."

That comment startled Evarts, but when he looked at her, she smiled in a way that conveyed that she might have been kidding. Why were they both fencing around the subject of their relationship? Did they even have a relationship?

He decided to get back to the task at hand. "Maybe the clue isn't in the files. After all, he waited a long time to give them to you. I'm beginning to think it must have been something he told you."

"I'm not convinced he left me a clue."

"Downloading the files meant he still had faith that you would eventually join him in the Shut Mouth Society. Think about your conversations with him. He wouldn't leave you in the lurch if something happened to him."

"He left me money."

"He left you more."

Baldwin frowned. But Evarts saw her face slowly relax as she mentally went over her history with her father. When she spoke, her voice was quiet. "I told you he once said our family had a responsibility to people who had no idea about the corruption around them. I've gone over all these conversations in my head, and I can't remember anything that helps. I didn't like being preached to, so I tuned out a lot. Maybe I missed something."

"No chance . . . rather, he wouldn't take that chance. Any other big birthday events?"

"No, I didn't even want his five million. On my other birthdays, I got pretty standard presents, if you consider Saks and Barney's standard." She laughed. "When I attended Berkeley, they tried to buy my affections with gifts in my name to the Sierra Club and the American Civil Liberties Union."

"The Sherman descendants helped found the ACLU."

"Good memory, but I've found no connection to the Sierra Club. I think they knew I'd return ostentatious gifts, so they put some of their charity donations in my name."

Evarts opened the computer lid and scrolled through the files once again. He sat back and stared at the ceiling. "I don't think this will get us anywhere. These files contain only the numbers associated with these accounts. Did your father tell you the name of the lawyer who drew up these trusts?"

"Why?"

"Maybe I can figure out a way for you to examine the full text. The clue might be buried in the legal jargon."

"A lawyer doesn't have them. They're filed away at the DTCC."

Evarts leaned forward with newfound interest. "What's the DTCC?"

"Depository Trust and Clearing Corporation. Some big building near Wall Street that—" Baldwin bounded off the bed. "Oh my god!"

"Everything might be together!" Evarts said.

"Of course. How stupid of me. I shut those trusts out of my mind."

"What does this company do?"

"I don't know." She grabbed the laptop and connected the phone line for dial-up access. Because of the slow speed, it took almost ten minutes for her to find their website. She turned to Evarts with a smile. "They store financial records and process transfers of assets for the big financial institutions. They're a nonprofit owned by all the big banks and brokerage houses."

"What's the address?"

"None listed. Security, I suppose, but I remember my father telling me they were in the financial district, near Wall Street."

"We can find them, but I don't think we can break in. We need to figure out a way to get you authorized to view those files. Does your family's lawyer have access to them?"

"No, but I do."

"What? How?"

Evarts had never seen her beam with such joy as she grabbed her computer bag and unzipped a side pocket. With abandon, she flipped through a bunch of small, stiff plastic cards and flung them around the room. One landed at Evarts's feet, and he saw that it was a frequent flyer card for one of the airlines. In a moment, she held up what looked like a library card. "My father made me sign a signature card when I was still in prep school." She waved the card. "This is the account number."

Chapter 39

· · · · · ·

In less than five minutes, they had thrown their few belongings into the Explorer and headed for the highway. They arrived in New York City two days later. Evarts wanted a base of operations away from the city, so they rented yet another cheap motel room in Newark, close by the airport. Baldwin insisted that they both dress businesslike, so the next morning they shopped. They didn't have time for custom tailoring, so it took most of the day to find appropriate clothing that fit well enough off the rack.

They went into the city by train the following morning and took the subway to the financial district. Evarts knew there would be some risk in attempting to enter the DTCC building, but they had kept an eye on the news and had seen the barest mention of the shooting in Boston and no mention of their names. He had also checked the Internet law enforcement web pages and found no reference to himself or Baldwin. He didn't know the security procedures for the building, but he didn't believe they could be too onerous. Besides, he wanted to see the documents firsthand, and he needed to keep Baldwin in sight so he could protect her.

As they emerged from the subway, Evarts considered how to find the right building. He decided the best way was to ask. With Baldwin at his elbow, he approached a Wall Street type and said, "We're lost and late for an appointment with a client at the DTCC. Could you tell us where it is?"

Without hesitation, he pointed down the block at a building that looked like all the others. "That's the DTCC."

"Thanks." So much for keeping the address secret. Baldwin had been right about dressing appropriately. People projected their own values on others dressed as they dressed.

The lobby looked like every other office building except that, behind the reception counter, no company name appeared blazoned in huge brass letters. Baldwin approached the woman behind the counter with her account card in hand. "Good morning. I'd like to access my deposit," she said in a slightly haughty tone.

"Good morning. Do you have an appointment?"

"No. My attorney told me yesterday afternoon that she needed to see the originals of my trust."

"No problem, but there might be some delay. May I see your card?" After she examined it, she said, "My, this looks tattered. You must have been with us a long time."

"My family has."

She pushed a larger card toward Baldwin. "Would you be kind enough to sign?"

"Of course."

After she compared the signature against her computer screen, she asked, "Have you been here before?"

"No. I'm preparing for probate."

"I'm terribly sorry, Ms. Baldwin. Unfortunately, we see many of those."

"May my fiancé accompany me?"

"Of course, if you sign a release. The elevator banks are behind me. Go to the reception area on the second floor. When one of our custodians becomes available, he'll escort you to your deposit. You'll have to sign another signature card upstairs."

Baldwin retrieved her card and perfunctorily said thank you. Evarts noticed that the elevator required a key to go to any floor other than the second. He also spotted cameras. He presumed they would be under surveillance everywhere but in a private viewing room, and they couldn't count on that.

The upstairs lobby had the ambiance of a private bank. The paneling, Persian rugs, and tasteful art were supposed to make a waiting client feel comfortable, but unobtrusive cameras in the corners had the opposite effect on him. He was beginning to worry that he had underestimated their security measures. They hadn't been sitting long when an impeccably dressed young man approached them.

"Ms. Baldwin, my name is Jonathon. I'll escort you this morning."

After Jonathon shook Baldwin's hand, Evarts introduced himself using his real name. He didn't think that Jonathon's first name familiarity went with the refined character of the Depository Trust, but nowadays everyone, including doctors, seemed to have adopted the informality of the waitress at Mrs. Olson's Coffee Hut. Only the police and the military continued to use proper titles and sir and ma'am.

Jonathon led them into a small anteroom that Evarts recognized as a mantrap—an elegant mantrap, but a mantrap nonetheless. The design of these rooms allowed people through an exterior door, but if they didn't present the proper identification, it kept them locked inside until the authorities could deal with them. Jonathon waved them into two office chairs situated in front of a glossy wood desk that supported only a telephone and a flat panel computer monitor.

Jonathon opened a drawer a few inches and slipped out two three-by-five cards. "Ms. Baldwin, we need you to fill out both of these forms, please."

The first was another signature card, and the other was a release form for Evarts's entry. After Baldwin filled them out and pushed them back across the desk, Jonathon said, "Thank you. May I see your account card?" After he glanced at it, he chuckled. "I haven't seen one of these in years. Our new cards carry a photograph, and a scanner reads the account information automatically." He nodded to indicate something behind them. "After we finish, would you mind if I take your picture? I can have your new card ready before you leave."

"Of course."

Evarts noticed admiringly that Baldwin didn't flinch or hesitate to agree. He had anticipated Jonathon's next request. He wanted picture identification from each of them. That was why he had used his real name. It was a gamble, but if they had his name on a watch list here, the game was probably over anyway. His concern grew, however, when he saw Jonathon hold the card by an edge and casually pass it below the edge of the desk while making distracting small talk. Their escort had just digitally photographed their identification, and a computer somewhere in the building now ran their names and images against a suspect file. Did the computer know every wanted person in the nation? Probably. Evarts told himself to relax—or at least to appear relaxed.

Jonathon glanced at the flat panel and said, "Aw, I see you're a police officer in California. Have you seen a system like ours before?"

"Nothing this sophisticated." Evarts evaluated Jonathon's tone but detected no alarm. "We're a small town."

Jonathon's composure perplexed Evarts. If the computer identified him as a police officer, then it must contain national criminal records as well. The Los Angeles Police might not have filed formal charges against him in the Rock Burglar case, but surely the Boston shootout marked him as a wanted man. He studied Jonathon carefully but didn't detect disingenuousness. Odd, but he concluded that his record must be clean.

"We have a lot to protect. One of our vaults holds nearly a trillion dollars' worth of old coupon bonds. Everything went electronic years ago, but we still have to deal with the old stuff. Antiquated paper."

"I like the sense of security that a physical piece of paper gives you," Evarts said. "I don't trust a bunch of ones and zeros spinning around inside a computer."

"A false sense of security," Jonathan answered. "Paper can be burned, stolen, or lost. Computer records can be copied." Jonathon made an encompassing wave with his arm. "We duplicate every computer record in this building and send a copy across the Hudson to live a lesser life in New Jersey at our Disaster Recovery Site."

"Sounds expensive," Evarts said to be social, rather than because he cared.

"Very. We spend an enormous amount of money making sure we can recover our records under any contingency. It would be a bad thing if a terrorist bombed this building, but it would be a disaster if we lost track of who owned America."

Evarts guessed that he said that several times a day.

After another check of his computer screen, Jonathon asked if they would like a private room. Baldwin answered that they might need several hours and asked if that would be a problem. Jonathon responded that they could stay as long as they liked. After taking Baldwin's photograph, Jonathon led them to a room that had a small aluminum table, two aluminum chairs with embedded black cushions, nothing on the walls, and a cantilevered metal counter. Jonathon closed the door, and Evarts turned the lock on the handle. He slowly walked the periphery, but seeing no surveillance devices, he realized the DTCC had used the Spartan décor to reassure clients of their privacy.

The doorknob jiggled and they heard a soft knock. Baldwin opened the door to a uniformed guard who wheeled in a trunk-sized metal box with built-in wheels and handle. Evarts was wondering how much the box contained, when the guard said he would return momentarily with the second cart. Evarts looked at Baldwin and they both grinned at each other.

After a second identical cart had been wheeled in, Baldwin removed a small key ring attached inside her computer bag and unlocked the side panel of both carts. When she opened the door, Evarts saw two drawers similar to a file cabinet. He heard Baldwin take a deep breath before she opened one of the drawers. It slid with the smooth motion of precision machining. Not surprisingly, the drawer contained file folders. Baldwin extracted the first one and lay it unopened on the metal table.

"I'm trying not to get my hopes up too high," she said.

"Too late for me. Open it."

She gently gripped the lower right-hand edge of the file folder and slowly lifted it open. She gasped.

"What is it?" Evarts asked.

"Lincoln's discharge from the Illinois militia," she whispered, barely breathing. Baldwin rifled though the folder. "These are Lincoln's preinaugural papers. They appear to be in chronological order." She quickly thumbed through all the documents in this particular folder. "My god, to a historian these are priceless, to a collector they're worth millions."

"And as a solution to our predicament, they're worthless. We need to find the William Evarts files."

"Can't I have a half hour to see what's here?"

"Of course … if you'll allow me to look through your other cart."

"I'm not sure I should let you forage through my birthright … unless you'll give me a full hour to peruse these Lincoln documents."

He made a show of checking his watch. "Deal."

Evarts quickly determined that the second cart truly held her birthright. File after file contained trust documents, contracts, real estate deeds, last wills and testaments, the provenances for dozens of artworks, and an aged box of heirloom jewelry.

"These are your family affairs. No Lincoln or William Evarts documents."

Baldwin had buried her head in a pile of papers. She made a distracted wave toward the cart in front of her. He opened the bottom drawer and immediately saw from the labels that these folders contained the William Evarts dossiers on the misdoings during Reconstruction. Without saying anything to Baldwin, he started reading from the front folder.

Two hours later, he said, "Sorry to disturb, but we need to talk."

"What's the matter?"

"These papers in the bottom drawer implicate people by name in the looting of the South during the Johnson administration, but I can find nothing that relates to the union or modern crimes."

She looked at the file drawer. "You can't possibly have read everything."

"I've flipped through it all."

She now gave all her attention to Evarts. "There must be something; otherwise, why would the union fear their disclosure?"

"Good question."

Chapter 40

. . . . . .

Baldwin had looked at only three of the dozen or so files in the top drawer, so Evarts started searching from the back. The last folder contained about thirty pages of code. At first, he wished he had brought a copy of *The Tempest* with him, but he realized these encrypted communiqués would probably not help in their battle with the union.

He heard a knock and Jonathon stuck his head in to say, "I'm going to lunch. Would you care for a break or would you like me to bring something back for you?"

"No. We're fine," she said.

"Any coffee out there?" Evarts asked.

"Coffee, tea, soft drinks. What would you like?"

Baldwin smiled sweetly. "Tea for me and if you have one available, a carafe of coffee for my friend here. He likes it black."

"Certainly." He disappeared behind the closed door.

Evarts jumped up and opened the door. "Excuse me."

Jonathon turned around to face him. "Is there a copy machine available?"

"Would you like one wheeled into your room?"

"That would be perfect. Thank you."

After he closed the door, Baldwin asked, "What should we copy?"

"The encrypted pages and the Evarts dossiers. I only glanced through them."

"And these." She held up several handwritten pages.

"What are they?"

"Letters to Lincoln from William Seward, secretary of state."

"Can they help us?"

"No, but I want to study them. They're not Illinois documents." She looked at the papers with a puzzled expression. "Lincoln probably stuffed his preinaugural papers in some closet, and a few administration papers from the early days must have gotten included accidentally."

"Any dark secrets?"

"I'd put them in the class of revelations. When Lincoln agonized over whether to reinforce Fort Sumter, Seward opened a back channel through a Supreme Court justice from Alabama who hadn't resigned. He assured Jefferson Davis that the fort would be evacuated. Of course it wasn't. Historians assume Seward acted on his own. Early on, he thought Lincoln weak and tried to set himself up as some kind of prime minister to act as the real head of the government, using Lincoln as a figurehead. Supposedly, after Lincoln discovered that Seward had made assurances without his permission, he engaged in a little political theater to put Seward back in his place. After being embarrassed in front of the entire cabinet, Seward became a loyal cabinet member." She waved the pages. "These letters say Lincoln knew all along. Seward explained exactly what he was doing."

"Why would Lincoln allow that?"

"To buy time. It paralyzed the Confederacy until Lincoln made a decision."

"Okay, so why the charade?"

"If it were official, then Lincoln lied. My bet is Seward told him about the back channel and Lincoln never responded. Seward took that as permission. Lincoln gave Seward free rein while it served his purpose and then later jerked him back in line." She shook her head. "Lincoln could be devious as hell."

An attendant wheeled in a copier, and Evarts grabbed his ancestor's dossiers to start the copying process.

They completed a quick search of the remaining files and copied hundreds of pages, while Evarts consumed the entire carafe of coffee. He suggested that they take two of the William Evarts originals that mentioned his investigational targets by name. Evarts explained that they should each hide one of the original documents and not tell the other about the hiding place. It would give them each a bargaining chip that couldn't be compromised by the other—the same strategy Douglass had used. She agreed but insisted that the originals be replaced with copies so the files in the cart remained intact.

"Let's see," she said. "How many hiding places are there in an Explorer?"

"Not now. In fact, perhaps never. Depends on whether we can settle some place for a while. For now, it's just an idea."

"Greg, I'm beginning to worry." She tapped the file in front of her. "The thrill of finding these made me forget that we came looking for a two-by-four to bludgeon the union."

"I'd prefer a small nuke." He looked at the remaining files. "It's here. We just haven't found it yet ... or we saw it and failed to recognize its significance."

Chapter 41

······

When they emerged onto the street, Evarts saw that the day had grown overcast and threatened rain. They returned by public transportation to Newark, carrying the box of document copies. Thunder rumbled in the distance, and the humidity made their new clothes cling uncomfortably to their bodies. In the room, he threw the box of papers onto the bed and said, "Let go eat an early dinner."

They found one of those chain eateries that looked like a cross between an upscale coffee shop and an uninspired restaurant. These establishments advertised themselves as family restaurants and then subtly promoted themselves as a respectable place to drink alcohol. As a cop, Evarts had seen too many automobile accidents to like the idea of taking the wife and kids out for the evening, getting a bit soused, and then driving them all home in the family sedan. He usually made it a practice to avoid these places, but it was close by the motel, and the sky continued to forewarn that a thunderstorm would soon be on them.

Baldwin sipped her wine and made a face. Evidently, the usual clientele had less sophisticated palates. Beer made life simpler. After finishing his drink, Evarts excused himself to make a telephone call. Using a calling card, he phoned Lieutenant Clark.

When Clark answered, Evarts said without preamble, "Give me the news."

"Good news or bad news first?"

"Give me the good. I need it."

"You're no longer a person of interest to the LAPD for the Rock Burglaries. They checked your whereabouts around the time of all the burglaries over the past three years and found no pattern that implicates you."

"And the bad?"

"Where are you?"

"Never mind that. I don't want to stay on this line long. Give me the rest."

"You got two days to get back to work, or the chief is going to suspend you again: This time as a disciplinary action. You better fly your ass back here. The chief wants you to bring back Baldwin as well. We still haven't solved that Douglass mess and she's a witness."

"I gotta go." Evarts had a premonition. "Hey, one more thing. You heard anything about a big shoot-out in Boston? Three, four people killed."

"Yeah. Some kind of botched drug hit. The dead all had long rap sheets."

"Any suspects?"

"The cops ain't got a clue. Who cares? Bad guys just shooting each other. Hey, are you in Boston?"

"No. Why does the chief want me back so bad?"

"We're getting killed on this Douglass thing. Now the mayor wants a cop who can claim to be his friend. You know, we're not a racist city and all that. He's rip-roaring mad. Can you fly back tomorrow? I'll pick you up at LAX."

"Tell the chief I'm on vacation."

"You'll be on suspension is what you'll be. Come on, Greg, where the hell are—"

"Gotta go." Evarts hung up.

When Evarts returned to the table, Baldwin asked, "Learn anything?"

"Plenty. I'm no longer a person of interest in that Rock Burglar thing, and someone managed the news media around the Boston episode. The dead have been identified as henchmen for drug lords, so they dismissed it as a gangland hit. That's why we've only seen subdued news coverage."

"Who'd cover that up?"

Evarts waved down the waiter and ordered another beer. After all, they didn't need to drive. A loud racket drew his attention outside, and he saw that rain pounded the cars and pavement. It looked like they would run instead of walk the hundred yards back to their motel.

He waited until the waiter had returned with his second beer before he continued. "The police would've easily reconstructed the scene as an assassination attempt, and although the dead killing team had drug-related police records, they would've pursued the targets as assumed gangland members. Our prints were everywhere, so someone squashed the investigation. Only the union had motivation for a cover-up, because if we got identified as assassination targets, it would lend credibility to the Shut Mouth materials—if we ever got to release them."

"Can they cover up a crime that significant?"

"Sure, with enough pull in either the mayor's office or the police department. I guessed as much when the DTCC computer let me into their building." Evarts took a long draw of beer.

"That's not all bad news. At least we're not being chased by the police." Baldwin studied him. "Why are you upset?"

"I discovered who planted that parking receipt at the Rock Burglary."

"Who?"

"Lieutenant Clark."

"He works for you, doesn't he?"

"Yeah, but the union must have got to him. Dickhead's older than me, so maybe he didn't want to wait around to see if I retired early."

Evarts watched the heavy rain hit so hard it bounced up almost a foot from the hood of the car outside his window. After another swig of beer, he continued to look out the window as he talked. "He told me to fly back and he'd pick me up at LAX. The bastard kept asking where I was, so how did he know I needed to fly? When he said I should get you back as well, it clinched it for me."

Evarts turned to Baldwin. "Nothing puts us together except forensic evidence in Boston, so I asked him about the shooting, and he knew too much." Evarts looked out the window again. "You've seen the television coverage. Barely mentioned. Why would a Santa Barbara cop know about a Boston gang shooting?"

"You need to hire a better class of subordinates."

Evarts laughed, but he didn't feel happy. "Civil Service regs. What's a fella gonna do?"

"What *is* a fella gonna do?"

"Thinking about it." He did. "I'm inclined to open a channel with Detective Standish but keep Clark on the line. He could prove useful if we want to feed the union misinformation."

"And when you get back, promote Detective Standish to Lieutenant Clarks' job. I liked her."

"I forgot. She interviewed you at the Douglass house."

"Yeah, she won't sell you out." Baldwin winked. "She likes you."

Chapter 42

· · · · · ·

A fter dinner they sprinted across the parking lot to their room. They got as drenched as if they had stood for five minutes in a full-throttle shower. When they got inside the room, Baldwin started cursing that she had been dumb not to change before the rain.

"Let's put on something dry, and we'll take these clothes to the dry cleaners tomorrow," Evarts suggested.

"They're ruined!" she shouted. "At least mine are. Since you don't care about your appearance, yours are probably fine."

He checked a sharp retort. "Why don't you go into the bathroom and change? You'll feel better after you're dry."

"I'll feel better after we get out of this mess. We didn't find anything useful today. Goddamn it, I don't—"

Just then a clap of thunder shook the room so hard that Evarts glanced out the window, expecting to see a tree incinerated. He heard another goddamn and turned around to see the bathroom door slam behind Baldwin.

He changed into a pair of shorts and tee shirt and hung his own clothes up to dry in the metal rack that served as a closet. The rack hung outside the bathroom door, and he heard Baldwin crying. When she finally opened the door, she was dressed in the beach gear he had bought her. She held the new clothes they had bought the day before in a wad and tossed them on the floor under the clothing rack.

"I'm sorry," she said. "You didn't deserve that."

He thought she looked forlorn. "What's wrong?"

"It's just such a letdown."

"It's the weather. It would depress anyone."

"This was our big hope. Since the beginning, we thought the Evarts documents would give us a weapon. Now—" She plopped onto the bed.

"I only scanned them. We'll study them more thoroughly in the morning." Hoping that talking about history would brighten her mood, he asked, "How do you think Evarts got hold of those Lincoln documents?"

"He probably found them in the White House basement or a closet after Johnson took control of the Executive Mansion." Her voice still had an edge, but she seemed calmer.

"That stuff about Seward was fascinating. Did you learn anything else today?"

"Learn?" He saw her mentally flip through the pages again. "Small details, confirmation of suppositions, but mostly behind the scenes maneuvering of public events already recorded by the press of the day."

"Any specific event?" Evarts saw that the diversion had worked.

"The 1860 race that elected Lincoln president. The files contained only letters from his political operatives, not his responses."

"Where would his responses be?"

"Lost, I suppose. The people who managed his campaign never passed them on to us. It would be like Lincoln to issue instructions that they be destroyed."

"A shut mouth man."

"Exactly. He always pretended that things happened accidentally or required very little effort on his part. He actually took meticulous care to orchestrate events. Lincoln agonized over speeches and then helped propagate the myth that he scratched them out on the back of an envelope. He also sought advice from everyone on his major addresses and then allowed each one of them to think they had contributed far more than they actually did."

She got up from the bed and went over to the tiny faux wood table by the window. "Caspar Weinberger once said it was amazing how much a person could accomplish in Washington if they didn't care who got the credit."

"But you found no more startling revelations?"

"Only that Lincoln knew his operatives' plans, but no historian believed him innocent of political maneuvering. The first step in Lincoln's plan was to convince his party that they had to win Illinois to gain enough electoral votes to take the White House. After he accomplished this, he persuaded them to hold the Republican convention in Chicago to help win the state. Once he gained that concession, he used local advantage to manipulate the convention to his ends. His strategy was to appear as if he wasn't running prior to the convention and to court delegates only as an alternative if the convention deadlocked. Then he engineered a deadlock, packed the galleries with loud partisans using forged tickets, and bought support by aggressively using patronage." Baldwin took a deep breath. "He suckered them onto his turf, quietly built a superb campaign team while he pretended to be a harmless hick, and then bribed his way past all the front-runners."

"So he captured the nomination," Evarts said. "What about the presidential race?"

"The convention *was* the race. Lincoln and every savvy politico knew that Douglas would split the Democrats, and whoever won the Republican nomination would win the White House. Lincoln only won forty percent of the popular vote to become our first minority president. The other sixty percent got split between Douglas and a proslavery Southern Democrat."

"I thought Douglas was proslavery."

"So did the northern abolitionists but not Southern Democrats. Douglas wanted to be president, so he curried favor with the South by engineering the Kansas-Nebraska Act. Later he tried to straddle the slave issue. Slaveholders on a roll would brook no wavering— none. So they convened a second convention, and two Democrats ran against Lincoln."

Evarts loved it when she got passionate about history. Her head bounced, her emerald eyes flitted to and fro, and her gestures became lively. Evarts must have smiled, because she said, "What?"

"You're beautiful when you're excited."

"I'm not beautiful." She took off her glasses and blushed. "Cute maybe, but not beautiful."

He leaned across the table and gave her a gentle kiss on the lips. As a reward, he received one of her wicked smiles. Evarts never thought history could be an aphrodisiac, but she grabbed his hand and drew him toward the bed. They made love for the first time since Des Moines. The thunder, lightning, deafening rain, and other dangers that lurked outside made the bleak room seem cozy. They felt protected and alone together. Instead of wild abandon, their caressing and quiet lovemaking drew them together in an emotional bond that fixed the evening in his memory forever.

Chapter 43

· · · · · ·

In the morning, Evarts went out and brought back coffee and pastries. They decided to work in the room on the material they had copied. The summer storm had cleaned the skies and streets but hadn't reduced the humidity. It would be a good day to stay indoors with air-conditioning.

Baldwin was already sitting at the little table when he came into the room. He handed her a cup of coffee and said, "I need to go to a bookstore and buy a copy of *The Tempest*."

"Already have it. I downloaded an electronic copy onto my computer."

"The whole play? I didn't know you could do that."

"Shakespeare's copyright expired centuries ago." She turned the laptop toward him so he could see.

Evarts sat down and sipped his coffee as he leafed through the encoded pages. Of the pages he had copied yesterday, one had two sets of numbers separated by white space. He suspected that the set of numbers at the bottom of the page were written in a different hand, so he wanted to start with that sheet. He found it and pulled the laptop toward him.

While he used the computer, Baldwin read the copies of the William Evarts documents. Translating the numbers on the bottom of the page took him two hours. By the time he finished, he was sure that he had gotten the message right. Now he knew for sure that the notes at the bottom of this page had been added recently.

He had made notes in a word processing file, and now he hit Save and stared at the screen a moment. He had found one more clue in an unending string of clues, but he wasn't thinking about unraveling the next level. He had to figure out how to tell Baldwin what he had discovered and in what sequence. He walked to the telephone, where he picked up a tiny tablet, and then returned to the table to make some notations. When he finished, he closed his work file and snapped the lid shut.

He stood again, stuffed the tablet in his back pocket, and stretched. "I'm going for more coffee. Want some?"

She had her head buried in one of the documents and just nodded.

Just as he was about to open the door, her voice stopped him. "Greg?"

"Yeah?"

"Did you read this document?"

He came over and looked down at it. "Probably not. I only scanned most of them. Why?"

"This puts a different slant on the supposed William Evarts deal. It offers an acquittal in the Johnson impeachment in exchange for dropping the treason charges against Jefferson Davis. A president for a president, so to speak. The document also talks about a cessation of plundering, but it appears at the bottom, almost like an afterthought."

"Doesn't that fly in the face of a grand conspiracy between a bunch of rich New Yorkers and aristocratic plantation owners?"

"Why do you say that?"

"Well, a bunch of Yankees wouldn't care about Davis, would they?"

"You'd think not, but Horace Greeley and Cornelius Vanderbilt were the moneymen behind the Davis defense. When the courts consented to bail, each of them contributed twenty-five thousand dollars—a huge sum in those days."

She seemed to puzzle that over for a bit. "If Davis escaped treason, then the rest of the rebellion leaders would probably receive pardons and get their plantations back. That would provide them the wherewithal to repay their New York debts." She swiveled around in her chair and looked up at him. "I'll bet Evarts and his advisors thought that if the Southern part of the coalition reclaimed their legitimate wealth, they'd quit stealing other people's money. It sure makes more sense than just getting an empty promise from them to quit stealing."

"But how could they pull off a deal like that? Wouldn't it take a lot of people in the know?"

"Not as many as you might think. Lincoln appointed the Radical Republican Salmon Chase as chief justice of the Supreme Court because he didn't want him as an opponent in the 1864 presidential race. Chase had been his secretary of the treasury and a royal pain in the ass because of his outsized presidential ambitions. The man would do anything to gain New York backing." Baldwin paused dramatically. "Chief Justice Chase presided over both the Johnson impeachment and the Davis treason trial." Then she waited another couple beats and added, "And William Maxwell Evarts defended Johnson and prosecuted Jefferson Davis."

"You mean Evarts was the one to let Davis go?"

"He pleaded nolle prosequi, or unwilling to pursue. But yeah, probably with the approval of Johnson and others, your great-great-grandfather was the one to give Jefferson Davis his get-out-of-jail-free card."

Evarts pointed at the paper in her hand. "And that document says it was a quid pro quo for Johnson?"

"Yes."

"Do you think the Shut Mouth Society got it wrong?"

"No, but they got outsmarted. The union predecessors got the plantations returned, freed their figurehead, crippled Johnson, and then continued to plunder to their heart's content—at least through the Grant administrations."

Evarts left the room deep in thought. He didn't know what to think about this new development. Up to now, he had thought his ancestor had been a crafty player in the highest political arena. Now Baldwin had intimated that these cagey union conspirators had gotten the upper hand on the Shut Mouth people right out of the gate.

He wanted more than coffee. He wanted to call his police department. When the dispatcher answered, he got put through immediately to Deputy Chief Damon.

"Where the hell have you been?"

"I thought you didn't want me around."

"Abraham Douglass is old news. If you remember, you have a job here. What is this, some kind of juvenile snit?"

"I have a personal issue. One I'd prefer not to discuss. Put me on vacation. I have three weeks coming."

"You're already on administrative suspension. I don't know if I can get it changed to vacation. Why'd you run?"

"Long story, but you've got to trust me for a few more days. I've got something I need to handle, and I want more time. Is it true I've been cleared of that Rock Burglar thing?"

"Yeah. But the chief's still upset that you took off. He thinks you might be hiding something else."

"My problem isn't police business. Can you put me on vacation? Talk to the chief."

"I'll try, but you're not giving me much to lay in front of him."

"Okay, listen, I got pissed off and went on a surfing trip along the coast. At first, I just wanted to clear my head, but now I've found a woman. One I think might turn into something serious, and I want to give it a chance. Get me some time … please."

Evarts listened to a long hesitation and then heard a reluctant, "All right."

"One other thing. I've been thinking about the Rock Burglar. Someone at the department tried to frame me. I want you to check the schedule of the rest of the force to see if anyone has a pattern that tracks to the robberies."

"You suspect someone on the Santa Barbara force?"

"I think implicating me might have been a diversionary tactic."

Damon paused again. "Okay. You might be right. I'll put someone on it."

"Can I make a suggestion?"

"Sure."

"Detective Standish."

"Good choice. She should be clean."

After Evarts hung up, he thought about what he had just done. Was it peevishness? If word got out that he had initiated a broad internal investigation, he would have trouble with his fellow officers. Unless they found something—then that news would override all else.

When he returned ten minutes later, he slid the cardboard coffee cup over to her and said, "I need to interrupt you."

She put her finger in the middle of the document to indicate where she had stopped reading. "What?"

"Put that down … please."

Now she looked worried. "What is it?"

"I have a message from your parents."

She looked confused for a moment and then glanced at the

computer. Her eyes looked scared when they returned to his. "You deciphered a message to me?"

"Yes. It's very short, but I thought you should read it before we try to figure out what the rest of it means."

"Give it to me."

Evarts pulled the tablet out of his back pocket and made a mental check one more time. The motel logo dominated the top of the paper, and the chain's contact information took up a good part of the bottom. He hadn't needed much room. He checked the two rows of numbers and the cursive note below.

41111, 124252, 221105, 1230118
214834, 512913, 512914, 121612, 121629

If find, then dead.

Daughter - Dear'st Love - Mother Father

He handed it to her and sat on the edge of the bed. She read the note, paused a long moment, and then took off her glasses and looked out the window. Evarts sat still and sipped his coffee as quietly as he could manage. After awhile, he saw her dry her eyes, with her head still diverted. She turned away from the window, and sympathy welled up in him when he saw her rueful smile. Without a word, she came over and sat beside him on the bed, leaning her head against his shoulder. They stayed like that for several minutes. She didn't cry, and he sensed that she didn't want him to pull her closer.

After awhile, she said, "That was sweet." Then she heaved a big sigh and added, "I assume there's more."

"Yes ... about the union, that is."

"That's what I meant." She kissed his cheek. "Let me see it."

"On the computer. I didn't transcribe it." They both went over to the table, and Evarts opened the file he had saved to the desktop. The screen showed three additional rows of numbers.

41213, 111522, 324216, 126131, 128944
416254, 414161, 222121, 22352, 122635
323116, 414161, 41411410, 5127127, 122635

Below, he had typed the three corresponding messages.

believe Dog lass told all
stuff at john she man
danger at lake nor man

"What do you think it means?" she asked.

"The first message seems obvious. Douglass was supposed to tell us what we needed to know, but he didn't sense the danger, so he played a little game with us to whet our appetites for solving the mystery. We failed to start this mission with a proper brief."

"Mission? Brief? You're reverting to your old army intelligence mindset."

He shrugged. "Secret codes and hidden files." He pointed at the screen. "I don't understand the second two lines, but I hope the 'stuff' reference means evidence against the union ... modern evidence."

"John she man?"

"I don't know, maybe a transvestite?"

"You're kidding."

"No. Cops call the client of a prostitute a john. This may be a lead—a sexual freak who we can find by checking police records."

She studied the screen a minute. "Do you think Shakespeare used the Sherman family name in his play?"

"What? No. Why?"

"Because I don't think my father found Sherman in *The Tempest.*"

Evarts looked at the screen again. "Damn it." He felt stupid. "John Sherman belongs to the Mute Council. Greene already gave me his name."

"Some code breaker you are."

"Now all we've got to do is find him?" He caught her smile. "You know, don't you? Tell me."

"John Sherman, who I assume is a descendant of all these other Shermans, is an influential congressman from Ohio. You should watch more news."

He read the screen aloud. "Stuff at john she man." He grabbed her shoulders and kissed her on the forehead. "A congressman. They gave the stuff to a congressman for safekeeping."

Baldwin suddenly looked worried. "What if they've already killed him?"

"Check the Internet."

Baldwin made a Google search and said with relief, "He gave a speech on the floor yesterday."

"Are you sure? Members can just hand speeches over to the Congressional Record and pretend they're doing their job while they sail around on some lobbyist's boat."

"No, he made a real speech. The *Washington Post* has a story on it. Big news. He slammed the Mexican Panther party for corruption. He's taking a lot of flack, especially from Hispanic activists."

"Thank god. How soon can you get packed? I want to get on the road to D.C."

"What about the last message line?"

"Piece of cake. Dog lass, Douglass. She man, Sherman. Nor man, Norman. The last line warns us about a danger at Lake Norman. With any luck, it's the center of the union."

She typed quickly and hit the enter key hard. When she tapped the touchpad at the first listing, the Lake Norman Chamber of Commerce website popped onto the screen.

"North Carolina," Evarts read over her shoulder. "Over five hundred miles of shoreline. That's a big lake."

"Smaller than all of North America."

"You got that right," he said. "Those sons of bitches are almost in our sights."

Chapter 44

· · · · · ·

"**W**here are we going?"

"A friend's house." He smiled. "This time we won't have to stay in a motel that counts its crummy towels."

"Who?"

"Steven Harding. A friend from when I lived here."

"Can you trust him?" She looked nervous.

"With my life." He gave her a pat on the knee. "And more importantly, with yours."

"How much are you going to tell him?"

Evarts had spent a lot of time thinking that through. "Everything. Steve and I ran several missions together. He's a good guy to have around in a fight." Evarts thought she still looked nervous. "Trish, we need help."

"I think we should talk to the congressman before we disclose anything to outsiders."

"I thought so as well...at first, that is. Trish, the congressman might be another dead end. I have people in this town I trust from my army days and—"

"You're going to pull others in?"

"No." He wished he had brought up Harding before they had rolled into Georgetown. "No, just Steve for now."

"What kind of missions?"

"What?"

"What kind of missions did you run with this Harding character? And don't give me that crap about a secrecy oath. People are trying to kill us. I want to know about Harding."

Without hesitation, Evarts said, "We ran covert insertion operations: small, highly trained teams that implanted surveillance devices in unfriendly or hostile locales. I ran the technical side, and Steve's crew took care of any trouble we ran into, but we were all trained to do any function."

"I thought the NSA could intercept any communications."

"Only transmitted communications. We were after private conversations. The kind that occurs between two people behind closed doors."

"You planted bugs?"

"In a way of speaking, but the stuff we have nowadays, you don't need to actually get inside, just close."

"So, you didn't break codes?"

"Oh, I did my share of that, but mostly I tried to pinpoint where we needed to insert close-quarters listening devices. Then I joined the missions to make sure they got implanted in the right spot and were properly calibrated. I mostly worked behind a desk, but Steve always played on the dark side."

Baldwin seemed to think these revelations over and then said, "How many times did you run into trouble?"

Evarts laughed. "Seemed like every time, but we only ran into the shooting kind of trouble twice." He looked at her. "Trish, I trust Steve when things get dicey."

Baldwin turned toward the side window, and when she spoke, she sounded like she was talking to herself. "'Dicey' seems like such a civilized term for what we're into."

Evarts had arrived at his destination in Georgetown. His friend from his military service had inherited a townhouse in the toniest section of this tony enclave. Evarts had lived with Harding during his last year in the service, and Harding had been badgering him to visit, but he never seemed to find the time—or perhaps the motivation. These were not the best of circumstances, but he looked forward to seeing his old comrade in arms again.

The street appeared empty and the house still, but Evarts thought that Harding could be home. People closed themselves off inside their houses in this neighborhood, and Harding had enough money not to work. Evarts parked at the closest spot he could find, which was nearly two blocks away. They grabbed their bags and walked back along streets lined with immaculate brick townhouses.

Evarts rang the bell. When no one answered, he stepped into a flowerbed and removed a loose brick in the planter, where he found the spare key. When he returned to the stoop, he checked the street and windows before inserting the key. After he unlocked the door, he said, "There's a security panel just inside the door. If he's changed the code, an alarm will go off. If it does, we walk away as calm as two residents taking an afternoon stroll. Okay?"

"What's he going to do when he sees you've broken into his house?"

"Give me a bear hug." He pushed the door open and keyed the old code into the keypad. A green light blinked on and he sighed with relief.

They stepped into the entry, and a burly man with a .45 hanging at his side suddenly appeared at the end of the hall.

"Steve. You didn't answer the bell."

"I was on the crapper." He rushed over and did exactly as Evarts predicted. He gave him a crushing bear hug that made it hard for Evarts to get a breath. "Damn, it's good to see you. Why didn't you call?"

"Long story, but we'll get to it. This is Patricia Baldwin. A friend."

"I hope she's just a friend," Harding said with a broad wink.

He started to embrace her, but she stopped him with a single uplifted finger. When he feigned disappointment, she touched him affectionately on the forearm and kissed him on the cheek. "I'm pleased to meet you, and I'll deal with Greg later for that 'friend' comment."

"Let me know if you need help. I've put this bozo in his place too many times to recount." He stuffed the .45 in his front waistband, and putting a beefy arm around each of their shoulders, he led them down the long hall to the kitchen in the rear.

"Coffee, beer?" He looked at Baldwin. "Diet coke?"

"Do you happen to have any port?" Baldwin asked.

"Of course. Did Greg tell you I was a barbarian?"

"He said something about me discovering for myself."

Harding laughed uproariously as he swung the refrigerator door open. He threw Evarts a beer and then pulled one out for himself. "Follow me," he said.

He led them into a sitting room decorated in a federalist style that would have looked appropriate in the White House. In a moment, he offered a bottle to Baldwin, which he held by the neck and cradled in his other hand. "Will this do?"

"You're an officer and a gentleman," she said.

"Not any more," he chuckled. "Let's sit on the patio."

The small enclosed patio nestled between perfectly manicured trees and shrubs. Along the surface of the brickwork, dozens of pots had been planted with colorful flowers, giving the private area a serene atmosphere.

"My compliments to your gardener," Baldwin said.

"I accept." He looked around as if seeing it for the first time. "These flowers are my children." He took a long swig of beer. "Now, tell me what brought you to Washington."

An hour later, Harding whistled and said, "That's a tall tale."

Baldwin spoke for the first time. "Unfortunately, it's more than a tale. It's our life."

"What can I do to help?"

"First, we'd appreciate lodging," Evarts said.

"That goes without saying. What else?"

"Nothing until we see Sherman. Then I'd appreciate your help in devising a plan."

"Sounds like you could use someone to watch your back."

"Steve, this is dangerous. A dozen people are dead already. I almost bypassed your hospitality."

"If you had, I would have beaten those union guys to the punch." He looked at his potted garden again. "I love flowers, but life has gotten just a bit dull. Let me in."

Evarts smiled. "I came here looking for a friend. Something in short supply lately. If I'm honest with myself, I came for more. I came hoping that we would no longer be alone in this fight." He hesitated. "Maybe I've been alone too much, even before this mess." Evarts tipped his beer at Harding. "I'd appreciate someone at my back."

"We'd appreciate it," Baldwin added.

"Then it's settled." Harding jumped out of his chair. "We need fresh drinks before we plot how to sabotage the Mexican elections."

Chapter 45

. . . . . .

John Sherman's office in the Cannon Building included just two rooms. The outer office had been equipped with four desks for his staff and several chairs for visitors. The room looked more than crowded. It looked a mess. Paper and people were strewn everywhere, and the competing conversations made it hard to see how any work got done. After a moment, one of the staffers turned his head in their direction to ask their business.

"We're here to see the congressman," Baldwin said.

"Do you have an appointment?"

Baldwin surprised Evarts by saying yes. The staffer looked puzzled but stood and asked their names.

"Patricia Baldwin and Gregory Evarts. He's expecting us."

The staffer disappeared behind the closed door of the second room. As he passed through the open door, Evarts saw three more desks crowding the inner office. People sat at two of them. Damn, how would they get any privacy?

When the staffer returned, he apologized and said the congressman would be with them as soon as he finished with another constituent. Then he suggested that before their private tour of the Capitol, perhaps they would like to peruse a book on the history of the building. Evidently, they wouldn't meet with him in his office. Evarts and Baldwin took seats amongst the bustling staffers and pretended to read.

They had taken a chance that Sherman would recognize one of their names and make time for them. Evarts thought it would be better if they didn't appear in his appointment calendar, so they had watched CSPAN until Congress recessed and dropped in unannounced. Unfortunately, he was with a constituent, but it appeared that he would soon be free and had decided to see them.

A half hour passed before Sherman came out. His age surprised Evarts. He guessed that the congressman hadn't yet celebrated his fortieth birthday. Sherman spent a few minutes saying good-bye to a well-dressed couple and then turned his attention to Evarts and Baldwin.

"I'm sorry, that appointment went a bit long." He shook their hands and introduced Baldwin to his staff as the daughter of a major contributor to his campaigns. "Well, are you ready for the tour? If you leave your purse in my office, we can get through security faster."

Baldwin hesitated and then handed her purse over. Evarts guessed it held several thousand dollars, but if you can't trust your congressman, whom can you trust? They had left their guns with Harding at a sidewalk café up the street in a yuppified residential area. Evarts hoped his friend wouldn't overdose on caffeine by the time they had finished their tour.

As they left the office, two U.S. Capitol Police officers joined them. "Since I recently started getting death threats, these two gentlemen have become my shadows," Sherman said. "Seems I upset some people with a speech I made several days ago."

"We read—"

Sherman interrupted Baldwin by saying, "Since 9/11, security has been upgraded. Cameras and microphones everywhere."

Evarts and Baldwin took the hint.

At the elevator, Sherman said, "We'll go to the basement and walk over through the tunnel." He hooked a thumb behind him. "Makes these guys more comfortable."

In the elevator, he told Baldwin how sorry he was to hear about her parents' accident, and he seemed genuinely sympathetic. The elevator opened onto a stark white tunnel that looked utilitarian, except for the children's artwork mounted along the corridor walls. When they got to the security checkpoint, Sherman led them around the line for the parcel inspection and directly through the metal detector.

Sherman carried on an effusive narrative about the history of the Capitol Building, how bills moved through committees, constituent services, and a few jokes that no doubt he used for every tour. As they approached the end of the tunnel, he pointed out a federalist-style wood cabinet that looked completely out of place in the austere corridor that was barren of any other furniture. He told them it contained gas masks.

The five of them crowded into another elevator, with Sherman chattering away like this was a routine visit by the family of a major contributor. When the elevator door opened, the metamorphosis from austerity to elegance took Evarts's breath away. He had been in the Capitol many times but never by this approach. It reminded him of how Gothic cathedrals used dreary low-ceilinged entrances to accentuate the grandeur of the nave. When he saw Sherman's smile, he knew the congressman had seen this effect on countless guests.

They did the standard tour of the House side of the Capitol, and they even sat for a few minutes in the gallery of the House of Representatives. Since Congress wasn't in session, they didn't stay long. They took another elevator, and then Sherman led them down a paneled hallway to a closed office door. "Could you wait here a moment, and I'll check to see if we can tour the Speaker's Office?"

After he returned, he said, "All clear. This is a special treat that I don't get to show every visitor."

When they entered the anteroom, Evarts noticed that the two Capitol Police officers stayed outside. Maybe they would get to meet in a private office after all. Sherman made a perfunctory introduction to the receptionist and then led them into a large conference room. Evarts stopped short when he saw Lincoln portraits and memorabilia on every wall. He almost laughed when he realized the appropriateness of the room, but Sherman led them out the opposite end of the conference room and through a pair of glass doors onto a small patio cantilevered high up on the Capitol structure.

"This is the Speaker's Balcony. You should feel privileged. You should also feel private. No one can eavesdrop on us here."

The balcony gave an elevated view of the Mall with the Washington Monument standing at the end like a giant exclamation point. Evarts wanted to enjoy the view, but he assumed that they didn't have a lot of time.

"We understand you have possession of evidence against the union."

"I do. Do you have the William Evarts documents?"

"We do. At least we have copies. The originals are safe."

"Copies should do." He turned to Baldwin. "Are you prepared to endorse the documents as genuine?"

"How soon?" she asked.

"Three days. I'll release my evidence tomorrow."

"You have a plan?" Evarts asked incredulously.

"I do now. A new one. I was chartered by the Mute Council to help collect and then hold the evidence until I turned it over to Ms. Baldwin, to be released with the historical records. When I never heard from you and saw that the Mute Circle had been murdered, I came up with a new plan. It's already in motion and too late to change."

"What is it?" Evarts asked.

"It started with my speech a few days ago. I accused the Mexican Panther Party of corruption and complicity with drug trafficking. It got the response I wanted."

"You wanted epithets hurled at you?" Baldwin exclaimed.

"Many and often. I'm the lead in every newspaper, talk show, and blog in the country. I've been called a racist, a demagogue, a McCarthyist, and a meddler in foreign affairs. I wanted the hullabaloo to reach a crescendo before I released the evidence."

"So it will get the attention it deserves?" Baldwin asked.

"Precisely, plus the hate mail got protection for me and my family. Without it, I'm sure I would already share the fate of your parents."

"You don't want the historical record released simultaneously?" Evarts asked.

"No. Dilute the impact. Orchestrated properly, we can be the lead story for over a week." He placed a hand on Baldwin's arm. "You should say you happened on these documents a while ago, and you kept them to yourself until you could authenticate them. When you read about my disclosures, you realized the connection and decided to bring your documents forward." He looked them both in the eye. "Publicity is our only salvation. Can you do it?"

"Yes, of course," Baldwin said. "I haven't really had time to authenticate them, but I have no doubts."

"They're genuine, I assure you. You won't be embarrassed."

"What do we do in the meantime?" Evarts asked.

"Keep your head low. These are dangerous people, as you well know." He handed Baldwin a small card. "That's my secure cell phone number, if you need to contact me. Try to use a pay phone."

He looked at his watch. "I don't have much time. I called a press conference so I could give an 'I got a list of fifty-seven names' speech."

"Then after the predictable uproar, unlike McCarthy, you'll publish actual evidence," Evarts said.

"This town loves political theater," the congressman said with a smile.

"Do we have time for a few questions?" Baldwin asked.

"Go."

"Why did the Society keep the Lincoln documents hidden?"

Sherman looked irritated with the question. "Because they're worth tens of millions. We don't have the resources of the union. We held the Lincoln documents in reserve in case we needed funds. Now we're going to raise suspicions if we dally, so do you have any questions about the union or the plan?"

"How is the Mexican election tied to the union?" Evarts asked.

"José Garcia has been a longtime member of the union. He started working for them over thirty years ago as a teller in one of their banks. Someone noticed that Garcia had brains and charisma. They pulled him out and sent him to school. Then at some point, they recruited him into the union, and ever since, he's been groomed for high political office. They got their chance with the ascendancy of the Panther Party."

"Are you saying the Panther Party isn't a union front?" Baldwin asked.

"It is now, but originally it was a run-of-the-mill populist sideshow. The union began backing it about fifteen years ago, when the Panthers started capturing local elections in southern Mexico. They managed to jockey Garcia until he became the standard-bearer for the party. In the three-way election next month, he's sure to win the presidency and control of the Mexican military and police functions."

"Aren't you leaving something out?" Evarts asked.

"Nothing crucial to executing my plan."

"Do you know the Greenes?" Evarts had grown annoyed and tried to keep his voice steady.

"Of course. We're all members of the Mute Council."

"They betrayed the Society," Evarts said.

The congressman gazed out at the Mall. Finally, he said, "We knew someone did. Damn." He kept looking out into the distance. "We haven't heard from our man inside the union since this trouble began. I suppose he's dead now."

"The Greenes told me the union was involved in drugs."

Sherman whipped his head around and gave Evarts a startled look. "You interrogated them?"

"Briefly." Instead of saying more, Evarts just gave the congressman his hard-ass cop stare.

Finally, Sherman said, "I didn't mention that because I was afraid it might scare you off."

"How is the union involved with the drug cartels?" Evarts asked.

"'Involved' is a wimpy word. The union is the power behind the throne. With Garcia in place, they'll rule the drug trade throughout the Americas."

"Which cartel are they aligned with?"

"All of them. At least all the big ones."

"All of them?" Evarts found this hard to believe. "You're not telling me the Mexican cartels cooperate?"

"No, not at an operational level, but they share the services of the union. They have no choice."

"What services? Weapons? Intelligence? Money? Distribution? What could the union possible hold over the cartels?"

"The union doesn't smuggle or distribute drugs. They sell the first three services you mentioned, but only one gives them their leverage over the cartels. Weapons can be bought on the worldwide black market, and officials can be bribed to gain information." Sherman gave Evarts a cunning look. "Money is the weakness the union exploited."

"Laundering?"

"How do you handle $142 billion a year? You need someone to launder it, move it across borders, invest it, and create clean little bundles that can be used for the big-time bribes. Only the union controlled banks and industries on both sides of the border that could disguise cash flows that large."

Evarts thought through the implications. "The union has control over the cartels' money, don't they?"

"Yes. They have custodial possession of billions of dollars."

"But the cartels are dangerous clients. They can turn vicious with the slightest provocation, so the union protects itself with secrecy, don't they? Do the cartels even know they exist?"

"Not by identity, at any rate. But you're right; they rely on anonymity for security. Oh, they have their own mercenaries, but they're no match for the cartels' thugs if they grow angry. That's why my plan might work. Their safety requires that they stay anonymous."

Sherman shifted his gaze between Baldwin and Evarts. "We need to leave this balcony. Any final questions?"

"What's at Lake Norman?" Evarts asked.

The question stopped Sherman. "Not the slightest. Why?"

Evarts ignored him and asked, "What's the name of the leader of the union?"

"We think a man named Branger might run it, but we're not certain."

"I am," Evarts said. "And he's what's at Lake Norman."

Chapter 46

· · · · · ·

Evarts and Baldwin walked east on Pennsylvania Avenue in the direction of the sidewalk café where they had left Harding.

Baldwin took his arm and laughed quietly to herself. "So Branger's at Lake Norman. Aren't you the smart guy?"

"You're not going to rub my nose in that she-man thing, are you? It still smarts."

"An odd choice of words."

"You *are* going to rub it in."

"For years."

"Well, I'm glad to hear you're optimistic about our survival."

"I like Sherman's plan."

Evarts walked a bit before saying, "I have reservations."

"Really? Why?" She seemed surprised.

"The congressman asked if you could do it, but he failed to explain what that entailed."

"What are you talking about?"

"The man is manufacturing a media maelstrom. Pretty competently, I might add. When you go public, you'll be sucked into the vortex. Press conferences, interviews with reporters, talking-head television shows, and you'll be besieged by other academics who will badger you for an early peek at the documents."

"Oh my god, you're right. I hadn't thought it through."

"It means coming out of hiding, which is fine as long as the union runs from the media's intense beam." He walked a few steps. "What worries me is that I don't know how the union will react."

"I know how they should react if they're smart."

"They're smart, so tell me."

"Get a bunch of renowned academics to challenge the meaning, relevance, and authenticity of the documents. Believe me, you can't hold the media's attention with an arcane academic argument."

"Can they do that quickly enough to blunt Sherman's strategy?"

"Have you seen a professor's salary? James Carville once said you'd be surprised what you could pick up if you dragged a hundred dollar bill through a trailer park. Well, try dragging a ten-thousand-dollar bill through any American campus."

"Okay, but what about Sherman's evidence? In truth, you're just a sideshow."

Before Baldwin answered, they saw Harding get up from his little table and walk toward them. Evarts noticed him look back and wave like he was saying good-bye to someone at the café, but he was really checking for activity behind him. When Harding reached them, he gave Evarts a big bear hug to disguise Evarts's reaching inside his friend's waistband to retrieve his SIG automatic.

"Well?" Harding said.

"Back to your place," Evarts said. "We need to do some planning."

On the drive back to Georgetown, Evarts and Baldwin explained their conversation with the congressman. Harding suggested they stop along the way and pick up Chinese food to take back to the house, and Baldwin insisted on buying. Harding scoffed at her, and Evarts thought it bizarre that two rich people would fight over buying a lunch that he could afford. When they entered the strip mall takeout joint, Harding reluctantly conceded that she could buy, but only if she let him order. Evarts made a theatrical groan when she readily agreed.

She smiled. "I know, he eats a lot."

"True, but I'm alarmed because he orders weird."

She looked at Harding. He winked and said, "Deal's a deal."

Evarts enjoyed her expression as Harding ordered dish after dish. Puzzled, she stepped back to get a clear view of the huge menu that hung above the counter. As Harding continued to order, she tapped him on the shoulder. He paused, faced her, and said, "Yes?"

She pointed up. "I don't see those items on the menu."

He looked up as if seeing the menu for the very first time. "That's for tourists," he said dismissively.

"I'm picky about what I eat," she said.

"I'm ordering over a dozen dishes. You'll find something to your liking." He shrugged. "If not, there's always rice."

"What was that last dish you ordered?"

"Chicken feet. They have a different menu for Chinese customers. You'll enjoy the pig's throat."

"Order lots of white rice," she said with a smile that acknowledged that she had been had.

Harding tuned back to the counterman and said, "Three orders of fried rice."

"You bastard," she laughed.

"Live a little. Try things the way nature intended. God made sugared soda pop, red meat, and beer. He drinks his tea hot and his wine red, and he made lettuce for rabbits."

Baldwin turned to Evarts. "Excuse me for ever thinking of you as an unreconstructed cowboy."

"You thought I was a cowboy?"

"You lamebrain," Harding said. "All women think we're good-for-only-one-thing retrogrades who behave like fifth graders on our first unsupervised recess. Hell, they see us as buffoons with our heads in a refrigerator and our ears tuned to a televised game. You don't think they build televisions into refrigerators for women do you?"

"That act work well with women?" she asked.

He laughed. "I get my share of dates."

"Really? Do you think it's because of your impeccable manners? No wonder you're not married."

That stopped conversation cold. Harding picked up one bag and shoved it in Evarts's arms, grabbed the other bag, and headed out the door.

Baldwin gave Evarts a questioning look, so he explained, "His wife died two years ago from breast cancer." He looked at his friend's back. "I never saw two people more in love or any husband who so readily accepted his lot as caregiver. He was by her side constantly at the end."

"Oh my god." She rushed after Harding. When she caught up, she put a hand on his arm to stop his progress. "I'm sorry. Greg never told me. I thought we were just roughhouse bantering. Please?"

"Forget it. You had no way of knowing. And you're right; it's an act. I like to shock people and sometimes I go too far." He hugged her shoulder with his free arm. "But give these dishes a chance. Despite its appearance, that's a damn fine takeout joint. Authentic as hell."

Evarts kept a couple paces behind them and let them talk as they walked toward the car. He wanted these people to like each other. He heard her say, "When will you quit surprising me?"

He laughed good-naturedly. "Tomorrow morning I promise to be perfectly predictable."

"And the rest of the day?"

He hefted the bag up and grinned. "That depends entirely on my mood."

Chapter 47

· · · · · ·

Baldwin had eaten delicately, but she had tried almost every dish. Evarts guessed she was still hungry because she had barely touched the fried rice. When they had rid the table of all the little white boxes and dirty dishes, Evarts pulled out the materials they had removed from the DTCC and shoved them over toward Harding.

After perusing the documents for a half hour, Harding said, "You can't just dump this thick stack of paper onto some innocent reporter's desk. You need a press release to go along with them."

"A press release?" Baldwin asked, a bit surprised. "Really?"

"Yeah, you gotta package news nowadays. Write a press release that tells the story the way you want it to read on the front page. Otherwise, the lazy will ignore you, and the industrious will study the material. A good reporter might take days to figure out the lead."

She looked at the large stack of documents and sighed. "How long?"

"Time?" Harding look puzzled.

"No. How long is a good press release?"

"No more than two pages. You don't want an academic synopsis, you ... well, to put it bluntly, you're handing the news media the spin you want."

"I'm not sure I can do that," Baldwin said.

Evarts decided this had gone on long enough. "I know someone who can write your press release, someone Colin Powell called the best military flack in the business."

"Who?" Baldwin asked.

Evarts pointed with the flat of his hand. "May I introduce you to Mr. Steve Harding."

"You? You scoundrel. I ate your damn food. I thought you promised no more surprises." She stood, arms akimbo. "Next, you're going to tell me that when they sent you on black bag jobs, you went undercover as a ballerina."

"Nope, wildcatter. I kept asking to be a ballerina, but the big boys had me typecast. I sure wanted to be backstage with limber women. Instead they kept sending me to godforsaken deserts to live with a bunch of putrid-smelling louts."

She tapped the stack of paper. "How long will it take you to write a press release?"

"Us … and it might take all night, maybe more to get it right. If we made it ten pages, we could probably finish in a couple hours, but a terse, carefully crafted message takes time."

He looked at Evarts. "To get this process rolling, Greg can run over to Kinko's and make twenty copies of the whole package. We tell our newspaper of choice that it has only a one-day head start before we blanket the major dailies with this stuff. That'll build a fire under their abundant posteriors. While your boyfriend's gone, you can give me the general gist, and we'll talk through various ways to dress this scandal so it makes the right people quake in their tasseled loafers." He winked. "Unless you and Greg are really just friends—then other possibilities come to mind."

She turned to Evarts. "Please hurry," she said in mock panic.

Evarts looked over the material they had brought out of the DTCC and separated the paper into three stacks: the encoded pages, the William Evarts documents, and the two original documents. He only intended to make twenty copies of the Evarts evidence, but that still comprised over two hundred pages. He would be gone awhile. Before Evarts left the townhouse, he had an inspiration and grabbed one of the two original manuscripts.

He found the Kinko's near Georgetown University bustling with students, faculty, and work-at-home professionals. After flagging down a harried store employee, Evarts secured an empty box that had previously contained ten reams of copier paper. He next stood in line and eventually got control of a self-service copier. For an hour, he told people who lined up behind him that he had a big job, but instead of a thank you, all he received was a series of irritated "how dare you" looks. When he finished, he hefted the now nearly full box and stood in another line for counter service.

After he made it to the front, he asked the attendant, "How much do you charge for data entry service?"

"A dollar per forty-five words."

He slid the original William Evarts document across the counter. "This is a historical document. Can I trust you with it?"

"We handle all kinds of valuable papers, and we've never lost a single one."

"Never?"

"Never. We do copy and transcription work for professors with years invested in their books and for attorneys working on Supreme Court cases. We don't lose material left in our charge."

"What if I get called away and can't get back right away? I travel a lot."

"We'll keep your work for a year, but we can also mail it to you anywhere in the world."

"Okay, please instruct the typist not to eat or drink while she works on this."

After Evarts filled out the worksheet and turned to leave, he received more irritated "how dare you" looks from the people in line behind him. He didn't blame them. He thought people insufferable who hogged the counter once they got to the front of a line.

By the time he made it back to the townhouse, he had been gone for over two hours. Baldwin and Harding sat at a table tucked into the bay window that overlooked the rear garden. They continued to pore over notes and both gave him a perfunctory greeting. Evarts set the heavy box down on the counter, pulled out a banded copy of the documents, and slid it onto the table in the breakfast nook.

"Two copies, please," Baldwin said.

Evarts slid another one onto the table and took a seat. They talked about strategies, tactics, and nuances until he grew tired of trying to catch up and went to the refrigerator for water. As he twisted off the top, he heard Baldwin say, "We don't want to dilute the focus on Branger."

"You found a Branger connection?" Evarts asked.

"Sort of," Baldwin answered. "I found a Charles Branger mentioned in the Evarts files. William Evarts had identified him as one of the ringleaders. With a little web research, we discovered that a Ralph Branger lives near Charlotte and is currently the chairman of a corporation founded right after the Civil War."

"Public or private corporation?" Evarts asked.

"Private and closely held. Family only," Harding answered. "Not real big. Sales around eighty million. The company makes furniture under a number of different brands, and as far as we can tell, they manufacture only in the U.S. and Taiwan. No Mexican operations listed. From our Internet research, it looks completely legit, and it certainly doesn't have the financial heft the union supposedly wields."

"Could be a cover. Most of the union enterprises are supposedly covert. What have you learned about this Ralph Branger?"

"An enigma. Very little information about him."

"So beside the fact that he runs an old business possibly started by a charter member of the union, what makes you suspicious of him?"

"Only one thing," Baldwin said. "The corporation, Dixie Furnishings Company, has been headquartered in Charlotte for a hundred and thirty years."

"Charlotte?" Evarts said. "North or South Carolina? I forget."

Baldwin did a truly awful imitation of a Southern belle. "Oh goodness, you men do need us womenfolk. My dear, Charlotte is in North Carolina, right next to Lake Norman."

Chapter 48

· · · · · ·

While Baldwin and Harding continued to work on the press release, Evarts checked the television to see how the news played Congressman Sherman's earlier press conference. In a few minutes, he called them in to witness the carnage. He flipped back and forth between CNN and Fox. Both news networks were having a field day. The anchors almost gleefully reported that a bigoted congressman had made ridiculous accusations against all Hispanics and against Mexicans in particular. With little else newsworthy going on, the networks filled the screen with smug talking heads who compared Congressman Sherman to Senator McCarthy. To drive the point even deeper, the stations frequently flashed up a still photograph of the congressman with his lips curled in a vicious snarl. Having just left the amicable man, Evarts wondered where both news channels had found the identical photograph.

"That's your ally?" Harding asked.

Baldwin laughed. "He's friendlier looking in person. He wants all this negative coverage so that when he releases the evidence tomorrow, the networks will have already made the story the cause célèbre of the moment."

"What did he say in the press conference?" Harding asked.

"They've shown only clips, but I gather he accused José Garcia and the Panther Party of being in the pocket of drug lords," Evarts explained. "I've heard no mention of an American involvement. He said he has names, but when asked, he made some evasive remarks about releasing evidence later."

Harding whistled. "No wonder they're comparing him to Joseph McCarthy. He's playing a dangerous game. They may vilify him beyond redemption."

"I hope he knows what he's doing," Evarts said. "Not one news commentator has even hinted that there might be a smidgen of validity to his charge of a corrupted general election in Mexico."

Harding shook his head. "In this narcissistic town, you try to never piss off the bureaucracy, and he must have made the State Department livid. They don't like mere congressmen creating foreign crises."

Evarts pushed the power-off button on the remote. "It's all the same. We better get to work." He turned to Baldwin. "I've hidden my original document. You might think about where you can stash yours."

She looked at the darkened screen, apparently lost in thought. When she spoke, her tone said she had made up her mind. "I'm taking mine to a professor at Georgetown. After watching this, I want the backing of a second opinion from someone with academic standing."

"Damn it." Evarts knew he should have anticipated that one of the documents would go to a professional for authentication. "I didn't think this through. We should've taken three documents out of the DTCC."

"You can't anticipate everything, and I can always go collect as many documents as we need. While we work on the press release, could you decode some of those encrypted messages? I want to use them to whet the appetite of this professor."

"Do you have someone in mind?"

She smiled. "Oh yeah. He tried to pick me up at a conference last year."

As Harding expertly prepared a late dinner, Evarts started decoding the pages of numbers. By the time they retired to the front sitting room with port and scotch, it was near midnight. Evarts took a small pillow from the couch and held it up in the air with a questioning look. Harding gave him permission with a nod, and Evarts placed the pillow strategically on the coffee table so that he could put his feet up as he had on many occasions in this house.

"How are you doing with that press release?" Evarts asked.

"Mostly wordsmithing left." Baldwin pointed at Harding. "Colin Powell was right about your friend here. An academic would never write such an alarmist first paragraph, but it'll grab the attention of any reporter. In less than sixty words, Steve laid out a vile conspiracy that threatens the democratic institutions of two nations. The rest of the release uses the documentation to tie several financial enterprises together, hints ominously about participation in drug trafficking, and implicates the most prominent families mentioned in the William Evarts papers. We mention the Branger family but don't specifically call out Ralph Branger."

"Good idea," Evarts said. "We have only weak circumstantial evidence. In fact, the whole case looks weak from this side. I sure hope Congressman Sherman has the goods on these people."

"He must," she said. "We're just supposed to be backup. What did you find in the decoded messages?"

"A very circumspect man." Evarts handed her his transcriptions. "I've only completed three, but my take is that Lincoln was in communication with a prominent abolitionist, probably in New York, and the series of messages represented a political cat and mouse game. We have only the New York side of the exchange, but the repeated requests to put abolitionists in the cabinet leads me to believe he never made the promise. My guess is that Lincoln wanted to enlist the support from Radical Republicans without committing himself to a particular course of action."

"That sounds like my Lincoln." She scanned the papers Evarts handed her and said, "This may not look like much to you, but these few pages will probably support three or four doctoral theses. Lincoln avoided hard promises, but he frequently insinuated agreement and then followed through unless circumstances changed. He always wanted an emergency escape route."

She read the sheets again and seemed to be talking to herself when she added, "He did appoint Chase and Seward to the cabinet, both ardent abolitionists." Then in a clearer voice, she said, "I know one thing—they'll certainly make my lecherous colleague at Georgetown drool."

Evarts turned to more practical matters. "Steve, what kind of weapons do you have in the house?"

Harding touched the .45 on the table beside him. "This is it, my friend."

"Do you keep in touch with any of the old gang?"

"Once or twice a year for beers. None are in the business anymore. Gary drives the NASCAR circuit now." Harding bounced out of the chair. "Shit! Gary lives in Charlotte. Maybe he can reconnoiter for us."

"Call him."

"It's the middle of the night."

Evarts gave him a look. Harding shrugged and left the room. He returned a few moments later with his cell phone in hand, scanning the directory. He plopped back into his easy chair and said, "His races are televised. Do you watch them?"

Evarts felt a pang of guilt. "Not often. I'm usually out of the house on Sunday afternoons."

"Yeah, right. And you don't have TiVo or even an obsolete video recorder."

"I watched a few times when he first made the circuit, and I checked the newspapers to see how he did, but I never could get into car racing." He actually hated car racing, but he thought it better to keep that opinion to himself. Surfers and car-crazed inlanders never got along, and if he was honest with himself, he probably had carried the unwarranted prejudice into adulthood.

Harding held the phone up. "It's ringing. Just so you'll know, he's seventh place in points."

Harding put the phone on speaker and Evarts heard, "Hello."

"Gary, this is Steve and Greg. Where are you?"

"In my rec room playing pool. How the hell are you guys?"

Evarts cut in. "Bit of a bind, but we need to talk in private."

"Hold on." After a pause, they heard a door close. "Okay, shoot."

"Do you have a landline we can call you back on?"

"Yeah." He gave them another telephone number.

"Ten minutes or so. We need to get to a pay phone."

"What's with all this cloak-and-dagger shit? You *do* know I race cars now."

"And I'm a police detective and Steve's a bum. We all have new professions. We just need some confidential advice."

"How confidential?"

Evarts hesitated. "This is life and death."

"Then I'll switch from beer to coffee and send these guys home. They were cleaning my clock anyway."

Harding closed the cell phone. "You go. Someone needs to stay with Trish."

Evarts considered all three of them going and decided that was foolhardy. "Where's the closest pay phone?"

"Use my car and drive twenty miles west. There's a persistent rumor that computers monitor every pay phone in the D.C. area. Use a prepaid calling card."

"Got one." Evarts bolted from the house and drove for forty minutes before he pulled into a strip mall. Gary Johnson answered his phone after the first ring.

"Gary, this is Greg. I need help."

"Police work, old business, or new trouble?"

"New. First, do you know Lake Norman?"

"I'm standing here looking at it. At least, I would be if it wasn't dark."

"You live on Lake Norman?"

"Most of the drivers do. Why?"

"Ever heard of a man named Ralph Branger?"

"Yeah, but we move in different circles. He's kind of a mystery man. I've only heard about him because he got into a row with the county over this *Gone with the Wind* style mansion he wanted to build on an outcrop that extends into the lake. Made the local paper, but he must have found the right politician to bribe because he built the damn thing. Big eyesore, in my opinion."

"Can you find out everything you can about him?"

"Surveillance or public records?"

"Public records only...at least for now."

"Okay. I got a couple days. I guess I owe you a favor or two."

"Be careful. If Branger's connected the way I think he is, he's dangerous. Drugs and other bad stuff. He won't take kindly to someone snooping around his personal life."

"I'm always careful. Probably why I haven't won but one race so far this season."

"By the way, congratulations on being seventh in points."

"Thanks. I'll send you some race tickets."

Chapter 49

. . . . . .

The morning news said that Congressman Sherman had called another press conference for ten o'clock in the morning. Evarts and Harding cooked a breakfast of eggs, bacon, potatoes, and toast. Baldwin ate half a cantaloupe and a dry double-toasted English muffin. By the time they finished the dishes and scanned the newspaper, it was close to ten o'clock, so they turned on the television in a small side room off the kitchen.

The preshow continued the attacks on Congressman Sherman and worked to set a high bar in case he actually did offer evidence to support his allegations. When the congressman appeared on the screen, he looked nervous and out of sorts.

"Gentlemen and ladies of the press, this will be a short press conference. Reasonable questions about what I'm about to deliver will be entertained. I stress the word 'reasonable.'"

He looked down at some cards he held in his hand. "Yesterday, I made some startling criticisms of the upcoming election in Mexico. I accused the Panther Party of being implicated with international drug trafficking. Today I'll present evidence supporting my allegations."

Evarts could hear a buzz from the off-camera press, and someone shouted, "Will we get a copy of the evidence?"

"Yes. At the conclusion of my remarks, copies will be distributed to all of you. But first, I want to address the slanderous accusations that I'm motivated by racism. I'll show that the corruption of the Panther Party emanates from these United States. That the real villains—"

The uproar from the press drowned out the rest of his sentence. Everybody shouted at once.

Evarts said, "He's lost control."

Sherman made an angry face that the press would surely plaster all over the media if he didn't present an ironclad case.

"May I continue," he said in a rough voice. "I'll answer reasonable questions at the end."

The press wouldn't relent, so he defiantly stood and waited until they quieted down enough for him to continue.

"Thank you. The documentation I'll distribute shows a financial trail that goes back to the nineteen twenties. A secret society—"

A chorus of groans came from offscreen.

"Excuse me, please! May I finish?"

Someone shouted, "Go ahead!"

"The secret society is called the union, spelled with a lowercase *u*. This secret organization has been in existence for over one hundred years and controls a fortune almost beyond comprehension."

This time laughter interrupted the congressman, but he pushed ahead.

"This secret cabal looted its original money during Reconstruction after the Civil War. In the nineteen seventies, they started to support the drug traffic trade, using their strategic investments in Mexico. Although controlled by Americans, the union has reached such dominance in Mexico that they now threaten to put their man into the presidency and control a sovereign nation."

Offscreen shouting erupted again. "Put your hands down," the congressman said. "I'll answer questions only at the end. Please. This is serious."

Sherman reached behind him and took a spiral-bound binder from an embarrassed-looking staffer. He held it above his head. "This document delineates financial transactions between six American corporations and key Mexican companies. In the early part of the last century, money flowed south, but since the eighties, great amounts of cash flowed north into the coffers of companies right here in the United States."

"That's called capitalism, Congressman!"

"Of the most vile sort. These money sums are far too large to come from legitimate sources. They came from drug cartels."

"Can you prove it?"

"Circumstantially. The amount—"

Laughter.

"The amount of money far outstrips the profits from these Mexican corporations. I'm talking about hundreds of millions of dollars annually. The union controls huge private companies on both sides of the border and uses them to launder drug money."

"Is this the same secret society that killed JFK?"

"No, but possibly Abraham Lincoln."

Huge laughter. That rejoinder had been an obvious mistake. Now they had him tagged for certain as a kook.

"What companies?" someone shouted.

"They're private and keep a low profile; however, one is an investment bank that *Forbes* ranks as number four in their list of the largest private companies."

"Name?" many shouted.

"Confederated Trust."

"Oh shit," Harding said. "That's an American business icon."

The incredulous reaction of the press resulted in more shouted questions. They wouldn't quiet down this time. Sherman gave his staffer a discouraged look and indicated he should pass out the spiralbinders.

"Questions. One at a time."

He had to wait several minutes until the confusion caused by passing out the binders subsided, and the reporters settled back into some semblance of order. Eventually, the congressman pointed to an uplifted hand.

"Mr. J. C. D. McGuire is chairman of Confederated Trust. Are you accusing him of heading up this so-called union?"

"We know he *does not* lead the union, but we also know he is a direct descendant of one of the families that plundered the South during Reconstruction and formed the union during Grant's administration." The congressman hesitated, and then gave a "what the hell" shrug. "We do believe J. C. D. McGuire is among the top echelon of the union."

The resulting blast of shouted questions made the other eruptions seem mild. "Are you prepared for a slander suit?" someone shouted without recognition.

"Is he prepared to explain the financial transfers listed in those binders?"

A barrage of questions followed, and then somebody actually tossed one of the binders at Sherman's feet, and it skidded across the platform. He looked down at it and immediately marched out of the briefing room.

"Damn it. Is that all he's got?" Evarts said.

"Maybe there's something more in those binders," Baldwin said hopefully.

"I doubt it," Harding said. "If there were, he would've beaten those assholes over the head with it."

An anchor desk replaced the raucous briefing room, and the bespectacled woman opened by saying, "Congressman Sherman from Ohio just made the outrageous accusation that J. C. D. McGuire, a respected businessman and generous philanthropist, is involved with a secret group of drug runners that Congressman Sherman claims controls the Mexican Panther Party and their presidential candidate, José Garcia."

Suddenly the televised picture split into four quadrants, with a face in each. The anchor, in the upper left window, introduced the three talking heads shown in the split screens and then said, "Let's ask our panel if the House will censure Congressman Sherman and whether his career can recover from this embarrassing episode."

Evarts turned the television to mute and asked Baldwin for the congressman's cell number. As she got it from her purse, Harding picked up the remote and turned on English subtitles. From what Evarts could read, the panel assassinated the congressman politically.

"Use my cell, not the landline," Harding said.

Evarts nodded, knowing that if they monitored Sherman's cell, a landline would be quicker to trace. The congressman answered in one ring. "Yes?"

"Gregory Evarts."

"I'm busy."

"Goddamn it, this'll only take a second. If that's all you've got, I'm not going to allow Patricia Baldwin to expose herself."

"Are you sure that she'll agree with that decision?"

"What do mean?"

"Your family shunned us. Patricia's family has paid the ultimate price in this war. She may be differently motivated."

"Have you seen the way the news channels are playing your press conference?"

"I would if I wasn't talking to you. This is a three-act play. The climax always comes in the third act. Ask Patricia to release the William Evarts papers tomorrow."

"I've seen the documents. What possible corroboration can they provide?"

"I won't say any more on this telephone."

"Then good-bye. We're outta here."

"Hold it. The William Evarts documents confirm the existence of the union in the late nineteenth century, and they also tie the current CEOs of all six corporations to that organization. Every last one of them is a direct descendant of an indictable figure in those dossiers."

Chapter 50

· · · · · ·

Evarts described his conversation with the congressman and then asked Harding, "Is that enough? Will it swing the media over to our side? All we have are some questionable financial transfers to six corporations led by men whose ancestors plundered the South after the Civil War."

"Hard to tell," he answered. "The congressman had a good strategy, but I think he underestimated the pack mentality of the press." Harding looked at the still-muted television set. "I wish I could see one of those spiral-binders." He nodded toward the press release he and Baldwin had been editing. "That's an art form. A black art, perhaps, but an art form, nonetheless. I sure hope the congressman had a good spinmeister."

"I'm going to get one of those binders," Evarts headed toward the door.

"You mean right now?" Baldwin asked.

"Yeah, right now. Before you become a media sensation, we need to know if this plan has a chance in hell."

"Greg, is this wise? They'll put it on the Internet soon."

He walked back toward Baldwin. "Sherman wants you to release your documents tomorrow. That means we need to make the decision tonight."

"I've already made—"

"Wait. Don't decide yet. I'll use the subway. I can be back in less than two hours. Steve can give us his view of the evidence, and the evening talk shows will give us a better handle on how this'll play out in the media."

"Greg, I've—" She stopped. After a moment, she smiled, leaned forward, and kissed his cheek. "Okay. Hurry but don't take any chances."

As Evarts walked to the subway, he called Congressman Sherman using Harding's cell phone. He asked to have three of the binders left at the security desk of the Cannon Building. Sherman sounded relieved that he wouldn't have to meet with Evarts and promised to have the binders ready for him. Not having to pass through building security and go up to the Congressman's office would save Evarts at least half an hour.

He actually made the round trip in under an hour and a half. On the subway back, he glanced through most of the binder. Without preamble, the document listed an array of financial transactions woven intricately into an impressive web. Evarts's concern was that few of the reporters would take the time to comprehend them. The second section showed how these transactions tied the six American corporations to the Mexican companies in a tightly integrated coalition. Sherman had built a great legal brief, but Evarts guessed it wouldn't supply the kind of sound bites and headlines the media needed to grab the attention of an audience afflicted with attention deficit disorder. The problem, as Evarts saw it, was that the media train had already left the station with scheduled stops at bigotry, dim-wittedness, and lunacy. They meant to destroy Congressman Sherman because he had the audacity to criticize a neighboring country they wished to pretend posed no threat. He feared that the introduction of facts couldn't derail this speeding train. Passion, rather than logic, often drove public discourse.

Evarts opened the front door and yelled out that he was back. No response. He quickened his pace through the hall and into the kitchen in back. No one. He ran up the stairs and checked the bedrooms. Still no one. Where the hell were they? He reentered the guestroom that he and Baldwin had been using and saw no clues as to her whereabouts. He checked the hall bath and saw nothing unusual. He had started down the stairs but suddenly reversed course and ran back to the bathroom. Everything was neat and tidy except for a tiny bottle of dry-wash antibacterial soap that sat in the center of the tile counter. Baldwin always took the hand soap with her to the gym. Maybe she pulled it out of the cabinet and then forgot to throw it in her gym bag. He ran into the bedroom and pulled dresser drawers open until he confirmed that her workout clothes were missing.

He had taken Harding's cell phone with him to the congressman's office, so he pulled it out and ran through the directory until he reached G. He quickly found the telephone number for Harding's gym and pressed the call button. In two rings, a receptionist answered, "Capital Fitness."

"Can you tell me if Steve Harding is at the gym? We were supposed to work out together, but I forgot what time I was to meet him."

"Just a second … yes, he arrived almost an hour ago with a guest."

Evarts felt more relief than he could have imagined. Damn them, they should have at least left him a note. "Thanks, can you give me directions?"

Evarts ended the call and decided he needed exercise, so he would run the six blocks to the gym. After he changed into shorts, tee shirt, and running shoes, he searched until he found a small backpack. He stuffed a towel, bottle of water, and his gun into the bag and slung it over one shoulder by a single strap. This arrangement might be uncomfortable while running, but he could never reach his gun if he needed it with both arms through the straps. Before leaving the house, he wrote a brief note, partly to let them know where he had gone in case he missed them, but mostly so he could be righteously indignant that they had left no note for him.

It took him about ten minutes to make the short run. The gym lobby included a full-circle wood counter enclosing three perfect bodies who handled customer requests and complaints. The twenty-something female greeter wore a beauty-queen smile designed to convince any male walking through the door that he had to join the gym that very day.

Evarts leaned against the counter. "I called earlier. Is Steve Harding still in the gym?"

"I don't know. We only scan customer membership cards on the way in."

The gym was open behind the circular counter, but Evarts didn't spot Harding or Baldwin. "May I walk around to look for them?"

"I'm sorry, but Capital Fitness is restricted to members and guests escorted by a member." The smile spreading across her face was so wide, it seemed her molars might show. "If you're considering joining our gym, I can have someone give you a tour."

Evarts smiled back. "Did I fail to mention that I was here for that very reason?"

She shoved a three-by-five card at him that probably earned her a two-dollar incentive. "I'll go get a trainer while you fill out this information card."

By the time she had brought back a trainer, Evarts had written some bogus contact information on the card. The gym had dressed the male trainer in a blue Capital Fitness polo shirt with sleeves cut so short and tight that they barely stretched over his Herculean biceps. He flashed a handsome smile that would have gotten him instantly hired at the hamburger emporium in Westwood Village.

"I can see that you work out. Let me show you why Capital Fitness won the Readers' Choice award from *The Improper Washingtonian*."

Evarts kept the trainer moving quickly by not asking any questions. Although he constantly searched for Harding and Baldwin, he never saw them. If they were still in the gym, they had to be in the locker rooms. He took a quick peek through the men's locker room and saw no sign of Harding. Damn, they must be back at the house already.

Evarts pretended to get a phone call, telling the trainer he had set his cell on vibrate. He walked out the front door, cell phone in hand, and called Harding's home landline. No answer. Where the hell could they be?

He walked back into the gym. "Excuse me, I forgot to ask about parking."

"All members get twenty percent off at the lot across the street and up one block." She pointed further up the street.

What she called a lot was actually a four-story parking structure. Evarts jogged up the ramps until he reached the fourth level. He had just turned the corner when he spotted Harding's white Lincoln Navigator. What he saw next caused him to swing the backpack free of his shoulder and put his hand inside to grip his gun. He checked left and right but saw nobody. He dropped prone and checked for feet visible under cars but again, nothing.

Rising to his feet, he returned his attention to Harding's vehicle. He hadn't been mistaken. Someone sat slumped over in the driver's seat. He approached carefully, his hand still on the gun inside the backpack. When he got closer, he was sure the body belonged to Harding. He took another quick look around and opened the driver's door.

As the door swung open, Evarts used his hip to keep Harding from falling to the ground. Keeping an eye on the garage, he pressed two fingers to his friend's throat and got a pulse—a very quiet pulse but a pulse nonetheless.

He would have felt more relief if he had not already scanned the rest of the car's interior. Baldwin was gone.

Chapter 51

· · · · · ·

Steve Harding had been drugged, evidently a weapon of choice for the union. Hurrying around the Navigator, Evarts struggled to get him into the passenger seat. He yanked Harding's legs around the center console and grabbed his shirtfront with both hands, pulling with all the strength he could muster, until Harding was positioned in the seat. He then leaned his friend's head out the door, pried open his mouth, and put his finger down his throat, forcing him to throw up. When Harding produced nothing but dry heaves, Evarts pushed him upright in the seat and closed the passenger door against his inert body. As he ran around the Navigator to get behind the wheel, he wondered how he would get Harding into the house. He exercised regularly, but his friend had to weigh over two hundred and fifty pounds.

Pulling out of the parking structure, he lowered the passenger window, causing Harding's head to flop outside like a dog excitedly taking in all the new scents. Evarts grabbed his shirtfront again and hauled him back inside the car. He doubted that the streaming air would revive him, but since Harding seemed to balance almost upright, he kept the window open.

Evarts grappled with the backpack until he got his hands around the bottle of water he had stuffed in it before he left the townhouse. It still felt cold from the refrigerator as he twisted off the plastic cap and poured the entire bottle over Harding's head. No response. By this time, he had arrived at the house and found a parking spot for residents less than a block away. What should he do? Harding appeared far more drugged than Baldwin had been. It could be hours before he started to come around. Evarts considered leaving him in the car to sleep it off, but until he could find out what had happened, he couldn't start looking for Baldwin. Suddenly he realized they might be looking for him. He had been so upset that they had grabbed her, he had forgotten about his own safety. He couldn't help her if he didn't start acting like a professional.

He immediately turned the ignition and drove away from the townhouse. He circled the block twice but saw no one lurking in a vehicle or on the street. They could be waiting inside the townhouse to ambush him, but they would have taken Baldwin to a different location. Besides, entering the house alone would be foolhardy. He needed Harding. Pulling into a supermarket, he found a parking spot away from other cars and reached for Harding's cell phone. He scrolled through the directory, looking for names he recognized. There were many. With each, he pressed the view button and dismissed anyone with an area code outside the district. He soon found his man and touched the green call button. It took six rings before Rick Matthews answered.

"Rick, this is Greg Evarts. Steve Harding and I need your help. Now."

"Where are you?" his old army buddy asked.

"Georgetown."

"I'm in Alexandria. I'll be there in half an hour."

"No. We'll come to you ... Rick, this is life and death."

"What ... never mind, do you have pen and paper?"

"Just give me the address." After he did, Evarts added, "Meet us at the curb, a white Lincoln Navigator. I'll need your help moving Steve."

Evarts cut off the call, started the engine, and wheeled out of the parking lot. He tried to think straight, but his anger got in the way. Damn. Why had he left Trish alone? Why had he been so stupid as to stay at a former address, even one that had never been documented as his residence? He stole a glance at Harding. Damn him. Why had Harding taken her out of the house? And how the hell was he going to get her back?

He drove a hairbreadth below reckless and pulled up to the apartment building in less than twenty minutes. Because he had ended the call so abruptly, Matthews was already standing in front of the building. Evarts pulled the big SUV alongside the curb in front of the fit-looking black man.

"Parking?" Evarts asked through the passenger window that he had left opened.

Matthews waved a remote. "Underground." He leaped into the backseat and immediately put two fingers on Harding's throat. Feeling a pulse, Matthews leaned forward and quickly examined Harding's body. Next, he cradled Harding's head in his palm and rocked it back and forth. "Drugged?"

"Yes. Hit the remote." Evarts had pulled down a steep driveway, his progress stopped by a white wrought-iron gate. Before he had completed the sentence, the big gate started to roll slowly to the side. Matthews directed him to a visitor spot next to an elevator.

The two of them each grabbed an arm and hauled Harding into the elevator. He seemed to breathe normally but didn't respond to their manhandling. When they finally got his limp body inside the small apartment, they eased him down to the carpeting.

"What happened?" Matthews asked.

"Not sure. We need to revive him to find out."

Without another word, they each grabbed an arm and dragged him into the bathroom. They struggled, lifting him up enough to get his bulky body into the narrow shower stall. Once inside, they just let him collapse into a sitting position.

"How long since he took the drug?" Matthews asked.

"My guess would be about an hour."

"He's out like a light. I think it's too early for cold water to do much good."

Evarts looked at Harding and reluctantly agreed. He wasn't going to come around soon. "Whoever did this kidnapped my girlfriend, and they're a nasty bunch." Evarts slammed the wall with the flat of his hand hard enough to leave an indentation. "Damn it to hell!"

"Come on," Matthews said. "Let's get the coffee going, and you can tell me what you know."

By the time they had started the coffee brewing and made ice packs with ziplock sandwich bags, Evarts had explained the broad outlines of the conspiracy and the abduction of Patricia Baldwin. Matthews said he would find the whole story fantastic were it not for the public rhubarb over the charges by Congressman Sherman.

When they returned to the bathroom, Harding hadn't moved. Impatient, Evarts turned on the cold water but got no movement.

"He's really out," Matthews said, after trying the ice packs under his armpits.

"Any ideas?"

"Only one you won't like. Give him time to sleep it off."

"Damn it, I don't have time. Let's try a shock treatment."

"That could be dangerous."

Instead of arguing, Evarts opened drawers until he found a hair dryer. In the kitchen, he used a kitchen knife to cut off the cord close to the appliance and then stripped the wire. When he reentered the bathroom, Matthews still had the cold water running to no avail. Evarts plugged the socket into the wall and approached Harding with the cord.

"Stand back," he ordered. Evarts barely touched the bare wire to Harding's wet leg, but he convulsed spasmodically. When he flicked the wire against Harding's arm, he heard Harding take a deep intake of breath. Evarts stood back with the cold water still running and watched. Soon Harding shivered involuntarily and kicked one leg. "Okay, let's get him up."

It took forty minutes of assisted pacing, alternated with hot and cold showers, before Harding could get down a sip of coffee. After another thirty minutes, he became coherent enough that they let him indulge in a hot shower until he quit shivering. After the shower, they stripped off his wet gym clothes and wrapped him in a big terry robe. In the kitchen, they made him pace while he sipped exceptionally strong coffee.

His first question was, "How long?"

"Over two hours since I found you."

Harding looked at his watch and shook his head. "Can't focus."

"Keep walking," Matthews ordered.

After another five minutes, Harding asked, "Trish?"

"Gone. They took her," Evarts said.

"Oh, damn." Harding sat with a dejected expression, but as soon as his butt hit the seat, he bounced up and continued pacing.

"Can you tell us what happened?" Evarts asked.

At least a full minute passed. Evarts began to think the question hadn't registered.

"She started her routine on the abs lounger, and I went to the weights. When I moved to the bench press, two gym rats offered to second me. My water bottle was on the floor behind and one of them must have slipped something into it while the other helped me with the barbell." He continued to walk back and forth in the small kitchen. "I began to feel woozy and told Trish we had to leave. After getting to the car, I don't remember a thing."

"Would you recognize them again?"

"You bet. When I was on the bench press, I looked right up into their faces."

Evarts couldn't think of a plan of action. Until now, he had been focused on reviving Harding enough that he could explain what had happened. Now that he knew, it didn't help. Should they go back to Harding's house? To what purpose? The union wanted the documents, so hopefully they would keep her alive to gain access to the DTCC. Should he plan an operation to intercept them in New York? Was there a way to find her before New York?

He finally thought about the question he had been avoiding. How long could she last under interrogation? She had a stubborn streak and a strong ego, but they got everything out of Abraham Douglass, who was equally smart and self-assured. They had also needed only an afternoon to break Douglass. The union had a predilection for drugs that could tear down a person's defenses. Combined with physical torture, it wouldn't take long. Evarts's army training had included simulated interrogations. Only the line of inquiry was simulated, not the drugs or techniques. Although he had hated the exercises at the time, he realized that the training had saved his life when he was able to recognize the early symptoms the Greenes' drugs had produced. The experience also probably helped him and Harding recover faster than if they had never been subjected to the treatment. Baldwin had some experience, both at the hands of the Greenes and with recreational drugs. Evarts bet she would buy them a little time but not much.

Evarts grabbed Matthews's elbow and led him into the living room. "Rick, are you willing to help me find Trish?"

"I'm insulted you felt the need to ask."

"These are very dangerous people. This is strictly a volunteer mission."

"I'm in. Do you want me to round up a few others?"

"First, let's create a plan." Evarts looked at Harding, still pacing in the kitchen. "Steve can handle himself now. I'll fill you in on the details after I make a call."

Evarts called Congressman Sherman's private cell.

"Yes?" Sherman sounded very irritated.

"Evarts. They grabbed Baldwin."

"What? Who?"

"The goddamn union, who else? They drugged her bodyguard and took her."

"What about the documents?"

"Who the hell cares about the documents? They've got Trish."

"Don't you understand? Without the documents, my plan goes up in smoke."

"Well, it's blown to smithereens. I haven't been back to the house, but I'm sure they wouldn't have left them behind."

The phone went quiet.

Finally, Evarts asked, "What are you going to do?"

The answer came immediately. "Collect my family and get the hell out of here. Good-bye." He hung up.

Chapter 52

· · · · · ·

Evarts had the most fitful night of sleep of his life and gratefully rolled out of bed at first light. Matthews woke early as well and kept him company in his anxious vigil. A few hours later, Harding wandered into the front room, but he remained unusually quiet.

Harding seemed to have recovered most of his faculties. Now it was Evarts's turn to pace the small kitchen. He felt impotent. He had wanted to charge over to Harding's home the prior evening, but his friends convinced him it would be a mistake. Instead, Evarts had briefed Matthews on the entire history since Santa Barbara, and they had talked over alternatives. They could come up with no action they could take until the union contacted them. Assuming they would.

That was the part that worried Evarts. He possessed only a single original document from the William Evarts dossiers. Was it enough? They had blunted Congressman Sherman's political assault and most probably had picked up all the copies from Harding's house. Did he still pose enough of a threat that they would contact him, or would they just dispose of Patricia Baldwin and discredit him in some way? The Rock Burglar episode certainly showed they used means other than violence.

Despite a light breakfast, Evarts's stomach felt sour and bloated from too much coffee and nervous agitation. He walked around the counter to the tiny eating area where Harding and Matthews sat silent at a small table. "Rick, you've got tons of computer gear in that extra bedroom. Does any of that equipment give you access to secure government files?"

"I have access to everything, including stuff I'm not supposed to know exists. What do you want to research?"

"Hell if I know, but I've got to do something. Maybe some agency has an ongoing investigation of the union or Ralph Branger."

Matthews gave him a sympathetic look. "I checked while you were in the shower. Nothing except for Branger's tax records. He consistently reports an eight-figure income, and there're no audits pending. On paper, he looks to be an upright guy."

"Shit." Evarts pulled over a chair and sat down at the table. "What else can we look at?"

'There's so much material on the drug cartels that it would take months just to sift through it."

"The union?"

"No references."

Harding cleared his throat. "Greg, I'm—" He choked. "I'm sorry. I never should've—"

"Steve, I understand," Evarts said. "It's not your fault. I was the stupid one. I thought your place would be safe because I haven't lived there in years. I was the idiot."

"But I should've known better than to take her out of the house."

"Steve, right now, I need you. We've got to get her back and self-recriminations won't help." Evarts was angrier than his words indicated. What he had said was true, but logic didn't overrule emotions. At least not this day. He knew it could have been him as easily as Harding. After all, he had visited the gym with Baldwin several times, but he had put the most precious thing in his life in the hands of a trusted friend, and that friend had failed him. Reason had nothing to do with how he felt.

Evarts changed the subject. "Rick, can you penetrate private corporate records?"

"Sure, with time. Which ones?"

Rick Matthews's specialty in army intelligence had been cracking computer systems and wireless communications. He knew more about cell phones than practically anyone on the planet, which was why his second bedroom looked like an electronic junkyard, with computers and communication gear strewn everywhere. Most of the devices were in some stage of disassembly, and Evarts found it hard to believe that Matthews knew which ones were operational.

"Confederated Trust. I heard on television that some guy named McGuire is CEO."

"That's J. C. D. McGuire, a legend in the investment banking world. This should be fun. I always wanted to—"

Harding's cell phone rang.

They all just stared at it. On the third ring, Evarts picked it up and checked the caller ID, but it said "restricted." He opened the phone and put it to his ear but said nothing.

After a moment, a husky voice said, "There's a package for you at Harding's house. Go pick it up."

The caller disconnected.

"What did they say?" The question came from Harding, who had finally come out of his daze.

"They left something at your house, and they want me to go pick it up."

"A trap?" Matthews asked.

"We should proceed on that assumption," Evarts said.

Harding went into the kitchen and poured himself more coffee. When he stepped back into the living room, he said, "We'll get her back. They're not supermen. They already made one big mistake."

"What's that?" Evarts asked.

"They left me alive."

Chapter 53

· · · · · ·

That afternoon, they approached the Georgetown brownstone from three different directions. Harding jumped a neighbor's fence and entered from the rear through his garden. Matthews scaled a trellis on an adjoining house and leaped onto Harding's roof. Evarts intended to approach the front door directly. On the way over, they had stopped at a RadioShack and improvised a makeshift communication system. Evarts waited around the corner until his friends called to say they were in position.

He heard Harding's voice first. "I'm in position and see no threats through the kitchen window."

"In position," Matthews answered. "Their surveillance point is across the street at 347 on the third floor. I see a man in the window with binoculars."

They had discussed the possibility of Matthews's spotting the surveillance from his rooftop vantage. Evarts heard Harding say, "Plan B."

Plan B called for them to take out the surveillance team and apprehend at least one of the men alive. Unfortunately, Plan B had no course of action except that Harding and Matthews would withdraw, and then they would all meet to figure out how to catch the watchers by surprise. The three had talked through several scenarios but had no firm plan.

They met at a rendezvous point in a pocket park two blocks away. Evarts asked Harding, "Do you know that house?"

"Yeah. Two years ago they converted it into apartments. The third floor has three or four studios."

"Security?"

"Buzz-in entry. Roof's probably secure. Best bet is to come in from the back."

"Or get a neighbor to buzz us in," Matthews offered.

"There's an old woman in the ground-floor unit. She owns the building and had it converted after her husband died."

"Does she know you?" Evarts asked.

"Yeah, but if I approach the building, I'll alarm the observation team."

They had previously decided that if they spotted a surveillance nest, Harding would become the diversion, and Matthews would act as point person in the assault. They hadn't decided on a role for Evarts.

"Wait a minute," Harding said. "Her husband was a dean at Georgetown. What if Rick pretended he had some personal item from her husband to return to her?"

"What item?" Evarts asked. They had nothing but weapons and communications gear.

"This," Matthews said. He took off his watch and handed it to Harding. "It's inscribed on the back: 'From the gang, good luck.' I can say they found it in his old office or somewhere, and we think it might be her husband's."

"That gets you in," Evarts said. "Then what?"

"I can handle whatever's in that room upstairs, if you two can keep them glued to the window."

Evarts didn't like Matthews going in alone, but he knew his capabilities, and he would be a stranger to the watchers. He also had the only silenced weapon, something he had appropriated from a hostile combatant when he was in the army.

"All right," Evarts said. "They know both of us, so we'll walk the block on alternate sides like we're casing the house before entering. Use the walkie-talkie to tell us when you're out of her apartment and on the stairs. Sure you can get through the studio door?"

"I haven't forgotten all my training. Let's go."

As Matthews approached the converted townhouse, Harding took a circuitous route around the block so that when the time came, he could approach from a different direction than Evarts. Splitting the watchers' eyes between the two of them would create a better diversion.

It seemed like an eternity before Evarts heard Matthews in his earpiece. "I'm climbing to the second floor."

"Hold," Evarts said. He had kept out of sight over a block away. "I'll be in position in two minutes. Steve?"

"Ready."

"She took the damn watch," Matthews whispered.

"I'll get it back for you later," Harding said.

"In position," Evarts said.

He turned onto Harding's street and made a show of looking into cars and at windows. He saw Harding approach him on the opposite side of the street. Their behavior should look normal. They had been ordered to the house, but the union knew they had professional training and wouldn't just barge in the front door. Hopefully, the watchers would stay behind curtains and track them as they reconnoitered. Everything depended on timing. Both he and Harding passed his townhouse and pretended not to notice each other.

Evarts had reached the end of the block and turned back toward the townhouse when he heard Matthews's voice in his ear. "Mission accomplished. I'll buzz you up."

Evarts resisted an urge to run back up the block. Harding arrived first and waited for him. Without pushing the button, they heard the door buzz and entered the building. When they got to the third-floor apartment, the door was closed. They crouched on either side of the door and drew their weapons. They couldn't rule out that Matthews had been forced to give them the all-clear message. Evarts took hold of the door handle and twisted it slightly to verify that it was unlocked. Then he nodded to Harding, and they burst through the door.

"Hi, boys," Matthews said, pleased with himself. Matthews had two men trussed up on the floor, with duct tape over their mouths.

"Have you decided which one to kill and which one to interrogate?" Evarts asked.

"Not yet. But I think they'll cooperate. They told me there's nothing in Harding's house except a package."

"Do you believe them?" Harding asked.

"Yeah, they said they were only assigned to call after you got the package. These guys are rent-a-thugs. Evidently the pros cleared out once they grabbed Baldwin."

"Rip the tape off," Evarts ordered.

Matthews picked the closest guy and tore the tape from his mouth.

After yelping, the man immediately started talking as fast as he could. "Please, this was supposed to be an easy gig. Just ask us anything. We'll tell ya what we know."

"Let me explain," Evarts said evenly. "I have a nasty background. I've been trained to take people like you apart. Your employers grabbed the only woman I've ever cared about. I'm telling you this because I want you to know I'm capable and motivated. Do you understand?"

"Yes." The one still taped nodded his head vigorously.

"Good. Who hired you?"

"A man named Greg Evarts, but I doubt that was his real name."

Bastards, Evarts thought. "How did they contact you?"

"They mailed us that cell phone." He nodded toward Matthews, who took a cell phone out of his pocket.

"I already checked," Matthews said. "Only one number in the directory."

"What were your instructions?"

"Watch the house and call that number when you entered. They sent photos of you two with the phone."

Evarts had already spotted the surveillance photographs on the table by the window. "How were you to be paid?"

"Wire transfer to an account number that we gave them when they explained the assignment."

"Have you ever seen any of the people who hired you?" Evarts already knew the answer to that question.

"No. Honest. Only the name … Greg Evarts."

Evarts made a signal, and the three of them retreated to the opposite side of the room. "What do you think?" he whispered.

"They don't know shit. Amateurs." Matthews sounded disdainful.

"I agree," added Harding.

"Any other questions you guys can think of?"

Both shook their head no.

Evarts walked back to the captives. "What's in the package?"

"We don't know. We didn't plant it."

"A bomb?"

"No. We were supposed to call again after you exited the house. They wanted to know if you appeared angry or grim or whatever. They seemed anxious to—"

Evarts didn't hear the end of the sentence because he had charged out of the apartment and barreled down the stairs.

Chapter 54

. . . . . .

Evarts fumbled with the lock on the door to Harding's townhouse. When he finally got the door open, he saw a Best Buy shopping bag tucked in the corner of the entry. He ignored the bag and raced through the rest of the house, dreading that he might find Baldwin's body. He found nothing new or threatening in the house except for the shopping bag. There were things missing, though. All their photocopies and notes had disappeared from the kitchen table, and Evarts didn't see Baldwin's laptop computer.

Evarts keyed the makeshift communication system. "House clear. There's a shopping bag in the entry. Do you read?"

"Copy. Should I come over?" Harding answered.

Evarts decided he wanted the company. "Yeah. Make sure our guests are secure, and then both of you come over."

Evarts went to the window and checked the street. Could the rent-a-thugs be a diversion? He saw nothing untoward. He watched Harding and Matthews casually cross the street and greeted them at the door. All three of them looked down at the bag.

"I don't think it's a bomb," Matthews said.

Harding leaned forward and peeked inside. "Merchandise boxes. The top one looks like a digital camera."

"Let's take it into the kitchen." Evarts wanted enough flat space to lay out the contents so they could all see.

In the kitchen, Harding reached into the bag and carefully extracted a box with "Canon" emblazoned on all four sides and placed it on the counter.

"Digital camera. The box has been opened," Harding said.

"What else is in the bag?" Evarts asked.

Harding looked. "A disposable cell phone, the kind parents buy for their teenagers. Plastic shell packaging, also opened. The sons of bitches threw in the register receipt."

"Pull it out."

After Harding extracted the cell phone, he said, "And a letter." He handed the plain white envelope to Evarts. "It's addressed to you."

Evarts hesitated for a nanosecond and then ripped open the envelope. Someone had handwritten the message in block letters.

LOOK AT THE CAMERA. YOU SHOULD RECOGNIZE YOUR WORK. WE WILL TRADE BALDWIN FOR ORIGINAL YOU TOOK FROM DTCC. USE CELL PHONE FOR INSTRUCTIONS.

Evarts read the short note a second time. It told him a lot. He felt heartsick. He knew what must have transpired to force Baldwin to reveal that he had an original document in his possession. He handed the note to Harding. "They broke her."

He reached for the camera box with an unsteady hand. He jockeyed the camera free from its Styrofoam brick, turned it on, and flipped the setting switch to view the stored pictures. Baldwin's face filled the little screen on the back of the camera. She looked distraught and in pain. Damn them. The next picture showed only her bare thigh. The image conveyed an unmistakable message: She had been shot in the leg. The last photograph showed her full body with her hands tied behind her back. It was framed to show that the wounded leg belonged to Baldwin. Her helpless, frightened expression made Evarts want to throw the camera across the room. Instead he handed it to Harding and went to the refrigerator for a bottle of water.

He took a long drink that emptied a third of the bottle. When he lowered the bottle, he saw Harding's sad eyes. "Steve, what's past is past. We need to focus on getting her back."

"How?"

"I need to make a call," Evarts said.

Matthews finished reading the note. "Don't you think we should talk first, go through the scenarios?"

Evarts had a thought and crossed his lips with his index finger. His friends immediately understood: The house might be bugged. Evarts opened the back door and stepped into the garden. Using a business card he had been given at the DTCC, he called Jonathon. After a short time, he stepped back into the kitchen to find Harding and Matthews visually checking for bugs.

Evarts picked up a tablet and pencil on a counter by the landline telephone. He wrote: "Called DTCC. Documents stored as long as fees paid. If payment stops—retain three years—then destroy."

Matthews immediately picked up the tablet and wrote, "They're going to kill her."

"Yes—unless we stop them," Evarts wrote.

Matthews nodded toward the door. They stuffed the camera and cell phone back into the bag and left. When they got on the street, Evarts asked, "Find any bugs?"

"No, but we should proceed as if they heard us," Harding said.

"What about our guests across the street?" Matthews asked.

Evarts didn't believe they could learn any more from a couple of thugs who had been rented for routine watchdog duty. "Leave 'em. If we're lucky, they'll starve to death."

As they walked the several blocks to the car, they reviewed their conversation in the house and decided that, if the union had planted a bug, the only important thing they learned was that there were three of them. This meant that the union might track down and possibly interrogate all of Evarts's old army buddies, so Harding started making calls to warn people.

As they approached the Navigator, Evarts signaled for Matthews to drive so Harding could concentrate on making the phone calls.

"Where to?" Matthews asked.

From the passenger seat, Evarts said, "Not your place. They'll watch it if they start checking my army contacts."

"Then how 'bout a motel in Arlington? Lots of D.C. tourists stay there."

"Yeah. Fine."

Evarts had never felt such despair. He also felt foolish and inept. He knew better than to just keep running. Sooner or later, one of their breakneck escapes had to fail. He should have found some way to attack, but the measured unraveling of clues had given him hope that they would uncover some final evidence to bring this nasty venture to a close. He had failed. Now he had to start acting smarter, or he would also fail the most important mission of his life. The fear that he might not rescue Trish made him heartsick.

"What're you thinking?" Matthews asked.

"That Trish is close." Evarts looked out of the car at the passing buildings.

"Because of the camera?"

Evarts continued to watch the buildings pass by his window. "Yeah. And the Best Buy receipt was local."

"We could run over to that store."

"They left the receipt so we'd do just that. Those bastards."

Evarts tried to understand his feelings. He had had men captured before and had ruthlessly tracked down their captors. This time he felt different. Worse. Way worse. Why did he feel this way? Then he knew beyond any doubt. He was in love with Patricia Baldwin. An odd word for him to even think, but he knew he didn't want to go back to the solitude he had convinced himself he actually preferred. He wanted a life with Trish. Did she feel the same? He wasn't sure.

He listened to Harding's end of the cell conversations for a while and then turned toward the window to hide a tear. He heard himself say, "I want her back."

Chapter 55

· · · · · ·

In Arlington, they found a high-rise Holiday Inn that catered to tourists. By the time they checked in, Harding had finished all the calls. They managed to get three adjoining rooms intended for families on vacation, so they had plenty of space. Each room had the ubiquitous small table with two chairs stationed in front of the single window, so they hauled another from Harding's room into Evarts's and gathered around the table.

Harding began, "If we can figure out a plan, I believe we can field a full platoon. Everybody wants in."

"Are you serious? Because I have an inkling of a plan."

"Yeah, Greg, I'm serious. If you want an army, you've got one."

"Are we going to call the bad guys?" Matthews asked. All three of them looked at the two cell phones positioned in the center of the table. The first one they had taken from the surveillance team and the other had been in the shopping bag. They had already checked, and the two phones had been preprogrammed with different telephone numbers. Since he didn't get a response, Matthews added lightheartedly, "In the movies, the good guy always calls the bad guy and surprises him by acting cool."

Evarts didn't answer for a moment. Finally he said, "They don't know what happened to their hired thugs and probably intend to stay away from the scene. They're anxious about me getting the package, or they wouldn't have left men watching the house. Why forewarn them? I like an anxious, unsure enemy. So ... no call, on either phone. What do you think?"

After both men nodded, Evarts asked Harding, "Did you call Gary to warn him?"

"Yeah, I called everybody."

"Did he offer any information on Branger?"

"Preliminary only. By most outward appearances, he's a responsible citizen and good neighbor. Branger has made generous donations to every charity, church, and cause within a hundred-mile radius.

Government finance disclosures showed that he makes maximum contributions to every politician in sight. Newspaper society pages are often filled with happy-face photographs from elaborate parties he throws at his country club for the hoi polloi." Harding checked the notes he had made on a small tablet. "North Carolina doesn't canonize its citizens, and they don't award knighthoods, but Duke University did confer an honorary LLB on our generous Mr. Branger."

Harding put the tablet on the table and nudged it away with two fingers. "There's only one chink in his good-citizen armor. Every three months, he entertains a dozen or so business associates, and at these little conclaves, some rather rough characters guard his house. One neighbor filed a police complaint that these guards physically threatened him, and a boater claimed that some goons on shore brandished automatic weapons when he drifted too close to the Branger dock. Gary also said the building permit included a subterranean gun range, dual electric feeds, and enough telecommunications bandwidth to service a bank."

"What about when there's no meeting?" Evarts asked.

"Evidently he still has guards around, but they pretty much stay out of sight. So much so, that it's hard to gage the level of security."

Evarts asked the next obvious question. "Is there a meeting going on now?"

"Gary drove by the estate yesterday, and everything looked quiet," Harding said.

"Does your inkling of a plan have anything to do with this Branger character?" Matthews asked.

"Yes." Evarts scooted his chair closer. "The way I figure it, the union already has possession of all of our photocopies, Trish's original, and Trish herself. Congressman Sherman has been written off as a kook. To completely eliminate the threat, they only need to get their hands on me and the document I hid. I suspect they're more interested in me than the document. They haven't remained secret by letting people that know about them run around free, especially law enforcement officials. The remaining documents will stay buried in the most secure depository in the country. My bet is that they plan to arrange a transfer in such a way that draws me into their clutches, after which, they'll destroy my original, and kill Trish and me. They know Trish hasn't designated an executor, so the documents will be destroyed in three years. Problem solved. On to world domination."

"So you don't intend to make the trade?"

"Losing proposition. Sherman said the union has mercenaries on the payroll. They've probably been doing drug deals for decades. They know how to set up a meet so their side walks away clean."

"If we don't meet, what's our plan?" Harding asked.

Evarts slapped the table. "We grab Branger."

"Then what?"

"That's the inkling part."

"Branger probably knows where they're holding Baldwin," Harding offered.

"Yeah, if we can somehow grab him without alerting the entire union, break him fast, and have a second team ready to pounce on the hideout, maybe, just maybe, we can rescue her. I want to snatch Branger, because they wouldn't expect it, and it puts us on the offense. But unless we can figure out a way to leverage it, I'm not sure it will get Trish back."

Evarts stood and paced up and down the room. He worried that he just wanted to strike back, that his desire for action made him embrace a foolhardy idea. He stopped his pacing in front of the table and looked down at his still-seated friends. "We don't even know for sure that Branger's in the union, much less running it."

Neither Harding nor Matthews responded, so Evarts began pacing again. He didn't have room for mistakes. One miscalculation would doom Baldwin, and the thought made his stomach draw so tight, he had to keep moving to relieve the ache.

Matthews shoved his chair back and rested his right ankle on his other leg. "You think all that protection at his house is just for him?"

That stopped Evarts in his tracks. He thought it through. "You're right. That house might be the nerve center for the union. All that telecommunications bandwidth must be for encryption."

Now Harding stood up. "Yeah, let's steal their business records *and* Branger."

Evarts felt unsure that his friends understood the extent of the commitment involved with an assault on the house. "Listen, the union may have started because the Civil War ruined the economic base of the South, but through the years, it has morphed into something far more sinister." Evarts made sure he had their full attention. "We might have to kill people. We can't attack the headquarters of a secret society that has Mexican drug connections and use stun guns. Some of us might die, and others might go to prison. The only chance for some of us coming out clean depends on finding incriminating evidence in that house."

The three men stood and looked at each other a moment. Then Matthews said, "Listen, this is going to sound corny, but I see myself as an old-fashioned patriot. I joined the army to protect my country. Then I trusted politicians to point me at our most dangerous enemies. All the while, these union assholes wrecked our country and my neighborhood from inside our own borders." Matthews took a step toward Evarts. "I may have gotten older, but I haven't lost my sense of duty. Greg, when I see a clear and present danger, I no longer need permission from some dumb-shit politician."

Evarts turned. "Steve?"

"I say, load up the car and let's do our planning on the drive down to Charlotte."

As they got up to leave, both the cell phones rang almost simultaneously. "Anxious buggers, aren't they?" Harding said as he shoved both ringing phones into his pocket. They were on the road in less than five minutes.

Chapter 56

· · · · · ·

The five-hour drive had been filled with cell phone calls to plan an operation. Harding got six of their old army buddies on the road heading toward Charlotte. The three of them plus Gary Johnson made ten. A team of four others gathered in the Washington, D.C. area to mount a rescue attempt in the event that Evarts discovered where Baldwin was being held.

Because they might be watching his house, Johnson had suggested that they meet at the home of a fellow driver on the NASCAR circuit. They pulled up to the house on Lake Norman just before eleven o'clock at night. As they got out of the Navigator, Harding whistled. "Have you ever seen so many toys?" he exclaimed.

Parked on the massive driveway was a forty-five-foot Diesel Pusher motor home with a Honda Pilot in tow, two foreign sports cars, and a pristine 1965 Mustang notchback. The open garage door revealed two all-terrain vehicles, a trailered bass boat, and a Mercedes AMG E-Class.

Gary Johnson answered the door and everyone quickly shook hands. The purpose of their visit had put a damper on what should have been a happy reunion. Harding even abandoned his normal bear hug greeting. Johnson waved them inside and started to lead them to the back of the house, but Harding stopped their progress by saying, "Gary, do you live like this?"

They all stopped and stared at the living room. Instead of furniture, the supposed front parlor contained a pool table surrounded by arcade video games and a foosball table. A vintage Harley Hog sat parked in a corner like a decorator item. The architect had probably assumed this would be the most formal space in the house.

"Naw. I keep my pool table in the basement. Come on. It's a nice night. We'll sit out back."

As they passed through the kitchen, they each grabbed a beer and then took seats outside around a wrought-iron patio set. A long wooden walkway extended off the patio to the lake, and despite the darkness, Evarts could make out a pontoon boat and a ski boat tied to the dock. "You racers sure like your toys," Evarts said.

Johnson glanced in the direction Evarts was looking. "We play for a living, so our playtime gets a little outrageous. That's why I'm still a weekend warrior, except for me it's in the middle of the week."

"What do you mean?" Matthews asked.

"I'm a brigadier general in the North Carolina National Guard. It lets me fly helicopters when I'm not zooming around a racetrack."

Gary Johnson had been the helicopter pilot when their insertion teams needed to come in by air. Evarts had always thought he enjoyed the ground-hugging flights a bit too much. He guessed car racing just gave him another way to get the excitement he craved.

"Where's your racing friend?" Harding asked.

"Partying at another driver's house. Lots of women. He'll spend the night, so we each have a bedroom and all the privacy we need to plot an assault on our illustrious neighbor."

"This is not a lark," Evarts said, a bit irritated. "He's dangerous and there might be killing."

Johnson dropped the comradely smile. "This woman's important to you?"

"Yes." He chose not to elaborate, but it occurred to him that, of the four of them, only Harding had been married. Maybe it was time for them to grow up. It was certainly time for him. What would he do if he couldn't save Baldwin? He shook the thought from his head. Then he had another.

"What kind of helicopter do you fly?" Evarts asked.

"Big old ones, unfortunately. The Guard doesn't get the latest equipment. Still a lot of fun though."

"Can you borrow one?"

Johnson laughed. "What do you have in mind?"

Evarts told them.

Chapter 57

· · · · · ·

Evarts knocked on the door with more trepidation than he had felt on any previous assignment. He glanced at Harding standing beside him. In prior operations, he had had no personal attachment to anyone but the assault team. This time, his concern for Baldwin loomed over everything he did and every decision he made.

Lake Norman had five hundred and twenty miles of uneven shoreline, with inlets and bays providing innumerable private building sites that were further protected from prying eyes by thick stands of trees extending all the way to the lakefront. Because of the curvy nature of the lake, driving around it took more time than direct routes by boat. When they had finally reached the access road to the Branger estate, they could see nothing from the highway except layers of trees. There was no hint of the vast mansion hidden beyond or that the property included a private inlet.

After driving the Navigator up the access road, Evarts had continued around a circular drive to the front of the house. No security gate had inhibited their progress. Evarts guessed that Branger didn't want his neighbors to think he had anything to hide, so instead of a gate, he probably relied on electronic measures and human guards. After he had parked near the front door, a man had stepped from around a corner to make himself visible but hadn't interfered with them as they approached the expansive white mansion.

The architect had designed an antebellum plantation house with a white-columned portico that stretched across the entire front. Evarts knew from the building plans that the part of the house facing Lake Norman looked identical to this side, with a common grand hall on the inside connecting the two "front" doors. Whether someone arrived by boat or car, the visitor had the impression of approaching the entrance to the house.

Planning the operation had taken two days. They had reconnoitered the Branger estate from the land side and from a powerboat. At the city offices, they had studied lot plats, architectural plans, and building permits. Their plan was good but depended on precise timing. He hoped his ploy to give the illusion of deadly force would work.

As he knocked again, Evarts wondered if he had hurried for surprise or because it pained him so much to consider Baldwin's plight. At this point, everything was in motion, and he had no choice but to push ahead. He squared his shoulders and reminded himself that if you don't have a choice, you don't have a problem.

After the second knock, a tightly dressed business-type opened the door. "Yes, may I help you?"

"We're here to see Ralph Branger," Evarts said.

"Are you from the community?"

"No."

The business-type looked perplexed when Evarts didn't elaborate. "I saw no appointments in his book today."

"We don't have an appointment."

The man glanced over Evarts's shoulders to verify that the guard was in place behind them. "I'm sorry, but Mr. Branger is very busy, and he sees no one without an appointment."

"Tell him Greg Evarts is here to see him."

The suited man motioned to the man behind them. "I'm sorry, but I'm going to have to ask you to leave."

"Your pay grade isn't high enough to make that decision. Close the door, let that goon keep an eye on us, and go tell Mr. Branger that Greg Evarts is at his front door." The man looked a bit confused and uncertain, so Evarts added a firm, "Now."

The man held up the flat of his hand to stop the advance of the guard and said, "Watch these two." Then he closed the door as instructed.

Evarts and Harding ignored the man behind them and waited patiently. This time two rough-looking characters opened the door with their hands theatrically positioned inside their windbreaker jackets. "Step into the foyer," one of them said without preamble.

As soon as they had stepped inside enough to shut the door, one of the men pulled out an automatic and leveled it at them. "Stand very still." The other bodyguard patted them down. He confiscated a cell phone from Harding's pocket.

"If I don't call every ten minutes from *that* cell phone, a helicopter gunship will take this place out," Harding informed him.

"Bullshit."

"You people know our army background," Evarts said. "Our friends like to blow things up, especially your sorry ass if my friend here doesn't make those calls."

"You want me to believe that your army buddies will launch a missile at the home of one of the most prominent citizens of this state. Give me a fucking break." He put the cell phone into his pocket.

"The gunship has Mexican markings and Russian ordinance," Evarts said with a smile. "All intercepted communications will be in Spanish."

That stopped him. He handed the cell phone back to Harding, who opened it, pressed a speed dial number, and simply said, "Emerald." Then he snapped it shut with relish.

The first bodyguard appeared unamused. He said, "Follow me."

They were taken into a handsome library. Unlike Abraham Douglass's dog-eared library, this one was used as a prop to stage Branger's guests before gracing them with his presence. After one guard left, supposedly to fetch Branger, the other took up a preposterously defiant stance in front of the door. Evarts and Harding ignored the overly dramatic gangster and scanned the room.

In less than a minute, Evarts pointed and said, "There's the camera." They had no time to waste. The other prong of their assault had already been launched. Harding walked over and stood beside Evarts. They both looked into the camera, and Evarts said, "Mr. Branger, we each have something the other wants. It's time to bring this long-running saga to an end."

Evarts turned from the camera and said evenly to the guard, "Where's the bar?"

The guard looked unsure for a moment and then pointed to a closed cabinet against the opposite wall. Evarts opened the cabinet and saw rows of expensive scotches, bourbons, and brandies. Only dark liquors: no rum, gin, or vodka. Branger was a man who imposed his taste on others. Evarts poured himself a short glass of single malt scotch and turned to the guard. "Bring my friend here a cold beer. Preferably Anchor Steam."

"Go to hell."

"If you're otherwise disposed, please ring for a servant."

Now he looked confused. Eventually, he rapped on the door with his knuckles and said through the closed door, "Pete, have someone bring a beer for our guest."

Suddenly, loud whacking noise assaulted their ears. The walls and bookshelves rattled so violently, it seemed as if the room were about to fling books in every direction.

"Relax," Evarts said to the nervous bodyguard. "That was just a demonstration flyby. We didn't want you to get the idea that we might be bluffing." He looked up at the ceiling. "Those old Russian choppers are sure noisy."

Actually, they were bluffing. This was Evarts's grand idea. Since Johnson knew the lake, he had insisted on leading the assault team that would approach by water. He had asked a couple of his pilots in the National Guard to do a low-level flyby. At first they resisted, but he assured them that, as their ranking officer, he would cover for them. They had finally agreed after Johnson put the orders in writing.

The helicopter had actually been an old American-built Sikorsky transport with its sound suppression turned off. Even if the crew had live ordinance, they would never have fired on a residential home under any circumstances. The point was moot because, unless there was an eminent threat, the National Guard didn't allow armed helicopters to leave government military preserves.

Evarts sipped his scotch and tried to look confident. In a few minutes, the door opened and an ordinary servant brought in a Dos Equis beer and a chilled glass. Harding grabbed the longneck and drank from the bottle.

After another ten minutes, Evarts was getting jumpy about the amount of time that had elapsed. He was about to try a more severe gambit in front of the camera, when the door finally opened. Two thick-necked brutes entered and patted them down again. Evarts took this as a good sign. Branger must have decided to meet with them. After they had passed inspection, one of the bodyguards rapped on the door twice. Evarts didn't know what to think about the person who walked through the door. A tight-lipped young man with short-cropped blond hair stared at them in a curious manner, with his head bent to the side like he was puzzled by some oddity. He didn't look to be over thirty and wore round tortoiseshell glasses, gray trousers, and a pink polo shirt that appeared to have been pressed. The young man looked like the nicely fitted-out son of a prominent country-club member.

Evarts stepped forward but didn't extend a hand. "Mr. Ralph Branger?"

"Why did you come into my home uninvited?"

"To barter."

"For what?"

"Are we going to play dumb, sir?"

He tilted his head again and studied Evarts. "I never play dumb."

Evarts pointedly looked at the three bodyguards in the room. "I presume I can talk in front of your men?"

"You may presume nothing."

Evarts decided to test Branger. "A fault of mine, I fear. And it seems I've made a mistake. No one so young could possibly run the union. If you'll excuse us, we'll depart."

"You really are a simpleton. How did you elude my men for so long?" Branger shook his head. "No matter." After pausing to adjust his prissy tortoiseshell glasses with two manicured fingers, he continued in a controlled monotone. "Mr. Evarts, I do run the union. It was a simple task to push aside the timid old men who presumed to ascend to the throne. To restore the South to the gracious glory that was once hers requires a man of courage, vision, and intellect . . . not purposeless pomposity."

Evarts started to speak, but Branger raised the flat of his hand. "You have intruded on my home. I do not abide that."

Evarts felt Harding tense beside him. He spoke quickly before events could outstrip his ability to manage them. "I apologize." He bowed his head slightly. "Not having been raised in the South, I may have overstepped proper decorum."

"Overstepped proper decorum? Forcing entry into a gentleman's home, threatening to blow it up, insisting on refreshments not offered by your host: You call that overstepping proper decorum? I call it trespassing, and in this state, we can shoot trespassers. Pete, kill these men and dispose of the bodies."

As his men drew weapons, Branger turned toward the door. "I

shall be in the bomb shelter in case these ill-mannered louts aren't bluffing."

"Yes, s—"

"Aren't you concerned about the original I took from the DTCC?"

Branger turned away from the door in a movement that seemed almost slow motion. Evarts thought he was going to smile, but instead his lips twisted into an unbecoming smirk. "I'm sure you buried it so deep, it will probably never be found. If someone does happen to stumble upon your hiding place, it will be far too late. This little episode with Congressman Sherman will be ancient news. No one will care a wit about a single old document with questionable authenticity."

He was turning toward the door, when Evarts said, "Two more signature cards have already been filed with the DTCC. Ms. Baldwin has authorized access for myself and another person. She's left instructions for this third person to turn over the entire contents to Congressman Sherman if she isn't heard from in seven days."

Branger faced Evarts. What he did next chilled Evarts to his very core. His thin lips curled in a grotesque manner that conveyed unbridled menace driven by an unstable mind. "Mr. Evarts, if that had been the case, I'm certain Ms. Baldwin would've already told us. She has been most cooperative." He adopted the odd tilt of the head again and then said to his men, while keeping eye contact with Evarts. "Pete, I believe my instructions have been clear. Please carry them out immediately."

In desperation, Evarts said, "Have I misunderstood Southern hospitality?"

Branger charged at Evarts until their noses almost touched. When he spoke, spittle sprayed Evarts's face. "You are not to speak of Southern hospitality or anything else associated with my homeland. You know nothing of our culture or way of life. You're both ill-bred white trash, and it's a sacrilege for you to be standing here. Your very presence dishonors North Carolina."

He took a step back but continued to glare. "Kill the woman too. Her first, so these make-believe heroes can see the results of their handiwork. A single shot to the back of the head, if you will, please."

"Yes, sir." The one called Pete pulled the hammer back on his .45 automatic.

"Trish is here?" Evarts blurted.

"Not for much longer," Pete said.

Chapter 58

· · · · · ·

When Branger left the library, Evarts was glad to see that one of the three guards accompanied him. He took a step toward the guard closest to the door. "Your boss is crazy, you know."

"Step back or I'll kill you right here." He laughed. "We already replaced this carpet once."

Evarts retreated. "Don't tell me you buy into this scheme of his to resurrect the antebellum South?"

"I don't buy into anything. Mr. Branger buys, and he's very generous."

"Then it's just business to you?" Harding asked.

"A damn good business. Mr. Branger runs a tight operation."

"Are all of Mr. Branger's employees moronic?"

The guards were too professional to take the bait. The one by the door made a sideways motion with his gun. "Just put your hands on your head and walk slowly toward the door. Any sudden movement will be very painful."

The first guard opened the door and positioned himself with half his body on the opposite side of the doorjamb in a way that protected him from a body blow, but didn't interfere with keeping his gun aimed at Evarts's center mass. The second guard kept his distance to the rear, with his gun leveled at Harding. Army covert-operations training included how to disarm an opponent without sustaining a lethal wound, but the techniques required close proximity. As Evarts slowly approached the doorway, the first man backed up to stay out of reach. These guards appeared to be experienced and thoroughly trained.

When all four men had transitioned into the hallway, the first guard said, "We're going to the basement. Down this hall and to your left."

Evarts had no intention of fighting these men. First, he had to know Branger's location. The revelation that they had transported Baldwin here gave him hope. All he needed was a little luck to go along with their plan. He stole a glance at his watch and almost groaned when he realized they had little time to discover Branger's position in the house. At least they were going to the basement, which Evarts assumed was the bomb shelter.

A few yards to the left, Evarts saw a grand staircase going up to the bedroom level and a closed door. The first guard commanded, "Hold up. Lean against the wall with your legs spread. Police position." After they had assumed the position, the guard opened the door to disclose a narrow staircase to the basement. "I'm going to be at the bottom of the stairs. If you'd like to come tumbling after me, I wouldn't mind a little moving-target practice." He disappeared down the stairwell.

The second man continued to keep his distance. "Okay, one at a time. Keep it slow and easy."

Evarts led the way down the stairs, which went far deeper than an ordinary cellar. At the bottom, he saw an unpainted concrete hallway leading left and right that ran far too long to be restricted to the foundation of the house. Perhaps they had been right. It looked like the basement could be a headquarters. It was hidden from sight, and it was certainly large enough.

The forward guard motioned them to follow him down the left branch of the corridor. When they had passed two doors, the guard punched a number into a keypad and pointed them through the third door in the long hallway. When Evarts passed through the steel cased door, the interior of the room surprised him. Large and indirectly lit, it reminded him of a movie set from *Gone with the Wind*. After the sterile concrete corridor, the heavy upholstered furniture, spindly wood pieces, patterned rugs, and life-size nineteenth-century portraits stunned his senses, but Evarts thought the décor leaned too heavily to maroon for his taste.

Branger suddenly opened a door at the opposite end of the room and showed surprise at seeing them. "*What* are you doing in my parlor?" he demanded.

"I'm sorry, sir. I must have misunderstood." The guard glanced back at his accomplice for support but received a noncommittal stony stare. Evidently he would have to face their boss's wrath alone. "I thought you said to take the woman as well."

"I pay well enough to expect a three-digit IQ." Branger's voice assumed the tone of a parent instructing a recalcitrant child. "I thought it clear that the sight of these men makes me nauseous. Take them to the shooting range. And if it wouldn't be too much trouble, would you mind tying them up? Once you have them secure, one of you may return to pick up the woman. When you come back, the polite thing would be to knock first. Then you may take the woman back to the range." Branger removed his glasses and excessively cleaned the lenses with an unsoiled white cloth from his pocket. "Do you need any further instructions?"

"No, sir."

"Good." He started to turn away but then rounded on his employee. In a chillingly cold voice, he said, "Never again presume that because I ask you to dispose of some discarded article, you may enter my private chamber unannounced." Branger slipped his glasses back on his face and returned the cloth to his pocket. "Are we *perfectly* clear?"

"Yes, sir."

Just as the guard turned around to escort them out of the parlor, Harding reached into his pocket. Both guards came instantly around on them, and Evarts could actually sense them squeezing ever so slightly harder on the triggers of their automatics. Harding froze in mid motion. Waiting until the guards seemed assured that they had control of the situation, Harding slowly pulled the cell phone out of his pocket with two fingers. "If I don't call, this house will be rubble."

"Then I shall build another," Branger said.

"When the authorities investigate, they'll find your command post down here," Evarts tried.

"The authorities don't concern me," Branger said dismissively.

Harding raised the collapsible antenna and flipped the phone open with his thumb.

"You ignoramus, there's no reception down here."

"Then you'd better call your contractor," Harding said. "Because you're going to need a new plantation house."

"I'm tired of these games. Take that phone away from him and get them out of here."

Harding raised the phone like he actually held a weapon. "Stand back. I can blow this house to smithereens as easy as one, two—"

Harding tossed the cell phone in the direction of Branger, and in mid flight a light flashed so white that all other colors disappeared.

Chapter 59

· · · · · ·

The flash grenade barely made a popping sound. On the count of two, Evarts and Harding shut their eyes and covered them with their hands to protect against the blinding light. They simultaneously sidestepped away from where they had been standing and ducked close to the floor. As soon as the flash dissipated, they attacked the two guards.

Evarts punched his target in the solar plexus with his two center knuckles. He knew he had pent-up energy, but he hit the man so hard that the expulsion of breath felt like a bellows. He next hit him in the windpipe with all four knuckles. Suddenly, the boom of gunfire assaulted his ears, so he grabbed the guard by his shirt and twisted around behind him. He immediately saw that Branger had somehow gotten hold of a .45 automatic and was now blindly spraying bullets around the room.

Evarts felt a bullet hit the guard he held in front of him as a shield. He didn't feel anything and hoped that Branger's automatic had been loaded with hollow points; otherwise, even the slow-moving .45 slug could pass through and hit him. He tried to push the guard toward Branger, but he collapsed instead of moving forward, and Evarts had to drop to the floor to stay behind his limp body. Luckily, in another second, the gun's slide locked open because Branger had emptied the magazine. Still blinded, Branger fumbled around in a table drawer trying to feel for another magazine. Evarts charged.

He hit Branger with a football tackle, and they both went tumbling to the floor. Evarts felt a sudden excruciating pain in his neck and reflexively rolled away from the hurt. In a split second, he rallied and came back at Branger with a punching fist aimed at his face, but Branger jerked and Evarts's glancing blow skidded against the floor. He raised his knee to attack Branger's groin, but Branger had twisted enough so that Evarts merely hit the inside of his thigh. Then he felt the jarring impact of a fist driven into the side of his head. Damn it. Branger knew how to fight. He had to win this quick.

Evarts bounced into the air and came down knee first into the center of Branger's chest. He heard a cry of pain and knew from his agonized expression that Branger had lost the will to fight.

Evarts scrambled back to the body of the man he had used as a shield and quickly found his pistol. He gave Branger a glance and saw that he was holding his chest and gasping, so he whirled toward the second guard in time to see Harding's great fist smash into the face of the already unconscious man.

"Steve, stop. He's out."

Harding hit him once more before the words penetrated his dark fury. He pulled his fist back and stared at the bloody, bone-shattered flesh that had been a face. When he saw no life in the slack features, Harding rolled off the body and slowly stood. After he reached full height, he kicked the man furiously in the head. "Fuck you."

"Get his gun, Steve," Evarts said.

"That's the asshole who drugged me in the gym." Harding picked up the gun from the floor and came at Branger with such intensity that Evarts thought he was going to kill him.

"Stop!" Evarts yelled. "We need him."

"That son of a bitch." Harding shook with anger.

Evarts grabbed him by both shoulders. "Get a hold of yourself. This isn't over. Do you hear me, Steve?"

"You're not going to let that bastard live are you? Our team's coming in. We don't need him."

"Goddamn it, Steve." He shook the bigger man. Evarts understood that Harding felt guilty for not protecting Trish, but he needed his brain as well as his brawn. "Listen. She's *here*. If we don't fuck up, we can get her out. Pull yourself together."

Harding looked at him with recognition for the first time. "Breathe," Evarts ordered. He looked over his shoulder at the other three men in the room. Both guards looked dead, and Branger still held his chest and groaned.

A sixth sense suddenly raised the hair on the back of his neck. Releasing Harding, he leveled the automatic at Branger. With his other hand, Evarts gave Harding a shove toward the door. "Check the hall ... be careful." He moved to the side to get a clearer view of Branger. "Stand up."

Branger continued to groan, but Evarts now knew for sure that he was faking. "Stand up or take a bullet to the leg. Now!" There was only one moment of hesitation. When Branger got fully to his feet, Evarts said, "Drop it."

Branger smirked and theatrically opened his palm to let a small black object clatter to the floor.

Without looking at the device, Evarts yelled over his shoulder, "Steve, he's set off an alarm with a remote. Can you secure that door?"

"No," Evarts heard from behind him. "The deadbolt requires a key on the inside."

Branger's smile turned sickening. "I raised an alarm and now that door can't be locked, even with a key."

Evarts stepped further away from Branger and glanced at the doorway. Harding had been peeking through a crack and opened the door enough to poke out the barrel of his gun. He fired two blind shots down the hall.

"That will give them pause for about twenty seconds," he said with disgust. "And the fucking door opens outward so we can't pile shit in front of it."

"We've considered every scenario," Branger said.

"Don't move," Evarts ordered as he sidestepped toward the door at the rear of the room. He opened it and stole a quick glance. He had hoped to find Baldwin in the room, but still he swallowed hard when he saw her. Reclining in a huge leather swivel lounger as if taking a nap, she looked inert, and her pasty white face displayed the slack features of the seriously ill. He scanned the apparent emergency bedroom and returned his attention to Baldwin. Despite her unconscious state, she was bound hand and foot. Evarts shouted at Harding, "No exit from the back room! Trish is here and appears drugged!"

As Harding marched across the room, he effortlessly grabbed Branger by the scruff of the neck and threw him toward the back room. "We can't defend that door. They can come at us from two directions. I'd throw a flash-bang grenade into the room."

The slight jerk of Branger's head told Evarts that's exactly what they intended to do. "Quick, into the back!" he yelled.

Harding literally threw Branger through the door frame and then took up a position on his knees, with one hand ready to slam the door shut when he saw the grenade fly into the outer room. Evarts decided he didn't have time to babysit Branger, so he pistol-whipped him unconscious. He next went to Baldwin, untied her feet, and used the rope to tie Branger's hands behind him. Damn, how much time did they have? "Buy me time!" he yelled at Harding.

As he ran into an adjoining bathroom, he heard a single shot. The bullet couldn't penetrate the steel door or the concrete wall, but hopefully the assembling assault team could hear the shot and would stop to try to figure out what it meant. Then he heard Harding yell at the top of his lungs, "Open that door and I kill your paycheck!"

Evarts rummaged around in the bathroom and found some cotton balls. He ran back into the bedroom and knelt behind Harding. While Harding kept his gun aimed at the door, Evarts stuffed two cotton balls in each of his ears. After he plugged his own ears, he stuffed Baldwin's ears and untied her hands so he could use the rope to tie Branger's ankles. Then he inspected the room. No exit, but he found a fully automatic rifle under the bed. He ran over and gave the weapon to Harding, who nodded in appreciation.

The plan they had devised yesterday called for them to try to isolate Branger while a small assault team broke into the house from the lake side of the mansion. With luck, their assault team should have taken the perimeter by now, but Evarts didn't know how long it would take them to find their way to the basement. They had to hold off until help arrived. That meant securing their position—not worrying about Baldwin. He ran back into the bathroom and soaked two washcloths. He stuck one in his shirt collar so he could pull it over his mouth quickly and threw the other one at Harding, who felt the wet cloth hit him and tucked it into his collar. They were as ready as they could get with the limited resources at hand, so Evarts took a position with his back against the wall next to Harding.

He had no sooner gotten in place, when the outside door opened a crack, and a grenade rolled into the outer room. Harding fired a three-shot burst and then slammed the door. Despite the cotton, the blast deafened them, and the reverberations shook the wall. Harding almost immediately opened the door and blindly spayed another three-shot burst. Evarts stood behind the kneeling Harding ready to fire, but he could barely see through the smoke. He soon made out two charging men, wearing full body armor and face shields. Both he and Harding opened fire, aiming for the unprotected legs. After that he couldn't recount what he did, only that his next conscious thought was that the .45's slide had locked back in the open position because the gun had run dry of ammunition.

After he picked up the other automatic from the floor and took aim, he saw the two men writhing on the floor. "Back off," he yelled at the men he assumed remained hidden in the hall.

The answer came immediately from behind the outside door. "There's no exit. Throw out your guns."

"We have Branger!" Harding yelled.

"And we have our orders. Next comes a bazooka. Throw your weapons across the floor so we can hear them!"

"Think they're bluffing?" Evarts asked, but Harding didn't answer.

Evarts ran to the recliner and lifted Baldwin to his chest. If they retreated to the bathroom, maybe help could still arrive in time.

Harding saw what he was doing and yelled toward the outer door, "Give us a second."

"No! Now!"

Damn. Evarts wondered how long it had been since they had first knocked on the door. He tried to glance at his watch as he carried Baldwin to the bathroom, but his wrist was wrapped around behind her. Time had stretched out so much that it seemed like they had been in the house forever. Evarts heard a gun clatter across the floor, and at first he thought Harding had surrendered. A glance showed him that he had thrown only the empty .45.

"I only heard one gun!" someone yelled.

Evarts unceremoniously threw Baldwin on the floor of the bathroom and ran back to the door to tap Harding on the shoulder. Harding immediately shot another three-round burst and grabbed Branger by his shirt, dragging him into the bathroom. Evarts leaped in just behind him and slammed the door. They each took a breath before they heard an outrageous explosion. No bluff.

Evarts heard someone shout "fuck" and realized that it came from him. Harding opened the door to rubble, smoke, and flying debris. Stumbling over pieces of wall and fractured furniture, Harding charged toward an upturned mattress. As soon as he hit the ground, he fired a single shot.

Evarts thought he was conserving ammunition until Harding

turned around with an expression that told him he was dry. Damn, damn, damn. All they had left was the automatic in his hand. No target was in sight, so he ejected the magazine, made a quick inspection, and slammed it back into the butt. Seven shots. He handed the gun to Harding and started rummaging around for additional weapons. Branger must have another gun squirreled away somewhere.

Gunfire. Lots of it. Evarts frantically increased the pace of his search. He threw over a nightstand and the drawer fell out to reveal another automatic. Then he heard the bark of a .45 much closer than the other gunfire. Harding was shooting. Evarts leaped back to what was left of the doorway and plopped behind the mattress with Harding. Without an instant of hesitation, he fired at the legs of one of the attackers, because his body armor and faceplates made a killing shot all but impossible.

Just then, the firing became unbelievably more intense, and the charging men fell spasmodically to the floor. After a moment, Evarts saw that his own assault team had arrived and taken positions in the outer hallway. Branger's men had been caught in a wicked crossfire.

It was over.

Chapter 60

· · · · · · ·

Only the firefight was over. The next hour was chaotic. The team secured the house and confirmed that no neighbor had raised the alarm with the police. The only audible gunfire occurred in the basement, which had been soundproofed because of the shooting range. The team quickly gathered up the bodies and hauled them to a storage area. The wounded received first aid in a barracks area next to the range.

Evarts carried Baldwin to an upstairs guestroom and laid her carefully on a bed. She remained in a drugged stupor, but her pulse seemed almost normal. He checked the bullet wound to her leg and discovered that someone had attended to it properly. He groaned audibly when he saw puncture marks on her arm. He hoped they had used only morphine to deaden the pain in her leg. Even so, she would probably have some trouble with withdrawal.

Unfortunately, he had other things to tend to, so he let her lie in the bed, keeping the lights on in case she regained some consciousness. This time he wanted her to sleep off the drugs naturally.

When he descended the stairs, he found Harding and Matthews waiting for him in the kitchen.

"Any coffee?" he asked, rubbing his ears.

"Brewing. How is she?"

"Out. We have work here, so I think we should let her rest." Both men just looked sympathetic in response. "What have they found?"

"An office with a secured computer," Matthews said. "That will take time. We also found a vault in the basement, but Branger won't give us the combination." He looked uncomfortable. "He insists on seeing you. I think he's got another card."

"Where'd you put him?"

"In the library. Tied up and under guard."

Evarts thought a minute. "Let him stew. I want a cup of coffee first."

"He acts as if it's urgent."

"He thinks he holds an ace, but unless I'm mistaken, it's a deuce. That coffee ready yet?"

Harding poured him a large mug of black coffee and then poured another for himself.

After an appreciative swallow, Evarts said, "Thanks." When Harding just shrugged, Evarts added, "I meant for the help here today."

"I know." He looked uneasy.

"What is it?"

"We lost someone."

"Who?"

"Gary."

"Shit."

"We all volunteered," Matthews offered.

Evarts turned his back to them and leaned against the island counter. After a few seconds, he muttered, "This isn't the way he should've died."

"No, it's not. But it's Branger's fault, not yours."

"Did he have a wife?"

"No. But a bevy of NASCAR groupies will be grief stricken." Evarts felt a hand on his shoulder. "Gary insisted on being a part of this, and I'm told he handled his part expertly." Harding paused. "He saved our lives. He's the one that charged the basement."

"That's supposed to make me feel better?"

"No … but I thought you should know."

Evarts drained the coffee mug before turning around and facing his friends. "We've got to do the rest of this right so people know he died a hero."

"What do you want us to do?"

"Rick, break into that computer but be careful. If I know Branger, he left worms in there that can be tripped with the slightest mistake. Don't underestimate the sophistication of these people." Matthews left immediately. "Steve, take control of the interrogations. Focus on drug connections. We need proof that these people were criminals. Next, try to get the hierarchy of the union. Since they only meet here quarterly, they're probably scattered all over the country."

"Which country?"

"Good point. Get some Mexican connections so we can justify

our actions to the State Department. Push hard but keep it clean. At least for now. Work the wounded first and promise relief from their pain if they cooperate."

"Gotcha. What are you going to do?"

"Get the combination to that vault."

Chapter 61

. . . . . .

"Hello, Chet," Evarts said as he entered the library. With all the planning activity in the last two days, he hadn't had time to meet face to face with all of his old comrades. "I see you've made our guest of honor comfortable."

Branger sat in a brown leather club chair with his hands and feet bound. He held a glass of water with both hands, and as Evarts approached, leaned over awkwardly so he could set the glass on a side table. "Tell this hireling to leave," Branger ordered. "You won't want him to hear what I'm about to tell you."

"This hireling, as you call him, just beat the snot out of your crew, so treat him with a little respect."

"I won't talk in front of this *boy*. Tell him to leave us."

Chet showed no reaction to Branger's racial slur, so Evarts tried to suppress his own irritation. When Evarts had planned clandestine missions, the army had allowed him to pick his own team, and Chet's name had always been at the top of his list. On two separate occasions, his life had depended on this black man's courage and wits.

Remaining outwardly calm, Evarts said, "Chet, can I borrow your cell phone?"

Chet reached into his pocket with his left hand while keeping his gun aimed at Branger with his right. Chet flipped his cell phone over to Evarts, who caught it with a smooth motion. He punched in a number and waited for an answer. When he heard a voice say hello, Evarts said, "Detective Standish, this is Greg."

"Yes, Commander," he heard her reply.

"Have you arrested Lieutenant Clark, and are my parents under protective custody?"

"Yes, sir. To both." She gave a brief recap of what had transpired on the West Coast that day.

"Excellent. I'll talk to you again in a bit." Evarts snapped the phone shut. "Now, what did you want to tell me, Mr. Branger?"

No smirk this time. In fact, the look of paralyzed dismay confirmed for Evarts that he had been right. Branger had left his parents alone so they would be available to use as hostages if all else failed. The examination of the calendar for the entire Santa Barbara Police Force had revealed that Clark had been the mole inside the department for the Rock Burglar. After his interrogation, Clark had turned state's evidence, and a combined task force of three police departments had made seven arrests and captured the entire gang. Evarts guessed that Branger hadn't needed to apply much pressure to further corrupt an already dirty cop. Fortunately, Evarts had figured out a few days ago that his parents' safety posed a personal risk if he ever managed to get close to the union. He had delayed Clark's arrest until the raid had been set so that Branger wouldn't be forewarned.

"If you have nothing else on your mind, Mr. Branger, I would appreciate it if you would give me the combination to your vault."

He gave Evarts and Chet a disdainful look. "I seem to have a lapse of memory."

Evarts pulled the leather ottoman out of Branger's reach and sat down. He stared at him for about twenty seconds before speaking. "Mr. Branger, you're a smart man. You've climbed to the top of one of the most powerful organizations on earth and—"

"Soon to be *the* most powerful."

"No, you're wrong about that. Let me explain why. You're sitting here under the presumption that there will be no hard evidence against you and that with your hundreds of millions of dollars—"

"Billions."

"That with your *billions* of dollars you can buy your way out of this mess. Let me explain why you can't. First, we assume that you planted worms deep inside your computer system that will erase all the data if we try to break through your security network. You know we're army intelligence. We penetrate these systems for a living. Right now, I have the best hacker on the face of the planet working on your computer. It may take him days, maybe even weeks, but he'll penetrate whatever safeguards you've put in place."

Branger looked smug. "He'll never get in."

"I should also mention that he's a black man."

Branger actually roiled with laughter, and only the binds seemed to keep him from bouncing out of the club chair. When he finally caught his breath, he said, "I can't imagine how you got this far. One of those cretins will fry my system and turn the records into gibberish. You're so naïve; I can't believe I'm tied up in my own library."

"Chet, could you hand me your gun? I'd like you to check with Rick on his progress." Evarts kept eye contact with Branger. "Feel free to tell Rick what our gracious host just said about him."

"With pleasure."

Just before Chet left the room, Evarts threw over his shoulder, "Chet, not too much levity. We have some serious work ahead of us."

He heard the door close and then Chet's laughter as he walked down the hall. Evarts just stared at Branger until the man finally asked, "What makes you so sure that boy can unlock my computer?"

"When he worked in army intelligence, the National Security Agency kept borrowing him. Now that he's out of the service, he works as a contractor for them. He does what they call destructive testing. Whenever they think they've got an airtight system, they call him in." Evarts smiled. "He has an unusual contract. He gets paid only if he breaks into their new system, and he hasn't missed a fat paycheck yet."

A look of concern flitted across Branger face, but he erased it almost immediately. "I'll bet you a thousand dollars he can't break into my computer."

"You sure you want to make that wager? You're already betting your entire future."

"I'd bet my life against the intelligence of a nig—" He gave a half smile. "Excuse me, a black man any day."

"This is the day." Evarts smiled. "Now, let's talk about the vault. I assume you've booby-trapped it with incendiary explosives. A series of false combinations or an attempted forced entry will cause a firestorm to envelop the interior of the vault and destroy everything inside." He let it sink in that he had anticipated the move. "I presume you're aware that fire requires oxygen. We've already discovered the air vent, and we've ordered equipment that will suck the air out and create a vacuum." Branger tried to maintain a poker face but his hands tightened in a tell. Evarts had guessed correctly. "We do this for a living. It may take us days to bypass your computer security, but we'll have that vault open tonight."

"Then we don't need to have this conversation."

"Time is of the essence. We don't know whom you may have

scheduled for a visit or if your alarm alerted others outside the house. You could make things easier if you gave us the combination."

"I have no reason to make things easy for you."

"I meant you could make things easier for yourself. Let me explain. We aren't turning you over to the criminal justice system. You have been classified as an enemy combatant and will be dealt with by the military."

"You can't do that." His eyelids flickered. "Get me a phone. I want my lawyer."

"Don't worry, we'll take you to your lawyer in a bit. Military police arrested him hours ago. You can talk to him in your cell… if you cooperate."

"You can't deny me legal counsel."

"Of course I can. You're a foreign agent."

"I'm an American citizen."

"The Supreme Court can sort that out in a few years. In the meantime, let me explain your alternatives. If you give me the vault combination, you'll go to a stateside military prison and share a cell with your attorney. If you continue to be uncooperative, then you'll go to a secret offshore prison, and your cellmate will be a huge nasty black man. We'll make sure he knows all about your opinions of his race." Evarts paused. "Do I need to say more?"

Branger couldn't have looked more frightened if he had been approached with a white-hot poker. "You wouldn't dare. You're just a damn city cop."

Evarts let his temper flare. "You asshole. You just did despicable things to the only woman I have ever loved. I wouldn't dare? Do *not* test the limits of what I might dare!"

Evarts stood and paced the room to cool down. He intended a little interrogation theater, but when he pulled the stopper off his anger, he surprised himself with how much he really wanted to punish this man. Forcing his emotions under control, he sat back down on the ottoman and purposely spoke in an even voice. "As for being a city cop; that's my day job. I also do contract work for the government. Did you think a bunch of army has-beens took out your team? This assault had the full backing of the Department of Defense."

"That can't be true. I would've been warned."

"I believe you have heard of the Shut Mouth Society. Did you think they were just librarians?"

"I—"

"Mr. Branger, I've been patient." He stood up and looked at his watch. "But your time is up. You have exactly thirty seconds to make a decision about your future cellmate."

Before the thirty seconds elapsed, Chet reentered the library. "Rick broke the security system before I arrived. He said he knew twenty kids who could've done a better job." He looked at Branger. "Just in case you think we're a bunch of bluffing cretins, your primary account appears to be in the Cayman Islands." He smiled and then recited the account number and exact balance from memory.

Branger looked shattered. Evarts had seldom seen a more crushed man.

Chapter 62

· · · · · ·

The water looked smooth as glass. Evarts loved an early morning that was overcast because it kept the wind from rippling the ocean surface. It was seven thirty, and he had been surfing for over an hour. He checked the flag on the lifeguard station, and it still dropped straight down: Not a whisper of wind. A low cloud cover made the sea look dark and heavy and as immutable as the earth. When the air was this still, Evarts sometimes found it hard to believe that a modest breeze could cause so much havoc with the surface of the ocean.

The smell of seawater, the feel of salt on his back, and the utter calm interrupted only occasionally by crashing breakers made Evarts feel at peace with the world. He looked out to sea to spot the next set. The waves were few and far between this morning, only about two to three feet. In these glassy conditions, the surf seemed to magically roll out of a flat, monotone backdrop, the overcast sky blending so evenly with the sea that there appeared to be no horizon line.

Normally, he preferred a point break, but on some mornings he just liked to play in the beach break in front of his house. Due to the smallish surf, Evarts had chosen one of his new long boards to ride. All of his boards were new, of course. When he had finally returned to his home two months ago, his garage had been cleaned out and his old quiver of surfboards stolen. Luckily, a neighbor had noticed the open garage and called the cops before someone penetrated the house. He found everything inside just as he had left it.

Other things had changed, of course. He had visited the Abraham Douglass grave site twice since his return. He had missed the elaborate funeral, but the time he spent with Douglass had usually included only the two of them, and he preferred to pay his respects in the same manner. Standing alone at the grave site, Evarts came to understand that their friendship may have been engineered, but he and Douglass had bonds that stretched back over a century.

Over the last months, he had argued, cajoled, and even yelled to try and get the government to take the actions he thought necessary. After he had broken Branger, they had gotten enough hard evidence to create the biggest scandal in the country's history, but the State Department had refused to add fodder to the horrible Yankee image south of the border. After weeks of negotiations, the Washington powers had finally come to a consensus that the best course of action would be to reveal the bust of a major money laundering operation and to disclose some carefully crafted half truths that would vindicate Congressman Sherman and restore his credibility. At least they had released enough information to insure that Ralph Branger would spend the rest of his life in prison for drug-related crimes. Mexican authorities had detained José Garcia, and his Panther Party had imploded after the government disclosed that the Yankee Branger had been financing Garcia. The existence of the secret society of the union, however, would be buried under so much governmental bilge that it would never see the light of day.

Evarts reveled in the news that Branger had experienced an emotional meltdown while in custody awaiting trial. At the house, he had broken Branger's will to resist with a string of bluffs, lies, and insinuations. The one thing he hadn't lied about was Matthew's prowess as a computer hacker. Evarts had discovered years ago that people who used a radical belief system as a shield fell apart if you could pierce the veneer of their convictions. Branger's collapse had started at the house and accelerated as he saw his impenetrable organization poked with holes from a dozen different directions.

Last week, the government had convened a grand jury. With the hard evidence from the house and Branger's continued cooperation, the demise of the union should be eminent. Should be. Evarts worried that the government's decision to focus primarily on the drug-related aspects of the union might leave elements of the secret society in place. In case the union wasn't completely destroyed, Evarts had taken a few precautionary steps to make sure they would never wield the same level of power again.

Evarts straddled his board and continued to wait for a wave. The sets had become even more inconsistent. He looked up and down the surf line and saw only one other surfer in the water over a hundred yards away. Many surfers liked the sport so they could fraternize with other surfers and enjoy the onshore clannish lifestyle. Few ventured into the water alone, but Evarts liked solitude. He had never feared being alone. Especially today. He needed to be by himself to figure out a few things about his future.

He spotted a bump in the ocean surface almost directly behind him. He lay down on his board and paddled several strokes to his right. He had judged right. As the wave bent in toward shore, the peak had shifted north. Evarts was in perfect position. He swung his board toward shore and made a couple of lazy hand-over-hand strokes until he felt the back of his board rise slightly and sensed a small acceleration. Then he made two deep, hard pulls to make sure he caught the waist-high wave. Suddenly movement enveloped his senses, and he snapped to his feet and slid down the face at a leftish angle. When he reached the trough of the wave, he used the momentum to gracefully swing the board around to the right.

He had done all this without a conscious thought, just an athlete's automatic reflexes in response to sensory input. As the board naturally climbed the face, Evarts saw that the wave would crash in a line too long for him to beat. Instead of pulling out, he ran to the tip of the board in the hope of getting a momentary nose ride. He had no sooner reached the nose than he saw a surfer's nightmare, a head in the water directly in front of him. Damn it, a swimmer. He stepped to the inside of the board, crouched, grabbed the rail, and pulled with all his strength toward the wave. The board pivoted on the nose in what surfers called an island pullout, and the tail section swung around in a swift motion. Evarts waited for the awful thud that meant he had hit the person with the back of his board. When the nose smoothly sank and the tailblock spun free, he knew he had missed the swimmer.

Evarts came to the surface with water and wet hair in his eyes, and it took him a second to shake his head so he could see.

"Trish? What the hell are you doing out here?"

"Bodysurfing."

"I almost hit you."

She laughed. "I noticed."

"Damn it. You scared the hell out of me. How's the leg?"

"Still kicking." She ducked under a wave at the last instant so that it would surprise Evarts when it blasted him from behind. As he turned around to paddle back out, she yelled, "A surfer who needs a board is a wimp!"

Evarts reached down to where his board leash attached to his ankle and ripped off the Velcro strap. With the board free, he pushed it toward shore in the next wave. He didn't bodysurf often, but he couldn't pass up the challenge. "Longest ride buys breakfast," Evarts said.

They bodysurfed for another half hour, and although he quibbled, Evarts knew Baldwin had won breakfast. They picked a rear table at Mrs. Olson's Coffee Hut.

"How's the book coming?" Evarts asked. When he had left to go surfing at about six that morning, Baldwin already sat in his library, enmeshed in writing her new book as she drank her morning coffee.

"Excellent. I can't wait to get back to it."

The preinaugural Lincoln papers had been announced to the press but not released. Baldwin had kept exclusive possession until she could finish a new book on his early political life. Most of the William Evarts dossiers from Reconstruction had been released, and historians around the country had begun to rifle through them with the gusto of children ripping open Christmas presents. Baldwin had told Evarts that a pile of new books about the Civil War period would hit the market soon. That was the reason she stayed on sabbatical: so she could work full-time on her book to beat the rush.

Greta sauntered over, carrying two steaming coffee mugs. "What'll ya have this morning, Trish?"

"Oatmeal and wheat toast."

"You got it, darling." She started to walk away.

"Hey, what about me?" Evarts asked.

Greta twirled around, threw out a hip, and placed a hand on her waist. "Bacon and eggs, over easy, hash browns, and rye toast. That right, mystery man?"

"White toast," Evarts said defiantly.

"White toast? Only wimps eat white bread. I'll bring you rye, hon." And she walked away without a backward glance.

"She's got your number," Baldwin said.

"I don't know. You beat me bodysurfing this morning. I may be on a white-bread diet soon." He grabbed the table edge to scoot closer but touched something under the table. He felt around with his fingers until he recognized the object and ripped a number 10 envelope free from the underside of the Formica table. "I forgot all about this," he said. "It seems like years since I taped this to the bottom of the table."

"What is it?"

"A copy of the code Abraham Douglass gave me with the Cooper Union address. I hid this encrypted page the first time we ate here together."

"I didn't see you do that."

"You weren't supposed to. At the time, I didn't want to alarm you."

They both just stared at the still-sealed envelope. Finally, she said, "You're right. It seems like such a long time ago, but it was less than three months." Baldwin's expression turned glum. "Greg, I went bodysurfing this morning because I had a piece of disturbing recall. I wanted to wash it away."

Evarts took her hand. "The doctor said this might happen, but if you can, leave it be. Some history deserves to remain buried."

"I—" She pulled her hand away. "It's like a scab I can't quit picking at. It's painful and I'd rather let it be, but I don't know if I can." She looked down at the table. "It's like my brain can't accept a blank spot in my memory."

"Then we'll deal with it. You're a strong woman."

"I don't remember much of it, but I can feel it." She looked like she might cry. "The emotions keep floating up: the fear, the humiliation. Greg, I told them everything."

"So did Douglass. So would I, had I been in your place. You were heavily drugged. The doctor said memories may resurface, but they will never be clear because your mind seldom had contact with reality. The emotions are a different thing. He said they might haunt you for years. I wish I could tell you that you can forget it or it doesn't matter or that it'll be easy, but those would all be lies."

She smiled wanly. "I'll tell you what you can tell me: Tell me you love me."

He grabbed both of her hands. "I love you."

"Then propose, hon," Greta said, as she placed their breakfast in front of them. "She's way more than you deserve, but you might get lucky."

"Greta, you're looking at the luckiest man in town. She said yes a week ago."

"Congratulations." She came around the table and kissed Baldwin on the cheek. "He's a great guy." Then she gave Evarts a stern look. "You devil. You knew what you were waiting for all along, didn't you?"

"Yeah, but I never really believed dreams come true."

They had set the wedding for the Friday after Thanksgiving. The date had been his idea, because his family had a tradition of gathering for Thanksgiving, and he wanted the holiday to always remind them of how close they had come to a different ending. Actually, they were both eager to officially cement their relationship, and they wanted to separate their future anniversaries from Christmas.

After Greta left, Evarts said in a hushed tone, "You know, you don't have to go the whole way. It's a lifetime commitment."

"Greg, I want to marry you." She smiled. "I have no doubts." Then the smile faded. "Do you?"

"I was talking about becoming the Keepers. We can still get married, but let someone else carry that burden." Not everything that came from Branger's vault and computer had been turned over to the authorities. In the future, the Keepers' duty would be to protect this new evidence in case the union ever resurrected itself. "You ran from the Society all your life. Are you sure?"

"I ran from something I didn't understand. Now I know." She took his hands and lifted until their elbows rested on the table. Then she leaned forward and kissed the backside of his hand. "I want to be the Keepers. If the union comes back, I want to know where I can get my hands on the wooden stake and the silver bullets."

She held his eyes. "Besides, fighting the union seems to be our fate."

Acknowledgments

· · · · · · · · · · · · · ·

I wish to thank Barbara Cunningham and Richard Bigus for all their help in bringing this book to fruition. A special thanks to Sergeant Gary Marshall of the Santa Paula police department for his technical advice and encouragement. I also appreciate the generous assistance of the docents and librarians at the various locales in the storyline. Any mistakes, of course, are my own.

Last, but certainly not least, I wish to thank Diane, my wife, who not only helped enormously, but put up with my moods and frustrations during the process of writing *The Shut Mouth Society*.

Printed in the United States
212887BV00006B/49/P